THE MISSING YEARS

LEXIE ELLIOTT

CORVUS

First published in the United States in 2019 by Berkley,
an imprint of Penguin Random House, LLC.

Published in trade paperback in Great Britain in 2019 by Corvus,
an imprint of Atlantic Books Ltd.

10 9 8 7 6 5 4 3 2 1

A CIP catalogue record for this book is available from the British Library.

Trade paperback ISBN: 978 1 78649 557 0
E-book ISBN: 978 1 78649 558 7

Printed in Great Britain by Ashford Colour Press Ltd.

Corvus
An imprint of Atlantic Books Ltd
Ormond House
26–27 Boswell Street
London
WC1N 3JZ

www.corvus-books.co.uk

For my sisters,
Tor and Hels.

And, always and forever,
for Matt, Cameron and Zachary.

THE MISSING YEARS

MY FATHER IS HAPPILY LIVING IN AUSTRALIA WITH A LADY called Sarah. Or Susan. They have a handful of charming children—with the exception of the last, who even in his early twenties is something of a handful (they call him their "late bloomer")—though of course my father struggles endlessly with thoughts of the child he left behind. But he's come too far to be able to see a way back to her.

ONE

The Manse is watching me.

At first I don't notice it, I'm too involved in my study of the impos-ing gray stone edifice before me. It's a tall structure—three stories, and the first two must have high ceilings—with a turret and stepped ga-bles like sets of staircases. *Grand baronial style*, I think, the half-remembered phrase leaping into my mind. I recognize the ground-floor bay windows that frame the wide doorway from the old battered pho-tograph that has traveled as far and wide as I have, but as I squint at them, I become aware of an acute, uneasy silence, as if the whole build-ing is holding its breath. There's a queer stillness to the dark, unreflec-tive granite, to the slate roof; as I lift my eyes upward, I notice that even the sky behind is still—still and leaden and looming. I turn my attention back to the windows, wondering whether the photograph I always keep beside my bed was taken in front of the left or the right one, and as I study them, I have the disturbing sense that whatever lurks beneath the flat, gray surface is stirring; the windows are craning forward, crowding toward me. I blink to try to find a wider perspec-tive, but then I notice that even the turret on the left is peering down; I have the sensation that it's swooping, rushing toward me, and my stomach lurches as if the lawn has dropped away beneath my feet. *The house means to swallow me,* I think with an irrational flood of panic, *swallow me whole—and then what?*

"Jesus." It's Carrie, my half sister, pushing her badly cut fringe out of her eyes as she joins me on the mossy lawn to survey the house. Her voice drags me back to normality with a hard jolt. I feel like I'm staggering from the impact. "This is a bloody castle."

"It's not so big inside."

I can feel her slanting gaze on me. "So you remember?"

Do I? Or have I created memories, built on the back of the photograph and the tales of others? Snatches of phrases, half-formed images, crafted in a child's mind into a castle worthy of the Brothers Grimm, the type of castle in tales that have nothing to do with fairies. I weigh my answer. I have an irrational feeling that Carrie isn't the only one listening. The Manse has been waiting a long time for me—a quarter of a century, give or take—but I imagine stone can be very patient.

I'm imagining rather a lot today. Tiredness from the long drive, presumably. *Stick to the facts, Ailsa.*

"Do you?" prompts Carrie.

"Yes," I say finally. "I remember. At least a bit."

Suddenly there is an earsplitting crack. Instantly I'm turning, scanning around, grabbing Carrie's arm with one hand to pull her with me. "Ailsa," I hear her say as I search the area wildly. Then, louder, more urgently, "Stop! It's all right. It's just a branch. On the oak. It broke." She catches me with her cool silver-gray eyes, so like our mother's, the only part of her that is. There's a drumming in my ears. It takes me a moment to realize it's my heartbeat. I take a breath, then another, staring into those pale eyes. "It's okay," she says gently. "Just a branch. Look." I follow her pointed finger. There's a very old oak tree that I hadn't noticed but somehow knew was there, to the right of the house. The lowest branch, thicker than the width of a well-built man, has cracked and is dangling at an odd angle. The twisted wood looks dead and dry. The tree is uncomfortably close to the house; its roots must be irreversibly tangled with the foundation. They must have burrowed into the dank earth, thin tendrils slipping through cracks in the brickwork below, growing and expanding over time, tightening around the bricks and pushing out the mortar, inveigling themselves until house and tree became irrevocably entwined. Rot in one can only lead to the same in the other.

The facts, Ailsa. Stick to the facts.

"Well," says Carrie, drawing in a deep breath. Her thin shoulders rise and fall with the draw of her lungs. "That was dramatic."

I'm not sure if she's referring to the broken branch or my reaction. I turn away to ward off her gaze. "Sorry," I say, looking at the tree instead. Only the broken branch appears dead; the rest seems to be thriving. "It was . . . Anyway. Sorry." I head for my little hire-purchase Golf before she can press her point, whatever that may be. "Time to move in, I guess." I throw a swift glance at the Manse as I open the boot of the car, but it's not watching, breathing, swooping or in any way exhibiting animated behavior. The facts: it's just a rather impressive old Scottish manor in the middle of nowhere that now happens to be mine.

———————

Except it's not. Not mine, not completely—and if you don't completely own a house, you might as well not own it at all, or so I discovered on meeting my mother's lawyer in his smart office in the City of London. I wasn't quite fresh off the boat (yes, boat) from Egypt; I'd slept two nights in my mother's and Pete's house in Surrey—my mother's very last abode, but never a home to me—but I was still adjusting to the cool, the lack of sunshine, the muted shades after color so intense it could hurt the eyes. The England I found myself in was lacking, whereas Egypt had been too much.

"Sell it?" The lawyer repeated my question, shaking his head. "Oh no. I'm sorry to say that with this type of joint ownership, there is very little you can do. You can't sell the property without the permission of the joint owner, you see."

"I can't . . ." His words took a moment to sink in. In fact the whole situation was still sinking in. Had I known my mother still owned the Manse? I couldn't say for sure either way. Certainly it wouldn't have been something we talked about. "I can't sell it?" He inclined his head apologetically. "What about renting it out?"

"No, I'm afraid not. Not without the permission of the joint owner."

"And the land?"

"No, not that either. Again, not without the permission of the joint owner."

"Even though that joint owner—my father—hasn't been seen or heard from for, let's see, *twenty-seven years?*"

"Indeed." Ignoring my caustic tone, he paused to remove his glasses and rub the bridge of his nose, then went on diffidently. "I don't suppose that you've had some slight contact with your father over the years?" His small myopic eyes blinked hopefully from his round face, putting me in mind of a mole. He must have been at least fifty, and he looked so much like how I would have imagined a probate lawyer would look that I could have believed I was on a film set and none of this was real. "A birthday card or something . . . anything . . . that you might not have wanted to share with your mother?"

I shook my head mutely.

"Ah," he said sadly. "That *is* a shame." I stared at him, but he was rubbing the bridge of his nose again. The gross absurdity of his understatement appeared lost on him. "Then the avenue that is open to you is to apply to the courts to rectify the situation; that is to say, to have his ownership share transferred to yourself. It would be under the Scottish Courts; you'd have to apply for a Presumption of Death. Our Edinburgh office would help you with that, though." Presumption of Death. I found myself imagining a form with those words in crisp black ink on stark white paper. How neat and tidy and definitive for a situation that was nothing of the sort. He went on, adopting an apologetic tone again: "I have to say that given the precise details of your father's disappearance, I imagine it might not be a straightforward process. It could take quite some months. Years even."

"Right," I said faintly while the Manse in my memory grew, expanding out from the photograph, hijacking my thoughts, my mind, my life. A house I hadn't lived in since my father disappeared and we fled from his absence—at least my mother fled, and I was dragged along, repeatedly bleating, *But, Mummy, when he comes back, how will he know where we've gone?* The lawyer looked at me sympathetically as I took a sip from the glass of water that had been thoughtfully placed in front of me, next to the square box of tissues. This lawyer was nothing if not prepared, though I doubted he had seen a situation quite like this before. "So what you're saying is that I own fifty percent of a property on which I have to pay one hundred percent of the maintenance bills, but there's nothing I can do with it?"

He placed the glasses back on his nose. "Nothing, I'm afraid." He paused. "Unless you want to live in it, of course."

I didn't. I don't. Yet here I am. Temporarily.

Carrie unpacks the food we bought en route at what Google had told us was the nearest supermarket, whilst I wander through the rooms; I suspect she is trying to give me space to unpack my memories alone. But any such memories, if they do exist, are keen to stay neatly parceled up. The kitchen is large, farmhouse style, and has an ancient-looking range cooker that I leave Carrie to tinker with. There's a boot room, a lounge, a formal dining room with what looks like original wood paneling and another reception room on the ground floor; all are dated, but clean and bright—there is nothing that gives rise to the unease I felt on arrival. The wide staircase up the center of the house with its stained wooden banisters catches at me—do I remember tumbling down those stairs to run out onto the wide lawn?—but I cannot tell which way to turn at the top to find whichever bedroom had been mine. There are three good-sized bedrooms on this floor, and a large family bathroom with a raised cistern and a chain pull on the toilet that seems fuzzily familiar. All the walls have been painted an off-white, and the furniture is a cheery pine. The impression is of a bright and breezy mid-level bed-and-breakfast. My mother was perhaps unaware of the legal position, or perhaps, characteristically, she chose to ignore inconvenient truths; in any case, according to Pete, she's been blithely renting out the place for years. The master suite is on this floor too, but I leave it for last and head up a much narrower staircase to the top floor, which is far less attractive on account of lower ceilings and small windows. There are three more bedrooms up here, of awkward shape, and another bathroom, and a door which on inspection is locked.

Locked. That puzzles me for a moment until I recall the managing agent telling us when we collected the keys that it's a storage room—most rented houses apparently have a secure area where the owners can leave some things. But what would my mother have left in here? As far as I know, she never came back to the Manse. Did we leave some things behind when we bolted all those years ago?

I try the door again, but there's no mistake: it's most definitely locked. The smooth round knob of the door stares unblinking at me as if it can see through me, right to the center of my unease. I can imagine that dull gold sphere growing in my mind, until it throbs and pulses and burns away other thoughts—but I won't allow it. I will get the keys and open it right away.

On the way back down the stairs, I hear a snatch of music. Carrie must have found a radio. She likes to have noise in the background, a television or a radio or an iPod with speakers; I'm learning these things about her. I suppose I will learn a lot more as we live together in the coming weeks. If she does live with me, that is—when I suggested she stay with me in the Manse, I was more than prepared for her to politely decline. I'm still half expecting her to announce that she's actually found a flat in Edinburgh for the duration of the play she's in, which would surely be much more convenient for her. I haven't lived with Carrie since I left my mother's home at eighteen for university, and I've probably only seen her three or four times since she went to university herself four years ago. My fault, entirely. I could have handled things differently. I should have handled things differently.

The master bedroom door is open (was it open before?) and it stops me in my tracks: from the hallway, I can see the spectacular view afforded by the wide windows, over the lawn and the road and out across the stream that's hidden by trees up to the craggy hilltops on the other side of the narrow valley. It's a landscape of moss greens and bracken browns and gray granite, with the occasional splash of bright yellow April daffodils. An ancient landscape: one that makes no attempts to hide its years, stoically unflinching and contemptible of the petty jealousies and small prides of those who walk across it. The house is well suited to it—not this version with its bright pine beds and whitewashed walls, but the one I saw when I arrived. The Manse that lies beneath.

I take a small step into the bedroom, and as I do, I am suddenly absolutely sure the bed will be to the right of the doorway, facing those windows: a memory is slowly unraveling, a memory of entering this room in dim light, of walking all the way around the high bed to clamber onto the other side—a big scramble for a little person—where my father lay, warm and solid.

But then I stop. The bed isn't where I expect it. It's at ninety degrees, the wooden headboard against the adjoining wall, a cheerful purple throw spread across the white duvet. The smell is wrong, too: there's the vaguest hint of something sickly sweet on top of a suspicion of stale cigarette smoke. I find myself putting a hand on the wall for balance. Florence and the Machine floats up from the kitchen, telling me I've got the love they need. Before I've made a conscious decision, I'm halfway down the stairs heading for the kitchen. Carrie looks up from inspecting the contents of a drawer as I enter. "This place is at least well kitted out for the basics," she says cheerfully, bumping the drawer closed with her hip. "I made you a cup of tea."

"Oh. Um, thanks." I had been planning to grab the keys and go straight back to the locked room, but I take the tea she is holding out to me. The source of the music is a battered analogue radio in the corner; I have an urge to turn it down, but I don't want to seem dictatorial.

Carrie picks up her own mug, cradling it in her long-fingered hands. All of Carrie is long: long fingers and long limbs. Even as a child, she was always the tallest in her class. She's thin, but her frame gives a sense of strength. Rangy, is what she is. We've never looked like sisters. "So," she says brightly, "you have a house."

I chink my mug against her own, which is almost empty. "Go me. I have a house." Neatly sidestepping first-time buyer status, I have at the age of thirty-four achieved what is, according to the *Financial Times*, the dream of my generation: I am now a homeowner. I don't even have a mortgage. "Not one with any value, to be fair, since I'm legally unable to sell it . . ." I have a house I don't know what to do with.

"Oh, you'll sort that out," she says. Then she goes on, in an uncanny echo of my own thoughts, "I was thinking, when were we last living under the same roof? It must have been just before you went to university, right?" A very different Carrie then: one without permanent smudged eyeliner and purple dye at the tips of her shoulder-length dark hair, one without a gaze that inexorably presses, silently demanding answers. The Carrie I last lived with was in love with ponies and Michael Jackson music and any makeup she could sneak from our mother; she was seven, the same age I was when my mother and I left Scotland, the age I was when my father left me.

"Right." Half a sister and half a house. And I don't quite know what to do with either.

"Is it strange, being here?"

"Not really. I don't remember much." She's watching my face as I answer; I fight the urge to turn away. If I was at work, I'd have my professional persona firmly in place: tough, capable Ailsa, ready for anything, nary a chink in the armor to be found. I can't be that person with Carrie—it wouldn't be fair—but I don't know what to be instead.

"I suppose it's strange how *normal* everything is inside. Very IKEA. I don't know what I was expecting, but I guess it wasn't flat-packed furniture and magnolia-colored walls."

She's nodding. "It should be all oak panels and stags' heads, like a hunting lodge. But I suppose Mum just wanted to make it rentable for as little outlay as possible." I tense at the mention of our mother: we haven't really spoken about her death yet, except in practical terms. And that one, brutal, phone call about the funeral, when Carrie made it quite clear she was at the adult table now:

It's on Friday.
Friday? But there aren't any flights, I don't know if I can make it back—
It's all fixed. Dad wants it then.
Pete does? But—why?
He wasn't sure you'd come. This way, if you don't, he doesn't have to explain.

But the Carrie that's here with me now is forging on. She has an energy I haven't seen all day. In the car from London she mostly slept. "What does Manse mean, anyway? Is it just a Scottish version of Manor?"

"Yes—no, wait." That's not quite right; something is nagging at my brain. "No, it's a house for the minister. I think."

"Bloody inconvenient for the minister, seeing as the church is in the village." I glance at my watch: just after six. Perhaps she's an evening person. I suppose that would make sense given all her evening performances. "I meant to ask—is there a bedroom you'd prefer me to take?" she says.

"Whichever. I don't mind." When I take a sip from my mug, the tea is only lukewarm and far too strong for my liking. The time nags at me: just after six, the news will be on. I could turn on the somewhat outdated television I spied in the lounge and see Jonathan reporting from Louisiana on the *Deepwater Horizon* oil rig disaster. But I know if I do that then Carrie will see me watching Jonathan.

Another half thing. Half a house, half a sister, half a boyfriend. A sly whisper tells me that boyfriends are just like houses: if you don't have the whole of one, you might as well not have one at all.

But no, I'm overdramatizing—half isn't accurate. Surely at least four fifths. And the rest isn't available anyway: no one could ever have the whole of Jonathan, because he has forever mortgaged part of himself to broadcast journalism.

I could tell Carrie I'm keen to find out what's happening with the volcano, which at least has the benefit of truth. Somewhere in Iceland a malevolent volcano is belching a vitriolic stream of fire, ash and lava into the jet stream, shaking the ground with malicious laughter at the havoc it is causing. Or maybe the volcano is the victim, cruelly assaulted from below by the magma . . . In any case, the resultant ash cloud has grounded all flights in and out of Northern Europe. It's been the headline news item for the last seven days and my own private obsession, given that it genuinely is the reason I missed being both at my mother's deathbed and funeral, regardless of whether Carrie and Pete choose to believe me. But if the television is still on when the topic switches to the other major headline—the oil rig explosion— Carrie's eyes will fill up with all the things that she hasn't yet found a way to say, and I won't be able to bear their weight.

"I'll leave the biggest for you then," she says.

It occurs to me that she's trying very hard. I am too, of course, but I hadn't quite expected her to make such an effort, and I'm not sure if her reasons are the same. I have no idea what the landscape between us looks like from her point of view. "I don't mind."

"Okay then. Well, I'll go and have a look round then and get settled in. Shout if there's anything you want me to help with."

"Okay." She heads for the door, mug still in hand. "Wait," I say reluctantly to her back. She turns inquiringly. "I don't want the master. You take it. If you want to."

She pauses for a moment as if about to ask something, but in the end all she says is, "Sure. I'll take a look." She doesn't know what to do with me, either.

———

The keys.

There are four on the key ring, plus a pink plastic fob labeled *The Manse* in a curling, jaunty script that in no way matches the building itself. I stand in front of the locked door on the top floor, eyeing the lock and the keys and trying to work out the match. It can't be the Yale key; this is not a Yale lock. Of the other three, one I know is for the front door, so that seems an unlikely candidate. That leaves a large black iron one that looks more like it would fit a garden gate, and a key very similar to the front door—one for a traditional lever lock. I try the latter first. No luck. The black iron one won't even fit the aperture. I try the front door key, and for a moment I feel a slight give— *Yes!*—but then it sticks. It's not the right key, either. I try the two lever lock keys again, just to make sure, but the door stays resolutely, rebelliously, locked.

The door itself seems to be constructed the same as every other door in the house: of fairly old, but solid, whitewashed wood. I could take an ax to it, if I had an ax (is there one in the boot room or the cellar?), and if I was on my own, perhaps I would, but I can just imagine Carrie's surprise if I started smashing the place up. Though perhaps I shouldn't have expected the managing agent to have a key: if the room is purely for storage of the owner's things, you wouldn't want the agent to accidentally give that key to a rental family. Probably I should be asking Pete if he knows where the key is. Irrationally it rankles that I've been beaten. The defeat is only temporary, but I know that somewhere in a deep, dark corner of my mind, that dull spherical doorknob is lingering malevolently and looking for the opportunity to spread its malice.

But there are other things to do, chief among them to decide where to sleep. I take a bedroom on the second floor that looks out to the back, principally because it's right next to the bathroom and has a large wardrobe, though the latter is unnecessary as I have brought so little clothing that I could have flown up with hand luggage only (if there were any planes flying, that is). My paltry wardrobe looks even more meager and pathetic hanging on the ill-assorted high street hangers that were in the wardrobe (Topshop, Miss Selfridge, Oasis: it's been years since I bought anything from those). Carrie has dumped her suitcase in the master bedroom, which has an en suite, so I feel able to leave my toiletries in the family bathroom. There's a full-length wall mirror in there that catches me unawares, causing me to falter mid-step; for a moment it throws out a stranger's image, but a blink later it's recognizably me peering back. I stare and stare at the mirror, trying to see what I had a fleeting glimpse of—not even a glimpse, the merest hint: me as other people see me. But what gazes back is entirely familiar: average height, average build, average brown hair (though I like to think it has a touch of auburn to it). Pale skin, paler even than the average Scot, but you might not notice that right now given the smattering of freckles across my nose from the Egyptian sun. Even my clothes are average: jeans and a lightweight linen T-shirt. Really, the only thing that's worth remarking upon is my eyes: almond shaped and green, with a distinct black border to the iris. Cat's eyes, Jonathan called them. My father's eyes, my mother once said. *For God's sake, you're just like your father. You even look like him. Those bloody eyes!*

Suddenly I hear Jonathan's voice floating up the stairs; it throws me for a moment before I realize Carrie must have turned on the news. My legs are taking me down the stairs before I've finished deliberating. Carrie is standing in front of the telly, the remote still in hand; she turns at my entry. "Jonathan," she says unnecessarily.

It's a live piece. I try to consider him dispassionately, as any other viewer would see him; but really, does anyone view him dispassionately, when we've all grown up with his serious expression and dry BBC English reporting from every notable event around the globe? A tall, slim man in his fifties with a decent head of gray hair and piercing pale blue eyes. A man with authority, a man of gravitas, but not without charm—charm of the old-school variety: terribly Britishly polite. He's not, though; not in private, with good friends, after a drink or four: then he's scandalously, wickedly indiscreet. It's a required characteristic of the perpetual bachelor, presumably, if dinner party invitations are going to be forthcoming after everybody else has coupled up: *Oh, we must invite Jonathan, he's always a scream.*

There are other versions of him, ones that nobody sees but me. Or whoever was there before me, or whoever might come after. Perpetual bachelor: he shouldn't be considered as such, given we've been together for nigh on a decade. But I know that's how everyone thinks of him. I am presumed to be a barnacle on the hull that will at some point be scraped off, while the ship itself blithely forges on.

On-screen the oil rig burns, the fiery plume impossibly tall, the black greasy billows above it so thick they appear solid. The Icelandic volcano is not the only part of the earth making its protest through the medium of a deadly cloud.

Now Jonathan is in the picture again. He's fielding questions from the news anchor in London, his hand straying up to his earpiece; there must be a lot of background noise. He's doing a good job—well of course he is, he's Jonathan Powell—and the professional part of my brain relishes the story. It's a newshound's dream: a complex human and environmental disaster with wide-ranging economic, political and environmental implications. I can just imagine the atmosphere in the newsroom, an atmosphere I've lived through so many times: so charged your skin prickles with it, like wearing a blanket of static electricity. At the beginning it felt like that for me all the time, but the human body can't handle that level of adrenaline for a prolonged period. At some point you have to become inured. But for a story like this, nobody would be immune.

"What time is it there?" asks Carrie.

"They're six hours behind," I say distractedly. Jonathan has his gravest face on, laying out the facts in a final roundup. Eleven people are missing; the rig is in danger of sinking. This is the hard news dilemma: usually every great story is a terrible one, too. Eleven people: I wonder who is waiting anxiously for them. Parents, siblings, young wives? I imagine pinched faces, gray-white with worry; a snot-nosed child, crying . . .

"When did he get there?" asks Carrie, her eyes on the television as Jonathan explains the next steps for the rescue operation.

"Last night, I think. He took the last flight from DC."

"So did he work all night?"

"Probably. I should think so."

"He doesn't look tired."

"He's used to it. He'll catnap." Everyone is tired in hard news, all the time.

"You guys must be so good at that," Carrie comments. "Catnapping, I mean."

"I suppose." Jonathan is offscreen now. I collect myself and turn my attention to Carrie. Conscious I've been giving her abrupt replies, I add, "I can do it just about anywhere. But I'm especially good in bed." The ribald joke slips out before I can stop it, a knee-jerk newsroom habit, where the mantra has always been that if there's an entendre that can be made double, by all means go ahead.

Carrie's eyes jump to mine in surprise, and she laughs. It's an appealing sound. I remember her giggle from when she was a child. Pete used to tickle her all the time: not the ribs as you'd expect— Carrie's weak points were her knees and her calves. She'd scissor kick and roll around, and the laughter would huff out of her in wheezes and bursts. It's gratifying to hear her laugh again. Perhaps she doesn't want to ruin the moment, or perhaps I was wrong earlier; either way, her gray eyes hold nothing but the return of my own smile.

Later I lie in the strange bed, curiously unsleepy for someone who claimed to be able to sleep anywhere. I texted Jonathan before I went to bed (nothing momentous: Arrived at the Manse. It's rather yellow. Knackered and going to bed, speak tomorrow. Stay safe xx), but he hasn't replied. There's nothing to be read into that, he'll be madly busy with the story. Not that it's a real story to me yet; it hasn't taken shape in my mind. Jonathan cautions all newsroom newbies to let the facts speak for themselves, but they don't, they never do. Facts need to be shepherded and woven into a tapestry of human reactions and interactions, and then they don't speak—they sing.

I check the time on my phone: 1:35 A.M. Abruptly I fling back the covers. There's no use denying it: I can't sleep. It's too strange, being here, waiting for memories to strike at any moment. All day long I've been simultaneously avoiding thinking about the past and straining to find something familiar; no wonder I'm too overtired to drift off. Even while trying to sleep, part of my mind has been mulling over whether this could have been my bedroom before. I grab my dressing gown and pull it on as I leave the room. Carrie has left the door to the master bedroom open, but I know she's in bed—I can just make out her rhythmic breathing. I stand in the hallway and listen to those peaceful breaths with a feeling of relief: that she's comfortable enough to sleep, that with her asleep, I don't feel her hovering around the edge of my consciousness. My eyes are adjusting to the dark and I realize she's left the curtains open as well as the door. There's enough moonlight that I have no need of the hallway light, even if I could remember where the switch is. The stairs are lit by the same moonlight, streaming in through the fanlight above the front door. In this silvery half-light, the house is different again, neither bright and breezy nor uneasily dark, but something . . . other. Something patient, comfortable in its own skin, authentic. I can sense that the well-worn wood of the stairs beneath my bare feet could tell many a tale, some of them presumably relevant to me. When I get to the ground floor, I don't grope for the light switch—I like this version; I don't want to chase it away with the glare of artificial light. Instead I wander slowly through the ground floor, trailing my fingers along the walls where the moonlight is painting them gray.

The linoleum floor of the kitchen is cold beneath my feet; I should have brought my slippers. I try two cupboards before I find the glasses. As I fill one from the kitchen tap, I look out the window, to the back garden. There's a wood that finishes at the low, crumbling drystone wall at the end of the lawn, some twenty meters away. I know from the boundary map the lawyer showed me that the wood is mine, and so, too, is the fishing lake that lies beyond it, but right now there's very little to be seen except extreme blackness where the moonlight can't penetrate—a true darkness that nothing can break through. I wonder what it would be like to walk through that wood right now. Oddly I don't think it would be terrifying. I expect it can see me now, the wood. I can almost feel its eyes upon me, like a prickle on my skin— not unpleasant, just a constant pressure. Not even a pressure, an aware- ness. I expect the wood saw my father, too, many years ago, perhaps filling up a glass from the kitchen tap just as I have done, or raiding the fridge for a late-night snack. I wonder if the wood knows what happened to him.

But now the cold of the floor is chilling more than just my feet, and my warm bed has a certain appeal. The kitchen table is strewn with miscellaneous items from the shopping that haven't yet found a home. I grab a roll of toilet paper, as there was no spare in my bath- room, and take that and the glass with me, focusing on not spilling the water as I slowly climb the stairs, still relying only upon the moon- light, and relieved to feel the warmth of the wood under my feet once more. When I get to the top of the stairs, I turn for my bedroom, but instantly I know there is something wrong. I couldn't say what, but I can feel it before I can see it . . .

There's a man in the hallway.

MY FATHER IS LIVING IN COLOMBIA. OR VENEZUELA. (REALLY, anywhere exotic without an extradition treaty where a dollar goes a long way.) He's lithely strong and has grown a beard which is more gray than dark now. He likes to lean on the balustrade of his veranda which overlooks the city as darkness falls. Sometimes there's a woman with him, but never the same one for long. He leans on the balustrade, a cerveza in one hand, and looks at the stars, and sometimes he wonders if his daughter is looking at the same sky.

TWO

For a brief moment of lunacy, a hope flares in me (*Can he really be here? Has he been here all along, all these years?*), but common sense douses that flame almost instantly. The adrenaline is already coursing through every inch of me; my skin is crackling with it. Fight or flight? I wouldn't hesitate to flee except this man is only paces from Carrie's doorway. I can't see clearly in the dim light—now I'm cursing the ridiculous flights of fancy that led me to leave the light off—but I have the impression of a young man, perhaps six feet; certainly several inches taller than myself. He's facing the door of the master bedroom—Carrie's bedroom—and even as my brain gallops through possible weapons (Knife from the kitchen? An umbrella from the hallway? Or even just throwing the glass I'm holding at him?), I've run out of time: he's turning his head toward me.

As we stare at each other, I have the impression of shocked gleaming eyes, and then I drop the toilet roll and reach out a hand, with astonishing certainty given my earlier ignorance, to find the light switch at the top of the stairs. He blinks and hunches away instinctively from the sudden flood of yellow light. I'm cataloging him for a police report: younger than I, late twenties perhaps, dark haired, dark eyed, clean-shaven with a completely nonplussed expression. He doesn't look like a burglar, and there's no crazed drug-addict look about him, either. He's not even dressed for a bit of light breaking and entering: his pale gray wool jacket is far too visible to be a sensible choice, and the jeans he's wearing look designer. But there's no question he's much bigger than I am—probably much faster, too—and he's horribly close to the room where Carrie is sleeping, peacefully oblivious. *Carrie. Please don't wake up, Carrie. Stay safe.*

"You're trespassing." I mean to say it mildly, as I don't want to antagonize him until I know what I'm dealing with, but my heart is thumping in my ears and I misjudge the tone; my words are sharply accusatory.

"Um. Christ. Yeah." He clears his throat and straightens up, running a hand over his face. "Look, I'm not a burglar or anything . . . Shit, this is awkward."

"I'll say." I register his accent: Scottish, from these parts I would guess. "What are you doing in my house? How did you get in?"

"Your house?" He blinks again.

"Yes, my house. You are in my house." Is he deranged? Does he not know where he is?

"As in . . . You're Martin Calder's daughter?"

"The very same."

"Christ." He looks stunned. Then he pulls himself together. "Jamie McCue." He takes a step toward me and sticks his hand out as if at a cocktail party. I'm not quite sure what's going on here, but I'm fairly certain burglars don't normally introduce themselves . . . unless of course that's what he wants me to think . . . "Ah," he says after a moment, dropping his hand. "Well. Aye, fair enough."

"Downstairs, please." I adopt the tone I reserve for errant interns in the newsroom. "Into the kitchen, where you can explain to me why I shouldn't call the police this very moment."

He nods resignedly, and I move away from the stairs, keeping my distance from him and keeping him in sight at all times. Once he's on the stairs, I dash into my bedroom and ditch the glass in favor of my phone, keying in 999 in readiness—though I don't press dial just yet—and then I follow him down the stairs. At the bottom of the stairs, I grab an umbrella, keeping it half hidden against my side. Every step away from Carrie's bedroom makes me lighter, more able to think clearly. I don't think he has any idea there's another person in the house.

He switches on the light as he enters the kitchen, and instantly the silver-gray oasis I enjoyed only minutes earlier is replaced by the relentless cheer of daffodil walls and bright red checked plastic table cover.

"Sit down." I don't say it as an invitation, but a command. I want him boxed in by the table, at a disadvantage if it comes to moving quickly. He pulls out a chair then sits, looking up at me searchingly as I remain standing near the door, the width of the table between us. He has a strong face, long and lean. The skin is taut over his cheekbones. His dark hair flops carelessly onto his forehead; he pushes it back and starts to say something, but I talk over him. "You've been here before." Unlike myself, he knew exactly where the kitchen light switch was.

He sighs. "Aye." He leans forward, propping his elbows on the table, focusing on me. This is his pitch moment—his chance to win me over, to stop me calling the police—and he knows it. "Look, I cannae apologize enough. I had no idea anybody was here—"

"That's hardly an excuse. It's still breaking and entering."

"Well, the back door was unlocked"—he catches sight of my expression and hurries on—"but that's hardly the point. You're right, there's no excuse. There *is* an explanation, though, if you're willing to hear it?" He looks up at me beseechingly. "Or would you rather beat me senseless with that umbrella you're hiding? I have to admit, it's way more threatening than the toilet roll you were carrying before . . ." He quirks his eyebrows upward, inviting me to join him in his humor. He's a charming man, this non-burglar before me. On another day, in another place, I might briefly enjoy allowing myself to be beguiled, but this is not that day or place. My face remains stony. "Look," he tries again, dropping back to earnest mode. "The thing is . . . we just live across the field there"—he gestures vaguely—"and I was looking for my sister. Fi. Fi McCue. You havenae seen her? She's about your height, brown hair, two years older than me."

It's my turn to be nonplussed. "Why on earth would your sister be here?"

"Because sometimes she comes here. Obviously not when anyone's renting it, you ken. She's . . . Look, ask anyone, she's completely harmless, she's a sweetheart, but she's . . ." He spreads his hands. "She's a wee bit . . . different. Not a tinnie short of a six-pack exactly but . . . a wee bit away wi' the fairies. I couldnae find her, and I thought she might be here. I didnae realize the house was occupied."

"She comes here?" I feel queasy at the very thought. What kind of person goes wandering through empty houses? And why?

"She has a thing about this place." He looks around the kitchen and then back at me. "The Manse. Always has. Sometimes I find her here. Usually in the big bedroom upstairs." I don't know what expression crosses my face, but he starts shaking his head. "No, Christ, no, nothing like that; I think she just likes the view. Look, everyone round here will tell you, she really is harmless. Ask anybody. Everyone knows her and everyone looks out for her; you'll nae hear a bad word about her. Really."

"How does she get in?"

"The back door doesn't lock properly." His expression turns earnest. "You know, you should get that fixed."

"You think?" I say dryly. I'm still revolted by the idea of someone wandering through the house; I have an image of a demented young girl leaping through the rooms à la Kate Bush in the "Wuthering Heights" video. But right now, what to do with Mr. Jamie McCue? Of course I have ample grounds to call the police, but it does seem somewhat unnecessary. On the other hand, what if this is part of something more sinister? I would need evidence to go to the police with. I look him over again, as if I can read a solution on his skin. He's self-possessed, I'll give him that: my scrutiny isn't fazing him. In fact, he's doing a fair bit of scrutinizing himself; his dark eyes are busily taking in every detail of me. I can't help wishing I was wearing something other than a drab toweling dressing gown, however securely I may have tied the belt. In jeans, a sweater and Converse trainers I might have felt less vulnerable to the inspection.

A loud beep makes me jump.

"Mine," he says, patting a pocket on his jacket and then pulling out a mobile. He frowns and scrolls down on it quickly, then his expression clears. "It's okay, we've found her. She's back at home now," he says, looking up at me with evident relief. He starts to push his chair back. "I'll get out of your hair then."

"Not so fast."

He pauses halfway to upright, his face wary. "You're not really going to call the police, are you?"

"No." He relaxes and stands upright. "But before you go, I want a confession."

"Come again?"

"A confession. Here, I've got a Dictaphone app on this." I raise my phone. "Just state your name and admit you were in the Manse without permission on the"—I glance down at my phone to check the date—"the twenty-second of April, and you acknowledge you were in the wrong and will never again return uninvited."

There's amusement in his eyes as he shrugs. "Tell me when you're ready."

I hit the record button and hold out the phone in his general direction. "Go ahead."

He begins in a mockingly grandiose baritone. "I, Jamie McCue, being of sound body and mind, do hereby declare that on the twenty-second day of the month of April in the year 2010, I entered the property known as the Manse without permission, whilst looking for my sister, under the impression that it was unoccupied. I offer most humble apologies for the unintended intrusion and promise never to do it again. I also promise to try harder to leave the toilet seat down, to attempt to keep my feet off the train seats and to try to curb my rants about the incompetent eejit who runs First ScotRail. Oh, and to floss more." I hit stop on the Dictaphone app, uncomfortably aware that my cheeks have flushed defensively. "Happy?" he asks, his dark eyes dancing.

"You want to be a little more respectful," I say severely, but in truth I know I've lost the upper hand now. "I could still call the police, you know."

"Well, that would be a real shame," he says, moving round the table. "We're neighbors. We ought to be getting to know each other." He looks back over his shoulder at me as he heads toward the front door. "Especially since our parents were pals, you ken."

I want to bite, really I do, but I'm determined not to give him the satisfaction. "Is that so? Well, good-bye then. I would say let's do this again, but really, let's not."

He glances at me as if he wants to say something further, but instead he turns back to the front door and opens it, peering into the blackness beyond. The frost-tinged April air has been waiting for its chance to enter; it wastes no time in enveloping me in its cold embrace. "You dinnae have a torch or something I could borrow? It looks like the clouds have come in now."

"Nope," I say cheerfully, starting to close the door on him so that he has to step out into the darkness. "Off you go. Night." I see the amusement gleaming in those dark eyes as I close the front door firmly on him. After a moment, I swing the door open again. "Oh, Jamie," I call. He turns questioningly. He's far enough away that I have to raise my voice. "Perhaps you'd be so kind as to make sure your sister knows the house is occupied."

I have the sense that he grimaces, but really it's too dark to tell. Still, his voice finds its way to me through the blackness. "Aye, for sure. Bye then."

There's a dead bolt on the front door that neither Carrie nor I had thought to use before we went up to bed. Now I shoot it firmly home. Then I check all the windows on the ground floor. Finally I confront the back door. Contrary to my night visitor's statement, it's not immediately obvious that there's anything wrong with the mechanism. At a loss for what to do, I shoot the dead bolt, then look around for something to jam the door for good measure, but nothing springs to mind. Reluctantly I admit defeat and head on up the stairs, though I imagine I'll be far too keyed up to sleep. I stand in the yellow light of the second-floor hallway, listening once again to Carrie's rhythmic breathing, and marveling that she has slept through this entire episode. I wonder what she will say when I tell her about it, and even as the thought passes through my mind, I realize I won't tell her. She would expect me to have woken her, and how could I explain why I didn't even think of it?

Carrie's steady breathing continues. I turn off the hall light then go directly to climb straight into my new bed in my new bedroom. If the Manse has anything more to say to me, it can wait for the morning.

———

I awake with the awareness that sleep has been a threadbare blanket, unable to block out reality: I've had an uneasy sense of exactly where I am all night. I'm rubbing my scratchy eyes and nursing a cup of tea at the kitchen table when Carrie wanders in wearing a fleecy dressing gown tied loosely over flannel pajama trousers and a thin-strapped camisole. Is this what she sleeps in, or is this simply what she pulls on in the morning? Yet another thing I suppose I will learn. How many pieces of the puzzle are required before the full picture emerges?

She runs a critical eye over me whilst yawning herself. "You don't look like you slept very well."

"You say the nicest things," I say wryly. "The kettle has just boiled. How did you sleep?"

"Like the dead." The phrase makes me flinch, but Carrie is busying herself with a mug and instant coffee, and doesn't notice. "It's so quiet here. Anyway, sleeping is never a problem; it's the waking up. Coffee is the only answer." She takes her mug and sits opposite me, pushing her fringe out of her eyes. There are remnants of yesterday's smudged eyeliner around her eyes, and her features are still blurred with the traces of sleep. It's like seeing her through a Vaseline-coated lens.

"You have a rehearsal today, right?"

"Yep. What time is it?"

I glance at my watch. "Just gone eight." Two in the morning in Louisiana. I check my phone again: Jonathan hasn't texted me back, or called. There's still nothing to be read into that.

She grimaces. "I'm cutting it fine." She takes a sip of her coffee and momentarily closes her eyes, savoring the taste. There's no apparent sign of the time pressure forcing her into action. The aroma of her coffee wafts across to me, but something else has become tangled in there, something stale lurking beneath the warm scent of the roasted grounds—

"Do you smoke?" I blurt out in surprise.

"Mmm? Oh no, I could never stomach the smell." Sleep lies like a fog around her; it takes a moment for her brain to process my confused expression. "Oh, the ashtray. Not mine." She points to the kettle, and her words finally make sense to me: there is a small brown earthenware ashtray on the counter beside the kettle. I stand up to inspect its contents; it's filled to the brim with cigarette butts. Carrie is still speaking behind me. "I guess it was left over by whoever rented this place last. I found it on the windowsill in my bedroom, but on the outside."

Left over by whoever rented the Manse last. Perfectly plausible, but my mind has skittered back to my would-be-charming night visitor: *She has a thing about this place. Sometimes I find her here. Usually in the big bedroom upstairs.* I feel a sudden rush of adrenaline: before I even have time to process the intention, I've grabbed the ashtray and dropped it in the bin. I sit back down opposite Carrie, my heart still thumping.

"Well, I guess you *really* don't like smokers." She has pulled the sleeves of her dressing gown over her hands, and she covers her mouth with both hands as she yawns. It looks like she's stifling a scream. "Is it still called a windowsill if it's on the outside?" she muses.

"What?"

She shakes her head. "Never mind. Just my brain waking up."

We sit in silence for a moment. Carrie is savoring her coffee, and I am trying not to see a wild-eyed young girl sitting cross-legged on Carrie's bed, smoke curling up from a lit cigarette. Though perhaps Carrie was right: perhaps it really was left over by the previous renters. But who smokes leaning out of an upstairs window? A rebellious teen perhaps? Though not the teenager that I was—like Carrie, I could never stomach the smell, so my rebellions came in other forms—but surely a teen would be camped in one of the smaller bedrooms? Then perhaps a parent of a young child, who is trying to quit. My own mother smoked, though not with Carrie; she quit when she was pregnant with her. She knew more about the ill effects then, I suppose. Or she cared more. I look across at Carrie again with so little of our mother in her features, and suddenly I'm wondering how much common ground we really share: three quarters of our DNA is different, and all of our upbringing. Surely we are far more different than alike—can we really find a way to connect after all these years? I cast around for something to say, something to distract me from the unease that has anchored itself around my breastbone, and catch sight of the kitchen clock: quarter past eight. If Carrie was cutting it fine before, she must surely be late now. "I can drive you to the station if you like."

"Oh, would you?" She brightens. "That would be great. I should get in the shower." She pushes back her chair, taking the coffee mug with her, then stops in the doorway, frowning. "Your meeting with the lawyer isn't until this afternoon, right? What are you going to do with your morning?"

What I want to do is get some good quality sleep, but I don't say that. "It's not till quarter past three. I thought I might go up to the hotel this morning. Take a look at the health club the estate agent told us about." She doesn't need to know that priority number one is actually to call a locksmith. Preferably one that can do the job this very day.

"If they have spinning classes, maybe I'll join too."

I am momentarily thrown. "You like spinning?" I would have picked her for a yoga enthusiast: all contorted positions and inner peace.

"Nope, not really. But yoga always seems like a cop-out, and I hate running with a passion, so . . ."

"Oh. Well, I'll check." My eyes follow her as she leaves the kitchen, the dressing gown flapping around her. There must be any number of times that I have watched her leave a room, probably thousands in the seven years our lives crossed over, but none of those half-remembered occasions have any relevance now. It's like studying for an exam and then finding that the curriculum has entirely changed. I'm starting from scratch.

MY FATHER IS LIVING UNDER AN ASSUMED NAME IN EUROPE. HE wears flash suits that jar with the years on his face and dyes his gray hair with Just For Men. He travels in and out of European cities with an extraordinary quantity of gemstones hidden about his person, doesn't file taxes and always has hard cash to hand. He drinks too much on his own in bars when he's away from home. He drinks too much on his own when he's at home, too, in his poky rental flat with barely any furniture and a gun in his sock drawer. It doesn't matter anyway. It won't be cirrhosis of the liver that kills him.

THREE

I drive Carrie to the station, marveling at her calm. We are well past *cutting it fine* territory now; we must surely be into *Oh my God, oh my God, I'm so late*, but the ever-increasing passage of time has had no impact on Carrie's leisurely rate of preparations. I can feel my own heart rate rising on her behalf, but perhaps schedules run a little differently in the theater. After I've dropped her off, I head for the hotel, the route no less tricky for having just navigated it in reverse. There's a beaten-up Land Rover ahead of me taking the same route at what seems like a suicidal pace. In minutes, it has gained so many twists and turns that it's lost to sight. Will I one day know the road well enough to drive it at that pace? God forbid the Presumption of Death process takes as long as all that . . . I wonder what I would have to go back to if I stayed here for all that time, but then I shut that thought process down.

I drive straight past the Manse's entrance, deliberately not looking at it; I'm feeling rather resentful this morning. Instead I force myself to concentrate on finding the hotel turning among the road's twists and bends. Just as I'm beginning to wonder if I could possibly have missed it, a rather grand wooden sign proclaims *Kingrossie Hotel, Equestrian Center* in elegant black script on a forest green background. On my right, the drystone walls have become an impeccable high lime-stone barrier, and there are even pavements instead of grass verges bordering the road. A mini roundabout appears—surely excessive for such a quiet route—and I navigate it slowly, craning my neck to look between the huge limestone pillars that flank the entrance, but the road through them curves away to hide itself behind the limestone wall, and all I can see are pine trees.

Soon there's another grand sign—*Kingrossie Hotel, Main Entrance*—and another roundabout, but this one isn't mini, and the center is adorned with low flowering bushes and plants. I turn right and find myself on a road, at least five hundred meters long, that runs through perfectly manicured lawns seamlessly blending into a golf course in the distance. Despite this being without doubt the straightest, safest road I have driven this morning, I pass signs every fifty meters or so cautioning of a five miles per hour speed limit, and deer crossing.

At the far end of the road is the hotel, a grand building that some-what resembles the Manse in style, but on a much larger scale. Newer wings have been added to both sides of the main building. Those slant toward me, giving the impression that the hotel is opening up its arms in invitation. The stone that gleams in the continued sunshine is the same gray as the Manse, and the roof looks to be the same slate, but this is a very different building. It welcomes.

Presumably one of the newer wings will house the leisure club? But I am curious to see the inside of the hotel, one of only two five-star hotels in Scotland, so I park in the well-marked visitors' parking and head for the main entrance, where a smiling doorman holds the enor-mous oak wood door open and welcomes me. The lobby area is large, with a crackling fire in the huge fireplace that presides over one end of the room—clearly big enough to roast one of those deer I was repeat-edly warned about speeding into—with sofas and armchairs grouped around it. Ahead of me is a large staircase with heavy oak banisters and a very muted green tartan carpet. I find myself thinking how magical this room would be at Christmastime.

On the left, from behind a long reception counter, a young blond woman in a gray skirt suit with a tartan scarf tied beautifully at her neck offers a smile. It's an elegant combination, smart and businesslike without overdoing the nod to Scottish tradition. "Welcome to King-rossie Hotel. Are you checking in?"

"Actually no. I've just moved into the area, and I'm considering joining the leisure club." I'm very conscious of the quiet of the lobby; I feel like I'm talking in church.

The receptionist—Elena, her name tag tells me—has already picked up a phone. "Certainly. I can call the club reception and see if someone is available to give you a tour." A young man in a white shirt and gray trousers with surprisingly unruly caramel hair has appeared at the concierge end of the counter. He gives me a friendly smile then busies himself at the computer.

"What name, please?" asks Elena, covering the mouthpiece of the phone with one hand.

"Ailsa Calder."

I'm disconcerted to find the young man has straightened up and is staring at me so intently that I feel myself recoil from the force of his gaze. As Elena makes the arrangements, he quickly collects himself and returns to the computer, leaving me wondering what on earth could have drawn such an extreme reaction from him. The only thing I said of any note was my name.

My name. Calder. Of course: after living so long with the disappearance of my father as a deeply private event, it's a shock to think that it might be a matter of common gossip here—a local tale that has no doubt grown with the telling. I have to resist the urge to bolt for the car. The receptionist appears to be on hold on the phone, so I flick unseeing through a rotating display of postcards that's on the counter, ignoring the concierge so definitively that I'm convinced he must know it's deliberate. Though surely I am being paranoid. Even if the name Martin Calder might ring a bell for a certain generation of locals, there's no reason that his daughter's name—my name—should have that effect, and Calder is a fairly common Scottish surname. But I didn't imagine the concierge's reaction. I finally sneak a glance toward him, but he's no longer at the desk.

"Miss Calder?" It's the receptionist. "One of our personal trainers can show you round in a few minutes. If you'd like to wait in the leisure club café?" Armed with a map, I head off in the direction she indicates and find myself spilling from the corridor into the café. My attention is immediately taken by the spectacular view across the valley through the floor-to-ceiling glass windows. It's the same view as that from the master bedroom of the Manse, except off-center, which gives me the feeling of something familiar but not quite *right*. The hotel must be set a little higher up the side of the valley than the Manse, and the higher angle of view allows me to see silver flashes of the little stream that runs through the trees at the bottom of the V-shaped valley. I look to the east, briefly wondering if the angle is such that I will be able to see the Manse—but of course I can't, otherwise the hotel would be visible from there.

"Stunning, isn't it?" says a voice at my elbow. I turn to find a young man in sport kit whose impressively bulging muscles are certainly a good advert for the benefit of the gym facilities, at least in the male physique. "I'm Jack. Can I get you a coffee or a tea before we take a tour?"

"Black Americano, please."

He signals the girl behind the counter, then we settle into two comfortable armchairs by the window. It's hard to take my eyes off the view, but I force myself to look around. There are perhaps a dozen other people here, ranging from mid-twenties to retirement age. Some are reading the paper, some are tapping on their phones, one has a laptop open. The village doesn't have a Starbucks. Maybe this is the local substitute.

"So you've just moved into the area?" Jack asks in an Irish brogue. He's leaning in, elbows on the low table between us, hands clasped a few inches below his chin as if waiting to prop it up. We cover the basics while we drink our coffees. He's a handsome man, though surely a good few years younger than me. Perhaps Carrie would find him attractive, though she probably has an inch on him. I realize I have no idea what type of man Carrie would be attracted to. I have no idea how she conducts her love life at all. Is she a serial monogamist, or a bed-hopper? Does she bring men home? I can't quite imagine giggling with her about her sexual exploits the morning after, but isn't that what sisters do?

"Field producer," Jack says with a slight frown, as if trying to get a grip on the words.

"Yes. For television news at ITV."

He looks impressed. I used to love this, the effect proclaiming my profession has: seeing my stock rise in the eyes of the beholder, watching the person reevaluate me. Television news seems to have just the right mix of glamour and edge to intrigue. But these days I find myself feeling a little cheap and showy. "Does that mean you travel a lot?"

"All the time. Totally unglamorous, I'm afraid." I know from past experience that if I downplay it any further I will sound patronizingly disingenuous, but it's true: my job is not glamorous. "We do get extra time off for the hours we rack up, though, hence the four months of leave."

"And you'll be here for all of that?"

"I'm not quite sure." I look out over the view again, with the sunshine now glinting off the topmost rocks of one of the craggy peaks across the valley. It's somehow terrible in its careless, rugged beauty. Though I never spelled out a time frame, I know Jonathan is presuming I will be back in London within a couple of weeks. It's an understandable assumption, as I've never taken more than two weeks off in a row since I started work. Carrie is assuming the opposite end of the range, though I've never explicitly told her that, either. Her play is scheduled to run till the end of July, and if she's still living at the Manse then, I suppose I will be too. If not . . . well, if I go to London it will be to leave it, to depart to cover another story, Jonathan's field producer once again. "Probably a couple of months," I say, opting for the middle ground, despite the fact that in this case the middle ground would satisfy no one. Myself included.

He's frowning again, like he's chasing down something in his head. "Do I recall hearing something about the Manse? Some kind of local story? Diamonds, or something?"

So it's confirmed: my family story is now local legend. I don't know why I hadn't expected it. Jack's eyes are clear, devoid of artifice—actually I'm not sure his range extends to artifice. I could easily duck this, turn the conversation elsewhere, but what's the point? And perhaps I'm still smarting at the concierge's reaction, ashamed of my own consternation. Perhaps I'm looking for a way to control the story. I opt for a breezy, flippant tone. "Yep. That's about my father, actually. He worked for a jeweler's in Edinburgh and disappeared twenty-seven years ago after a diamond-buying trip." I pause. Jack's eyes could not be any wider. "*With* the diamonds. He's never been found, and nor have they." His mouth has gaped open now, too. I give him a wry smile. "Go ahead and draw your own conclusions. Plenty of others have."

"Jesus." Jack has recovered his voice. "Jesus. I literally don't know what to say. Twenty-seven years ago . . . Wow. You must have been only a babe, surely," he adds with apparent innocence.

I laugh out loud, genuinely impressed by his recovery. "Ah, Jack. I'm glad to see you didn't sidestep the Blarney Stone." He grins back, tickled by my appreciation, then pulls a couple of forms out of the folder he has been carrying just as my phone starts to ring. I don't recognize the number, but the area code is local. Perhaps the locksmith I left a message for earlier. "Sorry, I think I need to take this." Jack nods agreeably and gets up to chat to a regular whilst I take the call.

It is indeed the locksmith, who sounds both local and like he has smoked from birth. As I launch into an explanation, my eye is caught by an explosion of color on the wall behind the serving counter. I'm at an angle and can't see the painting properly, but there's something naggingly familiar about it. I climb to my feet to get a better look. It's a reproduction of one of my mother's, dominated by a slash of vitriolic crimson among a maelstrom of black. I can see her now, a cigarette in one hand and a paintbrush in the other, with eyes only for the canvas.

"Still there, hen?" asks the voice of ten thousand cigarettes. *Hen.* It's been a long while since I've heard that.

"Sorry. Yes, I'm here." I'm still staring at the painting. "Sorry, what time did you say?"

"I can come now, otherwise it would have to be tomorrow. Are you home the now?"

Home. *Home the now.* He pronounces it *hame*, but the word still jars: the Manse is no longer my home. Home should be Jonathan's flat in London with high ceilings, questionable draft exclusion and his book collection dominating the living room, but of course, neither Jonathan nor I are ever actually there. And even after all these years, I still call it Jonathan's flat. If I could sell the Manse, we could pool our equity for a bigger place . . . There's an image of a house hovering just beyond the reach of my mind, a house that could be mine. I can't bring it into focus. "I can be back at the Manse in ten minutes."

"Fine then. I'll be just behind you; I'll see you in about twenty."

I disconnect, still looking at the painting. It might be good, but I can't tell. I can't see my mother's paintings the way other people do, can't divorce the finished product from the memory of it being painted: where we were living, where I was at school, which version of Karen I was dealing with. We were staying in a kind of artistic hippie squat when she painted this one, with an imprecise number of other people living there at any one time. No one cared what I did or where I was, nothing was ever clean and there was never any quiet. I was ten years old and I hated it. I belatedly realize the waitress is talking to me. "I'm sorry, what did you say?"

She smiles. "I was saying that the artist is local. She's quite famous, actually: Karen Innes, have you heard of her?" She waits expectantly, and I nod weakly. Karen Innes. My mother painted under her maiden name. It always seemed significant to me. "She was born here, you know." Actually she wasn't. She was born much farther north, near Aberdeen, where my grandparents lived until she was one or so, and to whence they returned when they retired. I don't have any urge to set the waitress straight. "We have some postcards here"—she indicates a small stand on the end of the counter—"and there's posters of her work in the hotel shop if you like it."

"Bloody disgrace is what it is." I swing round to find a shriveled woman in her sixties at the end of the counter, her pinched mouth incongruously painted in a red lipstick that clashes with her purple fleece and set in a hard line. "Look at this." She jabs her hand sharply at the postcards. "Setting up that wee bitch as if she was Scotland's own Picasso. Bloody disgrace."

I hear my own shocked intake of breath even as the waitress quickly jumps in with such perfect politeness that her dislike of the woman is all the more evident. "Good morning, Morag, can I get you anything?"

Morag snorts as her head moves in an odd tremor. "You can get rid of that rubbish for a start."

A lady in her forties is bustling up to her now. "For God's sake, haud yer wheesht, Morag. The poor woman's only just gone to the grave." She turns to myself and the waitress, embarrassment and exasperation warring on her face, even as Morag mutinously mutters something that might be *Hell mend her.* "I'm so sorry. She had a bad night." I'm too shocked to speak. What on earth did my mother do to incite such long-standing enmity?

"I've seen you before. What's your name, hen?" asks Morag suddenly, her narrowed eyes focusing intently on me. The *hen* isn't the same casual term that the locksmith used. This *hen* accuses.

"Morag!" exclaims her younger friend. Perhaps not a friend; she has the demeanor of someone who is there out of duty. A family member, perhaps. But Morag is undeterred, her eyes locked on mine while Jack advances on us, drawn to the commotion. I could refuse to answer; of course I could. Nobody would think anything of it; the waitress already has apologies tumbling out of her mouth. But somehow Morag knows who I am. I can see that. And I won't give her the satisfaction of thinking I'm ashamed of my name.

"I'm Ailsa Calder." The words are distinct, strong. They mean to be heard. "The daughter of Martin Calder and Karen Innes." The heads of the waitress and Morag's younger companion swivel toward me in perfect, almost comic, synchronicity, their eyes wide and mouths open.

"You've got a *nerve* coming back here," Morag spits. Her anger rocks me back. It's hard and ugly and spiteful, and it seems to fill her whole body; she's growing with it. The younger woman is scarlet with embarrassment as she tries ineffectually to tug her away—*Morag!*—but Morag isn't done. "You've . . . got . . ." The words are difficult for her to form, and a visible tremor is running through her right side. She's ill, I realize—seriously ill; and in an instant, every single cutting response that my brain is considering is rendered impotent.

"Morag, you can't speak to other customers like that," remonstrates the waitress with commendable calm.

"I'm so sorry," Morag's companion says. "Really, I'm—"

"What's going on? Is everything all right?" Jack has reached us now and is looking from one face to another as if something in them might drag him up to speed.

"I think I'd better leave," I tell him, with deliberate calm. "We can do the tour another time." I wave away the waitress's apologies with a rueful smile. I'm taking the moral high ground. I have to be absurdly beautifully behaved to maintain it.

"Are you sure you have to go?" Jack asks, keeping pace with me as I return to our table to grab my bag and coat. Morag's companion has succeeded in getting her into a chair near the counter. She's still shaking. "I don't want, well, whatever this is to have put you off . . ."

"It's fine. I really do have to get back. I'll come back tomorrow for the tour." I smile a charmingly magnanimous good-bye, but Jack's concern is evident in his eyes as he watches me go. I'm halfway to the exit when the concierge enters. He seems to be scanning the room as if looking for me, but surely I'm imagining it. Then his eyes light upon me and I'm positive that's exactly what he was doing. He even starts in my direction, but the waitress bustles toward him; he turns to her somewhat reluctantly and patiently listens, though his eyes flick repeatedly toward me until his attention suddenly sharpens at something she says. I pass within a few feet of the pair of them, close enough to read his name badge: *Ben Rankin, Hotel Manager.* Not the concierge, then—he's rather more important than that. As I pass, he looks directly into my face with startlingly clear blue eyes, the color of the glorious cloudless sky that awaits me outside. There's no malice to be found in his gaze, but I can't decipher any message either. And then the moment has passed and he's behind me.

Once in the car, I put my hands on the wheel and drop the persona, feeling the anger and upset bubbling inside me. I am not magnanimous. I want to scratch and tear and bite and scream. It is not *fine* that a strange woman was unspeakably rude both about my mother and directly to me. I'm so livid at the injustice of it, I can almost see the emotions swirling inside me, a scarlet and black tornado. But no, that's the painting I'm seeing. Even as rational thought regains a foothold and the bitter anger recedes, uneasiness wells up in its place. It's abundantly clear that I can't expect to fly under the radar here, but is everyone going to react to me like Morag? I'm abruptly aware that the sense of isolation I feel doesn't stem purely from the implacable scenery. I know no one here. I have nobody on my side. I might as well be ten years old again, back in the hippie squat.

A car pulls into the car park and jolts me out of my melodramatic wallowing. I start the engine, determined not to think of Morag. Instead I puzzle over the manager: *Ben Rankin.* The name tumbles over in my head for the short drive back to the Manse, spinning this way and that. If someone told me I ought to recognize the name, I'm sure I could convince myself I've heard it before, but I have no certainty. He knows me, though. I'm sure of that. But Morag knew me, too—and look how that ended.

The Manse knows me—it's waiting for me when I get back. I can feel its carefully reined in impatience in the silence that greets me as I cautiously enter, wondering which version will present itself. Malevolent, benevolent or indifferent: no matter which, at least the Manse knows where I am, I think, and then I stop myself. I'm building stories yet again. The house is just a heap of stones, and I am no longer ten years old.

MY FATHER IS LIVING IN A FLAT IN STOCKHOLM, AS HE'S CUR-
rently separated from his wife Agata. She kicked him out when
she discovered his previous family—not Karen and his daughter, but the family in Belgium that he left them for. He can tell
the separation is only temporary, though, as she's insisted he
sees a counselor, and who would care about that if they were
actually done with the relationship? The counseling sessions
are tedious, but the flat is close to the center of the city and he's
rather enjoying the freedom to explore Stockholm's nightlife
again. In fact, when Agata comes to ask him to move back in,
he's considering telling her that it's very important that he
takes this time to really address the root problems; that should
buy him both the balance of power and freedom until the end
of the summer. After that, who knows? He's moved before. He
can do it again. At least there are no kids this time. That's his
rule now: no kids.

FOUR

The attic room.

I'm standing at the open door, my hand on the now inert door-knob. Neutered by the efficient locksmith, it can no longer throb malevolently in my mind. After replacing the front and back door locks—*Ye cannae be too careful, hen*, the locksmith told me approvingly, which under the circumstances I heartily agree with—and checking all the ground-floor window locks were in working order, he unlocked the attic door in such short order that it seemed inconceivable I couldn't have done it myself. Now he's gone and I'm lingering in the doorway, surveying the room, which is really nothing special: just a small and poky space, with an empty blocked-up fireplace and a single narrow dormer window, that could use a good vacuuming to remove the dust. There's a handful of cardboard boxes piled haphazardly in the middle of the floor and a folded trestle table and discarded canvases and frames resting against one wall. A box room holding boxes: nothing special at all, and certainly nothing to be deserving of such mental unease. So why am I reluctant to lift any of the lids?

Perhaps the locksmith's behavior is to blame. *Some place, this*, he said, glancing around nervously. *Aye wondered what it was like inside, the things you hear . . .*

What things?

Ach, dinnae mind me, lass. I'm haverin' like a fishwife.

I shrug off my disquiet and step forward to confront the contents of the topmost box. Books, mostly paperbacks. Nothing literary, mainly best sellers in the Jeffrey Archer vein, though I'm literally judging these by their covers, as I don't recognize too many of the titles or authors. Who was the reader, though: my mother or father? My father, I decide—surely he would have taken a book on his many gemstone-buying trips, and I don't remember my mother ever losing herself in a book. I was a voracious reader in my childhood; I'd go through four or five books a week. When did that tail off?

The second box is the same, and the third. But not the fourth. It holds books, but not novels: these are scrapbooks, A3 size, bought in bulk, judging from the same dated floral pattern that rambles across several of the covers. The top one is labeled *May 1980–Dec 1980* in my mother's handwriting: the spiky *M* is unmistakable. I open it at random, the rough paper rasping at my fingers, and find myself in my father's arms. We're outside; he's sitting on a wooden chair in the sunshine with me in his lap, a relaxed smile on his face and a beer bottle in one hand. 1980: I must have been around four. I'm not smiling, and I'm barely looking at the camera, as if it caught me dismissing it as something of no consequence. *BBQ at the Haldanes* is scrawled beneath. The photos are stuck into the album by triangular corner stickers that are losing their stick; some are floating freely between the pages.

I turn the page and find my parents together in a selection of faded snaps, probably taken on the same day, though one is missing—three of the stickers have maintained their grip, but the photo is gone. In this sequence, my parents are lolling on a rug on the grass, my father resting back on his elbows. My mother has a perm and is wearing some kind of beaded bohemian blouse. She has her bare feet tucked sideways under her and a smile on her face; it's unmistakably her, but no version I ever met.

I close the scrapbook and take a deep breath as if I'm coming up for air. It takes a few more breaths before I come back to myself; I could lose myself in here, but in the end, what good would that do me? What I should be doing is sorting and separating—for recycling, binning or keeping—but that's too much to face today. As I'm putting the scrapbook back in the box, I notice a framed photograph tucked down the side. I pull it out warily, but all it shows is a group of people sitting round a dinner table after what looks like a well-lubricated dinner, judging by the glasses and wine bottles strewn across the table. It's a tableau that smacks of a special occasion, and my mother is at the center of it, clad in a geometric print dress and a big smile, in pride of place at the head of the table. I can make out my father, too, halfway down one side, the same compact, lean man from my bedside photograph, but this time he's leaning back in his chair, a glass raised in his hand, a smile in place between absurdly long sideburns. He looks happy, or he looks like he's trying to look happy. I don't recognize any of the other revelers. I rub the dusty glass with my sleeve, but there's nothing more to see. Like the other photograph, it's just a sliver of time. I can't divine a truth—any truth—from it, but still, I feel like I'm being sucked underwater. I cross quickly to the mantelpiece, which is thick with dust, to leave the photo there.

I'm almost at the door when it strikes me. The mantelpiece was thick with dust. I turn back as if to check. The photo sits on a gray-brown carpet of it, with the only marks of disturbance those that I just made placing the photo. The horizontal edge of the trestle table has the same layer. But the box lids weren't dusty. I look at them again. There's no discernible dust at all on the lids of the topmost boxes, and I'm sure that's not just down to having been disturbed by me. I would have noticed if I'd had to wipe dust off my fingers.

Fair isolated out here, said the locksmith. *You and yer sister mind take care.*

Someone has been here. It couldn't have been a tenant; the estate agent didn't have a key to this room. Someone has been through these things, these memories that don't belong to them. Someone had a key. To this room, and presumably to the rest of the house.

You want to get to know your neighbors, said the locksmith. *Glen Mc-Cue is a good man. That daughter of his is . . . well, you'll meet her. But Glen is a good man.*

Now I can see the young woman again. She's leafing through the contents of the boxes, taking out certain scrapbooks and carrying them down to the master bedroom, where she sits cross-legged on the bed to peruse them at her leisure, these instants of time that she has no right to, her uncombed hair wild about her, mixing with the smoke spiraling up from the cigarette resting in the ashtray beside her. I can feel my heart thudding in my ears.

But I've changed the locks. She can't roam through this house or these memories again. I've changed the locks.

I'm suddenly struck with an absolute need to escape the confines of this attic before it's somehow too late. I take the stairs two at a time and reach the kitchen before I realize I've picked up the framed photograph again; I have it in my hands. I dump it on the countertop and take a few deep breaths as if coming up for air—which in truth is exactly what it feels like. Upstairs I was certain of things that down here, with the light streaming in through the wide kitchen windows, seem ludicrous. Glancing at my watch, I see it's almost time for the lunchtime news. I'm in the living room turning on the television before the oddity of that occurs to me: surely I wasn't in the attic room for a whole three quarters of an hour? But my watch is right; it matches the time on the strapline that runs across the bottom of the news screen. The top story is still the malevolent Icelandic ash cloud— flights have apparently been resumed, though it's nothing like normal service yet, with planes and travelers stranded all over Europe—but the oil rig disaster is second in line, and suddenly Jonathan is filling the screen.

It's a live piece again. He's on a boat, the burning rig behind him. It's barely dawn there, and the dim light makes the fiery plumes even more striking. I can't deny it: it grabs at my stomach to see him there without me, but I'm not sure I'm equipped to interpret the feelings. It's all too tangled up between us anyway—the personal, the professional, the public and the private, the strands twisted again and again, with links grown over time from one to the other, like a helical coil of DNA. The DNA of us. His silver-gray hair is whipping around in the sea breeze, and he has his gravest face on. I can already tell that there are no positive developments on this story. The search-and-rescue effort is continuing, but the expression of the exhausted spokeswoman in a short insert clip betrays the fact that after nearly thirty-six hours, there can be no reasonable hope. The firefighting effort continues, too, but the rig is listing so heavily that it's surely inevitable that it must sink. I imagine it slipping soundlessly into the black depths, the incessant fires finally quenched, sinking down and down until it at last comes to rest—a metal skeleton in the ocean's cemetery. I imagine barnacles growing on it, some form of plant life, perhaps—but no, I've missed something with my daydreaming: it seems there is the possibility of a seabed leak, perhaps as much as eight thousand barrels a day . . . Now the skeleton is surrounded by clouds of thick oozing crude oil, streaming around its metal ribs on the way to the surface, a murky, greasy, billowing black cloud, seeking to stomp on all sea life.

But Jonathan has left the screen, and the focus is now on a petty political spat. I shut down the telly with the remote and sit for a moment, reluctant to head back to the box room. I feel curiously jet-lagged, as if I'm not quite in step with the world. Or perhaps it's that I'm not quite in time with the house. It hasn't escaped me that I continue to feel like I'm being watched. Or maybe observed is a better word: I feel like I am being analyzed. Which is wholly ridiculous. Clearly I need to eat.

As I'm trying to understand the hob in the kitchen with a view to making some soup, my phone rings: Jonathan. I feel something in me unwind as his name flashes on my BlackBerry screen. "Hey, you, I've just been watching you," I say lightly.

"How was I?" There's a smile in his voice, but exhaustion too.

"Good. Of course. Though more needed on the missing workers and the families, I think." The pinched white faces of the wives and children silently demand it. I don't know why he can't see it, why he can never see it.

"They won't find them. That's not the story now." He sounds testy. I won't be the first person to have told him that; I expect he's been on the receiving end of a pretty firm directive from the head of the newsroom as to where he should be focusing his time. He's building up a head of steam, though. I let him rant. It's not my job to talk him round this time.

"How's Rod doing?" I ask when he's finished venting. Rod is his field producer on this trip.

"He's not you." He's still testy.

"I'm reassured that you noticed." I've deliberately adopted an amused tone. Rod is fifty with a ginger beard and a large beer belly.

There's a whiff of a reluctant chuckle down the phone. "He really isn't you, though. He's good enough, I suppose, it's just . . . If I had to put my finger on it, there's just not the same attention to detail." *Or perhaps there's not the same attention to Jonathan.* A silence falls between us. I realize he's waiting for me to say something reassuring. Something like *Don't worry, it's only for a few weeks.* Or perhaps *I'll be back with you before you know it.* He can't ask me when I'm coming back, not without at least some sideswipe of acknowledgment of what brought me to Scotland—and he doesn't want to bring that up at all, because then I will remember what he said in the dim light of the hotel room in Cairo . . . I close off the memory, but I still can't find a voice for the platitudes. "Anyway," he says eventually. "How's the house?"

"Well, it could certainly use a repaint." I grab on to this subject like a lifeline. "It actually borders the land of Kingrossie Hotel—you know, the five-star golf place? I might be able to sell to them; I'm guessing they might want the fishing lake if not the Manse itself."

"You've sorted that certificate thing already?" I can hear the sudden hope in his voice.

"No, not yet. I meant when that's sorted out." A faint crunching noise grabs my attention. Footsteps on gravel, from the front of the house I think, though I'm slightly disoriented by the background noises coming through the phone. Someone is speaking close by to Jonathan—probably Rod. "I'm meeting the lawyer this afternoon." There's a sharp bang from the front of the house; I move to peer down the corridor to the front door. Something is lying on the welcome mat. Post, presumably. It must have been the postman.

"Good luck." Jonathan yawns down the phone.

"You sound dead on your feet." I'm closer to the front door now, and I can see it's not post. It's a newspaper. Presumably a freebie circular, since there would be no reason to pay for papers to be delivered here regularly.

"Yeah. But this thing is moving so fast." I hear a louder snatch of a male voice. "Look, I have to go. I'll call you when I can."

"Okay. Stay safe."

"You too." It's our habitual sign-off. Not *I love you*, or *I miss you*. We do say those, too, like all couples, but *Stay safe* is just for us. We initially became romantically involved when covering the Seattle WTO conference in 1999; it was my first experience of rioting, of the speed at which violence can rip through a crowd. I remember Jonathan's hand on my arm when I had to be separated from him, the intensity in his eyes as he said those words, the dryness in my mouth as I nodded back. *Stay safe*. Back then it meant everything. It doesn't quite seem enough, now.

There's something odd about the paper in my hand. I look at it more closely and realize that not only is it not neatly folded in half at the front page, as you'd expect from a new issue, but instead it has been roughly folded to quarter size at a different page. And it's old; the paper has yellowed. I look for the date: 20 October 1983.

October 1983. A month after my father disappeared.

I open the door and look out for a moment, but whoever put this through my front door has gone. I can hear nothing but a vague hum of traffic from the distant main road, and the inscrutable hills across the glen are keeping silent about whatever they have seen. I close the front door again. I have an idea of what I might be about to see, and it's right there when I open out the paper, circled three times in violent thick red marker pen: an article on my father. *No Leads in Case of Missing Jeweler.* It's a large piece on page three; I read it through quickly, then again, slower. The writer has done his level best to underline all the tawdry details without actually accusing my father of theft; professionally I can admire his agility even while despising his gutter journalism. To be fair, the police spokesman is quoted as saying that currently they are pursuing all avenues, but that doesn't counterbalance the four separate mentions of the diamonds. Karen and I are mentioned, too—"distraught wife and young daughter"—but only once. Abandoned family members are clearly much less interesting than a missing fortune in gemstones.

There's nothing in the article I didn't know, of course, but the article itself isn't the point. The point is that someone kept it: there's a fury inherent in that which stops my breath. Someone kept it, for over a quarter of a century, and still felt angry enough today to make sure that I saw it. The real message is very clear: I am unwelcome here.

I am unwelcome here. *As if Morag hadn't made that clear already . . .* For a moment I entertain the thought that Morag might be the anonymous donor, but then I dismiss it: she didn't look nearly well enough to drive herself, and I can't imagine the sensible companion with her allowing this sort of thing. No, there are at least two people who don't want me here, Morag and someone else. The wayward sister of Mr. Jamie McCue? The hotel manager? Someone else I haven't even met yet? It occupies my thoughts for all of the drive to Edinburgh, even though there's nothing to be gained from dwelling on it, and gradually resentment takes over from shock. Even though selling the Manse is exactly what I want to do, it irks me that by doing so I will make these awful people happy. One part of me wants to live happily ever after here, metaphorically sticking two fingers up to Morag and her anonymous co-believer every day with my vomit-inducingly perfect husband and children . . . Though I'm hazy on exactly how the husband and kids part might come to pass. And I'm not sure the Manse would want us anyway.

MY FATHER MAKES A LIVING CAPTAINING A TOURIST BOAT IN Mombasa. He's lived in several different places in Africa, but he feels settled in Kenya now; he can't imagine ever leaving. He has a decent place to live, and the job is a good compromise between a simple life and the comfort of sophistication: the romance of the high seas coupled with the commercial safety of the tourist trade. Nothing too complicated. If he had to explain in a few words why he walked away all those years ago, that might be it: it felt like life had become too complicated. A job, a wife, a mortgage, a child, friends, relatives, all with expectations; he was drowning in them, failing them all. He was losing himself. But that was then; he was a different person. He can only be who he is now.

FIVE

The wood—*my* wood—is a joy.

Wandering through the trees, I feel far more like myself than I have all day. It's being outside the Manse, I think. When I'm there, I can't help straining myself to tug on memories that tease, just out of reach. Even when I catch on to one, my mother and father only lurk in the edges of it, a solid adult presence that's peripheral to my childish concerns. I thought I had discovered a gleaming Technicolor memory, of my mother in the garden, but then I realized I was just seeing the tableau from the box room photos. Though perhaps in time I will believe it's a memory. How can one tell the difference?

I feel better when Carrie is in the house too. But Carrie is staying up in Edinburgh for dinner with the cast; she rang to say so. I wonder if this is just the start. In mere days she might not be coming back at all. I know she thinks I invited her here as reparations for not making the funeral, but that was beyond my control. And it's not an apology for all the times I didn't call or didn't visit. It's not even an apology for allowing my relationship with my mother to drive me away without thinking about what else I was leaving behind, because I truly don't know what else I could have done. What it is, is an attempt to start afresh, because we both might need someone we can count on in life. I thought I had that, but I was wrong.

So Carrie is in Edinburgh, and here I am walking among the trees—mainly oak and pine, I think, but horticulture is not my strong point—which create an almost closed canopy, though the tree trunks are widely spaced and the ground level is clear of bracken or bushes. Instead layers—perhaps centuries—of pine cones, needles and leaves have created a thick brown-red carpet that delivers a spring to each step. I ought to have a dog, I think. A black Labrador, perhaps; something that looks like a gundog—and then I laugh at myself. As if I have any idea of how to care for a dog. As if I even really know what a gundog does.

It takes me five or six minutes to get to the other side of the wood, so I estimate it to be roughly half a mile wide, or perhaps less, because I appear to have veered off to the west a little given that I've come out at that end of the fishing lake. The lake—*loch*, I should probably say—isn't large. It's broadly kidney bean shaped, roughly two hundred meters by one hundred meters. For a body of water located in one of the most spectacular areas of Scotland, it's curiously unpretty. There are no trees, no plants of any kind lining the water. I wonder if it was man-made. Walking around it is harder than expected, as in places the land rises very steeply away from the water into rounded hillocks, but there are a few areas of easy access, almost like dirt beaches, where I spot evidence of use: the odd empty crisp packet, a discarded can of Tennent's Special. In one bush I spy a lid labeled *PowerBait*. My fishing lake—loch—does not go unused, it seems. I try to imagine spending an afternoon casting a line here. I'm not sure I can think of a leisure pursuit more mind-numbingly boring.

Back at the start of my loop, I survey the loch again before starting back: I could sell it without a single pang of regret. Not the wood, though. I feel differently about that. My father must have walked this wood. He must have known the landscape, known the people. And they knew him. It's laughable that I hadn't put that together, that I hadn't considered I might encounter people who were acquainted with him. Were friends with him, even. *Our parents were pals, you ken.* Parents, plural. Perhaps not everyone will react like Morag, then. My parents had friends—the photos prove that. There are people who could tell me about them. About my father.

I could find those people. It's not why I'm here, but it wouldn't be difficult, and in truth it's exactly what I'm trained for. To ask the question, to follow the leads, to build up a picture, a shape of events; not just this happened, then this, then this, but a story. A coherent whole that answers not only the first question—*What happened?*—but the ones that follow. *How? Why?*

It's not why I'm here.

I've almost returned to the now-familiar garden wall when a small movement catches my eye. There's a cat, gray and sleek but slender in a way that suggests this creature has no intention of being merely a house cat, slowly stalking something I can't see. From the angle of the cat's gaze, I guess the quarry must be on the other side of the iron gate. The cat inches forward, her haunches bunched underneath and her tail swaying slowly but deliberately behind her. I try to spy whatever it is that she has spotted, but I can't see anything on the long expanse of green lawn. No doubt my eyes are less keen than hers, particularly in the fading light. I inch myself forward to get a better look, and she turns her head slowly to me then dispassionately returns her focus to the prey, which, judging by the cat's continued stillness, hasn't been scared off by my movement. The cat is now less than a meter from the gate, and what she is staring at through the ironwork ought to be only just inside the garden, but there's still nothing I can discern. The sun is beginning to set behind the Manse, in a glorious spread of golds and reds that the news reader earlier told me is in part due to the concentration of volcanic particulates in the atmosphere. I like it, this knowledge of unexpected consequences—it makes me appreciate the sunset more.

The cat, though, is not focused on the sunset. Instead she moves suddenly, not through the gate as I expected—the bars are plenty far enough apart for her to slip through—but leaping lightly onto the top of the drystone wall. She picks her way carefully around the top, repeatedly turning her head to focus on a spot within the garden. With the cat gone, I move toward the gate myself, glancing again at the Manse.

There's a figure in the attic window. In less than a heartbeat it's gone, without moving, as if swallowed directly into the air.

I strain to look closer, and there's nothing there. But there was— I'm sure of it. I'm almost sure of it. I had the impression of a slight figure topped by a triangle of hair surrounding a pale face . . . I stand in indecision with one hand on the gate, my heart thudding in my ears. I'm simultaneously absolutely sure I saw a person and absolutely sure what I saw was a trick of the light. But the twilight is taking hold, shifting and bending and filtering the light to a dark gray everywhere except where the remnants of that glorious sunset still linger. The cat pauses to consider me silently, or perhaps she's still looking at her invisible prey.

"There's nothing there," I tell her. "I've changed the locks." But I can no longer pick out her gray figure in this dusk. I shall have to leave this wonderful wood, go into the Manse, and I shall have to check every room, and there will be nothing there. I will know there never was, and yet the certainty of what I saw, what I know I saw, will sit in my stomach in a block of icy leaden dread.

With the Manse waiting silently for me to decide what to do, I take a breath, push the gate open and cross the garden briskly, determined not to look reluctant. The absurdity of that strikes me, and I almost laugh. Look reluctant to whom? Because now I am hell-bent on practical action, and in this no-nonsense spirit, it's easy to see that my mind conjured a female figure after the shock of the possibly charming Mr. McCue's nighttime visit and not only hearing about his alarmingly free-wandering sister, but seeing the evidence, too, in the ashtrays and the rifled box room. The back door is just as firmly locked as when I left it, and given the locksmith's visit, I know beyond a shadow of a doubt that nobody has the keys to this house but me. I turn on the kitchen light, and for once the immediate drenching in rational, cheerful *yellow!* is welcome. It carries me through the entire ground floor, room after room, where I snap on the light in each, check them over and move on with the lights still on, warding off the now near-total darkness that has descended. The stairs to the second floor give me slight pause, but I grab the poker from the living room and forge onward and upward, each step of the stairs creaking as I lay down my weight on it. The sound is like a dry chuckle from a rarely used throat. The Manse is laughing at me, but I can't be annoyed at that. I'm almost laughing at myself.

There's nothing on the second floor, except confirmation that Carrie's room gets better reception when my phone suddenly unleashes a torrent of text messages. The first beep of the sudden onslaught makes me jump, but the adrenaline wave subsides quickly. They're all administrative—confirmation of change of billing details for the phone and broadband. Nothing from Jonathan. I turn my attention back to the room. Carrie's bedroom is in the same muddle that she left it, the duvet tangled on one side of the bed and a hairbrush and makeup bag on the exposed bedsheet. Two of the drawers in her chest of drawers are half open. It would probably be possible to entirely ransack this room, and I would just put it down to Carrie's relaxed attitude to tidying up.

Only the top floor is left. I climb the stairs slowly, poker in hand, feeling less able to congratulate myself on calm rationality. Sheepishly neurotic might be a more accurate description. The poky bedrooms upstairs aren't a worry, and in any case, they offer scant concealment—in one glance it's obvious there's nothing and nobody hiding within them. It's the box room that looms in my mind. Of course it would be that room, with its cartons of who-knows-what waiting to drag me down into the past. No wonder my tired anxious brain placed a figure in that room, of all rooms. The door is slightly ajar, the hall light spearing inside in a single slanting stripe. I slip my hand inside without disturbing the door and fumble for the light switch. The bulb flickers mulishly for a moment then yields to give a steady glow.

I take a deep breath and fling the door open, brandishing the poker. The door bounces off a box and smacks the poker back into my face, right on the bony crest of my eyebrow, hard enough to make me yelp. If someone was watching, they would have found it hilarious, but at least I've already seen that the room holds nothing more than it did earlier today. I rub my eyebrow ruefully and look around once again, then move to the window, trying to figure out what I might have seen from where I was standing, if I had indeed seen anything. A box perhaps, maybe this one, topped by a rather bedraggled beige tasseled lampshade. It's not exactly triangular, but in the dim light, with a fleeting glance and a suggestive mind, probably anything can morph into any shape. It doesn't matter anyway. I turn for the door, then on second thought lift down the lampshade, and also the box it was sitting on, so there's no chance of making the same mistake twice.

Back downstairs I make toast for dinner and eat it in front of the television in the living room, channel-hopping until I find one on which *Dirty Dancing* has just started. I make it to about halfway before becoming aware of a sense of prickling unease. Glancing around, I realize I haven't drawn the curtains. The darkness seems to be staring in at me, but even as I tug the drapes shut, I can't help wondering whether that is the equivalent of an ostrich sticking its head in the sand—if there's something out there, shouldn't I be able to see it? And anyway, what if the something is inside rather than out?

There wasn't anyone in the box room. There couldn't have been. I changed the locks.

I return to the film and watch until the very end of the credits, well past the point of exhaustion, then I shove one of the new keys under the mat for Carrie and fall into bed, determinedly not thinking about the figure in the box room. Because there wasn't anybody there. I changed the locks.

MY FATHER IS LIVING IN DUBLIN. THERE'S SOMETHING ABOUT the city that reminds him of Edinburgh, and he always loved Edinburgh: so much friendlier than Glasgow, which is the city of grit, the one that the true Scots understand, feel the life-blood of in their bones—or so the folklore goes. It was in Edinburgh that he had the epiphany, a shining moment of clarity on a bright, blustery spirit-of-adventure day on Princes Street, with the castle standing proudly against the cloudless sky and a cold wind snatching at his clothes and hair, tugging him away; it was there that he realized he could simply unhook himself from his life and slip away like a dog slipping its leash. But once you unhook, you can never go back. He knows that now. He's not sure if he fully understood it at the time.

So he lives in Dublin, and likes it, though he's not Irish, but the Irish don't care; they love his enthusiasm for the country—and they need all the enthusiasm they can get, now that the Celtic Tiger has lost its roar and the recession is truly biting. He runs a caravan park that's owned by a big corporation and bemoans the increasing health-and-safety regulations that require him to post notices such as "Caution: floor may be wet" right next to the swimming pool. He hasn't remarried. There were several opportunities over the years, but he wasn't sure he could trust himself not to unhook again.

SIX

The station again.

Carrie called me to let me know she was on the train home, and I offered to come and pick her up. She was gone before I got up, but she left me a scribbled note on the kitchen table. If she were staying at home—her home, the house she grew up in—would she be calling Pete instead? Or her mother? I can picture her on the train, reaching for her phone to call Karen, then catching herself with a sharp intake of breath, and calling me instead. I find myself aching for her despite the fact that I have no evidence at all of this happening.

In any case, I'm leaning against the bonnet of my car, having climbed out to better appreciate the environment. It's actually a breath-taking waypost for a traveler to alight into. If it weren't for the thrum of traffic from the nearby A9, this could be the middle of nowhere—which, technically, I suppose it is. The road I drove in on stretches away from the low gray stone station building in both directions with only the odd fence or drystone wall to suggest that mankind has ever actually settled here. I try to trace the road with my eyes in the failing light, but it's impossible—my eyes are dragged to the craggy peaks which are darkening by the second, the definition vanishing until they become merely looming dark presences. I feel the weight of time here, of the years that have passed. This landscape has been old for a very long time.

By the time the train arrives, darkness has truly fallen. From a distance, I see the lights of the train and it's a jolt, a jarring thrust back into the twenty-first century. The metal-on-metal scrape of the train wheels whips through the rails ahead of the train itself, and for a moment I fancy the rails are alive, buckling and dancing with the intensity of the energy funneling through them. But the noise is changing; the train itself is drawing in. Seconds later Carrie steps out onto the platform, her black biker boots easily eliminating the ground between us with her long strides, and her hands thrust into the pockets of the open long gray coat whose tails are flapping behind her in the breeze. Individually everything she's wearing looks like it came from a jumble sale, but somehow when settled on her frame it becomes imbued with a slouchy elegance I could never hope to find. Perhaps I was already aware of it, but I feel like I'm recognizing it anew: Carrie is seriously cool.

We say our hellos and climb into the car. Carrie is already yawning. "Were you back late last night? I didn't hear you come in."

"Not too bad. One-ish. I prebooked a taxi back from the station." She yawns once more and throws a sideways glance at me. "You left all the lights on when you went to bed, you know."

"Did I?" I concentrate deliberately on backing out of the parking space. "I was pretty wiped, I guess."

"What have you been doing with yourself?"

Suddenly I can't think. What have I been doing? And how can whatever it is have taken all day? "Admin and sorting, very dull. And all of it seems to take forever. You'd be amazed by how much I haven't achieved today."

"How did the meeting with the lawyer go yesterday?"

"Fine. I guess. A bit strange." We're pulling away from the station now, and I marvel at the completeness of the darkness around us.

There's no moonlight to be found thus far this evening; Carrie would have needed a torch to navigate this had I not picked her up. The city dweller within me balks at the idea.

"How so?"

I shrug. "You know. Talking about my father. I don't usually do that." Talking about my father, without really talking about my father. We covered his date of birth, town of birth, occupation, last known abode; the barren facts that in no way construct a person. The lawyer—Mr. MacKintyre, a veritable mountain of a man—had them in the file already, but after so many years and now with a different plaintiff, a double check was warranted. I hadn't expected there would already be a file. "The lawyer met Mum once, actually. Years ago. She looked into the process too."

"Why didn't she go through with it?"

"That's exactly what I said." Though what I was thinking was less charitable: *Why couldn't she have cleaned up this mess herself?* Surely her mess, or his. Because the only other person that was there was a seven-year-old me, and I refuse for it to be mine. "But it was too soon. Without sufficient evidence pointing toward the person having died, you need to show they haven't been heard of for seven years. I guess she never got round to it when the seven years was up."

"That sounds remarkably like her." There's a caustic tone to Carrie's words that surprises me. I throw her a quick glance, but I can't deduce her expression in the darkness of the car interior. "Do you have to, I don't know, come up with a theory? For what happened to him, I mean?"

"I . . ." In front of me hang a hundred, a thousand, a million and more different possibilities. I almost can't see the road for the myriad of my father's lives playing out before me, like overlapping cinema screens, all that could have been, might have been, perhaps was, perhaps even is. All of the things I have imagined and all I haven't yet thought of. If I had to pick one, I might damn all the others. What if I picked the wrong one?

"Ailsa? Are you okay?"

"Yes. Sorry. No, we don't have to submit a theory. He has to speak to the investigating office, for completeness, but apart from that it should be . . ." I hesitate. Even now, I can't use the word the lawyer used: *painless*. "Straightforward. More straightforward than the lawyer down south seemed to think, anyway." I turn the conversation back to Carrie. "But what about you? How's the director? You've worked with him before, right?"

She talks and I listen as I drive. The car's headlights don't seem to extend nearly far enough in the darkness, and they have the odd effect of bleaching virtually all the color out of the grassy verges that are temporarily bathed in their light. I could almost believe we are driving in a black-and-white bubble. It's a shock to see the vibrant red and white stop sign that suddenly rears up in front of us.

"Where are the rest of the cast staying?" I ask.

"A mixture of flats and B&Bs in Edinburgh." She stifles a yawn. "We aren't exactly worthy of Judi Dench–style accommodation. Though they're all pretty close to the rehearsal venue, so at least they have the benefit of a short commute."

"Wouldn't you have preferred the shorter commute?"

"And have to endure Janey as a roommate? No thank you! This way I pocket the per diem *and* get to stay somewhere way nicer." She turns toward me suddenly. "Wait, you aren't trying to kick me out already, are you?"

"No! I just thought—well, this commute isn't that convenient for you. That's all." I feel her eyes upon me in the darkened interior of the car. I'm making a mess of this, I can tell. "Carrie, you're welcome at the Manse as long as you like. Of course you are. I invited you." She isn't speaking. Does she think that I invited her out of politeness? Does she think that I didn't expect her to accept? I didn't, exactly, but that doesn't mean I didn't want her to. I should have made a joke out of her comment, but it's too late now—by addressing it earnestly, I've given it credibility. I risk a glance at her on a straight section of the road;

when she sees me turning toward her, she looks straight ahead, tension somehow apparent in her profile despite her slumped position. I can think of absolutely nothing to say that will improve the situation. Our colorless bubble continues to eat up the meters and kilometers to the Manse.

"Well, okay," Carrie says finally, breaking the deafening silence.

I search around for some way to return the (slim) olive branch, if that's indeed what it was. "Oh, I went to the hotel yesterday, to see the leisure club."

She clears her throat. "Really?" Her tone is still belligerently neutral. "How was it?"

So I describe the hotel. I even tell her about the manager's reaction and the incident with Morag; I joke about not actually getting to see the health club. I'm overcompensating now, adding more color and detail than I ordinarily would, but little by little I can feel Carrie thawing out—and her hint of righteous indignation on my behalf is a reward in itself, so I tell her about the newspaper too. We're almost back at the Manse now. Turning carefully into the driveway, I have to slam the brakes on suddenly—"Shit!"—as the headlights wash momentarily over a figure in the driveway, a scant meter or so from my front bumper.

"Ow," complains Carrie, rubbing a knee which presumably connected with the dashboard.

"Jesus, I nearly hit them." My skin is still singing with the sweep of adrenaline.

"Hit who?"

"The man. Didn't you see someone?" I look around, but outside the bubble of the headlights, there is little chance of seeing anybody or anything clearly.

"I was checking my phone." She holds it up. "Did you recognize them?"

"No." I'm not actually sure I could give a description. Not terribly tall, though with the lights and the shadows, that could be debatable. I had the impression of jeans and a black parka with the hood drawn tight around the face, which, come to think of it, means I'm not even one hundred percent certain on the gender. "God, I hope it wasn't one of our neighbors. They don't need any more reasons to hate me." Though it seems an odd place for a neighbor to be, actually within the grounds, on the Manse's driveway. Perhaps the person was walking a dog that went roaming. I look around again and then put the car into first gear and inch gingerly down the drive.

"You must have left the lights on again," says Carrie in a mildly accusatory tone. I've been concentrating so hard on not running over any more neighbors that I haven't really looked at the house; I'm surprised to see a yellow glow emanating from within the utterly black mass that is the Manse—blacker even than the darkness that it sits within. For a second the light puts me in mind of a dragon: a fire within the belly of the beast. But of course it's sure to be something far more prosaic. An electric bulb, most likely the ceiling light on the second-floor landing. I must have left it on accidentally. Or perhaps I'm still subconsciously keen to keep the house lit, like last night. Though I thought I had turned everything off . . . I think uneasily of the figure I almost ran down. Then I remind myself that I changed all the locks.

"I guess your key worked fine last night," I say as I unlock the front door, not an easy thing to do in the darkness. I should install some kind of security light with a sensor, except of course I'm not going to be staying. Though maybe I should do it anyway, in case I rent the place out after all. Finally I have the door open and a draft of air licks over me, like the beast is breathing out. "I thought changing the locks was the safest thing to do," I add casually. "Who knows how many old keys are knocking around after being rented out all these years. I feel a bit better knowing just you and I have access."

"You can take the girl out of London . . ." Carrie says. She's not quite mocking, but it's not exactly friendly ribbing either. The thawing process is not entirely complete. "Probably sensible, I guess, though I doubt the Highlands of Scotland is fertile ground for intruders."

Actually very fertile seeing as we've had one already, I think with grim amusement. She has her back to me whilst she takes off her coat and hangs it on one of the hooks near the front door, so I don't need to hide my reaction. "God, it's Baltic in here. Is the heating not working properly?" Carrie asks.

"It should be. It was fine earlier." She's right, though: the chill I'm feeling isn't just the remnants of the cold outside. I've only been gone— what?—twenty-five minutes or so; surely the temperature inside couldn't have dropped this much so quickly? I glance at my watch and try to recall the heating timing pattern, then put a hand to the hall radiator. It still holds some warmth, but it doesn't seem as hot as I think it ought, given that the central heating should still be on. "I'll go check."

"I'll put the kettle on," Carrie calls after me.

The second floor, lit by the landing light that I must have indeed left on, is even colder. It's not hard to trace the culprit: the bottom half of the wide sash window in the bathroom that I've been using is a couple of inches open. Was it open this morning? I haven't ever opened it myself, and I can't believe it was left ajar all the time the Manse was unoccupied. Surely I would have felt a draft whilst I showered if it had been open then? The boiler is in a cupboard in the same bathroom. There's no light on it anywhere that I can see. I look in vain for instructions then tentatively press a button with a flame on it. There's an encouraging *whoof* noise, then a blue pilot flame obligingly appears in a tiny open window in the metal casing.

Coming out of the bathroom, I'm faced with Carrie's open bedroom door. That, at least, I'm sure has been open all day, offering a framed glimpse of the glorious view that lies beyond the wide bay windows. But now there is nothing beyond except a heavy pressing darkness. I have the uneasy sensation that mere glass can't possibly keep it out, that the darkness will find cracks to ooze through, an inexorable creeping blanket of dark absorption that will eventually snuff out all light.

Carrie is busying herself with mugs and tea bags when I get to the kitchen. "Sorted," I tell her. "I've boosted the heating now; hopefully it will warm up soon." She doesn't react, her dark head still bent over the mugs. I watch her for a moment, taking in her deliberate silence. It's effective, this passive-aggressive approach. She must have been an absolute joy to live with in her teenage years. I missed all of those. "We should go out," I say suddenly. "We could eat at the local pub or something—it's got to be better than freezing ourselves here. My treat. We can celebrate . . . I don't know . . ." I trail off. What is there to celebrate? We're only here because our mother died and somehow that prompted me to make a cack-handed attempt to reconnect with her. That, and what Jonathan said before I left Egypt.

But Carrie's head has lifted. "The Quaich," she says. There's more life in her voice now. The Quaich is the gastropub in the village. She's pronouncing it wrong, with a hard *k* sound at the end, but who am I to judge? I haven't lived in Scotland for twenty-seven years. "We could walk there, so we can both have a drink. We might even meet some of the locals." The locals. Locals like Morag, or the mystery newspaper-deliverer? I wish I could swallow back the suggestion, but it's too late, Carrie is glancing down at herself. "I'll go and change." Now she's looking me over, assessing my attire too.

"Me too." It hadn't occurred to me to change clothes for a dinner at the local pub, but Carrie's enthusiasm is a stiff wind. It's easier not to fight it.

Soon I'm opening the door of my meager wardrobe, hoping for inspiration, but the clothes inside have not miraculously transformed into designer garments. I opt for skinny jeans with a kitten heel, and a white silk shirt with a deep V at the front that Jonathan always approved of. I head to the bathroom and put on some light makeup—the faint bruise from the poker requires some more careful work with concealer—then on second thought apply some heavier eyeliner. *In for a penny . . .*

Carrie is exiting her bedroom at the same time as I'm leaving the bathroom. Once again she runs a critical eye over me. "Good," she says approvingly. "Though, I think . . ." She dashes back into her bedroom and returns with a long, complicated necklace of different-sized silver circular links, interspersed by chunks of what looks like green glass. It's far bigger and busier than the jewelry I would ever choose to wear, but I put it on obediently.

"Much better," she says with a satisfied air. "Here, look in my bedroom mirror."

I look at myself looking back at me. She's right: it does make a difference, turning a perfectly nice outfit into something much more stylish and considered. Carrie's tall figure is beside me in the frame, now clad in tight black jeans tucked into spike-heeled boots, with a sloppy maroon wide-necked cashmere sweater over the top. Her makeup is artfully edgy without being overblown. There's no question in which direction the eye is drawn.

Suddenly she throws an arm around my shoulders, easy to do from her height, and pulls me against her side. "Look at us," she says smiling. "The Innes girls, together again."

I can't spoil the moment. I let her infectious mood pull an answering smile from me, and I know better than to say, *I'm a Calder.*

MY FATHER IS LIVING IN THE LAKE DISTRICT. HE IS IN A CIVIL partnership with a man named Colin, and they run an organic cheese-making farm together. Sometimes he wonders what his life was like before whatever the accident was that robbed him of his memories, but he would never risk upsetting Colin by investigating. Colin says they ought to be grateful for their happiness, and he is, although he hopes it's not at the expense of anybody else's. The cheese-making is a little dull, truth be told, but it's lucrative, and they go on long holidays to the Bahamas. He feels grateful for what they have and doesn't often wonder if there's anything more.

SEVEN

If I'm harboring any stereotypical qualms about the Quaich being some kind of parochial tavern where the locals stop talking and stare when strangers walk through the door, those are dispelled the minute we enter. The room feels like an airy barn, with high timber beams spanning the broad space. On one side, there are square wooden tables and chairs laid out for dinner, with sparklingly clean glassware, and the other is obviously meant more as a drinking space, with large leather sofas in dark greens and browns flanking low wooden tables. A long bar runs along the entire back wall. Even for a Friday night, it strikes me as busy: all of the dining tables look to be occupied, and there are clusters of people on the sofas and at the bar. Not a single person looks round at us.

"God, I hope we can get a table. I didn't think to call and reserve one."

"Well, we can always have a drink at the bar if there isn't one immediately." Now that Carrie is over her earlier hump, she seems determined not to let anything ruin the evening. "What is a quaich anyway?"

"It's a sort of shallow cup," I say absentmindedly, trying to catch the eye of the waitress. "Always has two handles, and it's usually silver or wooden. I think it's mainly ceremonial now: the cup of friendship, that kind of idea. Ah, here we go." The waitress has spotted us and is approaching with a big smile which doesn't dim in the least even as she tells us it's a thirty-minute wait for a table.

"Why don't you settle over there and I'll get us drinks." I point out two unoccupied wingback chairs by a low table. "What do you want?"

Armed with Carrie's order, I settle myself on one of the high bar stools to wait for attention from the bartender, a pale beanpole figure in super-tight black jeans and a sleeveless black T-shirt who is almost as edgily cool as Carrie. The artistic type: I went through a phase of those at university. If this was fifteen years ago, and I had my way, by the end of the evening I'd be making his close acquaintance up against a wall in a storeroom, or a bathroom, or out back behind the bins. I can imagine it now, I can see it unfold, I can even see the pale of the skin on his stomach, the marks left there by his tight jeans . . . but in an odd way, that removes the desire. There's nothing new to be discovered. Instead I concentrate on trying to read the phrase tattooed down his ropy forearm in a cursive script. I can only pick out a word or two: *if* and *love*. What words could be so important, so monumental, so timeless that he's prepared to carry them with him forever?

A man has approached the bar, squeezing into the space between myself and another customer. He's looking away from me, over his shoulder, nodding in response to something a friend is calling to him. His height and his tousled caramel locks look disturbingly familiar, but I can't see his face. Then he turns back and looks directly at me, a ready smile already in place that turns abruptly to surprise.

"It's you," I blurt out.

Something lights in his clear blue eyes. "You remember?" he asks. His face is broad and open. Even the wayward locks grow away from it, declining to obscure.

"Seeing you at the hotel? It was only yesterday." Does he think I've forgotten the events of one day ago? He's wearing jeans and a smart light blue shirt now, but it's definitely the same man.

The light in his eyes fades, and he shakes his head. "Sorry. Yes, of course. I just thought . . . Sorry, where are my manners?" He sticks out a hand. I'm too puzzled to do anything except numbly shake it. His hand is warmer than mine. "I'm Ben. Ben Rankin."

"Yes." I'm too confused to follow the niceties. "What did you mean when you asked if I remember? Have we met before?"

"Yes. A long time ago. At least, we have if you're the Ailsa Calder from the Manse . . . ?" I nod blankly, and a smile tugs at his mouth. "I wasn't really in doubt. I remember those eyes." There's no hint of an attempt to charm; he's simply stating a fact. "I was a couple of years behind you at the local primary school. You were the queen of the monkey bars, as I recall." Instantly I'm transported back: I can feel myself swinging, getting the timing just right to release one hand and reach for the next bar, the cold metal slapping into my palm, my grip sure and solid. He's right, I was good at it; the best even. I can feel that certainty within the memory. But here and now, I'm still staring at Ben, despite the hubbub and the background music of the bar around me, trying to see the boy he must have been. There's something about his face: the openness of it, the directness of his gaze. There's a thread of something—not even a thread; a suggestion of a thread, gossamer thin, floating through my mind. If I chase it down it might break, or vanish entirely, or maybe it was never there in the first place.

"What can I get you?" interrupts the bartender.

"Let me get it for you," Ben jumps in. "What are you drinking?"

"Oh. Um, a vodka tonic for me and pint of lager for Carrie, but it's okay, I can get it . . ." But Ben is waving away my mild protestations and delivering his own order to the barman too, which is substantial: either he is on a mission or he is ordering for a large group. There's something odd about his accent, even in the few words he has uttered. Just when I think I have it pinned down, it throws in something new. He could be Scottish, South African, American or Australian. When he's done with the bartender, he looks back at me with those startling clear blue eyes. "Consider the drinks an apology. It was such a shock to hear your name at the hotel, I must have looked like a lunatic staring at you—"

"Yep, fairly lunatic-like," I say lightly, and he grimaces in apology.

"I was hoping to find you to explain. And then I heard there was a bit of drama in the café—I can't apologize enough. The hotel is actually known to be really welcoming. I'm so sorry you had a different experience."

"Don't worry, I'm not blaming the hotel. The staff couldn't have been nicer." I hesitate. "The woman . . ."

"Morag."

"Yes. Do you know why she was quite so . . . ?"

"I don't know. I wouldn't read anything into it, though—I know it's not really a valid excuse, but she's not very well." I nod, and he leans in conspiratorially. "Though she wasn't exactly a product of charm school when she had her full health, if I'm honest." I laugh, as he means me to, and he leans back again, shaking his head and smiling. "Ailsa Calder. Who'd have thought."

"I was only at the school for, what, just over two years. I'm surprised you remembered me at all."

"Well, there were only thirty of us in the whole school," he points out. I'd forgotten that, how small the local school was—and perhaps still is—but now it's flooding back to me. Thirty kids aged between five and twelve and two teachers. One classroom that could be partitioned into two, and almost always was. When it was your birthday, you had to stand at the door between the two halves, and the whole school would sing happy birthday, with extra verses, one of which the birthday child had to sing solo: *I'm only six, I'm only six . . .* I hated that—how was it any kind of birthday treat to have to *sing* in front of others? But Ben is still speaking. "And you disappeared in rather dramatic fashion, so I guess that helped the memories stick—ah, thanks, mate, what's the damage?" Ben picks out Carrie's lager and my vodka tonic from the drinks-laden tray the bartender has just pushed across to him, then pauses with the glasses still in his hands. "Look, I'm with a group over there"—he jerks his head toward a noisy group in one corner which is naturally cordoned off by a raised floor and balustrade—"why don't you come and join us? You can tell me what you've been up to all these years, and I can introduce you to some of your neighbors." He grimaces. "Nice ones, I promise."

"Thanks, but I'm here with my sister . . ." I gesture over at her.

"She's welcome, too, of course."

"Oh. Um, thank you. If it's okay with Carrie . . ." But I already know Carrie will be delighted to meet people. I glance back toward her table and find her watching me. She quirks up her eyebrows when she sees me looking at her and mouths, *Okay?* I nod and slide down awkwardly from the bar stool, then take the drinks off Ben. He's tall, Ben; even with my heels I have to tip my head back a little to look at his face.

"Okay. I'll go deliver these drinks, and I'll let you figure it out with your sister. No pressure. Except that I'm agog with curiosity about you. Dying of it, in fact. But really, no pressure." He's grinning as he says it. It seems as if his smiles hang around his eyes and mouth, looking for any opportunity to return. I can't help but laugh in response. I'm still smiling as I walk to the wingback chairs.

"You seem to have made quite the impression," says a wide-eyed Carrie, taking her pint of lager from me. "Do tell. Who is that?"

"That," I say, enjoying the revelation, "is the hotel manager I told you about."

She stops with her pint halfway to her mouth, a parody of astonishment. "You're kidding."

"Nope. It turns out we were at school together." I settle into the seat opposite her. I would never have imagined she drank pints. Some sort of expensive Czech bottled beer, perhaps, but not lager in a pint glass. I don't want to explore the layers of stereotyping exposed by my surprise.

"Wow." She looks across the bar at the rowdy group to whom Ben is delivering drinks. There's some fifteen of them, perhaps slightly more men than women at first glance. "And he remembered you?"

"Yep. I have that effect on people," I say, tongue firmly in cheek, and she laughs. "Actually it seems my family history is quite the local legend. Even the gym guy knew about it." I take a sip of my vodka tonic. Probably everybody in that group, if they are from round here, will know my story. For a moment I consider bolting, but there's no point in putting off the inevitable. "Ben's asked us both to go across and join them."

Carrie's eyes light up. "We should totally do that," she says decisively, then quickly backtracks. "That is, if you want to. If you just want to have a quiet drink, I'm fine with that, too."

I laugh. "Carrie, I know you're dying to meet the locals. It's okay to say it."

"Yep, I am. I'm not like you; I'm a people person, what can I say?" Now that I've let her off the hook, she's perfectly happy to laugh at herself, but her words catch at me nonetheless. *I'm not like you; I'm a people person.* I know I'll find them turning over in my mind later. But she's forging onward. "We're here for a while. It would be nice to have a few people I can grab a coffee or something with."

"Just a coffee? Or are you hoping for a little Highland fling? There's a fair few men to choose from right over there." I waggle my eyebrows suggestively, which for some reason sends her into reams of giggles. I feel a warmth inside me at that and half wish Ben hadn't invited us over—I'm not in any hurry to break up our tête-à-tête.

"Definitely no Highland fling," she says firmly, when the giggles have died down. "I'm off men." Before I can quiz her on that, she stands up and grabs her pint and bag. "Let's go join them then."

I follow her lean figure across the bar. Her hair is pulled back loosely in an artful mess, and her maroon cashmere sweater has slipped off one shoulder. Everything about her screams casual, sloppy sexiness; I see how it draws the eyes of almost every man as we cross the floor. It's a wonder we are in any way related.

MY FATHER WAS IN MI6 (ALL THAT TRAVELING WITH THE GEMS was actually a really good cover for being a spook). He was fluent in six languages and held black belt status in an unspecified martial art. As part of a major anti-terrorist operation, he single-handedly saved thousands of lives, but as a result became a target. His body has never been found, but the chatter that MI5 picked up at the time of his disappearance suggested that he was assassinated by a professional killer in Antwerp. Those who were closest to him in MI6 lament the fact that, for the sake of national security, his family can never know the true hero that he was.

EIGHT

Ben must have been keeping an eye out for us; by the time we reach the two steps to the raised area, he's waiting to greet us. "I'm Ben. You must be Carrie," he says, smiling and extending a hand to her. I see her take a deep breath and her shoulders shift somehow, a subtle movement, and then she puts out her own hand. Behind Ben I can see interested looks from his friends. They seem to range in age from early twenties to late thirties. "Watch your step there," he warns, turning to offer me a hand to steady me on the stairs. He has rolled back the sleeves of his shirt now to reveal tanned forearms. He certainly didn't get those from a Scottish winter. "Let me introduce you both to everyone, and then we can have fun watching you forget all our names. This is Fiona, Alistair, Gemma, Stefano, and here is—"

But I've stopped listening because over the shoulder of Gemma, or perhaps that was Fiona, next in line to be introduced is a face I've met before. My charming non-burglar, Mr. Jamie McCue.

"And this is Fiona's brother, Jamie," Ben is saying.

"Actually, we've met." Jamie steps forward with a handshake. Ben quirks up his eyebrows in surprise and Jamie obligingly explains. "We ran into each other near the Manse the other day and figured out that we're neighbors." Jamie's eyes are on mine as he pushes a lock of his dark hair off his forehead. There's a wariness within them, and also a touch of mischief, as if he's daring me to dispute his account.

Carrie glances at me. "You didn't mention that."

"Well, that's understandable," nods Ben sagely, saving me from having to reply. "Jamie is eminently inconsequential." The two of them drop onto a well-trodden path of mutual insults, and the moment to contradict him is gone. He's not as tall as I remembered, or maybe it's the combination of my heels and the fact that most of the men here look small compared to Ben. Like the other guys in this group, Jamie's dressed in jeans and a shirt, but the jeans are tighter, and the shirt is very slim fitting. Mr. McCue has an eye for fashion, I would think.

Carrie has been swept into a conversation with Ben and a few others, leaving Jamie and me to one side, half turned to each other and half watching the rest of the crowd. "So what are your plans for the Manse? A full London-style makeover?" he asks, the faintest touch of disdain in his voice when he says *London*.

I don't answer his questions because Ben's introductory words have just sunk in for me. "Which one is your sister?" I ask him abruptly.

This gets his full attention; his half-mocking grin drops abruptly. "Please," he says, laying his fingers on my arm. It's the arm that is holding my drink; I can't jerk away. His eyes are pleadingly insistent. "Dinnae say anything. Please. I dinnae want her upset. And we dinnae really broadcast her obsession with the Manse, you ken—"

"Which one is your sister?" I look around the group, as if to divine the answer for myself. Fiona. Which one is Fiona? None of the women here look like the "Wuthering Heights"-type figure I've imagined haunting the second floor of the Manse.

Jamie yields. "The one talking to your sister," he says dejectedly.

I glance across at Carrie and find her in conversation with an extraordinarily slight woman in her late twenties. She has a boyish build, almost entirely flat chested, without a scrap of fat on her, but there's a sinewy strength to the arms that are revealed by her sleeveless top.

She's in profile and I can't see her eyes, but her wavy, blunt bob-cut hair is certainly not as dark as her brother's. Still, I can believe they are related. There's something about the line of the nose, and a similarity in their compact, fine-boned frames . . .

But this, this is the woman who likes to wander through my family's house uninvited; the woman who is *a wee bit away wi' the fairies*. As I watch, Carrie laughs at something Fiona has said, and Fiona herself grins and turns a little more toward me, and I see the way her thick hair fans out like a triangle around her pale face. There's a sense of dread building in my stomach. I have to stamp on the urge to drag Carrie away from Fiona, out of the pub entirely.

"Please," says Jamie anxiously from beside me, but my eyes are fixed on Fiona and Carrie. "She's harmless, really. And this thing with the Manse and your father, it's just a fascination—"

I swing toward him. "My *father*? What do you mean, this thing with my father?"

"I didnae mean—" He's wretchedly uncomfortable now, his eyes jumping from me to the group, as he tries to project an air of casual conversation.

"What thing with my father?"

"Shh, please, I'll tell you, I promise—"

"Tell me now."

"Another time, I promise, just please, please, not the now—I cannae ruin Ben's birthday."

"It's Ben's birthday?"

"Guilty as charged." The man himself has joined our conversation, with a bottle of Peroni in hand.

"But then I should have been buying *you* drinks," I lament. It hasn't escaped my notice that Jamie has taken the opportunity to slink away from my side.

Ben shrugs. "Bar karma: it all works out in the end." Something beeps, and he pulls a phone out of his pocket and checks the screen. "Piotr is running late," he says.

"Tell him to take the back road," calls Fiona.

"Why?" asks Ben, but he's already typing with the thumb of the hand that's holding the phone, his Peroni held casually in the other.

She shrugs. "Not sure. But tell him." Now that the conversational groups have merged, Carrie and Fiona have blended into our circle.

"Done," says Ben, putting away his phone. "Anyway, Carrie—didn't you say you two were celebrating?"

"That's right," Carrie says brightly. "It's the first time we have lived under the same roof for over fifteen years. We thought it was worth celebrating." She holds my gaze and I can't read those gray eyes at all. Then she smiles, and something in me releases. I step forward to clink my glass against hers, and it's like I'm watching us through the eyes of our audience, this group of friends of Ben. We look like we have a past in common: shared history, whispered secrets. We look like we could be sisters.

The barmaid brings a bucket of beers and some bottles of wine. The alcohol flows, and the conversation too. Someone hands me a wine-glass and before long I've lost track of how many times it has been topped up. Ben has booked a large table for dinner and won't hear of Carrie and me eating separately. He shanghais the poor waitress into squeezing in another two seats, though from the way she hangs on his words, I suspect she would squeeze in ten more seats and the rest of the customers be damned if it got her another heartfelt thank-you from Ben—and I think he knows that too. I answer the same questions from several different people by saying the same things—my name, where I live, what I do: a micro manifesto of who I am—but no one digs fur-ther. In any case, it's a boisterous group and the conversation rarely runs straight; it follows any tangent that might lead to hoots of laugh-ter. When I glance across to see whether Carrie is okay, I see her hold-ing forth to Fiona and Ben, her audience in stitches. I suppose I shouldn't have doubted that the actress knows how to play to a crowd.

But . . . Fiona. Still talking to Carrie. She's hardly the unhinged nymph I had in mind, but now that I've seen her, that image is changing: now it's *her* that I see, sitting cross-legged on the bed in the master bedroom. One elbow rests on her knee as she taps the end of her cigarette against the lip of the earthen ashtray that lies on the bed in front of her. Her head is bent to the ashtray but as I watch it lifts to reveal her face, at the exact same moment as the real Fiona turns to find my eyes upon her. That triangle of hair, atop a slight body . . . I turn away quickly, unease pooling in my stomach again, and find Ben beside me. "Come sit next to me," he implores, ushering me toward a long table that must be set for at least twenty. "I haven't had a proper chance to speak to you yet."

"But it's your birthday." I resist the urge to glance back to see if Fiona is watching me. "I can't really take pride of place next to the birthday boy."

"Of course you can. And Carrie too. These reprobates get bored by me all the time; they'll probably welcome the break." He's pulling out a seat for me and I have little choice but to sit in it, with Ben on my left. As we're such a big party, we seem to be on a fixed menu: the waitress is already laying out sharing plates as starters, and stops to speak to Ben about something. The rest of the crowd is beginning to filter over too. There's a young couple settling into chairs on my right who are deep in conversation with the people opposite them. I turn to look directly across the table and find myself meeting the eyes of a dark-haired man in his late thirties to whom I know I was introduced earlier. He has an oddly creased face, like rumpled bedsheets, and eyes that are rarely still. Right now they're picking me over and he's making no attempt to hide it.

"Hi. I'm sorry, I can't remember your name." I'm aiming for disarming charm.

"Alistair. Alistair Jamieson." Is it my imagination or did he stress the surname?

"Ah yes! Ali."

"To my pals."

It might just be his broad accent, but there seems to be something truculent in his manner. It sparks a small rebellion in me. I resolve to use *Ali* regardless of whether he would like me as a *pal*. "Excellent. Ali. Sorry." I grimace theatrically. "I'm useless with names. I'm Ailsa Calder."

"I ken who you are. It hasnae taken you lassies long to get right to the heart of the community, has it?"

Definitely truculent. I play tone-deaf and smile brightly. "You sound like you grew up here. Did I go to school with you too?"

"Aye, you did." His lips twist sourly. "Though I'd lay money you only remember Ben."

"Actually I don't even remember him, really." There's a certain edge in my own words too, now.

"Shove up one, Ali, unless you want me to climb over you." It's Jamie, trying to squeeze between the wall and the table to settle into an empty chair.

"Thanks, but I can do without your arse in my face," Alistair—Ali—grunts, as he moves along one seat. Now he's facing Ben, and I have my intruder opposite me. This seating plan leaves a lot to be desired. "That your jeep out there, Jamie?"

"Aye, got her last week."

"Nice piece of machinery." There's the beginning of a sardonic smile hovering near Ali's mouth, and I realize he's caught the attention of a few others. I sense he's working up to something. "Couldnae help but notice her out there in the car park. Did you park her blindfolded with a ferret down your trousers?" A bark of surprised laughter escapes me to blend with the general hilarity Ali's words have prompted.

"Ach, away tae fuck." There's no aggression in the words; Jamie doesn't seem in the least bit riled. He hikes his chair in closer to the table and then looks across at me, a conspiratorial gleam in his eye. *We have secrets, you and I*, he seems to be saying. I look at my wineglass instead. It appears to be empty again. "So, Ailsa, what brings you to the Highlands? Are you just here for a short while or will you be staying?"

"It's temporary." On my left, I feel Ben turning away from the waitress and tuning in to our conversation. "I, um, inherited the Manse when my mum died recently"—I lift a few fingers slightly to acknowledge the murmurs of sympathy—"so I'm just trying to sort that out."

"With a view to what? Keeping, selling or renting?" Jamie asks.

"I'd like to sell. But there are a few legal hurdles . . ." I trail off and shrug.

"I'd love to talk to you about buying it sometime," Ben says seriously. Longer exposure to his laid-back drawl has given me no better understanding of his ever-changing accent. "I've always loved that place. I figure it could be run as a hunting lodge, under the same franchise as the hotel."

"Really? I may well take you up on that." Could it be this easy? Get the Presumption of Death certificate, sell to Ben? And then what—skip off back to London, leaving Carrie? "You know, my folks wanted to run it as a bed-and-breakfast when they bought it."

"When was that?"

"Just before I was born. My dad had a little bit of money from a relative that died and they blew it all on the Manse. It ought to have been a good investment but my mum was renting it out over the last twenty-odd years, and it never made much."

"It's never rented well," says Jamie. "I used to work at the estate agency that manages it, you ken. A place like that ought to have been picking up long lets, not just the odd week here and there."

Ali speaks up. "Maybe it's because of its history."

My eyes jump to his face involuntarily: does he mean my story? I know he's seen my reaction. There's a sly satisfaction to be read in his gleaming eyes, in the smirk of his mouth. "Really? What do you mean?" I ask with studied calm. There's an odd high-pitched beep that comes from the other side of Ben. I see Fiona glancing at her watch.

"He means its Internet history," interjects Jamie. He's certainly recovered his confidence. "Someone put a bad review on TripAdvisor, saying the place was really strange. Cold drafts, felt like they were being watched, like someone had been through their possessions—that sort of thing." His dark eyes are on me as he speaks, a hint of a secret smile within them as he adds with faux innocence, "Anything going bump in the night, Ailsa?" I know he means to reference his own midnight visitation, but now I'm wondering if he was wrong about his Manse-obsessed sister: maybe she doesn't only visit when the property is empty . . . I think of the figure that may or may not have been in the box room, of my own feeling of being observed, and an involuntary shiver runs through me.

Ben saves me from having to respond. "Rubbish," he snorts robustly. "Probably one of your lot at the agency trying to get some business from ghost-hunting nutters or something."

"I wouldnae put it past them," Jamie concedes, "but it backfired if so."

"I dinnae ken about the TripAdvisor thing," Ali says. "I was actually talking about the proper history of the place. You ken what Manse means? Good. So then the question is . . . where's the church?"

"In the village," I say, puzzled. "Just down the road from here."

"Nope. Well, aye, but that's not the original church. That one was built in the late eighteen hundreds. Where's the original kirk?" He glances around and a small smile touches his lips. He's in his element now that he's drawn his audience in.

"Go on," says Ben. "You know you're dying to tell us."

Ali throws him a grin. There seems to be genuine affection there. "Aye, well, it's actually a sad story. I would imagine Sassenachs such as yourselves"—he gestures at Carrie and me, and even that small motion is somehow patronizing—"dinnae ken much about the Jacobite rebellion—"

"1745!" calls out Carrie. "English oppression. Bonnie Prince Charlie, the Young Pretender, raised an army that was defeated at the Battle of Culloden." She catches my eye with a smirk. I raise my glass to her, surprised and impressed in equal measure.

"Top of the class," says Ali, inclining his head toward her, clearly rather impressed too. "So, after the battle, Charlie goes into hiding and eventually escapes—"

"To Skye, right? Hence 'The Skye Boat Song'?" asks Ben. He begins to sing in a surprisingly good baritone. *"Speed, bonnie boat, like a bird on the wing—"* Fiona joins her voice to his, and Carrie, too, in her wondrous alto; Ben starts to conduct with enthusiastic theatricality and now half the table has joined in, including me. *"—onward the sailors cry. Carry the lad that's born to be king, over the sea to Skye."*

"Give it a rest; this isn't *The X Factor*," the beanpole bartender yells over.

The song peters out but we are all giggling now, buoyed up by the togetherness of the singing. Ali waits a few moments until he has garnered sufficient attention again. "Aye, Bonnie Prince Charlie did indeed speed off to Skye, and then ultimately to France. But the Scotland he left behind was never the same. The Highland clan system was effectively outlawed, and a law was passed making it illegal to own a sword, wear a kilt or in fact wear any tartan at all. Even speaking in Gaelic was forbidden. And those laws were enforced, with gusto: the English were not taking any chances. Even the slightest whiff of rebellion about a man would result in death. Now"—his voice has dropped a little, forcing his audience to lean in—"legend has it that there was a pocket of strong Jacobite resistance right here. The village was smaller then, maybe only a dozen houses, and clustered much nearer the Manse than where it lies the now. When the English soldiers came to wipe it out, all the women and children went into hiding within the kirk—the church, you ken," he adds for Carrie's benefit. "The minister, though, was a sniveling, cowardly man. He'd thrown his lot in with the English early on and had been repeatedly preaching to his congregation that they owed obedience to the occupiers. When the soldiers came, the menfolk told them that the women and children had run into the woods to hide, but the minister revealed their true hiding place. For that, they spared him his life and his house. Then the soldiers went to the kirk and demanded that all the sons were sent out to be slaughtered along with their fathers, but the women refused. So the soldiers barred the doors and set light to the kirk." He looks around his audience. His jerky gaze has calmed, as if the act of storytelling has peeled him back to a quiet strength beneath. "It burned for three days, so unnaturally hot and fierce that nobody could put it out. By the time the fire died out, even the masonry had been reduced to mere rubble." I'm aware of the background murmur of the bar, but it's at a distance, as if we are in a bubble, where the only noise that matters is the de-spairing, terrified screams mixed with the cracking and roaring of the blisteringly hot fire that will not be appeased. "So the minister lived out the rest of his days at the Manse, without a kirk to preach in, for no one would rebuild it. But the spirits of those women and children never forgave him. He was haunted and tormented for the rest of his years. And even after he died, the Manse has continued to be haunted by the women and children who were lost in that fire."

There's a silence that sits over us all, despite the hubbub from the rest of the room. The laughter and the warmth of singing "The Skye Boat Song" might as well have happened years ago. "How is it that I've lived here for fifteen years and never heard that story before?" The question comes from someone farther down the table; I'm not sure who exactly.

"I ken it," says Fiona.

"And?" asks Ben. "Is there any truth to it?"

She nods. "There's something to it. Ali hasnae quite got it right, though." She sounds thoughtful. "The minister didnae betray his con-gregation. He saved some of the bairns—I dinnae ken how, but he put them out of reach." Ali doesn't dispute her. Somehow Fiona seems to have the authority on this.

"Ah, but then why would the Manse be haunted?" Jamie asks, winking at me to show his tongue is firmly in cheek.

"Is it really, though?" says Fiona in a musing tone. It sounds like she's taking the question seriously. I glance across at her in surprise, but she's partially hidden by Ben's lean bulk. All I can see are her fin-gers playing with the wax drippings at the base of a candlestick. Sturdy fingers, with the nails filed short. Despite my own flights of fancy, I know that if the Manse is haunted at all, it's by the non-ethereal, fully corporeal woman sitting to Ben's left. It doesn't seem any more comforting as a prospect than ghosts.

"Having spent two perfectly lovely nights in it, I can assure you the Manse is not in fact haunted," says Carrie pragmatically.

"Unless you're prepared to count a dodgy boiler as a manifestation of paranormal activity," I add.

Ben laughs, and suddenly the bubble bursts and the rest of the world rushes in, with its music and chatter, the clink of glasses and bursts of laughter. But I notice that Ali's looking at me again, in a return of that jerky gaze which makes me feel like I'm watching a movie shot in the handheld camera style where the frame never quite stays still. I pick up my wineglass. Somehow it's full again. I need to be careful—I can already feel the effects of the alcohol, how it loosens the way I hold myself together.

"All okay?" asks Ben quietly in words meant just for me. There's an intimacy in that, and in the heat that crosses the tiny divide between his thigh and mine, but a careless intimacy; I suspect he just can't help himself.

"Yes, all good," I answer with deliberate brightness, though Ali's story is still a fog around me, and Fiona's presence has become a dark, throbbing pressure in my mind. I look for an innocuous topic. "You know, I've been wondering. You don't exactly sound like you spent the rest of your childhood here." There's another digital beep and Fiona glances at her watch again. I glance at my own: a minute after ten.

He shakes his head. "I didn't. My folks got divorced when I was twelve and I went to live with Mum in Sydney, but I came back here every summer—every Aussie summer, that is, so over the Christmas holidays—so I kept up with all my Scottish mates. But yeah, the accent does kind of roam." I can see him as a teenager, moving effortlessly between worlds, his friendly, unruffled demeanor never faltering. *Hail fellow well met*: I always thought of that phrase as describing a particular type of bumblingly oblivious Englishman, but it fits Ben perfectly and he is neither bumbling nor oblivious. Nor, indeed, English—or Scottish, really. A mongrel.

"Sydney: gorgeous weather and beaches." I wonder if he surfs. He would be utterly at home on a beach; he has that air about him. Though he was not out of place in the hotel, and nor is he in this bar. But nonetheless, my mind is spinning out a scene of a younger, golden Ben horsing around in the water with friends, playing touch rugby on the beach, cycling to school with sand still dusting those tanned forearms. "Versus Scotland: rain and midges." I pretend to balance them, judging their weight with one in either hand, then I shake my head. "Nope, not following the logic here."

He smiles. The stillness of his gaze is in direct contrast to the constant movement of Ali's sharp, hooded eyes, which from time to time I can still feel upon me. "I think you're underselling the Highlands. I love it here. It's so . . . Actually, I'm not sure there's a word to describe the scenery, the air, all of this . . ." He waves a hand as if to pull the outside in. "And the people are great, really down-to-earth, plus my dad is here . . . So yeah, I've lived in a lot of places—I spent a ton of time studying and working in the States, too—but the Highlands kick them all into touch. It's so . . . raw." He's completely unpretentious in his quiet passion; it's infectious. I incline my head, accepting his points. I know what he means by raw, but it's not quite the right word. It doesn't convey the implacability of the landscape.

Suddenly there's a chorus of hellos as a tall, thin man with a lean, intelligent face appears behind Ben. "Piotr!" Ben says, standing to give him a greeting that lies somewhere between an arm wrestle and a hug.

"Sorry," Piotr says, in a marked Eastern European accent. "Accident on the main road, happened right in front of me. I had to wait for the police as a witness."

"Should have listened to Fi . . ."

"I always listen to Fi. I just didn't see the message until afterward." He reaches over to shake my hand. "Hi, Piotr."

I quickly rearrange my face from confusion to a smile. "Ailsa. And this is Carrie."

"She inherited the Manse," puts in Ben.

"The Manse? Isn't that where—"

"Sit down, Piotr. We're all famished waiting on you," Fiona interrupts. "There's a seat down the other end."

Piotr lifts a hand then moves off to find his seat. I stare after him, confused, then turn to Ben. "What was all that about the message and the accident?"

But Ben is settling himself down again, and either doesn't hear me or chooses not to answer. "Where were we?" he says. "What about you? Where have you been calling home for the last twenty-five-plus years?"

"Oh." I take in his deliberately bland expression and yield. It is his birthday after all; he should be able to talk about whatever he wants to talk about. Or not talk about. "God, everywhere. Nowhere. Literally." His eyebrows quirk upward inquiringly. "We moved around a lot for the first five years or so, then my mum settled in Surrey." He looks like he's about to say something about that, but I don't want to talk about my mother. I rush on. "Carrie is my half sister." I see Carrie turn her head and regard me coolly for a moment before she turns back to answer a question from the person on her right. It's the briefest of moments, but I register the complete lack of expression on her face, and at a stroke, the sense of connection from earlier is severed. I pick up my glass again, then put it down without drinking anything.

"And now?" Ben asks.

It's a struggle to regain the thread of the conversation. "Well, I've been traveling a lot with work since I left uni; it's hard to say what counts as home."

"No plans to make it the Manse?" He's smiling, and I smile back as I shake my head, but it hasn't escaped me that he, like Jamie, like Ali, has returned again to the same topic, and the leaden unease creeps back into my stomach. Even on a night away from it, meeting new friends, I can't escape the Manse.

MY FATHER RUNS A BEACH BAR IN VIETNAM. IT'S A RAMSHACKLE place, but popular with the tourists, of which there are more and more as the off-the-beaten tracks become ever more beaten. He hardly ever travels; after all, where do you go on holiday when life's already a beach? Though the more accurate reason would be that he's fairly sure his false passport would no longer pass muster. He has a wife and a child—everything he walked away from, in fact—and the odd furtive hookup with a tourist to keep things interesting, and this time round he's happier. Whether it's the place or the timing or a change in himself that's made the difference, he couldn't say.

NINE

Somehow it's past 1 A.M. and we are spilling into the breathless cold of the dark night. Carrie and I are losing an argument with Ben over the fact that he has picked up the tab for everyone, but won't hear of us paying him back. People are milling around in the car park, sorting out lifts, wishing Ben a happy birthday as they leave. If this is an average Friday night for the Quaich, the management must be very happy with the business.

"Everyone—at least, everyone who's left—is coming back to my place for a drink or two," says Ben to Carrie and me. But mainly to Carrie. "I think the single malt Ali has just given me might be the main attraction." He holds up an expensive-looking bottle in a presentation case. In the dim lighting of the car park, I can't see the brand, but it wouldn't matter to me anyway. I'm trying to work out who's left in the much whittled-down group, but I'm hampered by the darkness. There's Carrie and Ben and me, obviously, and Ali and Jamie—the latter smoking a cigarette at the bonnet of a jeep which, to be fair to Ali, does look like it was abandoned rather than parked—and Piotr, who I remember thinking at dinner looked more than a little enamored with Carrie. And Fiona. Still Fiona. I wish her gone, and the intensity of that feeling disturbs me. Though of course, this is her space, her homeland, her circle of friends. It's Carrie and I who should be leaving.

"So," prompts Ben. "A drink?"

I look at Carrie, who is looking at me. "Ugh," I say. "I'm really not a whisky fan."

"Aye, I figured." This is Ali.

"What's that supposed to mean?" The words slip out before I can stop them. I add a laugh, but it fails to soften the bite. I should have known he would consider my alcohol preferences as just another nail in the coffin of my belonging here. I can only imagine his disgust if he found out I also wouldn't vote for independence and I'm not comfortable in Glasgow.

He holds up his hands in mock surrender. "All right, all right, hen." His tone is so clearly patronizing that I feel a sudden desire to punch him. "Chill, lassie, I'm not trying to be arsey."

"Aye right, that'll be a first," snorts Fiona.

"Don't mind Ali," Ben says. "He's a softy inside really."

"Really?" Carrie laces the word with skepticism.

"Nope, not in the least," says Fiona, and the two of them begin to giggle.

"Thanks, Fi," says Ali in a surly tone. I can't tell whether it's for comic effect. "Fabulous to see I can rely on you for support after all these years."

Carrie and Fiona are giggling too much to reply, both sitting on the low stone wall that separates the car park from the pavement, bent over with their heads together. Apparently I'm not the only one who's had a little too much to drink. I move toward them, hovering indecisively. How to extract Carrie? Perhaps it's very simple. Perhaps I would be expected to herd Carrie home; maybe that's what older sisters are supposed to do. Or will she feel that I'm being overbearing? Does she in fact want to take Ben up on his unspoken intentions, despite claiming to have sworn off men?

"Are you a whisky fan, Carrie? Yes? Good lass." Ben turns to me. "And I have plenty else to drink besides whisky. My place is only another hundred meters or so; come for one drink, at least." I can't see his eyes properly in the dark.

"Oh shit, I left my coat inside," exclaims Carrie suddenly.

"Come on," says Jamie, leaving his jeep. "I'll help you look for it." He puts out a hand and pulls Carrie up to standing.

"Thanks," I say, throwing him a grateful smile. I watch them head back into the Quaich. I hear a snatch of a conversation—no more than a word or two, but I think I hear Jonathan's name and I glance to where Ben, Piotr and Ali have moved off to one side, involved in an animated conversation that is taking all of their attention. As I watch, Ali darts a glance at me with scornful glee, and seconds later his words float across the car park: *Jesus, he must be fifty if he's a day. Daddy issues, much?* A crimson wave of vitriol flows through me, almost blinding me. I have to take a few deep breaths before it recedes.

I turn away deliberately, toward Fiona. She's holding a cigarette now, an unfocused look on her face. I smell the smoke and it immediately puts me in mind of the Manse, and suddenly I can't stop myself. I sit on the uncomfortably uneven stone wall next to her. "Fiona." She turns to look at me, the small movement almost upsetting her balance given the alcohol we've all sunk. "I know you like to visit the Manse." Her eyes are trying and failing to focus on me, but I can see she understands. She knows what I'm talking about and she doesn't even try to deny it. My next words are hard and low. "I'm warning you. If you ever visit the Manse uninvited, I will have you arrested, do you hear me?"

She looks back at me, swaying almost imperceptibly. I can't see the color of her eyes in this light, and it occurs to me that I don't even know what color I should be seeing. The moment drags out. Then she carefully lifts the hand that isn't holding the cigarette and deliberately reaches out toward me with it. I try to pull away, aghast, but without standing up I can't get far enough away; almost in slow motion, I watch her hand get nearer and nearer to my face, unable to escape it. She pats me gently on the cheek. "S'okay," she says. Her eyes still aren't focused. "You 'n' me are going to be great pals."

I stare at her, almost shaking, both floored and furious in equal measure. "You're not listen—"

"Success!" I hear Carrie call, and I look up. She's exiting the Quaich, brandishing her coat, with Jamie behind her; there is nothing more I can say. I stand up.

"Do you want a lift home?" Jamie asks me. "It's all right, I wasnae drinking." He looks down at Fiona, still sitting on the wall with her head bent. "Unlike this one." His expression is a mix of exasperation and something else. I wonder what it's like, to feel tied to someone like this, someone who walks in your own friendship circles so that you can never quite escape. He becomes aware of the weight of my gaze and gives me a rueful smile and a shrug.

"Actually, that would be great." I smile back at him, a proper smile. It may be the first one I've bestowed upon him. "Right, Carrie?"

She sighs theatrically. "Much as I hate to say it, I do have a rehearsal to get up for in the morning." She turns to call out to Ben. "Can I take a rain check on that rather fine whisky?"

"Anytime." Then his gaze is caught by Fiona on the wall, and he leaves Ali and Piotr. "You okay, hon?" he asks, hunkering down.

She slings an arm round his shoulders. "Happy birthday, Big Ben. Ding-dong. You're going to have a good year." That annoying beep comes again from her watch. Nobody reacts.

"Up you come." He has her on her feet now, though I doubt there's much weight on them; it's all being supported by Ben. "Is that a fact? A Fi fact?"

"A Fi fact. Incontrovertible." The last word is slurred almost beyond recognition.

Jamie has unlocked the jeep. Ben helps Fiona into the passenger seat, then turns to Carrie and me with a rueful smile. "You're sure I can't tempt you both with a nightcap?"

"Another time," I say.

"Definitely, there will be plenty more opportunities. Well, I'll see you both soon." There's nothing to be read into his words—he's not putting any particular emphasis on them—but his eyes rest more heavily on Carrie. It occurs to me that I've never been in a social situation such as this with a grown-up Carrie before. It occurs to me that it would be Carrie with whom the bartender would be looking for a knee-trembler in the storeroom, and it's suddenly clear to me that my place in the world has shifted: I thought I was *here*, but actually I'm *there*, only I don't yet know what *there* is like.

"Hop in," says Jamie, a touch impatiently, and we do. As Jamie pulls out of the car park, my attention is taken by Fiona. From my vantage point behind her, I can see her reflection in the wing mirror. She has wound down the window and has her head turned to the stream of chilly night air, her hair blown back from her face, her eyes closed as the air streams in. She could be asleep, except I can see that her lips are moving, though I can't hear any sound.

In a matter of minutes we are back at the Manse, once again lit from within, but this time deliberately—Carrie and I left the hallway light on to welcome us home. Jamie is enough of a gentleman to hop out of his seat and open the car door for us. Carrie thanks him prettily then calls an unacknowledged good-bye to Fiona. Then she heads rather unsteadily for the front door whilst hunting in her bag for her keys. Jamie offers me a hand to help me out of the car.

"Thank you," he says quietly. "For not saying anything. She's doing better . . . I mean, she shouldnae really drink—Ben's never a great influence for that—but it was his birthday and all . . . Really, she's doing well."

"Don't mention it." Instantly there's a feeling of guilt clawing up inside me. Though I doubt Fiona will remember our confrontation in the morning anyway.

I want to ask Jamie what he meant before, but as if reading my mind, Jamie says, "I will explain; I promise. But . . ." With a rueful smile he gestures at Carrie, struggling at the front door with her keys, then at Fiona, possibly passed out in the passenger seat. "Can I pop round for coffee sometime?" He smiles gratefully at my nod and touches my arm gently. "Night, then."

"Night." He's turning away when his words from earlier register with me—*She shouldnae really drink.* Does he mean she's on some kind of medication? I'm suddenly appalled at myself. Did I really just threaten a mentally vulnerable individual? Then Carrie manages to open the front door, allowing a slice of yellow light to wash out over the driveway. It's the only light I can see in the 360 degrees of darkness that surrounds this house, and I feel the impact of that. We are a long way from city-living here, from the kind of living I'm used to, with an untold number of people within a couple of hundred feet who could potentially be called on for help should the situation warrant it. Here I could scream to the heavens and not a soul would come running. Our very closest neighbors are a good mile away. Even in a car, that would mean several minutes at least before help arrived—and that's supposing you could actually raise the neighbor on the phone in the first place, given the dodgy reception . . .

Jamie is climbing back into his seat now. "Thanks again for the lift," I call.

"Anytime." I watch his taillights disappear down the drive. The night is still, with only the fading engine sounds disturbing it. There are stars in the sky in a way that you never see in the city, thousands and thousands of them, in sprinkles here and cloudy nebulas there. I can't reconcile the serene beauty of this nightscape with the roiling, burning furnace of gases that science tells me is the cause of these elegant pinpoints of light. I watch the sky for a few minutes longer. Nothing moves.

The Manse that I eventually enter is warm; I feel its heat encircle me and instantly I'm yawning. Carrie is already in the kitchen, filling up the kettle. She's put the radio on low on some kind of channel where there's a lot of talking. It's very soporific. "Tea?" she asks. "Or straight to bed?"

"Tea, please. And a large glass of water, I think."

"Me too. I'm not quite sure who was topping up my wineglass but it always seemed to be full." She yawns, too, covering her mouth delicately with one hand. I think of a cat. "I had fun, though. Did you?"

"Yes, I did." *Did I?* There was plenty that should have been fun, or at least pleasant, but I can't shake the presence of Fiona from the evening; she is threaded through every scene. But Carrie looks like she's waiting for more from me, so I add, "Everyone was really nice. Well, maybe not Ali."

"Yeah, he seems to be an acquired taste." I smile at her caustic tone. "He's funny, though, in that biting kind of way. Hey, do you want to know where I got my Jacobite history from?" There's a sly grin hovering round her mouth as she looks up at me from pouring out the hot water. I nod obligingly. "I don't know if you went to the loo while we were at the Quaich, but the Ladies is papered with snippets of Scottish history. I read it just before we all sat down."

I can't help laughing and she grins back broadly, while trying not to spill the tea she's handing me. I wonder how many cups she drinks a day; she seems to be permanently either drinking or making one. We sip the hot tea in companionable silence, leaning against the kitchen counter rather than sitting down at the table. If I sat down I might go to sleep right there.

"Jamie seemed quite taken with you." I look at her in surprise. Jamie? I would have imagined if she had said that about anybody, it would have been Ben; he spoke to me more than Jamie did. As if reading my mind, she says, "Well, Ben too, but I gather from Ali he's quite the player, so . . ." She shrugs dismissively, and the maroon sweater slips off one shoulder; if Piotr could see her now, he would be even more lost. And Ben, too. "But Jamie was looking at you most intensely."

She's looking at me intensely herself, now, trying to gauge my reaction, with no idea that she's got the wrong end of the stick. Jamie isn't the least bit interested in me romantically; he's simply very interested in making sure that I keep his secrets. Well, Fiona's secret, really. But regardless, she has obviously picked up on something. There must be some kind of undercurrent of collusion between Jamie and me. I look for a way to dissemble. "I rather thought Ben was more interested in you. And Piotr was thoroughly smitten."

She smiles. "He's sweet. But not really my type." I note that she didn't comment on Ben. What is her type? I wonder. Carrie could be a player, too, perhaps even ought to be a player—she has all the where-withal and no reason not to use it, though I have never really seen her in action, so to speak. But she has put down her empty mug with a clunk. "Right. And so to bed. To sleep, perchance to dream," she proclaims, though the delivery is marred by another catlike yawn.

"*Hamlet.*"

"Yup." She runs her tired eyes over me even as a third yawn takes over her mouth. "You know, you look exhausted too. You should sleep in. I'll try not to wake you in the morning."

"I'll try." Then, without thinking I add, "Wait."

"What?" She pauses in the act of pushing off the counter.

I say the words before I can consider them properly, before I can paralyze myself by overthinking. "Do you miss Mum?" I shake my head, frustrated. Of course she misses her mum; she didn't have the complicated relationship with Karen that I had. "I mean, *how* do you miss Mum?"

She settles back against the counter and looks at me carefully, or as carefully as her bleary eyes can manage. "It's not . . . it's not every minute of every day. I think I would miss Dad that way; he's the one I've always called first. But Mum was . . . well, you know." She smiles ruefully as if I must know what she means, but I'm not sure I do. "Certain things remind me, I suppose. But really I think I miss the . . . the certainty most."

"Certainty?"

"You know, feeling that everything is going to be all right, that there's always a safe place, that all will be as it's meant to be." *You know.*

But I don't know that feeling. I never have. "They say you truly grow up when your parents die. I know I'll be worrying about Dad more now, too." The rueful smile comes out again. I wonder if that's why she's here—here in the Manse—beyond the per diem saving and the benefit of her own room: she's become acutely aware that one day we might be all each other has. Or am I projecting my own thoughts upon her? She looks at me with her disquieting eyes. "You miss her, too." Her words are perfectly balanced, halfway between a statement and a question.

"I wasn't sure I would," I admit. "We only spoke a couple of times a month." Logistical calls. *I'm flying out to this place. I'll be gone for this length of time.* That kind of thing. A courtesy, at best, since it was much better to call Pete for anything practical.

"Do you wish you'd come back?"

"For the funeral?" I can see Jonathan in the hotel room in Cairo. "But you know it was impossible. I tried everything—"

She's shaking her head. "I meant before. For longer than a couple of days every third Christmas."

I chose to ignore the bitterness. "It wouldn't have changed any-thing." My throat is tight.

"Maybe." It's not an agreement; there's a stubbornness to the word. It hangs between us and refuses to budge. I take a sip of tea in silence. "I'm sorry," she offers, after a moment. "I'm just tired. I know it's dif-ferent for you; I know it's always been different. But I miss her. I know you do too."

I nod slowly. "Yes. But I don't—I don't have the words for it." I think for some reason of my mountain of a Scottish lawyer. *I'm sorry about your mum*, he said in a thick gravelly brogue. *You must miss her.* It sounded like an order: must I? And then I found that, in fact, I did. How odd that the gap that's left is larger than the space that was oc-cupied. "I don't know how to *help*. You or me."

She's smiling again, but the rueful edge has gone. "I like that you want to." *I like that you want to.* It's a simultaneous warm hug and a cold glass of water to the face. Both steal my breath. But why should she be able to rely on my good intentions? I've never been around to be relied upon before. She's yawning again. I fight to keep my voice even. "You're done in. Go on up to bed; I'll lock up."

"Yep." She pauses by the door on her way out. "Are you sure you're okay?"

"I'm fine. Sleep well." The radio is still playing, giving the illusion of company, but I'm no longer in a kitchen in Scotland. I can feel the cool of the hotel room in Cairo, the shade inside in contrast to the brightness framed by the linen curtains, like an old sepia photograph set against a saturated digital image. I can see Jonathan in profile bent over the desk, irritably trying to reach over the back of it to plug in his laptop. *We have to go,* I tell him urgently. *We can't wait this out; we have to take a car, a boat, whatever. We'll have to go overland to England.* He looks across at me, startled, a lock of his gray hair flopping onto his forehead and his hands still busy with the plug. *I can't go too. I have to be in DC,* he says. *She wasn't* my *mother.*

He apologized. Of course he apologized, and Jonathan's apologies are works of art; they are three-act plays. He apologized, and I accepted that apology, therefore it must be over and done with. Except that I still feel the ring of those words. I still feel the weight of the abrupt realization of where I stand in the pecking order of Jonathan's life, the realization that if this, my mother's sudden death, is not significant enough, then there is nothing I can ever do to move up the order. It can't be that I didn't know that before. I moved the goalposts. Was it the news of my mother's death that did that, or were they already stealthily inching out of their long-held positions? Had I already begun to suspect that if I stopped moving, there might be nothing of substance in my oh-so-busy life?

The program has moved on to a news update: the *Deepwater Horizon* search-and-rescue operation has been suspended; the oil rig itself sank yesterday afternoon. It sank, and I didn't know. Ordinarily it would be inconceivable that something newsworthy would have happened—would have happened almost thirty-six hours ago—and I wouldn't know. An image pops into my head immediately, of the burning oil rig, its thus-far indefatigable fires finally quenched by the rolling seas as it slowly slips under the water with stately majesty. I could turn on the television and see it for myself, live or recorded, but I'm far too tired. Instead I check all the doors and windows and turn off all the lights on the ground floor, and start to climb the stairs.

There's a strong smell of cigarette smoke.

A wave of adrenaline races over my skin that makes me freeze then whirl round, looking right, left, expecting to see a slight girl with triangular hair and a lit cigarette . . . but then rational thought kicks in. I'm right next to the coats hanging neatly on their hooks by the front door. I sniff mine, and then Carrie's. It's faint, but there's a definite scent of stale tobacco. They must have picked up eau-de-tobacco from the people smoking outside the Quaich, given that smoking is banned inside pubs and restaurants in the UK. I take two steps away from the coats and sniff the air again. Nothing. I climb the stairs to my bedroom. Then I go back downstairs and turn all the lights back on before I finally go to bed.

MY FATHER IS LYING AT THE BOTTOM OF THE ALBERT CANAL, near Hasselt. It might as well be a river as a canal, it's so much wider than what is conjured by the word "canal" in the UK. Not that that matters to my father, seeing as he's dead. One supposes he might prefer to be resting near the more picturesque parts—near Smeermaas perhaps—but as fate would have it, he has settled a stone's throw from the industrial zone, where the view rather disappoints in comparison to the rest of the canal route. His death, as deaths go, was a little disappointing, too: a sudden hemorrhage in the brain, causing him to topple into the water whilst taking a pleasant night stroll along the towpath; he was dead before he could even drown. He would have preferred a demise with more substance and flair.

TEN

I wake with my heart thumping, utterly disoriented, to a shrill, ear-splitting beeping that's extraordinarily loud. I fumble for the bedside lamp switch and fail to find it, then give up and leap out of bed to switch on the ceiling light and grab my dressing gown. By now my brain has identified the cacophony: it's a smoke alarm, one downstairs from the sound of it. I'm sure it's coming from the ground floor. I can't smell anything, though. I slam on the hallway light and take the stairs two at a time in my bare feet. There's no mistaking the source of the unceasing screech: the unassuming round white alarm clinging to the ceiling of the kitchen. The objectionable din it's emitting isn't helping me think clearly, but I can't smell smoke, or gas, and I can see from a glance that all the hobs are off. Certainly there's no visible signs of a fire. My only focus now is turning the bloody thing off.

I have to stand on one of the kitchen chairs to reach it, and even then it's a stretch. There are arrows on the alarm: a clockwise turn should release the cover. As close as I now am to the source, my ears are actually hurting. I can't believe Carrie isn't downstairs by now; surely nobody could sleep through this? I'm straining to turn the cover and at last I feel it give and come away in my hands, and as it does so, I'm suddenly aware of an undertone of buzzing and then—*dear God*—it's raining flies down on me, angry fat black bodies falling on my face, in my hair, buzzing round my neck, down inside my dressing gown, dropping onto my feet, their petroleum-swirl blue-black bodies bristling with fury as they taint me with their germs with every contact. I've dropped the cover and I'm scrubbing frantically at my face and hair in a cloud of the insects, almost toppling off the chair as I bat them away. In a panic, I drop down to the floor and feel some bodies squelch beneath one bare foot; I can feel myself start to retch as I tip my head upside down and rake my hands through my hair, even as I become aware that the awful din has stopped and that the sound I can now hear is my own shrieking. With an effort, I cut it off, only for the shrieking to be replaced by whimpering, then I run out of the kitchen and straight up the stairs to the full-length mirror in my bathroom.

There are carcasses of dead flies on the shoulders of my dressing gown; there are dead flies still caught in my hair. There's an acrid taste of bile in my mouth as I grab a hairbrush and furiously drag it through my hair while simultaneously stripping off the dressing gown. I'm almost crying with revulsion now, naked and shivering with the dressing gown discarded at my feet among a scattering of the lifeless black flies. One vile creature is still moving on the white porcelain of the bathroom sink, slowly and dully, as if unsure if it's worth the effort. I grab the bottle of hand soap and use it to squash the fly mercilessly, then hurl the bottle at the bin in the corner. It misses, clattering loudly off the rim. The noise comes as another jolt.

I need to calm down.

I take several deep breaths and look at myself again in the mirror, scouring my naked image. I could barely be more of a disaster—my eyes are red and my face and neck are blotchy, I've managed to scratch myself in several places in my haste to brush off the revolting creatures and my hair is sticking out at ludicrous angles—but at least I can't see any remaining insects on me. And then I look at my feet and see a squashed body, oozing out yellow innards, stuck to one of my big toes, and I have to rush to the toilet to physically retch.

When I've calmed myself a little, I clean the carcass off my toe with some toilet paper. Then I look in the mirror again, taking deep, slow breaths. I will have to go back downstairs. I will have to clean up the kitchen. How on earth can it be fair that I am dealing with all of this whilst Carrie is peacefully sleeping?

Actually, how can that even be possible? I suddenly feel sick with dread. Heedless of whether I might be stepping on any more insects, heedless of the fact that I'm stark naked, I dash from the bathroom. I cross the hallway to her bedroom door, which is ajar, and push it gently open, painting the floor with an ever-widening trapezium of light from the hallway. She has left the curtains undrawn again and the blackness is peering in. It takes a moment for my eyesight to adjust, but soon I can make out a hump in the bed. She is sleeping on her back, one arm tucked up under the pillow, her head turned away from where I'm standing. I can't hear her breathe—and then I do, a long, peaceful huff out. I stand for a moment, and as I do, my eyesight adjusts even further, and I can see that she has earplugs in.

Earplugs.

Jesus.

Even so, it's still a marvel that she has slept through all this. Maybe the alcohol is playing a part in her oblivion, too. I back carefully out of the room and go to find myself some clothes to wear to set about the unenviable task of cleaning up my fly cemetery of a kitchen. It turns out there's insect spray under the kitchen sink, which is useful because some of the creatures aren't quite as dead as I would like. I can't imagine how all of these fitted in the small smoke alarm—there are hundreds of them. When I'm finished, I feel vaguely light-headed from the spray and the kitchen is spotless, but my skin is still crawling and my hands feel itchy and raw, as if they're reacting to the chemicals of the spray.

It's just gone 3 A.M. now. I put myself in the shower and wash my hair twice. It's such a relief to feel the warm water flowing over me, taking away the contamination and the revulsion. It can't wash away my thoughts, though. *I should leave here. The locals don't want me here, I don't want me here and even the Manse itself doesn't want me here. I should leave tomorrow; I can do all the Presumption of Death stuff from a distance.* And then I think of Carrie, and I know I won't leave. Not until she does.

A scant few hours later I wake to the faint sound of running water. The light is slanting through the gaps around the edges of the thin curtains. I lie still on my side staring at the stripes of light on the chest of drawers and let reality soak into me. It's been the kind of sleep that wipes memory clean of the where and the when; my brain needs time to get up to speed. I push my hair out of my eyes and find that it's damp, and with that, the events in the kitchen come rushing back in.

The running water has subsided: Carrie is out of her shower now. I feel an urge to be in her company, as if that might reassure me that— what? That I haven't done anything unforgivable? The vague sense of wrongness that sits within me reminds me of my university days, when it was the done thing to drink beyond one's sensibilities at least once a week; the self-loathing that curled in my stomach each morning after, the inherent mental shudder when recalling the lack of control, was somehow never enough to prevent the next binge. The wine is to blame for my unease, surely. The wine and the undercurrents with Carrie, with Jamie, with Fiona.

I pull myself out of bed and head for the kitchen, where there's not a single fly carcass to be seen, and no lingering chemical smell from the spray either. Carrie must have been through the kitchen already; the empty insect spray can is nowhere to be seen. She's also replaced the cover of the alarm, which I'd left on the kitchen table; I was too tired to deal with that too after all my cleaning. The sun streams in at an angle through the rectangular leaded windowpanes, anointing bright diamond-shaped patches on the tile floor, the red-checked plastic cover, the daffodil walls. The sunshine is just another layer of artifice, I find myself thinking. Another way to hide what lies beneath.

Carrie joins me when I'm contemplating the contents of the fridge, wondering whether my stomach might consider scrambled eggs a good or bad idea. "Morning," she says. She seems suspiciously bright in comparison to yesterday; perhaps the shower has woken her up. "I thought you were going to sleep in?"

"Morning. There's some coffee on the table for you." I close the fridge door and stifle a yawn. I don't think I'm quite ready for eggs. "You slept through quite an eventful night."

"What do you mean?" She glances round from filling the kettle at the sink.

"I got woken at 3 A.M. by the smoke alarm going off." I gesture up at the ceiling. "This one. Quite the racket it made. It turns out the unit was full of flies. God, it was horrible. They must have been nesting in there or something. Cluster flies do that, I think, or maybe they were a different variety . . . They were everywhere. They got in my hair, my clothes . . ." I'm shuddering. Carrie is staring at me, openmouthed. Then she looks around, as if searching for evidence. "I cleaned it all up. Didn't you wonder why the smoke alarm cover was off?"

"What are you talking about?"

"The cover. I left it on the table."

"This is the first time I've been in the kitchen this morning."

"But . . ." I stop talking and look at the back door. There should be a black bin bag there full of a day or two of trash topped off with fly carcasses, knotted at the top to stop any creatures that somehow survived my chemical assault from escaping. "Did you take out the bin bag?"

"No, I told you, this is the first time I've been in here this morning. What's going on?"

"I don't . . . I don't know." I'm opening the cupboard under the sink. There's no insect spray there. Where did I put that?

"Did you have some kind of weird dream or something?"

"No!" She recoils at my tone, and I stop myself, then go on less vehemently. "No. It happened. Feel, my hair is damp. I had to take a shower afterward, to wash off all the . . ." I shudder again. She reaches out a hand and scrunches a handful of my hair. "See? Damp."

"Yes." I can't read anything in her gray eyes.

"Someone must have been in here."

"Maybe. Or—"

"Or what? You think I took a shower in my sleep?"

Carrie shrugs. "It doesn't sound any stranger than your version, which has me sleeping through a smoke alarm, and disappearing bin bags," she says flatly.

"You'd been drinking and you wear earplugs in bed." My words are level, but I'm not attempting to keep the bite out of them.

"Even so." She isn't backing down. "And wouldn't you have woken me anyway?"

"There didn't seem to be any point. I was dealing with it." She spreads her hands, her jaw set stubbornly, and I am filled with a stinging, furious resentment. I turn to stare out of the window as I fight to collect myself.

"Do you want a cup of tea?" she says quietly after a moment.

I take a deep breath and turn back to the kitchen. "No, thank you," I say with studied politeness. She nods calmly, then bends to look in the cereal cupboard. "I thought we bought—ah, here it is." She pulls out a packet of Special K and sets about finding a bowl and spoon. I lean against the counter and watch her, trying to let the negative emotions flow out of me. There's a fluidity to her movement, yet every action is economical: precisely what is required and no more. The sophisticated veneer of last night's clothes and makeup is gone. With her hair still shower-wet and her face scrubbed entirely clean, even of her habitual eyeliner, she has the skin of a child, perfect and pore-free. She could be a different person, or the same one, freshly reborn. Just looking at her makes me feel more aware of how tired I am, and of the age gap between us.

"Anyway, it was a good night," Carrie offers into the silence, as she sits at the table. Her gray eyes are fixed on me, giving nothing away. "A nice bunch."

"Yes." Would I feel the same doubt as Carrie if the situation were reversed? Possibly, but that doesn't make it any less hurtful. "Jamie's sister was pretty wasted," I add. Carrie's mouth is full of cereal now; she makes an indistinct noise in response. "Did you speak to her much?"

"A bit. She seems fun."

Oh God. I imagine Carrie inviting Fiona over. I imagine their heads bent together, their faces hidden by their hair as they shake in shared giggles. I imagine Fiona in this very kitchen, the smoke from her cigarette spiraling lazily toward the ceiling. "Really? I thought she was kind of odd. And what was it with that bloody watch beeping every half hour?"

"Oh yeah, I asked her about that, but it was at the end of the evening. I didn't quite catch the gist of what she was saying." She gestures with her spoon, as if it's an extension of her hand. "Something to do with not having a grip on time." She shrugs. "But by that point I'm not sure any of us had much of a grip on time."

I digest that for a moment. "Jamie said she's a bit . . . unpredictable."

"Did he? I'm not sure they get on that well, so I wouldn't set a lot of store in what he says. Anyway, what are you doing today?"

"Decluttering the attic, food shopping. Welcome to my glamorous life." I pause for a moment, considering whether to offer to take her to the station, and then mentally slap myself for my petty reluctance. "I'll pull on some clothes and give you a lift to the station, though, if you want."

"Really? That would be great." She tosses a grateful smile to me, and is about to speak when her phone, lying faceup on the checked table cover, begins to chirrup insistently. I see her eye the screen for the caller ID, and grimace. "Sorry, I have to get this." She pushes back her chair and picks up the phone, and as she does, I see that odd movement of her shoulders again: not a shrug exactly, it's not pronounced enough. It's more of a wriggle, or a slight shimmy. "Graham!" she exclaims into the phone, a wide smile fixed in place. "How lovely to hear from you." She's leaving the kitchen now, but her words float behind her. "Of course I'm up. I've got rehearsals to get to . . . Yes, that's right, Edinburgh . . ." I look around the now-empty kitchen, with Carrie's bowl abandoned on the table. She's left the cereal cupboard door open; I noticed that she did the same yesterday. Jonathan would hate living with her. I close the cupboard door and take myself upstairs, still surprised by how perky Carrie is this morning. Certainly she's a far cry from the woman who was desperately in need of a caffeine infusion two mornings ago. She's even exiting her own bedroom, coat on and bag at the ready, when I emerge from my own, a mere ten minutes later.

"Look," she says. "I must have missed this one." She's holding something in her hand, balanced on her flat palm. It takes a minute for my eyes to adjust to the relative darkness of the hallway after my bright bedroom; I can't immediately identify what it is. And when I do, I feel my stomach wrench and knot.

"Where did you get that?" I bark, staring at the ashtray in her hand. There are six or seven butts in it.

"On the windowsill of my bedroom."

"Your bedroom . . . What, the outside sill?"

"Yes, like the other one. I must have overlooked it." She cocks her head and then sighs. "Ailsa, don't be building this up into something it's not. I just overlooked it the other day." There's no judgment in her tone, no accusation in her eyes, but all the same, I know it must be there. I can feel the stiffness in my face. She sighs again. "If there was anybody out there having a tab, he or she would have to be BFG-sized to put an ashtray on my windowsill."

"Or be inside, not outside."

"But you locked the doors last night, right?"

I nod.

"Well, then."

"So, what, you think I'm being delusional? That Ali's story spooked me and I'm inventing ghosts?"

She doesn't let her voice rise to my challenge. "Not Ali's story. I just think that maybe you're overtired. You said yourself you haven't been sleeping well."

"I just haven't got used to the Manse yet."

"You told me that before we even got to the Manse."

I turn for the stairs, exasperated, even though it's true. I haven't slept well since I took the call from Pete telling me my mother had died. Carrie follows me down to the ground floor after a beat or two. I busy myself finding my own keys, then I go outside and unlock the little Golf just as my phone starts to ring: Jonathan.

"Hey there," I say, inordinately pleased to hear from him. It feels like an expression of support in the face of adversity. "I wasn't expecting you still to be up." Carrie is outside too, now. I mouth *Jonathan* at her and hold up two fingers. She nods and starts locking up the Manse.

"I'm almost not. Just climbing into bed as we speak. I wish you were here with me—not that I'd have enough energy to do anything about it."

This is more affection than Jonathan usually displays on a phone. I wonder if he really is missing me more than either of us expected, or if he's trying to make amends for Egypt. Today, I'll take either. "Me too." My words are almost engulfed by the yawn that overtakes me. "Crawling into bed with you has a lot of appeal right now." I've wandered away from the Golf as we're speaking. I look back at the Manse, up to the second floor, to the windows of Carrie's master bedroom. She's right: only a giant could place an ashtray on that windowsill. From the outside.

"Really? What dreadful plans do you have for today that lying beside an itinerant fifty-something reporter seems preferable?"

"Admin." He groans sympathetically. "Oh, I wanted to tell you—I met a guy last night in the pub that might be interested in buying the place."

That wakes him up a bit. "That sounds promising. Can you run the legal thing and a sale process in parallel? With the sale pending the legal resolution, I mean?"

"I hadn't thought of that. I'll ask my lawyer." It's a good idea. If Mr. MacKintyre okays it, I could call some estate agents this afternoon to at least get a valuation on the Manse. "You sound a bit less fraught than yesterday. Is it going better with Rod?"

"I'm getting a bit more used to him. Or him to me." I can hear his breathing down the phone. He will be lying on his back in bed now, probably with his eyes closed, his head on one side and the phone resting on his cheek. "Maybe it's good for me." He yawns. "Change is as good as a holiday and all that."

"In that case I'd better start putting out feelers to work with other people when I get back—"

"God no! You're too good. I'd never get you back, and my ego couldn't cope with that. It's fragile, you know." I can almost hear his self-deprecating smile.

"Ah, so what's sauce for the gander isn't sauce for the goose, then?" I know I'm smiling myself. I hadn't realized how much I'd missed our banter.

"Absolutely correct. I'm not too proud to admit it."

My roaming has taken me over by the oak. The branch that broke is lying on the ground now. It's large, about the diameter of a soccer ball where it has splintered away from the tree. I kick at the ruptured end absentmindedly, and some of the dry, pale inner wood shears off. There's something pale shimmering inside. "Still there?" Jonathan asks.

"Sorry. Yes." I'm peering more closely at the inside of the branch now. "I should let you and your fragile ego get some sleep." It looks like cotton wool, but . . .

"Night."

"Night—Jesus!" The line goes dead as I jump back from the branch. It's full of writhing white larvae, each at least a couple of inches long, their glistening bodies wriggling blindly over one another. Their skin is translucent, like uncooked prawns; one can infer movements beneath the membrane. They are from the dark, dank, fetid underbelly of the Manse, from the rot at its core; I can feel them crawling over me, through me, even though I know I'm not touching them, and then I can feel the flies again, tangled in my hair and crawling malevolently across my skin . . . Nausea begins to threaten my throat.

"Ailsa?" calls Carrie from beside the car, dragging my gaze round to her. "What is it? Ailsa?"

I've got a grip on my breathing, and my heart rate is slowing, but the nausea remains. I head back to the Golf, fighting down the bile. My forehead is clammy. "Sorry. Coming. There was . . . some kind of bug larvae or something in that dead branch." I feel myself shuddering involuntarily. "Really gross, I have to say." Carrie looks at me thoughtfully but doesn't say anything. I duck into the driver's seat, thankful for the safety of the car around me, thankful for the process of preparing to drive, which means I don't have to see Carrie watching me.

"Still no flights?" asks Carrie, peering out of the window.

"I don't think so." It's a beautiful day, breath-stealingly cold but bright and clear; the kind of day where one can see so very far that the curve of the earth is evident and it seems ludicrous that anyone ever thought the world was flat.

"It's weird not to see trails in the sky," Carrie muses. "Everyone was talking about it at the funeral."

I tense a little. Is bringing up the funeral another veiled rebuke? "I suppose I wasn't the only one whose travel got scuppered by the volcano."

"There were a lot of condolence cards from abroad." I sense rather than see her shrug as I'm concentrating on the road again. "But I don't know if those people would have come anyway. I didn't really know who most of them were. Dad said they were from the art world. Or from before she had me. One guy made it. From Denmark, I think. Or maybe the Netherlands—he got a ferry. Dad said he was a big collector, pretty much launched Mum's career. He said you might remember him." I can feel Carrie's gaze on me. "A big guy. Like a rugby player build."

I rack my brains as much as I can whilst keeping the car on the road. "It doesn't ring any bells." Or rather, it rings too many: to an eight-year-old, every man is tall. "What was his name?"

"I don't remember. I'll have to ask Dad. Anyway, he talked about her a little—Mum, I mean. The way she painted, staying up all night to finish pieces . . . It didn't sound like her at all."

"Well, Pete was a civilizing influence, I guess. She was different before."

"Before your dad disappeared?"

I shake my head. "I don't remember her much from then." Only that bright, shining garden image that surely isn't a memory at all; it's too distinct. Some memories of my father in the Manse have been returning, but they're all tactile: the feel of crawling into bed to cuddle into him, the weight of the kiss he dropped on my head as I ate my cereal. My mother wasn't the tactile type. "The guy from Denmark was right, whoever he was. I have plenty of memories of her staying up all night painting. Her coping mechanism, I guess. Or her escape . . ." That's a Karen, and a period of time, that I do remember. Chaotic, shambolic years . . . She was angry back then, tight-lipped and hard-eyed with rage. Presumably there was grief in there, too, but I was too wrapped up in my own loss to appreciate hers.

"You've never told me anything about that time." Carrie has unbuckled her seat belt and turned toward me in her seat, her gray eyes settled upon me.

"Well, it wasn't exactly a barrel of laughs." Her lips twist sourly at my knee-jerk flippancy and she turns away; I have to put out a hand to stop her. "Sorry. I didn't . . . Sorry. Though it really wasn't." She turns back, waiting for more. And she has a right to more, I suppose. "Didn't Pete ever tell you?" She shrugs. I can't tell if that means he did or didn't. "Well, we had no money. Like, zero; the bank account ran out pretty quick. And there was no family to help. Mum's parents had already died, and my dad's parents had never been fond of Mum— there was no way she was going to ask them for help. They would have told her to give up painting and get a proper job . . ." A not unreasonable viewpoint. "So. Anyway. She was trading on old favors and friendships for places to stay. I went to a new school at least twice a year. You can imagine how thrilled I was about that." Different places to live and different Karens each time, a new spin to the story, a reinvention with every new location. I deliberately move onto safer ground. "But then she met Pete." I expect her to smile at that, but she doesn't. She just nods, like she's slotting a piece of a puzzle into place. I try to conjure up the Karen that Carrie must remember, but it's impossible. To all intents and purposes, Carrie and I had different mothers.

A flash of moving color catches my attention. "Shit, that's your train. Go!"

"Yikes." She's already half out of the car, but she sticks her head back in to say, "Thanks for the lift."

The platform extends beyond the station itself in both directions. I'm able to see Carrie climb onto the train before it draws slowly away. I can't see her once she's aboard; the reflection of the bright sunlight on the windows prevents it. I wonder if she's sitting by the window, waving good-bye to me, but by the time the thought occurs to me, it's already too late to wave back. It feels significant, as if it's an omen of things to come between us. Perhaps I'm destined to forever be a little too late.

When I get back to the Manse after dropping Carrie off, I climb on a kitchen chair and reach up to rotate the smoke alarm cover. It slides and releases just as I remember it, but without the same angry buzzing. In fact, the interior is suspiciously clean, and there's an empty space where the nine-volt battery should be. I have a quick hunt through the kitchen drawers for any spare nine-volt batteries, but to no avail, so I climb back onto the chair. When the cover is once again fitted into place, I can no longer avoid thinking about the implications.

Either someone was in the house and removed the evidence of the fly incident at some point between 3:30 A.M. and 8:30 A.M., or Carrie is right and I'm delusional. I'm not sure which is worse. In any case, I start with the ground floor, moving systematically through the entire house, checking every possible access point—which as a course of action, I think with grim humor, has the benefit of fitting neatly into either hypothesis—and simultaneously sweeping for any more overlooked ashtrays. But at the end of my search, I haven't found any ashtrays or any obvious entry points. I remind myself that doesn't mean there isn't one. Though who would go to the trouble of breaking in purely to move things around, and why? The newspaper-deliverer? But this is an extraordinarily subtle form of intimidation. It doesn't seem to fit with the naked vitriol of those angry red pen circles.

But it must have been someone, because I couldn't have dreamed the flies. I couldn't have.

MY FATHER IS A SKI INSTRUCTOR IN A RESORT IN CANADA. IN the summer he's a rafting guide. He has a girlfriend called Crystal who teaches yoga and believes deeply that the only way to save the planet is through vegetarianism, which is a philosophy that, except for the odd bacon sandwich, he largely buys into. He never talks about his life before, and he barely even thinks about it. It's like he was a different person; it's like he was born anew on the night he decided to leave. Sometimes he's confronted by artwork produced by his ex-wife—that's how he thinks of her, as his ex-wife—and he congratulates himself on being able to be pleased for her success, in an objective, unemotional sort of way. He doesn't think of his daughter at all, not since he concluded that she was never actually his.

ELEVEN

Mr. MacKintyre—my lawyer—calls me later that morning. It's a wonder that he not only gets through, but that he can also hear me. On almost all of my calls, I can hear the person at the other end perfectly, but intermittently they have trouble hearing me. It hasn't been helping my progress on the mountain of administration that seems to be involved with inheriting a house. But in truth, that's not the only thing that's been hampering my efficiency. I feel like my brain has been split in two, with half of it trying to concentrate on the job at hand and half unable to drop the mystery of the missing fly evidence.

But Mr. MacKintyre disturbs this lack of industry and gets right to the point. "I've located the police report," he says. "It turns out I know the lead investigator; I play golf with him occasionally, as it happens. It was Glen McCue." I can hear the expectation in his voice.

"McCue." I can hear the locksmith's gruff voice: *You want to get to know your neighbors. Glen McCue is a good man.* McCue is surely a common enough surname round here. The combination of Glen and McCue, though, that can't be common . . .

"So you do know him? I thought you might; he lives in your area."

My area. As if any of this landscape could ever belong to anyone. "He's retired now, of course."

Our parents were pals, you ken. Surely the investigating officer wouldn't be a friend of the target of the investigation? "Does he have kids in their twenties?" I ask neutrally, with a sense that the world is narrowing, ruthlessly and irrevocably, to a focal point that I'd rather wasn't me.

"Yes. James, I think, and, what is it . . . Rhona—maybe Shona, or . . ." I can almost hear the furrowing of his brow.

"Fiona," I offer reluctantly. There's a sudden thump from upstairs, and I glance upward as if I can see through the ceiling.

"Aye! That's the one. So you do know Glen. Haven't you ever discussed—"

"No, I don't know him." The thump comes again. A door, perhaps. The Manse possesses eddies and air currents that challenge the laws of physics. "I've only recently met Fiona and Jamie. Socially." I start to climb the stairs, phone to ear.

"Always a small world."

"Yes." Before I can stop myself, I add, "Though I wouldn't want to paint it." It's a knee-jerk reaction, one of Pete's much-used jokes. Mr. MacKintyre gives a gruff surprised bark that I can only assume is his version of laughter. I hurry on. "I'm sure I could ask Jamie if I could speak with him as a courtesy, to let him know you'll be in contact." Now I'm the one that's surprised: where did that offer come from?

"If you like," says the lawyer. "I imagine he'd like to meet you in any case." Would he? I don't have enough detail to flesh out a story. Or rather, I could create far too many from what I've got; there's nothing to sway me in one particular direction over another. Glen McCue and my father knew each other, but were they acquaintances, or true friends? Was he, perhaps, closer to my mother? Or was it Glen's wife that was the connection, and if so, to whom? These thoughts, and others, are bubbling up inside me, jostling to be heard. Were they always there, sealed tight in a lightless swampy corner deep among my entrails? "Well," says Mr. MacKintyre, when I don't speak. "I'll get in touch with him directly in any case."

"Thank you." I disconnect with an overwhelming sense that it's too late, the die has been cast. But it's just a few questions, that's all. It's hardly monumentous.

I shake myself of the fancy and instead look around the second-floor landing. All doors are closed except the one to the family bathroom. As I watch, it moves gently in an undetectable breeze. I cross to it and close it with a firm hand, then push hard against it to test it. It holds fast. But by the time I get to the ground floor, it's thudding again.

———

Later, Carrie calls from the train. I offer to come and get her from the station, and she protests, though her lack of conviction shouts above her actual words. We drive from the station in a near perfect rerun of the previous day, except it's not dark as yet. The road is becoming more familiar to me, though I'm nowhere near ready to try it at the break-neck speed of that beaten-up Land Rover.

Carrie tentatively offers to make dinner, which I interpret as a peace offering to salve the flares of tension between us. I offer to help, of course, but she won't have any of it, so I sit at the kitchen table while she preps, and before long it's like our tense exchanges never happened. She has the radio on—of course—and the kitchen is warm from the oven and filled with the smell of the garlic bread that's baking in there. We talk about her play, all the gossip among the cast. She's funny, Carrie, in a very different way to, say, Ali. There's barely any teeth in her humor, even when she's sending up the pretensions of her theater luv-vie colleagues, but it speaks volumes of her talent for quiet observation. The Manse feels different with her in it, too, I realize. There's less thudding, for one thing. It feels more . . . what? More like a building—a house—should feel.

"Oh, forgot to tell you, my lawyer called." She has her head down, chopping chilies on a wooden board. "It turns out the investigating officer for my father's disappearance was none other than Glen McCue."

She pushes her fringe off her forehead with the back of the bent wrist that holds the knife and shakes her head blankly. "I don't—"

"Jamie and Fiona's father."

That at least stops her in her tracks. "You're kidding."

"Nope."

"He's a policeman?"

"Was. He's retired now."

"Wow. Talk about close to home. Will he have to be involved with all of this?"

"A bit. I shouldn't think it will be too onerous though: most likely just a phone interview." She's stirring the chopped chilies into the sauce, her back to me. "I was thinking someone ought to warn him it's coming, though," I say casually. "I don't suppose you got a phone number from Jamie last night? He could pass on the message."

"No, but I got Fiona's. My phone is—oh, right there." She points with her knife at the kitchen table, barely looking round. "But I'm seeing Fiona tomorrow. I could tell her then if you like." She's one hundred percent focused on the sauce as she says this. I have the feeling it's deliberate. I consider, then discard any number of possible responses whilst my mind revolts from the same image as last night: Carrie and Fiona, their heads together, giggling at the kitchen table. Even to my-self, it's hard to explain the *wrongness* I feel about that, the dank cold dread that pools in my stomach.

"Well, thanks. Yeah, that would be great," I say eventually, be-cause there is nothing else that I can say. I'm too aware of the fragility of the truce that we're enjoying. Somehow I know it will be shattered if I start casting aspersions about Fiona. "No rehearsal tomorrow then?"

"We're getting Sundays off. At least for now."

Tomorrow is Sunday. I'd rather lost track. "So are you . . . are you going for coffee or something?"

"She invited me to see the equestrian center." She's draining pasta now, in movements that are smooth and economical. A small hum escapes her to thread itself around the tinny melody emanating from the radio. It occurs to me that Carrie is enjoying herself. She actually likes to cook. The concept is extraordinarily alien to me.

"Does she work there?"

"Yep, right from when they started it up, on and off. I don't think it's great pay, but she loves working with horses. When she heard I used to ride a bit, she invited me." The pasta has made it to the plates now; she ladles the spicy tomato sauce and prawns on top. "God, I can't actually remember the last time I was on a horse," she says reflectively, standing momentarily still. Her expression is uncharacteristically anxious. "I'll probably make a complete fool of myself. And it sounds like Fiona was practically born in the saddle."

"Isn't it like riding a bike?"

"Oh, sure, absolutely, if the bike has a mind of its own and is stronger than you to boot." She grins ruefully, and the anxiety is gone from her face. "Oh! I almost forgot the garlic bread."

We eat in silence for a while. It's not quite companionable silence; it's more that each of us is lost in her own thoughts. I'm thinking about the newspaper, and the bin bag, and Jonathan, and ashtrays full of cigarette butts, and what Glen McCue might or might not be able to tell me; I'm thinking about the Manse and how it feels without Carrie and whether or not I saw an intruder in the box room. I realize I don't have the slightest idea what Carrie is thinking about, but for once her gray eyes are unfocused, without their usual forensic bent.

Carrie's pasta is delicious, but I'm eating mechanically. I put down my fork. "You know, I was thinking perhaps I should talk to Glen McCue myself. Maybe you could ask Fiona if she could give him my number." It feels like asking for a favor, and the last thing, the absolute last thing that I want to be is beholden to Fiona. But the destination of my train has changed, and I can't seem to climb off it. "If he's happy to speak with me, that is."

She looks over the table at me, and the focus has returned to her gaze. "Are you sure you want to—"

"No." It comes out a little harsher than I'd intended. I try again. "No. But it seems like I'm going to."

"Dad was a bit worried this might happen."

"Really." For once she can't hold my gaze. They've talked about me, Carrie and Pete. I bet she told him about my "delusions" of last night. I wonder if she also mentioned the lights I keep leaving on. If she knew about me also checking the rooms and the locks, too, then they'd really have something to chew on together.

"He's just worried being here would stir things up for you." She waves a hand and somehow conveys that "things" mean the Manse, my father's disappearance, even my relationship with my mother. Though perhaps I'm overinterpreting. There's an uncharacteristic anxiousness around her eyes. She doesn't want to upset me, I realize; she's choosing her words carefully, and the thought warms me. "Maybe it's not healthy to revisit it. What's done is done and cannot be undone and all that."

"*Macbeth*," I say reflexively.

"Mmm. And look how that turned out."

"You're right. Absolutely right. Most likely any minute the wood outside is going to up and march and overthrow our dear monarch."

We're both laughing now. "Yeah, okay, it's not the best analogy," she admits.

"Nope." I'm still smiling as I start to wash up the pans in the kitchen sink, looking out over the back garden. It's twilight again, the same strange light in which I saw the cat. And the figure at the window upstairs. And in fact I can see the cat again. She's on the wall, just like before, padding softly along the top, circumnavigating the garden. Her head is turned like before, too, to focus on the same spot, but this time I can see that there's something there: a small bird, something like a jay perhaps, though I can't really tell in this light. It's far away, but from its jagged movements I get the impression that it's injured.

It keeps hopping as if trying to take flight, but doesn't seem able to actually take off.

I start to turn to Carrie, to point out the peril that the bird is in, then I'm suddenly gripped with a fear that I'm imagining the entire tableau. But I must have grown still enough to catch her attention. "Is there something out there?" asks Carrie.

"I'm not sure . . . I thought I saw—"

"Look, a cat! There on the wall."

The relief is unexpectedly staggering. Carrie can see it. There is a cat and she can see it. "Yes! That's it. I guess it's stalking the bird."

"What bird?"

"At the end, not far from the gate. Look." I'm pointing and she's following my finger with her gaze, but she shakes her head.

"Your eyes must be keener than mine; I can't see anything." She turns away, then adds slyly, "I expect you're going long-sighted in your old age."

"Fuck off." She laughs. "Maybe if I go out there I'll scare the cat away." I'm already unlocking the back door. Even though I know it's coming, the chill still feels like a surprise. I've left my slippers inside, so I have to gingerly navigate the short stretch of gravel in bare feet before I reach the damp, cold grass of the lawn, lit only by the light from the kitchen window and open door. The cat is still on the wall; it hasn't pounced yet. "Shoo," I call. It regards me unblinking. "Shoo!" I try again louder and add a sudden sweeping movement, but the cat is undeterred.

It's getting darker by the second, but I can still see the bird. Perhaps I ought to pick it up, take it inside or something . . . I'm not at all sure what one is supposed to do with an injured bird. City living hasn't equipped me to deal with this. I move toward it slowly, hoping not to scare it even more. It's still trying to fly, but its attempts are becoming more feeble. I'm perhaps ten meters from it now, on an exceptionally soggy patch of grass that is surely soaking the hems of my jeans. The damp cold squelching beneath my naked feet is deeply unpleasant.

Suddenly there's a long shadow in the rectangle of light cast from the kitchen door. I look back to see Carrie framed in it. "Is it still there?"

"Yes," I say, but then I turn back to the bird . . . and it isn't. "Wait," I say in confusion. "Did you see it fly off?"

"I couldn't see it in the first place, let alone see it flying off."

Surely in its weakened state it couldn't have gone far. I look around, but there's no sign of it. To be fair, I can no longer see the cat either.

"It must have hopped away," I say, more to myself than Carrie. The darkness is becoming complete; there are no stars in the sky tonight. I look around a little more and then yield to the cold and the advancing black and head back toward the welcoming light of the kitchen. I see the glow of inhuman eyes and realize the cat is still on the wall, still focused on where the bird was. It's only because I'm looking at the cat that I catch a glimpse of the missile that's hurtling through the air toward me, and duck sideways in time for it to glance harmlessly off my arm.

"Fuck!"

"What was that?" Carrie calls.

I pick up the object, which is in fact a stone that has rolled harmlessly across the lawn to lie in the rectangle of light from the back door, throwing a shadow much larger than its own self. It's flattish, not even the size of an egg, and not terribly heavy, though I daresay I'd have felt its impact well enough if it had hit my head. It's almost certainly a piece from the drystone wall. "Who's there?" I call out, trying to peer through the darkness, trying to triangulate the source, fighting the instinct to run for the safety of the kitchen. It must have come from behind the cat, beyond the garden wall. "I'm warning you, I'll call the police." My words are immediately swallowed by the darkness. The cat's inhuman eyes blink at me once, and then she chooses to disappear. Without conscious decision, my legs are backing me slowly toward the light that Carrie is standing in. I daren't turn my back on the pitch black. "I'll call the police," I shout again, even as I continue to retreat.

I'm on the gravel now, crunching awkwardly backward over it in my bare feet. The darkness mocks me with its silence.

"Jesus. Did it hit you?" asks Carrie, ushering me inside. She's locking the back door and shooting the dead bolt for good measure. "Are you okay?"

"I'm fine." I show her the stone I'm still holding, rubbing my thumb over its rough surface. "It's too small to do much damage. I don't think it was really meant to hurt me." *Just scare me.* I take another look out the kitchen window, but the pitch black of the night has a firm hold.

"But who the hell is out there throwing stones?" Carrie's eyebrows are pinched together in concern. "Is there a teenage delinquent problem here that I don't know about?"

"If there is, I haven't heard of it either." A thought occurs to me. "I suppose it could be the person who delivered the newspaper." Though the vicious scarlet circles around the article suggested a stronger intent than throwing little more than a pebble. That person would have thrown a boulder.

"Should we report it?" asks Carrie as I try to wipe off my feet with kitchen roll.

"I don't know what the police could do. I didn't see anything."

"I suppose." I can see she doesn't like the feeling of helplessness. That makes two of us.

MY FATHER IS DEAD. HE WAS MUGGED IN ANTWERP FOR THE money in his wallet, but the thieves got rather more than they bargained for when they discovered the diamonds on him. They were minor criminals, nothing major-league yet, but the oldest of them—a hard-faced youth not yet turned twenty— had aspirations. He knew that a theft of gemstones would attract rather more police time and effort than a stolen wallet, and therefore their choices were to either eliminate the crime, by returning everything to my father, or eliminate the witness of the crime. He didn't find it a difficult choice, which is how my father's body came to be tossed into the Albert Canal, where it currently lies beneath layers of silt and detritus. That same hard-faced youth has killed many times since, but he remembers my father's murder with particular fondness on account of the extraordinary stroke of luck that led him to that unexpected windfall.

TWELVE

Fortified by scrambled eggs, I enter the box room the next morning armed with damp kitchen roll with which to attack the dust, and with a marker pen and a plan: I will check the contents of every box, without sorting them through; the sorting can come later (I stomp firmly on the question of when that later might be). I start by scribbling *Charity* on the boxes of books, wondering as I do so whether a charity shop will even want them—after all, isn't everyone reading on a Kindle these days? The box of floral scrapbooks gets the label *Albums* and no further scrutiny, and another box gets the same treatment. Two boxes are full of dated household items: a clock, a couple of ornaments, a random collection of utensils and a lamp base that might go with the beige tasseled lampshade. I scrawl *Dump*.

There's a white A4 envelope on top of one of the boxes, marked PHOTOS, DO NOT BEND, that was sandwiched in between two boxes and exposed when I lifted down the lampshade and the box it was on, though I was in no mood to take a look at the time. The envelope is addressed to M. Calder, but the flap is still sealed. I slide my finger under the corner of the flap and tear the envelope open to pull out the contents, which comprise several aerial photos, standard eight-inch by ten-inch size. I take them over to the window in search of more light. It's the relative position of the oak tree to the house that I recognize first: three of the photos contain the Manse. In one, the Manse is in the center. In another, a much smaller Manse is at the bottom of the frame, and the shot also comprises the wood and a portion of the loch. In the last, the Manse is at the top and the frame captures the road and a stretch of the side of the valley, down to the river. The other two don't show the Manse at all; I'm not sure, but I think they might be of farther up the valley. I look in the envelope again. There's no note, or indication of who sent this, or why. I wonder if it arrived after he disappeared. I suppose my mother must have had to deal with a lot of his correspondence. Perhaps she didn't care to open something that was so obviously not administrative.

I straighten up then stretch, looking out of the dormer window toward the trees that are gathered at the end of the garden, as if waiting for a chance to enter. Suddenly a flash of movement off to the left catches my eye: a red and black football. It sails through the air then lands only a few meters short of the stone wall that encircles the garden. The ball is followed in short order by a small dark-haired boy, perhaps six or seven, in navy blue tracksuit bottoms and red jumper; he runs to the ball, picks it up, then looks hesitantly at the stone wall. Even at this distance I can tell he's warring with himself. A sleek black Labrador bounds into view and looks up at him expectantly. As I watch, the boy visibly makes a decision and his face clears: he drop-kicks the ball over the wall. It bounces twice in the garden—my garden—before rolling to a stop beside the leg of a bench that rests on the opposite side. There's no question that the kick was deliberate. He begins to purposefully scramble over the garden wall. A burst of laughter escapes me.

I get to the back door only moments after he has rapped on it, but it takes a good ten seconds of fumbling with the still stiff new dead bolt before I get the door open. "Hello." I'm cautious with children, as they're not my natural milieu. I'm never entirely sure how to pitch my approach, but smiling seems a good start. He's a stocky little mite, this one; thoroughly robust looking, with ruddy cheeks on his otherwise pale skin, and inquisitive dark eyes to match the dark hair.

"I'm awfy sorry but my ball accidentally landed in your back garden," he says. Very much a local boy. *Awfy*, not *awfully*. Ball pronounced like *baw*.

"Accidentally, of course." My lips are twitching. "Could happen to anyone, I suppose." He looks at me warily but relaxes when he sees my smile. I stick my hand out. "I'm Ailsa."

He shakes it solemnly. "I'm Callum. I stay across the field." He waves nonspecifically behind him. The phrases of my early childhood are coming back to me. Not *Where do you live?* but *Where do you stay?*

"We're neighbors then. I would love to invite you in, but I don't think your parents would like you to enter a stranger's house all on your own." I pause. "Are you meant to be out alone?"

"I have Toast," he says defensively.

I look at him blankly. "Toast?"

"My dog." He steps back, looking around for the Labrador and frowning. It's fascinating to watch him, every thought and emotion writ clear on his little face. "Oh, I forgot, she willnae come in here." Before I can ask what he means, he rushes on. "And anyway, Mum's friend is looking after me. He'll be along in a minute. He wants to see you anyway."

Right on cue I hear a deep voice calling exasperatedly, "Callum! Callum! What did I tell you—" I'm fairly certain I know who owns that voice.

"It's all right," Callum calls back. "She's here."

I lean out of the doorway, holding on to the frame with one hand, and am confronted by the sight of Ben placing one hand on the wall then athletically vaulting over the entire thing. "Hi, Ben," I call, with a wry smile.

He's smiling back at me ruefully. "Hey there. I did tell Callum that it would be much more polite for me to call ahead and see if you were amenable to visitors, but apparently he couldn't wait—"

Callum is shaking his head in vociferous denial. "I could wait, but my ball landed in the garden—see?" He points over at the football.

"I do see. I see that you're shamelessly beyond redemption." His words are stern but he reaches out a hand to tousle Callum's hair, and the boy's face splits into a grin.

"Seeing as you're both here now, would you like to come in for a drink and a biscuit?" If we have biscuits . . . I'm mentally reviewing the shopping haul—I think I saw some Hobnobs in there. Carrie's choice; I don't buy biscuits for myself.

Callum looks up at Ben, and Ben nods his approval, dropping a hand on Callum's shoulder. It's not overbearing, or proprietorial; it's more a gesture of solidarity. "Yes, please," Callum says eagerly, and I step back into the kitchen, holding open the door and ushering them both in. Callum bounds in, then stops abruptly. "But . . . but it should-nae look like this," he says uncertainly.

"Callum!" admonishes Ben. Once again I'm reminded of how tall he is. It's more apparent in the close confines of the kitchen than it was in the garden.

"It's okay, I totally agree. Rather . . . yellow, isn't it? The decor doesn't really fit the outside." I smile at the boy, and he smiles back, relieved not to have offended. "Go ahead, sit down. We're not really set up for small people, I'm afraid. I can do milk, water or fresh apple juice, but no squash or anything more exciting." I start to hunt down the biscuits. "We do have . . . yep, here we go. Hobnobs." Carrie has obviously had a go at these already; the packet is at least a third gone. I place it on the table and Callum looks at Ben questioningly.

"It's okay," Ben says. "You can have a couple." The boy's hand snakes out, whip fast. "A couple is two, by the way," he adds drolly, looking pointedly at the boy, who wrinkles his nose, then thanks me through a mouthful of biscuit.

Mum's friend. What does that translate to in adult vernacular? They certainly seem unrelated, with Callum's dark hair and eyes in clear contrast to Ben's pale blue eyes and much fairer hair. And whereas

I already know that Ben tans well, without even freckling, Callum possesses milk-pale skin.

"Thanks again for the other night," I tell Ben, pulling out a chair to join them at the table. "Did you do much damage to the whisky in the end?"

He grimaces. "To the whisky, and the bourbon, and some rather fine brandy I was keeping for a special occasion . . . so I was somewhat jaded the morning after. I suspect Ali took the brunt of it, though. I don't think he surfaced till the afternoon." He runs an assessing eye over me. "Anyway, how are you settling in?"

"Oh, fine," I say, brightly.

"Do you remember it much?" Ben's eyes are wandering over the kitchen now.

"Not properly. Bits of it, here and there." I look around the kitchen myself, as if another look at the walls might suddenly unearth some recollections. Though there may be no recollections to unearth. Perhaps my brain was too amorphous, too young, too *new* to know how to lay down lifelong memories. "Do you want a tour after your coffee? I mean, if you really are serious about buying the place."

"That would be great, actually."

Callum has already finished his allotted two biscuits, and a glass of water also, and is eyeing the hallway with evident curiosity. "Do you want to go off and look around by yourself?" I ask him. Callum looks at Ben, whose expression seems inclined toward no. "I don't mind," I assure Ben. "I can't think that there's anything dangerous, which probably means there's nothing especially interesting for him either, but he's welcome to take a look."

Ben half nods, half shrugs, and Callum instantly slips off his chair, throwing a quick thank-you over his shoulder as he disappears. I turn back to Ben, a smile still lingering on my face. It seems oddly intimate, now, to be sitting at my own kitchen table having a coffee with a man, practically a stranger. I hear Callum thumping up the stairs, then the sound fades, as if the Manse itself is deliberately cocooning us in the peace of the kitchen. I look for something to say. "He seems a good kid."

Ben smiles and snags himself a biscuit. "He is. He has his moments, but yeah, he's a good kid. He's Fiona's, in case you didn't know," he adds. My eyes snap to him, but he's stirring milk into his coffee and doesn't notice my consternation. "Though I suppose there's no reason why you would know." I'm putting them side by side—Fiona and Callum—in my mind's eye, or at least I'm trying to, but I can't make the image of Fiona stick. She veers nauseatingly in and out of focus, whereas I can see Callum solid and pin sharp. "She's a single mum. I help out where I can."

Which means Ben is babysitting so that Fiona can meet with Carrie. I feel a distinct unease at the thought of the trouble she's gone to—arranging childcare—in order to meet up with Carrie. Unless perhaps she's working today anyway . . . "Where's the dad?"

Ben shrugs. "No idea. Nobody knows who he is." He half smiles at my open mouth. "She won't say."

"She won't say? But surely she'd want child support payments." I process that for a moment. "Maybe she doesn't know."

Ben shakes his head. "Nope, Fiona isn't like that, and believe me, this place is small enough that every single hookup is big news." The mild grimace that temporarily crosses his mouth suggests firsthand experience of that. "I didn't even realize she was pregnant. She was working at a stable up north for a few months and then came back with Callum, but she must have been pregnant with him before she left. As far as I can gather, it's an immaculate conception."

"Yeah, I've heard that one before." His lips twitch at my cynicism. "I get the impression that you guys are close."

"We are. We've been friends since we were kids. We didn't hang out so much in our teenage years—she went a bit wayward then, and I'm that wee bit older, so we weren't quite in the same circles, but after that we got close again, and now she's one of my best friends. But Callum's father is her own business, and she hasn't chosen to say, so . . ."

He shrugs, an exercise in coordinated movement: the corners of his mouth curve up exactly in time with his shoulders. "I can see the reporter in you is deeply unsatisfied with that," he teases.

"Deeply." In fact, I'm amazed by it. If she hasn't told anyone, then presumably she hasn't told Callum, either. I wonder if he's old enough to ask difficult questions, and if so, how does she respond? My experience of children isn't vast, but I rather think the sturdy little mite currently roaming through my house is very much capable of demanding answers.

"Fiona seems a little . . . I don't know how to put it . . ." Even though I've been desperate to broach the subject, I don't quite have the words for it. But Ben is already nodding.

"Yeah, I know, she's wired a little differently. But she's a top lass. You just have to get to know her. And make allowances with time." *Make allowances with time?* I shake my head blankly. "She has something called dyschronometria," he explains. "Among other things . . . Anyway, she can't understand time; she has no concept of how much of it has passed. It makes her memories difficult too—she has no idea how recently or long ago something happened, and she can't put anything in order."

Suddenly the watch makes sense. "So that's why all the beeping."

"It helps her keep track. She's actually pretty good at work; there have only been one or two issues as a result of it. Technically I'm her boss—or her boss's boss, I suppose—but I mostly leave the equestrian stuff to her manager, since he knows what he's doing." He shrugs. "Once you know about the dyschronometria, you find a way to work around it."

"I've never heard of it."

"It's not common. Sometimes it can happen after a blow to the head."

"Is that what happened to Fiona?"

He spreads his hands expressively as if to say, *Who knows?* "Nobody is sure. She remembers blows to the head, more than one in fact, but she doesn't know when they happened, or even if they're significant. I mean, if you were anything like me, I bet you bumped your head a ton in childhood . . . She could have been born like this, and it just wasn't obvious until the age when you're supposed to be a bit more responsible."

Dyschronometria. *Something to do with not having a grip on time.* "How does it impact Callum?"

"Not as much as you might think. He has to be more organized than you'd expect in a kid that age, but she has calendar reminders for just about everything in her phone. Between the two of them, and her dad, not much slips through the cracks."

"They live with her dad?" *Glen McCue.* Our nearest neighbors.

He nods. "It's a good setup. She gets a bit of help with childcare."

"And Jamie?"

"Yeah, he lives there too." His tone is decidedly neutral. Despite the banter I've heard between them, I wonder how well Ben and Jamie get on. And I wonder if Ben knows about Fiona's obsession with the Manse—it doesn't seem my place to tell him, especially if Fiona keeps away from now on. If I thought she was responsible for the missing bin bag, then I wouldn't have such scruples, but she was barely able to stand at the end of that evening, let alone break into a house—she can't be responsible for anything more than the ashtrays full of cigarette butts. And in any case, I can't imagine Ben would take kindly to me saying unflattering things about one of his closest friends. Still, I wonder if Fiona remembers my warning.

The silence stretches out between us as Ben finishes his biscuit. I drop my eyes to my mug, to my fingers wrapped around it. I'm suddenly very conscious of where my gaze alights, of where it is seen to alight. There's nothing exceptionally flirtatious in Ben's manner, no change to his usual laid-back demeanor, but still, I know there's something there, hovering. I know that if I were to reach for it, if I were to deliberately hold his gaze, the very air between us would change, each atom suddenly charged, no longer floating aimlessly but instantly imbued with the sole purpose of creating a conduit between us. We are bound within a cocoon. I am too aware of him, and he of me, and the Manse is aware of us both.

Suddenly Carrie's words echo in my head: *I gather from Ali he's quite the player.* I wonder whether Ben was hoping to see me or Carrie today. Surely Carrie, from the way his eyes lingered on her the other night. It should be Carrie here now, not me. I would prefer it to be Carrie.

I stand up abruptly, under the pretext of taking my mug to the sink, then lean back against the counter and survey him. He's sitting back in his chair, his legs sprawled in front of him, one of his hands resting on his thigh and the other on the table, his long, slender fingers playing with the teaspoon, turning it over and over lengthways. He glances at me with irises the blue of a springtime sky, and I know he knows why I moved. "So," he says, clearing his throat. "Do you own your place in London? House prices there are horrendous, I hear."

The moment has passed. The air is just air; there's no conduit and no charge. "It's my boyfriend's flat. He's had it for over twenty years."

"Ah yes, Carrie mentioned the boyfriend. Jonathan Powell, no less." His lips twist wryly. "No run-of-the-mill London wanker-banker for Ailsa Calder—no, you had to get yourself a national treasure. How are the poor Scottish menfolk to compete with that?" I find myself giggling at his theatrical chagrin. Ali is right. Ben just can't help himself being a player. "Did he never marry, or is he divorced?"

"Divorced. It only lasted a couple of years. Though he has a son from that marriage—Anthony. He's"—I screw up my face, doing the math—"gosh, he must be twenty-nine now." Kind, unassuming Anthony is twenty-nine. Time flies . . . Over the decade or so in which I've known him, I've only spotted the slightest hint of resentment toward his largely absentee father. Perhaps it's just as well. He doesn't possess the backbone to hold Jonathan to account.

"And do *you* want kids?" Ben asks. I stare at him, trying, not for the first time, to envisage it: a baby. A baby with Jonathan. I try to imagine him holding it, burping it, giving it a bottle, but nothing comes. My oh-so-fervent imagination is always sadly lacking on this exercise. Ben makes a motion with his hand. "I'm sorry. I didn't mean to overstep the mark."

"No, don't be silly, I just . . . You know, to be honest, I just don't know. I can't quite imagine it."

"But you must remember Carrie being born."

"Oh, totally. She was gorgeous, of course."

"Of course." He's smiling, as if we are somehow sharing the joke of Carrie's evident attractions. I realize that, here, Carrie and I are seen as a unit. A compliment to one is a compliment to the larger whole. The casual assumption that we already are what I hope we might become throws me off-balance. I struggle to bring myself back to the conversation. "So yes, I know what it's like to have a baby in the house. I just can't quite imagine the baby being mine." That's not quite true—I almost can. I can almost feel the weight and warmth of a small bundle snuggled against my chest. What I can't quite imagine is Jonathan there too.

Suddenly Callum spills into the kitchen in a whirlwind of noise and movement. "Uncle Jamie is coming up the drive," he says importantly.

"Goodness, I'm popular today." Ben looks at me thoughtfully but doesn't say anything. "Come on, Callum, we'd better invite him in."

"He doesnae like biscuits," Callum says as we walk through the hallway to the front door.

"Really? I didn't think it was possible to not like biscuits."

"I guess he likes other things instead."

"Like what?"

Callum pauses, his brow furrowed. "Fruit?" he hazards. "I dinnae ken."

He slips his hand into mine just as I unlatch the door, so I'm looking down at him in surprise as the door swings open. His hand is warm and sturdy, the skin supple and soft. The trust implicit in that simple action floors me. "Hiya, Uncle Jamie," he says.

I look up to catch a flash of chagrin on Jamie's face, which is quickly replaced by a smile. "You've got visitors, I see; hiya, Callum. Ailsa, I can come back."

"Not at all. The more the merrier. Come on in. Tea?"

"Ah, an invitation," he says, grinning cheekily. He's just as well put together as the previous occasions: slim-cut jeans and a very smart navy down jacket. "Well, in that case . . ." He makes a big show of stepping over the threshold, and I roll my eyes at him.

A sudden gust of wind slams the front door hard, almost catching Jamie's heels and making Callum jump, his little hand squeezing mine. "Wow. The back door must be open," I reassure Callum. "Anyway. Tea, Jamie?"

"I'd love one."

"Was the back door open, Ben?" I ask as we reach the kitchen. If it was, it's closed now. "The front one nearly took our heels off."

"No," says Ben, pushing his chair back to stand as Jamie leans in to shake his hand. "The draft must have come from somewhere else. How's it going, Jamie? Not at work today?" He's perfectly genial, but he's not warm; the handshake is not the welcome Piotr got. I can't tell if that's because Ben resents the interruption or if he resents Jamie in particular.

"No, I'm not doing weekends anymore."

"What do you do, Jamie?" I ask.

"I'm going to see Toast," Callum says to me, half a statement and half a question, and I nod my permission as he releases my hand.

"Day trading," Jamie says. "Equities." I start making tea for Jamie, only half listening to his reply as I keep an eye on Callum through the window. Somehow the existence of him, in the garden, completely changes the feel of the Manse. It should be a family home, I think. It was once. It should be again. "I used to work weekends at the estate agents', an extra pair of hands to show the houses, that sort of thing," Jamie is saying. "But it's going well enough on the trading that I dropped that."

Callum has reentered the kitchen. Ben pushes his chair back and stands, stretching briefly. "I'd better get you home, Callum." His shirt rides up, and I see a flash of lean tanned stomach, with a dusting of golden brown hairs running a trail into his jeans. I look away quickly, feeling like a Peeping Tom, especially conscious of Jamie's eyes on me. "Can I have a rain check on that tour? Maybe I can take your mobile number and we can sort it out for another time?"

"Sure." I reel off my number for him to type into his phone. Jamie settles into the same chair that he sat in on his midnight visit, and swaps a thank-you for the tea I hand to him.

"Hey," Ben says suddenly, pulling my gaze back to him. His attention has been caught by the dinner party photo which is still sitting on the counter. "You know, that's my father. I should have told you; he knew your mother pretty well. Look, this guy, farthest right. Next to Ali's folks, actually."

I move to his side to see whom he's pointing at, then take the photo from him and tilt it. I can't see any particular family resemblance between Ben and his father, but Ali's father is unmistakable. They share the same dark, rumpled features, though his father is a big man, both tall and broad, whereas Ali has inherited the smaller frame of his mother. The photo suddenly has added significance. All those friends, together in the same room, enjoying one another's company, and only the other night, over a quarter of a century later, their offspring were doing the same in the Quaich. It feels like looking into an infinity mirror: the same image repeating endlessly, getting smaller and smaller, until the end of light and time.

"I can't see Glen there, or your mum," Ben is saying to Jamie. Jamie reaches out a hand and I pass him the photo. "Maybe it was taken after she died. Come on, Callum, we'd best get going."

"It was lovely to meet you, Callum," I tell him.

"I liked it, too," he says with an endearing earnestness. Then he pipes up again, in the blunt way of children. "I like the dining room best. It's how it should be."

"Me too." He's perceptive, this little mite.

"Was the gold writing always there?"

"What?"

"In the corner, just under the window." I shake my head blankly. "You'll have to look at it. I cannae read it; it's too curly. And . . . and I'm not very good at reading. My teacher thinks I could be dyslexic," he says dolefully, as if it's a death sentence. "I have to go for an *assessment*."

"We talked about this," Ben says gently. "It's not a bad thing. It's just different. And they'll give you extra time in exams if it's diagnosed."

Callum looks thoroughly disgusted. "Why would I want exams to take even longer?"

I meet Ben's eyes over Callum's head, stifling a laugh. He throws a hand in the air as if exasperated, but it's belied by the amusement in his face. I've opened the back door now, and Toast's head is just visible above the garden wall as she stands anxiously awaiting her master. "Why wouldn't Toast come in?" I ask Callum.

"None of the animals will."

"What?" I scan his expression for some kind of explanation, for the hint of a joke waiting to step out, but his little face is still shiningly, earnestly clear. I think of the cat circling the garden, never actually setting a paw inside, despite the bird . . . "But no, that's not right; there was a bird in the garden only last night. It was injured, poor thing."

"Oh, that was from before," says Callum, unconcerned. "Or later." I look at Ben again, confused, but he has turned back to say good-bye to Jamie.

"Thank-you-for-having-me," Callum sing-songs at me, clearly a learned phrase, before I can press the point.

"Thank-you-for-having-me-too," parodies Ben. He's through the door now, squinting against the sunshine as he looks back at me. The fine creases that form around his eyes when he smiles are even more evident in the bright light. It reminds me that he's only a couple of years younger than myself. I wonder if his charm will prevail as he ages. I think of Jonathan, several trips round the sun past fifty. I didn't know Jonathan when he was Ben's age, but nonetheless, I can see similarities. The same charisma, the same inability to switch it off.

I watch the pair of them cross the garden and leap the wall together to be greeted by the excitable Toast. It's a thoroughly heartwarming image—the tall athletic figure of Ben next to Callum's sturdy little frame, and the midnight black dog leaping around them—made all the more so by my brief window into the unselfconscious affection between them. I turn back into the kitchen, carefully locking and dead-bolting the door behind me.

Jamie is finishing his mug of tea, an unreadable expression on his face as he gazes at the photo. He looks up as I join him and flashes his most charming smile. "Peace at last. Though I suppose it's a lot quieter here than wherever you live in London?"

"A lot quieter—" Suddenly there is a thud from upstairs. "Well, apart from the slamming doors . . . But yes, generally a lot quieter, though somehow I'm not sleeping well. I guess I'm not used to the house yet."

"Will you be here long enough to get used to it?"

"No." I think of Callum in the garden. The baby that Jonathan and I don't have, that I can't envisage, could play in that garden. "Well, probably not. Though I suppose it wouldn't be the worst thing in the world to use it as a holiday cottage. If it's going to make next to nothing if I sell it, maybe I ought to hang on to it after all." I look around the kitchen again. "And redecorate. Anyway, you were going to tell me about Fiona's obsession with the Manse and my father."

He grimaces. "Aye. Look, I dinnae want to make a big deal out of it or anything." He pauses, and I incline my head noncommittally. He sighs. "Aye. Well. It's just . . . Actually, this is harder than I thought to explain. It's . . . just that Fiona thinks that our dad isnae her dad." He looks at me expectantly. I shake my head, uncomprehending. He sighs again. "She thinks he was *your* dad. She thinks her dad was Martin."

"*What?*" I stare at him. There's something guarded about his eyes, like he's reining in more emotion than he wants to show. "Is that even possible? How old is she?"

He nods. "It's possible. I'm twenty-six, so she's twenty-eight—born 1982. Your father didn't disappear until late 1983, right?"

"Yes, but that's like saying he could have fathered any child in the region born prior to the date of his disappearance plus nine months. I mean, it's technically possible, but that doesn't mean it actually happened."

He extends a placating hand. "I know, I know—believe me, you're preaching to the converted. But she has it in her head. She's always had it in her head . . ."

"But why?" The door upstairs is banging at intervals just long and uneven enough for me to think that it might have stopped before each new thud.

"I know, it makes no sense. There is no reason. She just . . . I dinnae ken why. She just somehow got the idea in her head and it never left. I cannae remember a time that she didnae believe it."

"Does your dad know she thinks this?"

"Christ, no, that would destroy him. Fiona is his wee girl; she can do no wrong. Especially since she produced Callum out of the blue. My dad is gaga for that wee lad. And believe me, she's smart enough to know which side her bread is buttered on." His expression is rueful as he says this, but it's not completely convincing. I suspect Jamie's ego does not take kindly to being the less favored child. "I'd never tell him. Though it's been hard over the years; she can be quite hurtful. And with all the other problems she already has . . . You probably noticed her behavior the other night, right?" I shake my head, not sure what he means. "How she was watching you?" I hadn't noticed that, but then I was busy trying not to be seen watching her, worrying about my own subtlety. I'm so deeply unsettled now that it's a struggle to stay in my chair; I want to get up and pace. Jamie's still speaking though. "It's because she thinks she's your half sister." *Half sister.* The words jolt me.

I already have one of those. Do two half sisters make a whole? "And normally she's fine, really she is, but with you suddenly here, God knows what is running through her brain . . ." He drags a hand through his hair, then takes a deep breath. "I was thinking . . . ach, it's a horrible imposition, but . . ."

"But what?"

"I thought maybe . . . It's going to sound nuts, but I thought maybe if we did a DNA test, if we proved to her that the two of you are *not* related, then maybe she might, I dinnae ken, let it go or something—"

"No."

"Aye, I figured you'd say that, but please just take a moment to think about it—"

"No." His shoulders droop at my blanket refusal. "I'm sorry, but even doing a test suggests the idea has some credibility. Which it doesn't. I don't see the point in pandering to the delusions of an obviously sick girl. I'm sorry." I stop myself abruptly. I shouldn't have to apologize for refusing to be dragged into this ludicrous nonsense. "Is she on some kind of medication?"

"Well, sometimes that stuff works better than other times." He blows out a long breath. "Aye. Well. It was worth a shot. I just thought I had to ask. What with you actually being here and everything."

"Yes." We sit in silence for a moment. He seems smaller, somehow. Like the fight has gone out of him. "It can't be easy, living with her," I venture.

He smiles gratefully despite his dejection. "Well, no. It's not. And to be honest, I dinnae really have anyone to talk to about it. It's a pretty small pond here, and it's not fair to slag her off to folk who are her pals, too. She's mostly really good at keeping things under wraps, so they might not even believe me anyway. There's a lot of loyalty round here; my dad makes sure of that. Even when there was all that trouble with the police when she was a teenager, and then the social services investigation over Callum . . ." He sees my confused look. "Oh, it was nothing. He rolled off a bed when he was just a baby and ended up with a head injury. So then there was an investigation for negligence, and what with her police record . . ." He grimaces. *Police record? Social services investigation?* I suddenly realize I have my mouth open, and quickly shut it, working hard to find some equanimity. "It took all of Glen's connections to get *that* cleared." *Glen.* Not *Dad.* "Harassment, it was, he said . . . Anyway, my point is that everybody round here knows about the dyschronometria, and they're really protective of her. I would sound like . . ." He trails off.

I find myself nodding. "I noticed that with Ben." I've only been here a few days, and already I can tell that Ben would bridle if I tried to say anything uncomplimentary about Fiona.

He leaps gratefully on my confirmation. "Exactly! Look, Ben's a good guy, though nobody is such an open book as he makes out that he is—but I'm not trying to slag him off; I'm just saying it's not the easiest. And everyone round here thinks Glen is a saint for taking me in at all. Oh—you dinnae ken? Fiona is my half sister. Same father, different mother." His lips twist ruefully. "I'm the by-blow. I was dumped on him when my mam died, which well and truly scuppered his plan of refusing to acknowledge my existence."

"Oh, Jamie." Now the use of *Glen* instead of *Dad* speaks volumes. I, of all people, can empathize. Pete was nothing but kind to me, but Carrie came along when I was eleven, and my pubescent hormones still manufactured all sorts of slights, real or imagined. Carrie was a *choice.* I wasn't Pete's choice; I came with my mother. By then, I wasn't sure I had ever been my mother's choice either.

He shrugs, and aims for a jovial tone. "Aye, well, we all have our crosses to bear." He pauses. "Look, do you think you could see your way to keeping this private?"

"I'm not exactly planning to tell all the locals someone thinks my father was playing away. They already think he was a thief, I bet."

"Aye. Well. Thanks for that." It doesn't escape my notice that he hasn't contradicted me on the thief part. He half shrugs and smiles.

"Well. At least I have you to blether to now." I smile back. I can't think when I was the person that somebody turned to, in a nonprofessional context. There's a pleasure in it that I hadn't appreciated.

———————

Later, Carrie comes back, buoyant of spirit and flushed of cheek after her ride with Fiona, and asks a dozen questions about Ben and Callum and Jamie's visit. I'm vague on Jamie, but I do my best on Ben and Callum—even so, it quickly becomes evident my answers are wholly unsatisfactory to her. For my part, I want to know about her time with Fiona, what they talked about, how she conducted herself, but I don't know how many questions are too many, so I hardly ask anything at all. It's bedtime before I remember to look for Callum's curly writing. I switch the light on in the dining room, then cross quickly to draw the curtains to prevent the blackness peering in on me. *In the corner, just under the window.* I can't see anything anywhere along that wall, but the curtains I've just drawn fall below the windowsill. I have to lift them up and scan the wall behind a section at a time, and even then I nearly miss it: faded cursive script in gold paint, maybe half an inch tall, barely distinct from the warm hue of the wood paneling it has been inscribed upon. Callum's young eyes must be far sharper than mine, or perhaps it's more visible in daylight. Though now that I can see it, it appears to be gaining in luminosity and it seems ludicrous that I could ever have missed it. I can understand why Callum couldn't read it, with the loops and curls and each *s* written to look like an *f*:

Love makes a furnace of the soul

I trace the lettering with a finger, as if I might learn something from that, then snatch my hand back, suddenly worried that I might damage it with the oils in my fingertips. Carrie has already gone to bed, otherwise I would show her this. Who wrote it, and why did they feel compelled to do so? *A furnace.* It's such a specific word, and yet I don't understand. Was it written in quiet contemplation or is it an anguished cry for help? Did the author mean a cozy living room fire, warm and inviting on a winter's day, or a raging incinerator, reducing all it swallows to ashes, to atoms even, in seconds? I think of the oil rig, blazing with a fury beyond comprehension as it slides below the black surface of the sea. I think of the words tattooed down the pale forearm of the bartender. I think of the furiously buzzing flies. I don't understand any of it, least of all the roiling unease in my stomach, as if the very ground beneath me was bucking and shifting. I stretch out a tentative hand again, and the angry buzzing in my head increases even as the bile rises to my throat, and before my fingers can touch the lettering, I have to run from the room to retch repeatedly into the blessedly quiet cool bowl of the downstairs toilet.

MY FATHER IS LIVING IN ORKNEY UNDER AN ASSUMED NAME. HE ran off with the local woman with whom he was having an affair for the previous two years, and they had two children together, but now that the children have grown up, she has left him for the man who runs the Orkney Film Festival. He always liked the film festival, but it rather takes the edge off now to see her there with him; he's thinking of leaving Orkney. His art gallery can be managed from a distance in any case. He would like to know what his daughter is like—he even knows where she works; he could get in touch—but he can't help thinking what a disappointment he would be to her. It all feels like too little, too late.

THIRTEEN

Carrie assures me that she passed on to Fiona both my number and the message for Glen McCue, but my phone doesn't ring. It doesn't ring on account of Jonathan much, either, even though the *Deepwater Horizon* story has moved past the stage where he needs to be in Louisiana and he's now back in Washington. It seems my phone is particular about when it chooses to perform its sole required function. Some days all calls get straight through. On others, they stack up and blurt out all at once in a series of missed call messages, though none from Glen McCue. It always rings for Carrie, though, who calls me every day from the train. We have developed a rhythm, Carrie and I. And the Manse, too, to an extent, though it doesn't keep time very well. Maybe it has dyschronometria, too.

Carrie's phone, on the other hand, has no trouble in ringing. It rings on account of Pete, on account of her agent, on account of friends. It rings on account of Fiona, once, while we're watching a film together: I see "Fi M" pop up on the screen. I pause the film, but she gestures for me to keep watching and takes herself out of the room in one sweeping movement. I'm about to hit play again when something flashes in the corner of my vision, at the window or just below it. I turn toward the wide bay window framed by its open drapes; once again, darkness has fallen without me noticing. What did I see? Something pale: white, perhaps, or a very weak yellow; something moving, just the fleetest of impressions. But there's nothing to be seen except an oddly misshapen reflection of the lit room superimposed on the darkness by virtue of the old, uneven glazing. I can see blurry versions of the television, the sofa, even a bleed of gray that is myself, hovering uncertainly in the glass as I peer outside. Snatches of Carrie's words reach my ears, too indistinct for me to follow the conversation, as I continue to look. Perhaps it was an animal, or a bird. An owl, I suppose, at this time of night. If it was anything at all, that is. *Anything going bump in the night, Ailsa?*

I shake myself and pull the curtains, carefully making sure they meet in the middle, without a square inch of the window left uncovered. I must get better at drawing them before it gets dark if I'm going to exhibit this ridiculous paranoia every time the sun goes down. Carrie is still on the phone, sounding so much more at ease than I ever could. I call people purely to make plans to see them; in truth, the phone makes me uncomfortable. I feel like I'm operating blind, cut off from all the additional feedback that helps me make sense of the truth that lies beneath what people say. I press play on the remote and try to reengage with the plot of the film, which isn't entirely fixed in my head, but Carrie returns to the living room and I pause it again to ask with deliberate nonchalance, "Was that Fiona McCue?"

"Yes." She sinks back onto the sofa, pulling her feet up under her. "Oh, she said her dad will be at the hotel leisure center tomorrow morning. He'll be in the café around ten if you want to speak to him."

"Oh. Well, that's . . . that's good of her," I say awkwardly. "Thanks."

Carrie looks across at me and I busy myself placing the remote on the coffee table, precisely in line with the grain of the wood. "You don't like her, do you?" She sounds almost as if she's speaking to herself.

I can feel the flush spreading across my cheeks. "I've hardly even spoken to her."

"I know. Which makes it even more unfair that you don't like her."

I could try to equivocate, but she would see right through me. "It's just . . . from what I hear, she's a bit . . . unstable."

Carrie snorts. "Unstable, my eye. She's about the most grounded person I've ever met." I can see she's already gearing up to a robust defense.

"Well, maybe you haven't got to know her properly yet."

"What, and you have?" she challenges. I knew this would happen.

"No, of course not, but I think you'd have to accept that Jamie knows her pretty well." Jamie's getting to be quite the regular here. He often pops by for a coffee and a blether, as he puts it. It's a new experience for me: an entirely nonprofessional, non-amorous friendship. My job is social—very social, in fact. Every posting comes with a ready-made gang of journalists and crew keen to hang out. It's fun while it lasts, but nobody ever looks back. "And Jamie says—"

"Whatever he says is bollocks," she says flatly. "I told you they don't really get along. There's nothing unstable about Fiona."

"Really? Is that when she's on her medication, or off it? Or when she's wandering through the Manse when it's unoccupied?" The words have marched out of my mouth before I can stop them, followed instantly by a twinge of guilt for breaking faith with Jamie. Though surely my first concern has to be Carrie's safety . . .

"What?"

"I saw her here. Up in the box room."

Carrie pauses. "You saw her here. You're one hundred percent sure you saw her here." She reads my face, and her own erupts in exasperation. "No, you're not, are you? My God, Ailsa, will you just listen to yourself? Where's your famous journalistic reason and impartiality?"

"No, I'm not certain, but who else has that style of haircut?" Unless it was the lampshade after all . . . but I'm certain. I'm almost certain. "Who else would it be? She didn't deny that she comes here, and someone had been through those boxes. There was no dust on them." I take a breath and try to lower my voice. "Okay, I'm not certain, but it fits. She's always been obsessed with this place, apparently."

"Are you kidding? Everyone round here is obsessed with this place! I am telling you now, Ailsa, that if you are not prepared to be civil to, and about, the people I call friends, then you're not the person I thought you were. And . . . and I'm not prepared to live with you if that's the case." She cuts off her uncharacteristic outburst abruptly.

My breath catches as I stare at her. She's fiercely tight-lipped, her shoulders rigid with fury and resolve. It's not a bluff; I can see that in her stone-gray eyes even though she's refusing to look at me. She would actually move out over this. And if she moves out—what then? We would see each other as we always have, from time to time, when I'm in the country. Siblings, but distant. Half sisters, less than half, nowhere near the whole. I can hear her now: *Family? Well, there's only Dad and me now, really. I do have a half sister, but we don't really talk.* "Well . . . I'd be very sorry if you did. I don't want you to move out." She looks at me, but nothing has softened. She needs more. And it's not as if she's being unreasonable—I'm the one with the inexplicable dread. *Nearly inexplicable dread.* I'm the one who's being unfair and unreasonable and impressionable and all the things that are so far from my normal level self that when I sit back and look at myself, I almost can't find me. How did I get to here? And why can't I just get over this unease? "I wouldn't have asked you to stay if I didn't want you here."

"You never cared before." The words are stony. They have to be, to force their way through the tight hard line of her mouth. It's the same resentment, that same issue every time: that I left, without a backward glance. I've been tiptoeing around it. I've been handling her with kid gloves, and suddenly I'm tired of it. Maybe she'll never get over it. Maybe we'll never be anything more than distant siblings. And if that's the case, we might as well have this fight now.

"All right then," I challenge her. "Let's talk about that. I was eighteen and I left for university. What would you have had me do? Stay at home until you were eighteen and ready to leave yourself?"

"You could have come home at holidays! You could have called! You could have come to my concerts and plays, like you used to!"

"Concert and plays? I was trying to start my own life. I wasn't your parent, Carrie. That wasn't my job." I hear my own words, the harshness of them, but I'm no longer interested in sugarcoating.

"You don't get it. That's what you were like to me. Mum was—well, Mum was Mum, but you were always there. And then you weren't." She turns her head away, but not before I see the teardrop suspended from one of her eyelashes.

"You don't get it either, Carrie." My throat is tight now. Her tears have done that. "It seemed to me that you had everything; what did you need me for? You had Pete, and Mum was so much more involved with you than she ever was with me." It never occurred to me that Carrie could have felt neglected by Karen too. Maybe our mothers weren't as different as I thought. "I felt . . . I felt so *jealous* sometimes of the attention she gave you." I feel mean even admitting it now, just as I felt small and mean at the time. What kind of person is jealous of the love given to a child?

Carrie glances at me, simultaneously dashing a hand at one eye. "Really? She must have been pretty bloody absent with you then."

"Well, yes," I say ruefully. "She really was." And suddenly we are both laughing, though her eyes are overbright, and I suspect mine may be too. I take advantage of the moment to shift the focus. "About Fiona, I'm just . . . I'm worried for you, is all. I can't promise to like her, but I promise I'll be civil. Maybe even friendly." For Carrie, I will absolutely try. For all that she is the reason I'm here, it has still taken me aback how much I don't want her to leave. I must be growing accustomed to our rhythm.

Her lips begin to curl. "Well. Best not overpromise."

"True. Civil it is."

She smiles properly, just a small one, but the tension has left her shoulders. She reaches forward for the remote, then pauses. "Oh, I meant to say, that cat was out there again. I saw it while I was on the phone. It's getting kind of weird. Though no stone-throwing that I could see, at least."

"Did it come in the garden?" The cat comes by most evenings. I've never seen it set even a single paw on the lawn.

"No, it stayed on the wall, looking into the garden. The same as before."

I know what it was looking at: the injured bird. Sometimes I see it, sometimes I don't. The first time—well, the first time I saw it again, hopping desperately in exactly the same spot, still unable to take off—I couldn't believe my eyes. And I know I'm right not to believe them. I know the bird's not there, it's never there, because Carrie has never seen it. The cat is there, though, since Carrie has seen it, too. And the cat sees the bird, so how can the bird not be there? But still, I know it's not. And if the bird's not there, were the flies ever there? Was the figure with triangular hair ever there? But if they were there . . . if they were there, what does that mean? Are they part of a larger whole? Are they connected to the newspaper and the stone-throwing? Is this all I have to face, or are these incidents just a portent of what is to come?

Then Carrie presses play and I force my overtired brain to drop this feverish endless loop.

The next morning, I open the front door to take Carrie to the station and find a raven on the doorstep.

At first I think it's the injured bird from the garden, the one that I might or might not have seen. But it's much bigger, probably over a foot tall, and most definitely dead. I stop short and lean forward to take a closer look and then have to grab the doorframe to stop myself nose-diving into the carcass when Carrie cannons into me, her face in her phone.

"What's the—oh!" she exclaims. "Yuck!"

"Yep." I'm irrationally enormously relieved that she can see it too, even though it's not the injured bird. "I think it died a while ago. Look, there are maggots." Part of the belly of the bird has been torn open, and there are pale yellow bodies squirming in the opening. A shudder runs through me.

"Well, that's fucking disgusting."

"Quite." I find my lips are twitching. Even my melodramatic tendencies can't withstand the fresh air of Carrie's blunt appraisal. I straighten up and look around. "I wonder how it got here." Carrie looks confused. "Well, it wasn't here yesterday, and since it's been dead awhile, it didn't just up and walk to our doorstep."

"Maybe that strange cat brought it? Or another animal? A fox, or something?"

"Could be." I think of my unease in the living room. Did I see something bringing it then? Could the cat carry something of that size? Surely it would have had to have dragged it? I can't see any drag marks in the gravel. "Come on, let's get you to the station on time. I'll clear it up later; it's not like it's going anywhere."

I go straight from dropping Carrie at the station to the hotel café, and get there a little after nine thirty. There's no reason to be so early, but also nothing but a maggot-ridden dead bird waiting for me at the Manse, so the hotel café wins. I enter through the dedicated leisure center entrance this time, which takes me past the pool, where I linger for a moment. There's a lady in her fifties with dyed blond hair piled atop her head doing head-up breaststrokes, and a pale, leanly muscular man with heavily freckled shoulders doing laps in an economical front crawl, but neither of them could be Glen.

The view from the café is just as breathtaking as before, despite it being an overcast day with early-morning fog lying in wisps at the bottom of the valley. I order a black Americano from the same waitress and read the newspaper, glancing up every time I hear footsteps. None of them belong to a man in his sixties. I can't imagine that Glen Mc-Cue will be anything other than civil with me, but I still can't seem to get through a whole article. By ten minutes to ten I've given up on reading and am trying my hand at the cryptic crossword instead, but

I can't concentrate on that, either. My bladder is also feeling the effects of the large coffee, but I don't want to go to the bathroom in case I miss him.

At five past ten, a man enters who falls into the right age category. He scans the room then nods sharply at me and heads unsmiling directly toward my table. I stand up to greet him, and have a few seconds to study him before he's upon me. Not as tall as Jamie but built just like both of his children, wiry and compact. I hold out my hand. "Mr. McCue?"

"Aye." His grip is strong but brief. He looks like a man with a deep mistrust of anything frivolous. He pulls out a chair and sits opposite me, assessing me with sharp eyes that look as if life has bleached them of color. He has an extraordinarily weathered face, with skin like thick leather, and his dark gray hair is trimmed down to mere millimeters, military fashion. "Well. There's barely an ounce of your mother in you, is there." There's literally nothing I can think of to say to that, but it doesn't matter because he turns away to address the waitress who's approaching in his thick local accent. "Aye, hen, gie me a latte and one of them billionaire shortbread slices."

"Thanks for meeting me." There's something about his very presence which makes me feel instantly lightweight, as if nothing I could ever say or think or do could ever be of any import.

"Nae trouble," he says, unsmiling. "My grandson would have been most upset with me if I hadnae."

"Callum? He's such a sweetie." I've seen him a few times since his ball landed in my garden: once in the village with a lady I didn't know, and twice when he crossed the three fields between our houses and came to the Manse by himself, Fiona having phoned ahead to make sure Carrie was looking out for him. I would have thought Carrie was more child friendly than myself, but for some reason it's my hand Callum reaches for and my lap he scrambles into, and my heart feels defenseless each time.

"Aye, well, he likes you. And your biscuits." I laugh, and the edges of his mouth lift briefly. A hard man to warm to, then, but perhaps not without kindness. "How are you settling in at the Manse?"

"Fine." I start to shrug, then wonder if he will disapprove. It seems like he's the sort of man who would disapprove of elbows on the table and shrugging and addressing men of his generation as anything other than *sir*. "It's only temporary, anyway."

"Ah. So you're going to sell it, are you?" I nod. "Fi was born there, you ken."

"What?" I look at him, bewildered. Surely he doesn't mean in the Manse?

The corners of his mouth curl upward again, but with less warmth. "Aye. In the house itself. 1982."

"But—wait, I would have been six. I was living there then." How could she have been born there?

"She came early and too quick. I was away, following up on a case. We werenae expecting a bairn to arrive then. But she did . . . and Mary—my wife—couldnae get to the hospital, so she went to the Manse looking for help. It was the summer, though, and you were all away." He scratches his head. "Aberdeen, I think, visiting your grand-parents or the like." I nod. Both of them died before my father disappeared. I only have vague memories of visiting them, and most of those are of the long and tiresome car journey to get there. "Anyway, she didnae find any help there after all, and then it was too late."

"So, your wife, she had Fiona on her own?" It's a horrifying thought.

"Aye. In the dining room. We tried to pay your dad for the replacement of the carpet but he wouldnae hear of it."

There's approval in his voice for my father's refusal. I try not to think of the state the carpet must have been in to need replacing. Dear God, I hope it has been replaced at some point since . . . "But . . . how did she even get in?"

"I cannae remember." He looks sideways, as if the mountains beyond the glass that protects us might give him the answer, then gives up. "Ach, it was a different time. Everybody left spare keys outside, under a flowerpot or a mat. Anyroad. She loves that house, does Fi. Always has. If she was able to, she'd buy it off you in a flash." I can hear Jamie as if he's right next to me: *She has a thing about this place. The Manse. Always has.* I find I'm wrapping my arms across my stomach as if I'm physically chilled. It's a struggle to pull my attention back to Glen. *You promised Carrie*, I remind myself. *Benefit of the doubt and all that.* "Roy tells me you need the Presumption of Death certificate to be able to sell."

Roy is my lawyer, Mr. MacKintyre. "Yes. Without it I just own half the Manse." Which half, I wonder feverishly. I can't possibly have the dining room, not now that I've heard about the carpet, and not the box room, either. Is there any room that could be mine?

"Well, I told him that there's been no new evidence." He's eyeing me carefully as he speaks. There's only the barest hint of blue in the steel of his irises. "In my opinion, your father is most likely dead."

It takes a moment to find my voice. "Based on what?" I ask, trying to sound like we're discussing the relative merits of, say, taking the A9 to get to town as opposed to the back roads.

"Are you sure you want to talk about this? I'll answer any question you have, but you ken, I'm not really the sugarcoating type—"

No kidding. "I'm sure."

He looks me over again then sighs in a *your funeral* kind of way. "Well, you have to look at the push and pull factors. For example, were your parents happy in their marriage—"

"Were they?"

"Not especially." His words are blunt but delivered mildly. "But not specifically unhappy, either." He pauses for a moment, checking my reaction, then evidently decides it's safe to continue. "Your dad was a friend of mine; we would run together. I cannae do it now that my knee isn't what it was . . . We even did a couple of half marathons together." I'm looking at him in frank astonishment. I can imagine Glen running—he has a spare efficiency to his wiry frame—but I didn't know my father had been a runner. Perhaps still is a runner, somewhere.

"We'd have a pint and a blether from time to time and the idea just came from there. We were training for the Glasgow marathon when he disappeared."

"Did you do it without him?"

He shakes his head. "It wouldnae have been the same." I nod. It seems respectful that he didn't do it, like he was acknowledging the importance of what had happened. Life can't just go on regardless. It shouldn't. "So what I'm saying is I ken what I'm talking about, and not just from the professional side. He wasnae having an affair or anything, if that's what you're thinking." He's looking at me sternly now, like a school teacher belaboring the point. But I don't feel the slightest bit ashamed: of course I've considered that. I even wondered in my more adventurous period whether promiscuity could be an inherited trait. "We never found any evidence of that. They had their moments, your mum and dad, but that's marriage." He shrugs. "You ken how it is."

I don't, actually. Quite apart from not being in a marriage, I rather doubt that my relationship with Jonathan is typical. On top of which my parents were hardly a good example, and I could never quite understand the dynamic between Pete and my mother. "What caused their particular *moments*?" A *furnace of the soul*: perhaps my parents' love was more the incinerator type. Perhaps it had already burned itself out by then.

"Ah, thanks, hen." He stirs a sugar into the coffee that the waitress has just delivered and then continues. "Mostly your mum wasnae very happy here. You'll ken they met at Saint Martin's, all very arty-farty, antiestablishment, what have you." The set of his mouth tells me exactly what he thinks of the artistic community. "Then Karen gets pregnant with you. They get married and end up in rural Scotland with your dad going to work every day in a suit and tie." His mouth twists sardonically in his leathery face. "I doubt it was exactly what your mum thought she was signing up to."

"What did my father think?"

"Oh, he loved it here. Loved his job; he was doing well there. Mr. Jamieson had a lot of time for him—"

"Jamieson?" Where have I heard that name before?

"Aye, his boss at the jewelers. Jamieson & Sons." I nod and he goes on. "Aye, well, he loved the land, loved having you, loved the house—that was another bone of contention, mind. Your dad was fascinated by it. He was even researching the history and the like, but your mum couldnae stand the Manse. Not at first, like, but over time she grew to hate it. She wasnae one to keep her thoughts to herself, your ma. We all heard about it." I grimace faintly and his lips twitch in another humorless smile. "It was getting to be more of a wedge between them as time went on. If it had been your mum who disappeared, I'd have said you'd find her alive and thriving in some hippie commune in South America or somewhere. Your dad, though." He pauses and takes a bite of his caramel-and-chocolate-topped shortbread. I watch him whilst he chews. "Aye, well, your dad . . . It just didnae stack up. I couldnae believe he would leave." He shakes his head and takes another bite, and for a moment his businesslike facade slips, revealing something altogether more bleak. It takes him an unusually long time to get through his mouthful. "And your dad was a smart man," he continues suddenly, as if he hadn't paused. "He regularly carried two or three times the value of the jewels that disappeared with him. If he was planning to do a runner, surely he would wait for a bumper occasion?"

I nod as if I'm letting that sink in, though of course I've envisaged that scenario, and more, many times. "You said my father wasn't having an affair. What about my mother?"

He inclines his head a little, acknowledging the point. "Aye. Well. Maybe." It sounds like *mebbe*. "It wouldnae have surprised me. She was young and a bonnie lass; she liked to be center of attention and she wasnae short of admirers. There were a fair few who might have been holding a torch for her." He shrugs. "We looked into it at the time, but there was nothing . . . definitive. And even if your dad had found her up to nae good, I doubt he would have upped and left immediately. Not without at least packing a bag, or his research."

"Unless he had some kind of mental breakdown."

"Aye, possible. But I didnae see him as the type." What is the type? I wonder. Does he think he can read it on a person's skin, in the way they *blether*, in the way they drink their pint? Though Glen was a policeman for decades, he probably knows more about human psychology than I'm giving him credit for. "The problem for the investigation was that we couldnae pin down where he went missing from. We couldnae trace him after he flew back to Edinburgh Airport. And to be honest, he might not have been on the flight. The computer was down that day in Antwerp, and check-in was a disaster. It was some lassie ticking the passenger name off on a list and then writing the boarding pass with a Biro. The on-plane head count was off from the list count by three. You couldnae take off like that now, but this was the 1980s." He grimaces and spreads his hands. "There wasnae any CCTV in operation back then. He could have got on a bus or hopped in a taxi or just walked out of Edinburgh Airport. Or maybe he never flew back to Edinburgh at all. All we know is he didnae take his car; we found that a couple of days later in one of the airport long-stay car parks. With a flat battery."

None of this is new to me, exactly, but it's the first time I've ever had it delivered straight. I can't quite pin down how I gathered the information I do know. I have hazy memories of the first few days after he went missing, of being sent to another room when somber hard-faced men came to speak to Karen, of flattening myself against the wall near the doorway to listen in silently. I suppose I also asked my mother later what they said, though I can't imagine she was very forthcoming. I know I must have read the newspapers; there was a particular line that got tangled in my seven-year-old brain: *The police are appealing to anybody with information to come forward.* The somber hard-faced men were the police that were appealing, my mother said, but they didn't seem very appealing to me. I worried that anybody with information would be too frightened to come forward.

Probably one of those men was Glen, come to think of it. I find I'm rubbing my forehead between my eyebrows, as if trying to erase the faint frown line I've recently noticed I'm developing. I drop my hand to my lap. "So, what do you think happened? Did you have a theory? An accident? Foul play?"

"No grand theory." He's frowning himself, now. "Often you get a pretty good idea of what's happened; it's just whether or not you can prove it. You'd be surprised how seldom the police are surprised." I suspect he's used that line before. For all that he seems to eschew frivolity, I can sense a touch of the showman. "But on this one . . ." He shakes his head slowly. "I dinnae think he left. Not voluntarily. I think if your dad could be here now, he would be. So . . . aye, accident or foul play, one or the other." He eyes me carefully again. "He'd be right proud of you, I bet. Fiona says you're a big shot in television."

His words trip me up, robbing me of the questions I had waiting in line. It seems an oddly personal thing for him to say among this no-frills discussion of my father's disappearance. And . . . really? How can he tell my father would be proud? Of course he would be, in the versions of my father's life where he's the man Glen describes. But there are all the other versions I've considered, jostling for space in my head, where Glen is simply another person who didn't understand the true nature of my father. I choose to step right over that quagmire. "I'm in television, yes. Not a big shot, though. More of an air rifle than a cannon."

A bark of gravelly laughter escapes him, and I find a smile for him. I like that he tried to be kind, I realize. Though he makes me feel a bit like a schoolgirl again, craving approval from authority. By the time I was at university, my antiestablishment tendencies had come to the fore, and I had no such esteem for authority. Or maybe it was my mother's antiestablishment tendencies bubbling up inside me. The thought throws me off-balance. I want to feel that I am *me*, created from pure air, my genes unsullied by ancestry. I want to feel that my thoughts and reactions and decisions are mine and mine alone. But being here, in Scotland, in the Manse of all places, has me feeling the

weight of my DNA, of the history and memories and behavioral pat-
terns it carries. Of the impact it has had, or might yet have, on what I
think of as *me.*

"You have a sister, I hear."

I take it he thinks we've exhausted the subject of my father, and in
truth, I'm not sure there is anything left for me to ask. Nothing he can
answer, at any rate. "Yes, Carrie. Half sister, actually. But of course you
would know that."

He nods. "Aye. Do you get on?"

"Em, yes. I guess." It's not a question I was expecting. "Living
under the same roof as adults is . . ." I think of our argument, of Carrie's threat to leave. I think of all the things I know about her now, the
trail she leaves behind her, of open doors and objects, proof of where
she has traveled. I think of her need for company and noise, the way
they transform her: *I'm not like you; I'm a people person.* I wonder what
she would say in my place. "Well, it's new for us. But . . . yes, I guess
mostly we do."

"That's good." He looks at his empty plate for a moment then
nods, a tiny motion, as if it's for himself alone. "That's good. That's
something."

———

I try to call Jonathan from the car park of the hotel before I leave. It's
an utterly stupid thing to do, because it's the crack of dawn in Washington DC. I realize that just in time to hang up before voice mail
kicks in. Though hearing his familiar BBC English on his voice mail
would have been better than nothing. I'm craving some kind of lifeline
to the present—the past seems to be all but swallowing me up. Instead
I drive slowly and carefully back along the winding road to the Manse,
pondering the fact that for once in my life I have too much time to
think, and yet I'm not using it to think about anything productive. I
should be working through where I want to take my career or using
this time apart from Jonathan to try to untangle how I feel about him,

about us, about the future, and instead I'm rummaging around in events of the past, and worrying about flies and birds and intruders that may or may not exist outside my brain. I park up in front of the Manse, eyeing it mutinously, but it doesn't take the bait. It's just a pile of bricks, after all.

A pile of bricks with a dead bird on its doorstep. Only—the carcass is no longer there. I look around, somewhat nonplussed, in case an animal has dragged it and dropped it somewhere else in the vicinity, but I can't see any sign of it. I start to poke in the overgrown flower beds at the end of the front lawn before the absurdity of that strikes me—am I really spending time hunting down a maggot-ridden carcass that I didn't want to have to dispose of in the first place? I still have the echo of Carrie's dispassionate assessment in my ears—*That's fucking disgusting*—and I can just imagine her reaction to its unexpected disappearance: *Good riddance!* I should be considering it a bonus that I don't have to clear it up. It's not like with the bin bags; those were inside. Surely some animal has taken it and is currently delighted with the ready meal. I scan the garden one more time, but a black heap of feathers fails to suddenly appear, so I give up and head into the Manse. It's not like with the bin bags. It's not.

MY FATHER LIVES ON THE STREETS IN NICE. THE WEATHER IS generally warm, which is kinder to rough sleepers, though in latter years he has seen a growing threat from the influx of violent gangs from eastern Europe. On the days when he is able, he draws chalk pictures on the pavements, copies of old masters created from memory, although he couldn't tell you where or when he learned to love these paintings. He couldn't tell you much about himself at all. The chalk drawings can win him enough to buy a decent lunch or a bottle of wine, but the days when he is able to draw occur less and less frequently. There's a fog that has invaded his mind, that's been there for a great many years, growing and expanding to cloak more and more of his synapses with every passing week. One day he will lie down to sleep on a bench, and only his heart, not his mind, will wake up.

FOURTEEN

The next evening we spend together, I show Carrie the inscription, and she shocks me by saying, "Mum told me about this!"

"What?" I've climbed into one of the high-backed dining chairs, my feet tucked under me.

"I'd completely forgotten about it." She reaches out a finger to touch it, to trace it, a half smile on her face. Like me, she stops before she makes contact. "She said she lived in a house with a strange inscription, that the man she was living with was obsessed by it." She glances at me, realization dawning. "Oh my God, she meant your dad."

It had never occurred to me that Mum would have talked to Carrie about the Manse, even obliquely. "What else did she say?"

"I don't know . . . that it was a strange house. She couldn't sleep properly in it. She said she first started painting in that house—here, I suppose—because she couldn't sleep." She looks at the inscription again. "A furnace of the soul," she murmurs dreamily. "That's the kind of love I'd like." She cocks her head as she looks at me, a wicked gleam in her eye. "Does Jonathan make a furnace of your soul?"

"No, thank God! It doesn't sound terribly . . . sustainable."

"Sustainable! Aren't you the die-hard romantic!" Carrie is laughing at me, as I meant her to, but I'm not being entirely flippant. A furnace surely can't last. It makes me think of the newsroom phrase: *burned out*. Like the oil rig, like the missing kirk, until all that is left is a blackened husk of the original, all energy and passion and ability to *care* vaporized by the infernal fire. "Seriously, though, did you never just meet someone and know? Who they were inside and that you were right for each other? Someone you'd trust to be on your side come what may?" Is she talking about something current, or in the past? I wonder. There's something around her eyes . . . I can't tell if she's wishing or remembering.

"I kind of like to know the whole story first."

Carrie shakes her head, amused. "Nobody ever knows the whole story. Not even the people in it." She looks at the inscription again, and I see a distorted reflection of her dreamy smile in the old, uneven glass of the window. I get up to close the curtains before darkness can take its hold. "This house," she says, shaking her head. "Everybody I meet round here is always talking about it. Like they can't leave it alone."

Like picking a scab, I think. "Well, hopefully that will translate into offers when I put it on the market."

"Do you have any idea of what it's worth yet?"

"I spoke to a couple of agents again today. They both said roughly the same price"—I name a figure that widens her eyes—"but it depends very much on the market. It's such a specific property. It could get zero interest or it could end up in a bidding war."

"Well, for that kind of money, I can see how it might stick in Ali's throat."

I shake my head. "Ali's? Why Ali's throat?"

"Well, because . . ." She sees my blank look. "Shit, I thought you knew." She takes a deep breath. "He's Ali Jamieson. His family owned the jewelers."

"Jamieson & Sons." I groan aloud—I've been rather slow on the uptake. I remember Ali's truculent emphasis during our introduction. It didn't mean anything to me at the time, but it should have. Once again I have the feeling that the world is narrowing to exactly the pinhead that I'm dancing on. "Fuck. Who told you?"

"I overheard that bitch in the village shop saying something, and I asked Fi about it."

"What did she say? The woman from the shop, I mean."

Carrie is squirming a little. "It doesn't matter. I don't suppose she's a barometer for public sentiment; she's just a busybody. I guess you already heard the kind of things she says about Fiona." I don't know what she means, but it seems wiser to keep my mouth shut. Though it does suggest that perhaps Jamie was a little wide of the mark about the local loyalty to his sister . . . "She can go on for hours about each and every resident, and none of it is nice."

"Still, out with it."

She tries to meet my eyes, but can't, and abruptly caves. "She said . . . she said it's disgusting you being here. Flaunting your life of Riley up at the big house at the expense of good honest folk like the Jamiesons."

"She said that to you?" I'm truly appalled.

"No, not to me. I don't think she realized I was there."

"Life of Riley?" For a moment I can't think what on earth this charming-sounding woman could have meant, and then I twig. "Oh, I see. Hardly. Life of squalor, more like, at least until Mum started selling paintings. We'd hardly have been squatting if we had half a million's worth of diamonds to live off."

"Did you really have to squat?" asks Carrie quietly, almost apologetically, but I'm on a different track.

"Oh God. My lawyer told me that the firm went bust after . . . afterward. The insurance company found a technical loophole to wriggle out of and wouldn't pay up, so they had to file for bankruptcy." I hadn't considered it from their angle before. Jamieson & Sons lost an employee and the diamonds, and then their whole business. Even if they didn't believe my dad was a thief, they would have to be pretty hacked off at the way things had turned out. "No wonder Ali doesn't like me." He certainly hasn't improved in any of our subsequent encounters; I've seen him a few times, and he's been no better than grudgingly civil.

"He just needs to get to know you," she says with unexpected loyalty. Then she more or less contradicts herself by adding, "But the Manse is the thing, though. Everyone thinks it's a real prize and you're sitting pretty in it."

"Some prize. It hardly rents at all, and I can't even sell it yet."

"Even so, it's part of local legend round here. I'm not sure you're going to want to know this, but . . ." I can see she's going to tell me anyway.

"But what?"

"I think half the locals around your age lost their virginity in the Manse."

"*What?*"

"One of the stable girls was laughing about it when I went to the equestrian center. Did you know Mum didn't rent it out for the first decade or so? It was just empty, and not terribly well secured; all of that got sorted once she decided to rent it, but until then it was apparently a piece of cake to get in. So if you were a pair of horny teenagers looking for a place to be alone . . ." She lifts her eyebrows expressively, amusement radiating from her gray eyes.

I look around involuntarily, as if I might see a couple of spotty-faced, loved-up teens going at it behind us. "Fuck!"

"Quite." Suddenly we are both giggling. "Apparently the man at the estate agent said that Mum's decision to rent out the Manse did more for lowering the teenage pregnancy rate round here than any school sex education program could have."

"Christ." I shake my head, still smiling. There's something oddly reassuring about the idea of the Manse as a haven for hormonal teenagers seeking to indulge their sex-obsessed tendencies. It's so *normal* it's almost wholesome, and that makes the Manse seem wholesome too. I can't imagine any level of hormones would entice teenagers to undertake their initiation into the delights of sex in a place that feels sinister. Though that suggests once again that it's all in my head . . . I shake off that disquieting thought. "Do you think that counts for or against it in an open-market sale?"

She grins. "Definitely for." Then she cocks her head. "Have you considered *not* selling?"

"What, staying here?"

"Yes. It's not like you really stay in London, is it? You don't really live anywhere."

I leave a small pause before I answer her. "I live with Jonathan."

Even as I'm saying it, I can see the holes in the sentiment. Carrie looks like she's about to say something but thinks better of it. Instead she turns back to the inscription. "A furnace of the soul," she says again, barely audibly, and I'm almost sure there's something she's not telling me. Many things, perhaps. We've been eating together, and watching television together most nights—the news or a film—and we've been talking, but never about anything important. I wonder if the pitfalls we're each avoiding are the same ones. Maybe we're not navigating the same landscape at all.

Days pass. Then weeks, and we develop a rhythm, Carrie and I. Fragile, to be sure; and nascent, but nonetheless a rhythm. I pick Carrie up from the station, we might or might not go to the leisure club, we have dinner together (Carrie cooks; I wash up) then watch some telly or occasionally we meet some combination of Ben, Ali, Fiona, Piotr and Jamie in the pub. But abruptly that fledgling pattern is broken. Carrie rings, as she always does, and instead of discussing her day, instead of waiting for me to offer a lift, she tells me she's staying up in Edinburgh for the night, doing something with some of the cast. I'll be on my own in the Manse tonight.

I place my phone carefully down on the dining room table after she's disconnected, and look around me thoughtfully. I've taken to doing any necessary admin in here, partly on account of the practicality of the big table on which to spread out all my papers, and partly because of the view. This room looks across the rear garden, toward the lawn that acts as a welcome mat to the wood that I am growing to love, but more crucially it looks away from the valley floor and the spectacular mountains that rear beyond it, their very impassivity somehow drawing the eye and refusing to release it.

She sounded different, Carrie. It wasn't a conversation in which I felt questions were welcomed—probably there was someone with her. I wonder if there's one cast member in particular that she's more keen to spend an evening with. There's a hint of . . . something. I don't know what. A softness round her mouth when she's thinking and doesn't realize I can see her. Perhaps someone has indeed lit a furnace in her soul . . . Perhaps these nights in Edinburgh will become more frequent, and I'll be spending evenings alone more often than not. It's an unsettling thought. The Manse is different with Carrie in it. It keeps time better, it hides its other faces, the bathroom door stays closed and the boiler flame doesn't snuff out. It behaves like the mere pile of bricks it ought to be.

God, I will have to cook.

I head to the fridge and eye up the contents despairingly. It's by no means bare, but everything in it requires effort: chopping or prepping or frying or grilling or possibly all of those; Carrie would know. But the fridge door has been open too long; it begins a low accusatory beeping. I close it and consider my options.

Fuck it. I can buy a microwave meal at the village shop.

I decide to walk, even though it briefly crosses my mind that I might be exposing myself to more target practice from the mysterious stone thrower. It's still light, though, so it seems unlikely. Regardless, I find I'm constantly looking around to check behind me, even as I berate myself for allowing the stone thrower this victory over me. There's a brisk breeze that chills my cheeks and tangles my hair, but I'm warm enough inside my coat and I feel more awake than I have all day. Mostly I have to stick to the road, which has lumpy grass verges instead of pavements, but the road is so seldom used that I don't worry about traffic mowing me down. Closer to the village, a narrow pavement replaces the verge and the odd car passes me. Several hundred meters farther, the houses begin. At first they are boxy new-build houses laid out around curving crescents, but along Front Street, where the village shop is to be found, the buildings are much older, low squat structures with narrow windows and thick walls in local stone with slate roofs. It's not a busy street—I'm the only person on it—but there are a few cars parked in front of the shop and the post office.

I'm only thirty meters or so from the shop when Carrie exits it.

I nearly call out, then I stop—it can't be her. She's in Edinburgh. But nobody else has biker boots and a gray coat that flaps out around the legs; it's unmistakably her. She has a bottle of wine held by the neck in one hand and a plastic bag in the other, and she doesn't look up the street toward me. Instead she strides purposefully to one of the parked vehicles and climbs in. The car pulls away and is no longer shielded from my view by other parked vehicles. I can see it properly as it drives away from me down the long, straight road that is Front Street. It's Jamie's jeep.

It takes me a moment to realize I've stopped dead on the pavement. She lied to me. I resume walking and try to sort out what I've just seen. Why would she feel the need to lie? Does she think I would be jealous about Jamie asking her out? What on earth would give her that impression? I have Jonathan, after all—well, I have as much of him as is available, and I'm not even sure I want that, but I'm hardly on the prowl. The shopkeeper—a busty woman with impressive biceps who may or may not be the bitch that Carrie referred to—throws out a cheery *hiya*, and I find a vague smile for her in response. I don't understand what's happening. It almost hurts to breathe.

Perhaps she didn't lie. Perhaps she was planning to stay in Edinburgh, but her plans changed. I glance at my watch. No, she must have been on the train already when she rang me. She lied, and that one thing, that single small thing, has in a stroke replaced the solid ground beneath me with quicksand.

"That looks healthy."

Ben. Nobody else has an accent that covers three continents in three words. I look up and find him smiling at me down the shop aisle, dressed in jeans and a casual hoodie and his fingers looped loosely through the handle of a carton of milk. The sleeves are pushed back on his hoodie. I'm not sure I've ever seen him with those tanned fore-arms covered. I look back at what I'm holding. Microwaveable chicken tikka masala. "It has no added sugars," I rally.

"And no nutrients either, I bet. Is this how the Calder sisters live?"

"Carrie's not a Calder." I take a breath before that can truly bite and rush on. "And actually, it's just me tonight, and I couldn't face cooking, so . . ." I raise the microwave dinner with a rueful smile.

"We can't have that. Come have dinner with me."

My eyes leap to his. His sky blue eyes are smiling at me as if what he has suggested is perfectly innocuous. Which it ought to be, but it's not. I'm sure we both know it's not. I'm almost sure we both know. "What, now?"

"Why not? It doesn't sound like you have other plans."

"No, but—"

"Are you scared I might seduce you?" He waggles his eyebrows so ludicrously that I can't help but laugh, and once I'm laughing, I can hardly say, *Yes, that's exactly what I'm scared of.* Though the thought of a few more hours away from the Manse and some company to take my mind off Carrie's duplicitous behavior certainly holds an appeal . . . "So?" he prompts, sensing weakness.

"Where would we go?" It's not a yes, I tell myself. I'm still fact-finding.

"There's a good Thai place in the next village. Do you like Thai food?"

"Yes—"

"Excellent." He's thoroughly pleased with how this is turning out and not in the least bit ashamed of showing it. "Shall we drop your car back at yours and go together in mine?"

"You're railroading me," I say plaintively.

"I am. I totally am." He holds his hand up as if admitting guilt, then grins and reaches for the meal I'm still holding. "Just go with it."

It turns out it's remarkably easy to do exactly what he suggests. I relinquish the meal, and he replaces it in the freezer. "Okay, but I'm paying. After all, you paid for both Carrie and me on your birthday."

"Fine by me."

"And actually, I'm not in the car. I walked here."

"Great, we can go straight there and have a drink beforehand if you're not hungry yet." He pauses. "You stuck to the roads, right? Good. The path by the river is really slippy at this time of year. Normally you can walk up as far as the waterfalls—not beyond; there were landslips there years ago, so it's not passable—but right now you can't even get to the falls." He's moving down the aisle toward the cashier, who, from her evident interest, has been listening to our entire conversation. I'm fairly certain she's the woman Carrie so charmingly described. "So do you need anything from home?" I shake my head. "Okay, great, we'll go straight there."

"Just the milk, Ben?" asks the cashier.

"Aye, just the milk, Jean," he says pleasantly. "Oh, have you met Ailsa? She's staying up at the Manse with her sister."

"Nice to meet you, Jean."

"Nice to meet you, hen." She has exactly as strong a handshake as her biceps suggest. "You just missed Carrie."

"Oh, did I?" I attempt to sound vague.

"How are you both settling in at the Manse? Must be a big change from your city lifestyle." There's no sour note in the way she says *city lifestyle*, but somehow I can hear it all the same.

"We're fine. It's so beautiful up here."

"Aye, you wait till you've lived through a winter and then see how you feel." She pauses. "Sorry to hear about your mother. I knew both your parents, you ken. Your mother, she was life and soul of the party." She shakes her head. It's not clear whether she approved of Karen's party animal tendencies. "Aye, life and soul."

Ben glances at me then rushes in. "Aye, well, you have a good night now, Jean." He starts to usher me out.

"You too," calls Jean from behind me. "Enjoy your dinner."

He herds me toward his car, a very smart BMW convertible. I wonder how many times he gets to put the top down living here. "Is it going to be all over the village by tomorrow that we're having dinner together?" Not that I care, really. There's no point in caring, especially when I'm being talked about anyway, it seems.

"Of course not." He unlocks the car and opens the passenger door for me. It's an oddly old-fashioned gesture. I wonder if they teach the staff to do that at the hotel. "It'll be all round the village by midnight latest. By tomorrow the story will have expanded; we'll have been having rampant sex in the kiddie playground. Probably on the seesaw. Or maybe the slide."

"Not the swings?"

"Too conventional. We like our gossip a little more avant-garde here."

He pulls away from the curb and performs a neat U-turn, heading back toward the Manse and the hotel, but takes a right turn just outside the village. I dislike being driven as a rule—I've been in too many cars in too many countries where the drivers appear to operate as if there are only two options, flat out and full brake—but Ben is a smooth driver, and I'm able to relax. I find I'm wondering what Jamie and Carrie are up to tonight. I wouldn't think he would want to conduct a romance under the unflinching eye of his father. Perhaps he'll take her out for a drink or a meal. Oh God, what if they're at the same restaurant? How on earth would I deal with that? How would Carrie deal with that, and Jamie? I would think he would be embarrassed not to at least have given me an inkling that he wanted to ask my sister out, in all our "wee blethers." Or perhaps not. We've never discussed that sort of thing . . .

"Bloody hell!" exclaims Ben, as he turns a bend to find a vehicle careening erratically past us. "Someone's on track for an early death."

"I've seen that Land Rover before," I say, craning my neck to look back, but it has already disappeared round a corner. "Do you know the driver?"

He shakes his head. "I didn't see, it came on us so fast. And every third car is a Land Rover round here."

"Do I need to buy one to fit in?"

He grins. "I'll not deny it, it really might help."

We talk about his travels, where I've been for work. I'm too on edge from having seen Carrie to try to be funny or smart or deep; we just talk. He's easy to talk to. Though in only minutes we're entering the next village and he's drawing up to park on the street just along from the improbably named Ballashiels Thai. As I climb out, I sur-reptitiously scan the other cars. There's a Mini and a Volvo and a couple of Land Rovers—of course—but I can't see a shiny new jeep.

"Is this okay?" asks Ben, opening the door to reveal a warmly lit space with ten or so wooden tables and brightly colored cushions scattered on the bench-style seating. About half of the tables are filled, even though it's reasonably early.

"Looks lovely," I say genuinely.

A middle-aged Thai lady bustles up to us. "Ben! Welcome back. How've you been?" Her accent is an unexpected surprise—broad Scots, but from farther north than here, I'd guess. There's almost a Scandinavian lilt to it. "Table for two?" They swap news as we're led to a table near the back, then she bustles off to get us some drinks.

"Is there anybody in this area you don't know?" I tease.

He smiles. "Well, it's a pretty small world here. Which has its pluses and minuses."

"At the moment I think I'm only seeing the minuses."

His eyebrows quirk upward. "Sounds like you're thinking of something specific."

I shrug awkwardly. "I guess I'm just not used to people knowing about my father. And it sounds horribly selfish, but I hadn't really considered that it would have had an impact on other people. Other than me and my mother, I mean." He's still looking at me quizzically. "Well, Ali seemed to dislike me from the off—"

"Ach, he doesn't mean to be rude—"

"Yes, he does," I say mildly.

"Okay, yes, *sometimes* he does, but he's a good guy underneath it all. He's just . . . complicated." He cocks his head. "Why, are you thinking it's related to your father?"

"My lawyer told me Jamieson & Sons went under when the insurance wouldn't pay after the diamonds went missing."

Ben snorts. "They went under because Ali's dad started drinking like there was no tomorrow and finally left his mother. Which was something of a problem for the operation of a family-run business. Granted that all happened about the same time, but I think they would probably have weathered the insurance storm if Ali's dad had had his eye on the ball."

"Oh." I digest that for a moment. It shouldn't make me feel lighter—I shouldn't feel in any way responsible for my father—but it does. "Does Ali see his dad now?"

"Sometimes. He's dried himself out and is living on the Continent. Sometimes Ali goes across to see him. The whole thing was pretty brutal on him at the time."

"Yours seems an odd friendship."

"I know." He cocks his head, thinking about it. "We've been friends since school. Pretty much day one. Ali was this weird, surly, geeky kid, all elbows and knees. One of the older lads tried to steal this toy Ali loved—*really* loved, I mean, like he couldn't stand to be without it—just for a laugh, and I punched him. The other kid, I mean, not Ali." I can imagine him as a boy—more than that, I can almost remember him—with his straightforward view of the world. The other kid deserved a thump and he got a thump, and then it was done, with no hard feelings. For Ben, at least. "Didn't exactly go down too well with the teacher, mind, but Ali became an instant fan." The warm light reflects in his blue eyes as he smiles ruefully. "He was too bright for primary school; it wasn't the most fun for him. He's actually the smartest person I know, and really funny. And one hundred percent loyal." I can see how that particular trait would chime with Ben, with what he values, with how he sees himself: he's a knight of Camelot, riding in, sword aloft, to do the right thing no matter what the consequences. "But Ali . . . well, he's also a very complicated guy. And like his dad before him, he likes his drink . . ."

"You sound like he's your responsibility."

He shrugs. "I think we all have people in our lives that we feel a responsibility to, whether related or not." But of course Ben would feel that way. He takes care of people: Ali, Fiona, Callum, the hotel guests. I don't do that. For a long time I didn't have the luxury, and now that I'm trying, I don't have the training. I bet Carrie wouldn't be telling lies if he was her brother and she was his sister. "Loyalty is key, right? You stick together come what may." There's an unusual intensity in his eyes as he asks me, "Don't you think?" I'm saved from having to respond by a waitress appearing to take our order.

Later, when we've eaten a frankly delicious meal, and the lights have been turned low to favor tea lights on each table, we stay on. Ben has coffee, which I've declined in the hope I might sleep easily tonight. Instead I twist my glass by the stem, watching how the flickering light flows through the butter yellow wine, and find myself thinking of liquid autumn sunlight streaming through the leaf canopy in the wood behind the house, even though I haven't seen that wood in autumn—at least not for twenty-seven years. Then I find myself saying what I was determined not to. "You know, there's something odd about the Manse."

"Odd how?" I can see he's acutely interested. "Fiona says it's a special place."

"Why is she the oracle on it?" I can hear the peevishness of my tone. It makes me feel mean and small. And guilty—I promised to be civil. Even if Carrie is lying to me, it was still a promise.

"Because she knows more about it than the rest of us, I guess." It's not an evasion but it's not exactly the most forthcoming of answers.

"And what does she say is special about it?" I'm overcompensating now, trying to make myself sound open, nonjudgmental.

His lips curve upward in an echo of his shoulders. "Lots, but it'll all be too woolly for you." He's definitely teasing me this time.

"Try me anyway."

"Well. It's about time . . . Time is different there, she says. It moves at a different pace. She thinks . . ."

"What?"

"She thinks . . ." He makes a small movement with his fingers, as if he's reluctantly yielding. "She thinks it might be folded. Time, I mean. Like, I don't know, a long sheet of paper. But she thinks it's folded there. Multiple times. So that different times touch one another."

I stare at him. "You're kidding." But I think uneasily about how I've been thrown by the passage of time in the Manse, how my own sense of it passing and the movement of the hands of my watch can be so different.

"I told you that you wouldn't like it." There are crinkles at the corners of his eyes. I can't tell if it's my consternation that amuses him, or that he had correctly predicted it.

"The woman who can't tell a minute from an hour has a theory that involves time? And you believe her?"

"I believe that she believes it. She sees things differently to everyone else. And who knows . . . Anyway, you don't have to believe everything your friends believe. You just have to believe in them."

"You know that's kind of nuts, right?"

"Believing in your friends?" He's teasing me again. It creates intimacy—as if any more were needed given we've just finished a candlelit dinner à deux. I ignore him, and after a second he goes on. "Is it, though? It's no more nuts than believing in God, or homeopathy, or that you'll have seven years' bad luck if you smash a mirror."

"But those aren't measurable. Time at the Manse is. It's not like I spend a day there and five minutes passes elsewhere."

"She says it sort of lurches to get back in sync. It's like the other times that touch there drag on it a bit. Like there's resistance."

I think of Callum and the injured bird. *That was from before. Or later.* She must have infected her son with her warped thinking. Only I've seen the bird, too. Or have I? Did I see it the first day and then reconstruct the image in my mind on subsequent occasions? It was always the end of twilight, almost into night proper. The brain can make extraordinary leaps when trying to make sense of limited information in crepuscular light. "Doesn't sound ideal for a prospective hotel property."

He smiles a little at my caustic tone. "I'll take my chances. How is all of that going?"

"It's fine." I spread the fingers of the hand that holds the wineglass in a *What can you do?* gesture. "It's a process, the Presumption of Death thing. We're working through it step-by-step."

"I suppose it's bringing up memories."

"Not of my father, or not anything new, at any rate. But I guess it's helping make sense of some of the memories I had of the house itself, and the landscape." And of the police visits, and my mother's barely reined-in hysteria.

"Did you . . . did you think he was alive somewhere, when you were growing up?" His attention is on his coffee. He only looks up when he's almost finished speaking.

"Of course, at first—after all, I was only seven when he disappeared. Less so, as I got older, I suppose."

"Do you think it would have made a difference to you if you'd known for definite? Either way, I mean?" But he doesn't actually mean either way. I can see it in his eyes; Ben thinks my father is dead. He thinks he's always been dead.

"A difference to what?"

He shrugs. "To you. Your life. Your choices."

I almost laugh. I can't think of a single thing that wouldn't have been different, if we'd known for sure what had happened. My relationship with my mother, my desperation to get away, my personal interactions and relationships, or lack thereof . . . I would have to have been utterly lacking in self-awareness not to have considered how my father's abandonment has impacted me psychologically. Even when I was screwing my way through university I had a fair idea of why I might be doing it.

Ben looks at my face. "Yeah," he says, almost to himself. There's an uncharacteristic bleakness to the set of his mouth. "I suppose not knowing was the worst thing." I look at him, temporarily at a loss for what to say. It feels like *he's* grieving, over what happened to *me*. He visibly shakes himself. "Anyway. When does Carrie's play open? We should organize for a group of us to get tickets. I could borrow a minibus from the hotel or something."

I grab on to his change of gear gratefully. We talk, and he listens when I speak and somewhere inside me there's a twang, like a tuning fork has been struck deep in my stomach and I can feel the reverberations. It should be Jonathan here; it should be Jonathan hearing what I have to say. The wine has gone to my head now, but there's a clarity too. I would swap them, I think. I would have Jonathan in exchange for Ben, in exchange for anyone; today I would swap them. After a few more dinners, a few more glasses of wine, more seconds and minutes and hours of these calm sky blue eyes—or other eyes, as Ben is not the point; the point is that Ben is *here*, where Jonathan should be and is not and never will be—at some point I would no longer choose to swap. The wine is allowing me a certain honesty: we will not last through a long separation, Jonathan and I. Both of us are too good at learning to survive wherever we happen to find ourselves. And then I think: I already knew that, and yet I chose to separate us anyway.

It's not late when we leave, not even half past nine. The darkness hasn't had a chance to thicken, and the headlamps of Ben's car cut through it comfortably. The radio came on automatically when Ben started the car and is now playing something I know from my university years but can't name. Something that conjures up late nights writing essays in my student halls of residence, fueled by caffeine. Portishead, maybe. Or Massive Attack. I am warm and well-fed and full of wine; it would be easy to settle into the snug hold of the leather seat and drift off to sleep, but Ben mutters under his breath, and I glance across to see him frowning.

"What's up?"

"Just the tire feels a little heavy. Maybe a bit flat. I'll check it when I drop you off."

We're already crunching onto the gravel of the Manse drive. There's a light on inside, but there always is now, even in daytime.

"I'll open up and put more lights on, then you might see the tire better," I offer.

"Thanks."

The night air is warmer than on previous nights, but it's still chilly after the warmth of Ben's car. I can hear Ben opening and shutting the boot of the car as I struggle with the key. I think again that I need to get a security light, and then I follow that with the thought that I won't be here long enough to take advantage of it. But perhaps Carrie will be here without me. The whole house to herself and no reason to lie and sneak around . . . Once I get the door open, I put on the lights in all the rooms that face the front.

"How's that?" I call from the doorway, but I have to fling up a hand to shield my eyes. A car is turning into the drive, temporarily dazzling me with its headlights on full beam. It parks at an angle behind Ben's BMW, engine and headlights still on, but the latter are no longer aimed directly at me. Ali climbs out of the driver's seat, accompanied by a thumping wave of what sounds like German electronica.

"I thought that was you," he calls to Ben. Then he adds grudgingly, "Hiya, Ailsa."

I raise my hand in half-hearted acknowledgment.

"I'm on my way to meet Piotr in the Quaich. I thought I'd see if you want to join us." He's aiming this directly at Ben, with no attempt to include me in the invitation, but Ben looks across at me nonetheless.

"I'm good, thanks. I think I'll have an early night," I call.

"Your loss," says Ali cheerfully. "You got a problem with that tire, Ben?"

"Didn't feel right on the way back." Ben is peering at the front left tire. He has a light jacket on now, presumably pulled from the boot. He gives the tire a couple of kicks. "Seems okay, though."

"This car is too much of a thoroughbred for these roads. You want to get yourself a jeep like Jamie's. Where were the pair of you coming from, anyway?"

"Ballashiels Thai."

"Romantic dinner for two?" He raises his voice. "What will the esteemed Mr. Powell say about that, Ailsa?"

"He'll be sorry he missed out. He loves Thai," I respond with deliberate sweetness.

"Aye, that's exactly what I'd say if my girlfriend was having dinner with Ben."

"Stop being a twat, Ali," Ben says. He leaves off from inspecting the tire and approaches the front door. The yellow light which spills around me shows a rueful grimace on his face. "Sorry about this," he says quietly. "He's just being . . . Look, it's just Ali. You have to get to know him."

I wrinkle my nose. "If it's not compulsory, I'll pass, thanks."

He doesn't bother trying to dissuade me. "Thanks for dinner."

There's no step up to the front door, but the lawn slopes down away from the house, so I don't have to look up as much as usual. His hair is lit golden by the light from the hallway behind me, but his face is in my shadow. I'm aware of Ali's eyes upon us both. "No, thank you for saving me from a night of nutritionless microwave food," I say brightly.

"Night then." He leans in carefully and kisses me on both cheeks. I can feel the soft grain of his skin, the warmth of the contact, and yet it feels curiously formal throughout. He crunches across the gravel to round the bonnet of his car, then suddenly stumbles. "What the— Christ!"

"What's up?" asks Ali, from the open door of his own car.

"Come and look at this." He's leaning over a dark shape.

"What is it?" I call, but Ben doesn't answer. He's fiddling with his phone. The next moment a beam of light emerges from it. Ali is beside Ben now, blocking my view of whatever they are leaning over to look at; I catch a glimpse of bright fur and hear Ali mutter, *"Fuck."* Curiosity pulls me out of the warm doorway into the cold night air.

It's a fox. An absurdly healthy-looking fox, except for the fact that it's dead. It looks like it could have been frozen whilst running.

"Poisoned, do you think?" asks Ben grimly.

"Probably," says Ali. His tone is neutral but somehow I can sense an anger beneath it. He fishes out his own phone and trains another torch beam upon the carcass.

"You mean, deliberately?" I ask. Ali is concentrating his beam around the fox's head. Now that I'm looking for it, I can see a rim of dried foam around its muzzle, like the ring left behind from a bubble bath.

"Could be. It's not legal, but the farmers dinnae take kindly to foxes getting among the sheep. Especially now, when we're coming into lambing season. The farmer next to our place is blatant about it. I cannae think who'd be doing that round here, though." He looks around, frowning, as if the culprit might suddenly step out of the darkness, then shoves at it with his foot. "It's stiff now. Must have been here a good while."

I can't help wishing that he would move the torch away from the single open sightless amber eye. I'm shivering. I wrap my arms across my middle.

"You okay?" Ben asks me.

"I'm just cold." Though in truth the healthy-but-dead fox is simultaneously more upsetting yet less revolting than the raven. "It's my second cadaver of the week, actually. There was a dead raven on our doorstep the other morning." Ben blinks in surprise. I look down at the fox again. "At the risk of sounding selfish, I really wish this had found somewhere else to die. What am I supposed to do with it?"

"Dinnae worry about that. I'll get rid of it," Ali offers, in a surprisingly kindly fashion. "Do you have a bin bag or the like?"

I nod and we turn for the house. "I don't know how we didn't see it in the headlights when we arrived," I muse. The men dutifully wipe their feet on the mat before traipsing behind me through the hallway to the kitchen. I start to rummage beneath the sink. "Will this do, Ali?"

"Aye. What did you do with the raven?"

"Nothing. I didn't have to; it wasn't there when I got back from giving Carrie a lift. I suppose some animal carted it off for its dinner." I turn to Ben with a forced smile. "I guess this puts paid to Callum's hypothesis that animals won't come in here." Even mentioning Callum brings a warmth to me.

"Callum said that?" says Ali. His voice is oddly neutral.

"Yes, he said that was why Toast wouldn't come in the grounds. I keep forgetting to quiz him on it." Ben and Ali are exchanging glances. "What?"

"Nothing," Ben says, but his eyebrows are drawn together, and there's an uncharacteristic uneasiness in the set of his mouth.

"Come on, what?" They look at each other again. "It doesn't seem like nothing. Look, guys, I'm the one who has to live here." *Temporarily.* "If you have something to say, for God's sake, spit it out."

Ben looks at his friend as if for approval but if Ali gives any sign, I don't see it. "Callum is . . . Callum is usually right, on animals," Ben says quietly. *Right, on animals.* What does that mean? "And Ali and I were looking on TripAdvisor the other day, just for research if I'm going to buy it, trying to figure out why the Manse hasn't been renting."

"And?"

"There are reviews from people with pets. It's supposed to be a pet-friendly rental, but their pets . . . their pets wouldn't sleep in the house. Wouldn't even set foot in the grounds unless dragged in, actually, and then they'd run straight out first chance they got. One of the guests parked their car on the verge of the road and the dog slept in there each night."

"I see."

Ali finally speaks up. "What we mean is, well, the fox and the raven, they wouldnae have come in here—"

"So you think someone brought them in. Yeah, I grasped that."

Ali and Ben exchange glances again, and then Ben tries this time. "It's possible that, well—"

"That someone is trying to scare me out of the Manse." Ben blinks in surprise, though whether it's in response to my words or flat tone, I can't tell. "Yeah, I grasped that too." I turn for the kettle. My mind is running down several different paths, all at once, like a set of rats in a maze. Someone is trying to scare me. If the TripAdvisor reviews are true, if Callum is right, someone is trying to scare me. Toast wouldn't come in, and the cat never does—someone must have served me up two dead creatures in one week . . . But then again, Callum could be mistaken, and the TripAdvisor reviews could be malicious inventions, and the raven and the fox could just be dreadfully timed unfortunate incidents. But there's the missing bin bag, and the missing insecticide, and the person who might or might not have been in the house—if they happened at all . . . except I couldn't have imagined the flies. Surely I couldn't have imagined the flies. And I didn't imagine the stone that was thrown. And even if the TripAdvisor reviews aren't genuine, perhaps they were written by someone trying to scare me off . . .

I can't sort it out. It's all too muddled.

"Why, did something happen?" asks Ben from behind me, with surprising perception.

"Yes. A few things, actually." I look for a way to buy time. "I think perhaps we should all have a coffee."

Ali looks at Ben and sighs. "I'd best gie Piotr a bell and tell him we're not coming."

MY FATHER IS IN A CARE HOME IN ANTWERP. HE SPEAKS SO rarely that the staff haven't worked out that he isn't Belgian. He's been categorized as having Alzheimer's, though given he's been in precisely the same condition for many years, it must surely have been the early onset kind, which seemed a tragedy to the staff in the early years but less and less so as time passed. Twenty-seven years ago, he was found in a physically and mentally traumatized state in a backstreet, dressed in a suit without any belongings or identification, but carrying a local newspaper from Ghent, which led the police to believe that's where he came from, and to this day the staff in the care home call him Mr. Ghent. He's still mobile, but he can't manage the most basic of his own needs himself and needs twenty-four-hour care. The staff don't mind him in the slightest, though—he's not violent, or vocal, or prone to wandering. He's so little trouble, one could forget he's there.

FIFTEEN

We sit at the table, the three of us, with a mug of coffee in front of
Ben and me and tea in front of Ali. The mugs are part of a white
china set, with various depictions of dogs cavorting round each one,
and are wholly unsatisfactory, spindly where they should be solidly
reassuring, and too hot to hold. If I were to stay, I would replace these.
If I were to stay, which I won't. Someone or something doesn't want
me here.

Ali clears his throat in a series of staccato half coughs. I'm trying
not to look like I'm watching him closely, but I am. I'm watching Ben,
too. "Where's Carrie?" Ali asks, looking around as if she might suddenly appear.

"I don't know." I see a flash of something—what?—cross Ben's face
as I answer Ali's question, and then he clears his features. It's too deliberate, out of keeping with his natural openness. Jamie's words float
up to me. *Nobody is such an open book as he makes out that he is.*

"I've never been in here," says Ali, looking around. "Apparently my
dad wanted to buy it when it came on the market—when your folks
bought it—but my mum wasnae having any of it. Too isolated."

"I think my mum ended up wishing they hadn't." Both men look at me cautiously. Perhaps that didn't come out as drolly as intended. "It's weird that we didn't see the dead fox on the way in," I say again.

"I must have been too focused on the tire," Ben says, absentmindedly rubbing at his neck where the collar of his light jacket touches it. He got it from the boot of the car, I remember. What else could he have taken out of the boot at the same time? Or perhaps Ali had the fox in his car. It wouldn't have been difficult for Ben to let him know we were on our way back. Or maybe it was there all the time, and we just didn't see it.

"So what's been going on?" Ali's jerky gaze is roving over my face. From his expression, I think he's trying to be solicitous. It doesn't sit well on his features.

"I'm not sure exactly." I look at my coffee in its too-slender mug and try to create a plan. What to say, what not to say, how to be. The interviewer's dilemma: what is the right question and how should it be asked? "I'm worried you might think I'm overreacting. I probably am overreacting." It's easy enough to see why Ali might hate me, why he might be stirred into acts of pure hostility. It's less easy to see why Ben would do any such thing. Unless he wants to buy the Manse so badly that he's willing to scare me into selling . . . Oddly, that's quite a reassuring thought. If that's the aim of the harassment, then I'm surely not in any real danger.

"We promise to be nonjudgmental," says Ben, with a ghost of a smile. There's concern in his eyes. I can believe that he's worried about me, that he wants the best for me. He must be an excellent guest liaison up at the hotel.

I put down my coffee mug. *In for a penny, in for a pound.* "The night we got here, there was an intruder." I've got the attention of both of them. "It turned out to be Jamie." Ben's mouth is slightly agape, and Ali's eyes are still for once, fixed on me. "He was looking for Fiona. Apparently she comes here sometimes, has some kind of obsession with the place." Ben has started to protest, but I cut him off. "Even her dad said so. She was born here, in the dining room." I find

I'm shuddering, thinking about that carpet stained with blood and amniotic fluid . . .

"I didnae ken that," murmurs Ali, but I forge onward.

"Anyway. I had the locks changed. But I still kept feeling like I was being watched—I still do, actually. Then after your birthday, Ben"—I nod in his direction—"the smoke alarm went off in the middle of the night. It was . . ." I swallow. "Horrific. Thousands of flies rained down on me, it seemed like. Cluster flies; I looked it up the next day. They like to be somewhere warm. Maybe the battery was giving off heat or something, I don't know. They got everywhere, in my hair, all over the kitchen . . . I had to use most of a can of insecticide to clear up the mess. When I finally went to bed, I left the bin bag with all the dead flies in it by the back door ready to go out. I left the insecticide spray and the smoke alarm cover on the kitchen table. The next morning the smoke alarm cover was back on and the bin bag and the spray can were gone, and Carrie hadn't touched any of them; I checked. Then someone threw a stone at me when I was outside in the garden one evening; I didn't see who. Then the dead raven and today the fox."

"Christ," says Ali, with the air of a man who's just got rather more than he bargained for. "But . . . the flies couldnae be planned."

I shake my head. "No, I don't think they could." He's quick, Ali. "But maybe someone took advantage of that situation. They would have had to have been watching the house to know to move that stuff."

"If that's true, it can't have been Fi," says Ben unequivocally. "She could barely stand at the end of that night."

"True." At least, I think it's true. It occurs to me that Fiona could be a very good actress. Did she really drink that much, or did she merely pretend to? But I'm being ridiculous: Fiona couldn't have known Carrie and I would be joining them that evening. Still . . . I try for an innocent tone. "Did either of you two know about her obsession with this house?"

Ali shakes his head, and Ben does, too, after a beat, but then he says reluctantly, "Well, I knew she liked the building." His eyes roam around the kitchen, as if he's trying to see it afresh. "But lots of people do. It's the most impressive piece of architecture around here, barring the hotel. And like I told you tonight, she thinks it's kind of special."

"Ah yes. Time folds here."

"Dinnae mock," says Ali seriously. "What happened at the kirk—if anything could stick a pin through all time, it would surely be that."

I sigh. "Not you too?"

"There are more things on heaven and earth and all that. And anyway, there are plenty of genuine reviews online suggesting that this place is haunted."

"Maybe. Or maybe there's one person posting lots of malicious reviews online."

"Maybe." But his face tells me I haven't convinced him.

"What did you mean by what you said about Callum and animals?"

"The wee lad has a gift with them. He'll be a vet, or a horse trainer, or something," Ali says. It doesn't surprise me. I can imagine a grown-up Callum as a vet. There's something straightforward and calming about him. The animals would surely sense they're in safe hands.

Ben nods. "If he says they won't come in here, I would bet serious money he's right."

"So you think someone brought the raven and the fox here."

Ben's nod is a slow considered movement, Ali's a hurried jerk. It's startling how unalike they are, in every way. There's Ben with his caramel hair and face as open as a windswept moor, sitting back in his chair, facing the table squarely, his mug cradled in his palm. Whereas Ali, dark and twitchy as ever, is hunched over his mug, his eyebrows so low they blend with his eyelashes. "Obviously the question is who," Ben says.

Ali grunts. "To state the bloody obvious." He looks at his coffee, then mutters, half to himself, "I suppose if someone brought it here, it could have come from anywhere." Then he looks at his coffee again. "You got anything stronger? That is, if I can crash at yours, Ben, and Ailsa, you dinnae mind us leaving our cars here overnight?"

I push my chair away from the table and head for one of the kitchen cupboards. "Fine by me. I think we've got—ah, here." I pull out a bottle of Glenmorangie and put it on the table in front of them, and take a seat again.

Ali picks it up immediately with an appreciative nod. "I thought you didnae like whisky."

"I don't. Carrie picked it up." Beer, whisky—Carrie's drinking habits have been full of surprises for me.

"Good taste, your sister," comments Ali. *Half sister.* And it doesn't look like I know even that much of her. "She willnae mind?"

I settle back at the table with a shrug. "She's not here." Where is she? I wonder again. "I can always buy a replacement bottle."

"Glasses?" asks Ben, standing up. "No, don't worry, I'll get them." He heads to the cupboard I'm pointing at. Ali's hooded eyes follow his friend across the kitchen with an intensity that catches me by surprise. Then his gaze stutters back to me and the moment is gone.

"So, who?" says Ben again, when he and Ali each have two fingers of amber in their glasses.

"You tell me. I'm the newcomer; the only people I've spoken more than three sentences to are those I met in the Quaich the other night. And Callum, and Glen McCue."

"It's not going to be any of that list," declares Ali.

"Maybe," I say, carefully stirring my coffee that needs no stirring. Ali glares at me. "Maybe?"

I have the attention of both of them. "It did cross my mind that it could be either of you." I throw in a smile to lighten it, but nonetheless, Ben's eyes leap to my face. He looks oddly stricken.

Ali, on the other hand, is instantly furious. "How d'you figure that? You saw Ben find it. He almost bloody tripped on the fucking thing."

"I didn't see it when we came in. Ben could have had it in the back of the car the whole time. Or you, Ali." Ali looks faintly repulsed by the suggestion. Ben could be carved from marble. "It seems to me that you, Ali, haven't been my greatest fan from minute one, and that Ben would rather I hightail it out of here and sell him the Manse. So, it could have been either of you. Or maybe you cooked this up between you to get rid of me."

"You're a fucking piece of work, you ken that?" Ali stands up abruptly, almost knocking over his chair.

"Relax," says Ben laconically. He has recovered himself, but now I can't read his expression. It's disconcerting on his ordinarily open countenance.

I start to speak, but Ali can't be derailed. "Relax? I dinnae have to listen to this bint tell me she thinks I've been launching a hate campaign for no reason. You can fucking well clean up your own fucking fox corpse, you—" He stops, and then starts to laugh, in a cold high chuckle. "Ah, but not for no reason, am I right? You think it's a revenge campaign, on account of your thieving father." The vitriol in his voice—*thieving father*—robs me of everything I was about to say. I wonder that Ali can look at me at all with that hatred for my father wrapped up inside him. He searches my face, his own expressing a warring mixture of triumph and something else. "You do, don't you?" Indignation. The something else is indignation. It's more convincing than any words he could say. "You've got a fucking low opinion of people if you think—"

"She doesn't think that," breaks in Ben mildly. "Not really. She'd hardly be confronting us about it alone in an isolated house if she thought that. After all, who knows what we might do to her if we really are harassing her." He looks at me pointedly. "Right, Ailsa?" I nod numbly, though his logic is flawed; without knowing the aim of the harassment, it's unclear whether I'm at risk or not. But I'm still stuck on *thieving father*. Suspecting that a lot of people feel that way is very different to hearing it in person. "Ali, sit down," Ben commands. "She was just thinking aloud. Right, Ailsa?"

"Right. This *bint* was just thinking aloud." It comes out with deliberate tartness, now that I've refound my voice.

Ben barks a surprised laugh, and I'm taken aback to see that even

Ali finds a reluctant smile touching his lips. "Ah. Well. Sorry about that." I look at them both in bafflement for a moment, then find I'm inclining my head and smiling, too. I don't quite understand how insulting Ali has brought more civility from him toward me than I've ever seen before, but somehow it has. Ali hooks his chair with his leg and sits down again, a touch sheepishly. I look at Ben. His face is carefully blank. It's oddly chilling.

"All right," says Ben. "So if we can proceed on the basis that neither Ali nor I are out to bury you under a heap of dead animals, who else might be in the picture?" I raise my eyebrows but don't say anything, and I watch his face, waiting for the penny to drop. Now there's no longer a lack of expression; I can see every thought. "No, wait . . . you don't mean . . ." He trails off.

"She wouldnae," says Ali stoutly. And then, after a beat, "And anyway, it couldnae be her. She was too smashed to go stealing bin bags, remember?"

"That doesn't rule her out from fun with animal carcasses."

Ali's mouth twists. "You have a hell of a turn of phrase."

"I'll take that as a compliment."

"Dinnae," he says sourly, but there's a gleam in his eye. He likes this, this back-and-forth on the knife-edge of too much. He gets a kick out of it.

Ben ignores our traded barbs. "Come on, is it actually realistic to suggest that there's more than one person terrorizing you?" he objects again.

I pick up my mug and take it to the sink. "It doesn't seem realistic to me that there's anybody terrorizing me at all." But the alternative—that I'm imagining things—is too unthinkable. For me, at least; Carrie was certainly thinking it with the flies. "But nonetheless I found myself ducking a stone in my garden. Are there problems with gangs of kids round here?"

They both shake their heads. "There are barely enough kids round here to make up a gang," Ben says.

"Fi, Jamie, Piotr, Glen . . ." Ali counts them off on his fingers. "Do you ken anybody else?"

I start to shake my head and then stop. "Well, there was that woman at the hotel who was rude about my mother."

Ben winces even as Ali asks, "Who was that?"

"Mor—" I start, but Ben is speaking over me.

"Your mum," Ben says gently to Ali.

"Ah fuck," says Ali dismally, scrubbing his face with his hand. "Holly—my sister-in-law—said she'd gone off on one, but I didnae get the details." He turns to me. "I'm sorry about that. She has Parkinson's. And dementia too, now, we think."

"I didn't know. I'm sorry."

"Not half as sorry as she is," he says dismally, but there's no meanness in his words. "But it wouldnae be her; she's all talk and no trousers. And she's not allowed to drive anymore, so she couldnae even get herself here." He thinks again for a moment. "It doesnae make sense. Nobody has anything to gain."

"You said you've felt like you were being watched. Have you actually seen anyone?" Ben presses on.

I hesitate. "Once," I admit. I hesitate again, remembering that triangular shape. "I thought I saw someone . . ."

"Where?" asks Ali.

"I was at the end of the garden. I thought I saw someone inside. In the upstairs window." I'm leaning against the countertop now, and I find myself throwing an involuntary glance out the kitchen window, as if I might see myself at the end of the garden, looking up. "In the box room. It was locked before I got the locksmith over, but when he opened it up, there was dust everywhere, except on the boxes."

"Christ," says Ali faintly. Then he rallies. "You need some security cameras. We sell them at the shop; come and see me there tomorrow and I'll sort you out." My face must be showing my ignorance, because he explains. "I've got a hardware shop in town. The *other* family business," he adds, with unexpected humor. "We've got a whole line of this stuff, motion sensors, the lot. I've even got a guy who will fit it all for you. Here." He fishes in a pocket for his wallet and pulls out a card to hand to me. *Alistair Jamieson, Managing Director, Jamieson's Hardware.*

"Thank you." I'm unexpectedly filled with something that might be approaching warmth for him. I put the card carefully on the counter. "You know, Ali, you're in danger of being nice to me."

He grunts. "Dinnae worry, it willnae last."

"I wouldn't vote for Scottish independence."

He groans theatrically. "And that's it. No more Mr. Nice Guy. Fucking Sassenach," he mutters, half smiling as he reaches for the bottle again.

"Fucking Sassenach bint, surely."

"Aye, that too."

"Carrie's not coming back tonight?" Ben asks. I shake my head. "You shouldn't be here alone," he says, with sudden authority. He means to railroad me again; I can feel it. He will suggest he stays here too, or that I stay at his. "Don't try and be a hero about it. Better to be safe than sorry. I've a perfectly decent spare room."

"Wait a minute, I thought I'd just bagged the spare room," argues Ali, through a yawn.

"You can have the sofa," Ben tosses back.

"He can have the spare room. I'm not staying." They both start to argue, but I speak over them. "I'm not trying to be a hero, honestly. I just think . . ." What do I think? Do I really think either of these men mean me harm? I look at them both as if I can see their intentions on their faces, but there's nothing but tiredness on Ali's. And Ben is once again giving nothing away. "I don't think I should leave. If someone is trying to scare me out, they should see that it's not working." If I let myself leave now, I might never return—especially if it's all in my mind. I can't allow myself to be chased out of here. The decision shouldn't be tied up with Carrie, but somehow it is—it would feel like giving up at the first hurdle. On both Carrie and the Manse. "Anyway, if the pair of you are leaving your cars outside overnight, surely that will deter any harassment."

They look at each other again. "I suppose," concedes Ben. He glances at his watch. "Don't you need to check on your mum, though?" he asks Ali.

"Nah, my brother or Holly are checking in on her tonight."

Presumably she's on her own too, since Ali's father upped and offed to continental Europe. It's odd to think that we have something in common, Ali and I: we both grew up without a paternal presence. I reach for the photo of that immortalized dinner party that hasn't yet left the kitchen. "Is this your mum?" I'm pointing to a small but curvy woman with a smile on her face who's standing next to Ali's dad. Even though I'm looking for similarities, I can't see how she turned into the shriveled old woman, with her spiteful pinched mouth, that I encountered in the hotel.

Ali takes it and squints slightly. "Aye. And my dad. Was that taken here, aye? God, she looks young then." There's a sadness around his eyes, and concern in Ben's as he looks at Ali.

"Funny to think our parents all knew one another, and here we are, having a drink together," I muse.

"That might be odd in London Town, but it's pretty much par for the course round here," says Ali, putting the photo down. "Very hard to escape the sins of our fathers when everybody around knows exactly what they were." He glances at me. "Shite. Sorry. Let's talk about something much less controversial. Like, erm, Scottish independence or something," he says, tongue in cheek.

"I'm against, as Ali well knows," says Ben, in a screamingly obvious attempt to reinforce the change of subject. He takes the bottle that Ali pushes toward him. "You sure you won't have any, Ailsa?" I shake my head.

"Fucking Aussie," grumbles Ali. "Three of us here born in Scotland, and I'm the only one with any national pride. It's a disgrace."

"It's common sense, is what it is." Ben clinks his glass against Ali's. "Ali's a hopeless romantic, you see."

"That's exactly what I thought the first time I met him," I say. They both grin at that, and I wonder what this little tableau must look like from the outside. Friends sharing drinks in the warmth of the magnolia kitchen, laughing and smiling and teasing. I glance out of the window, but all I see is the golden glow of the reflected room. If there was anyone out there in the darkness looking in, I wouldn't be able to see them.

I wake in the morning to the sound of a car on the gravel, followed by the fading thrum of the engine as it leaves along the road. I've slept unexpectedly solidly; it takes a minute for my brain to fire up. Possibly it's hindered by the pounding headache I'm experiencing, which feels akin to a hangover, though I don't deserve one after only a couple of glasses of wine at dinner.

Ben or Ali, I realize. One of them must have been collecting his car. I don't know enough about cars to be able to determine which from the vehicle noise. I don't want to be undressed and unshowered if the other knocks on the door when picking up the remaining vehicle, so I reluctantly head for my bathroom and find Carrie's open bedroom door staring insouciantly back at me across the landing. I wonder again where she can possibly be waking up. Perhaps she and Jamie went to a hotel?

I make it down to the kitchen, clean and dressed, just before there's a rap at the front door. There ought to be a peephole in the door, I think, as I swing it open. A peephole, and security cameras and possibly a full troop of highly trained security guards on rotation. I'll settle for the security cameras, though. It's Ben that's waiting for me on the doorstep. Ben and no obvious sign of any animal carcasses of any kind.

"Morning. Coffee? Scrambled eggs?"

He glances at his watch. "I wouldn't say no to both, actually. I don't start work till eight thirty." He looks a little like last night's Glenmorangie has taken the shine off him. "How did you sleep?"

"Pretty well," I admit. Probably better than I have on any previous nights, if I'm honest. I peer past him, into the sun-strewn front drive. I can only see Ben's BMW. "Did I hear Ali picking up his car earlier?"

"Yeah, he was opening up at the shop this morning, so he came ahead of me."

In the kitchen I twist the dial to turn on the radio and focus on the scrambled eggs, one of the few dishes I'm confident about, while he picks up yesterday's paper, which is still lying on the table. When I place his plate in front of him, he smiles his thanks, then starts eating in a dedicated, thoughtful way without seeming to notice the taste at all. I get through two thirds of my own portion of eggs then realize I'm no longer hungry and put my fork down. "What's wrong?"

His eyes jerk to my face. "Nothing . . . nothing." After a moment he puts his own fork down and yields with a gesture as if to say, *Okay, fine*. "It's just . . . I guess in the light of day, with no whisky—"

"It all seems a little unbelievable?" He doesn't quite nod, but I can see that I'm right about what he was thinking. "Yes, believe me, I get that feeling too." Though not when I'm alone in the Manse. Not when the darkness presses and I lock all the windows and doors and then worry that I'm locking something *in* rather than keeping something *out*. "What did you guys do with the fox?"

"Ali's taking it to the vet later, to see if it was poisoned."

"That's good of him."

"Like I said, he's a good guy, really."

I purse my lips equivocally—*We'll see*—and he laughs, though I can't shake the feeling that something more is bothering him. But I can't follow up on it because his phone suddenly springs to life. I clear the plates with half an ear on Ben's side of the conversation after I hear my own name. "No, I'm at Ailsa's . . ." He deliberately rolls his eyes at me, half embarrassed as he says, "No! I slept in my own bed, thank you very much . . . When? Sorry, I'm on all day today . . . I take it Jamie and your dad can't?"

Fiona? I mouth at Ben. He nods and puts a hand over the mouth end of his phone. It's a curiously old-fashioned gesture, as if he's used to using the ancient barbell style of receiver. *She needs someone to sit Callum*, he murmurs back at me.

I'll do it, I find myself mouthing. You couldn't interpret that as anything but a thoroughly civil offer, I think with grim humor. Friendly, even.

"Hold on a moment, Fi," Ben says, and drops the hand holding his phone to the table. "Are you sure? It's just till lunchtime; Jamie or Glen can pick him up then. There's a problem with one of the horses, and Fi needs to be there—"

"It's fine. He's never any trouble."

He shoots me a smile full of grateful relief, then returns the phone to his ear to deliver the good news. I find I'm at once filled with warmth at his care for Callum and wracked with guilt at having considered that he might be behind the strange events. The empty Glenmorangie bottle from last night is on the counter, but the recycling box is already full. I carry it to the back door, intending to empty it into the large bin out back, and try to unlock that door one-handed, balancing the box against my hip and swearing under my breath at the stiffness of the new key.

Ben is off the phone and hovering behind me. "Do you want—"

The lock finally gives. I swing the back door open and am about to step out when my eyes alight on a black mass of feathers, right in the middle of the doorstep. I dump the recycling box abruptly on the kitchen floor. There's a distinct chink of glass on glass, but it doesn't sound like anything has smashed. "Oh, for fuck's sake. Really? Again?"

"What—oh." Ben is standing beside me now, peering down on the bird. It's clearly the same one. If it's more decomposed than before, I can't tell. Even the maggots look to be squirming in the same way. But the wings have been forced to spread out, as if in full flight. "Christ. That's . . . Christ. You know, I can't believe an animal arranged it like that."

"Me neither." I turn away abruptly and stomp across the kitchen to pull open a drawer. The anger inside me is threatening to come out through tears, and I won't allow that.

"What are you doing?"

"Looking for something—no, don't touch it," I say, forestalling him as he hunkers down as if to grab the mass of feathers. I finally find what I'm looking for: a large, robust safety pin. Ben looks at me curiously as I reach for the block of yellow Post-it notes and the Sharpie pen that sit on the windowsill of the kitchen. I scribble on the topmost note, then grab the Marigold washing-up gloves that are sitting by the kitchen sink and force them on. I'm powered by pure fury now.

"What are you—" starts Ben, but he gives up as I push past him, kicking my slippers off at the door. I grasp the bird round its neck and march barefoot to the bench that sits on one side of the garden, where I dump it. It's unexpectedly heavy. And awkwardly stiff, and it's beginning to smell. I'm breathing through my mouth rather than my nose, and my feet are cold and wet. But I get to work.

Ben has followed me out. "Jesus," he says faintly, as I push the safety pin into the flesh on the breast of the bird, and I think that perhaps I can rule out Ben; he's far too uncomfortable around the bird to have had anything to do with placing it here. The resistance is not what I expect, there's more of it to begin with and then suddenly much less—the pin abruptly moves more freely. Even so, it's unexpectedly difficult to angle it correctly so that it exits where it needs to in order to properly secure the note; the Marigolds are slightly big for me and make me clumsy, but after a couple of attempts, I finally manage it. I take a step back and survey my efforts. The bird is lying on the seat of the bench, one wing slightly outstretched, its ravaged abdomen with the sickly maggots on display but its breast mainly concealed by the note. The yellow paper is somewhat crumpled from the execution, but there's no doubting what I have written in bold black capital letters:

FUCK OFF. I'M NOT SCARED AND I'M NOT LEAVING.

"Subtle," comments Ben.

I look up at the sky. "It better not be about to rain; the ink will run." The sky is almost entirely covered by gray cloud, but it doesn't have the leaden heaviness of an imminent downpour.

"Not today or tomorrow, according to the forecast. I think your message will reach the target."

I head back into the kitchen and strip off the Marigolds, washing both them and my hands in the kitchen sink. Ben follows me in and locks the back door behind us.

"I'm sorry," he says after a moment.

"For what?" I'm drying my hand on a none-too-clean tea towel, still too white-hot with rage to step outside of myself and look at him.

"For earlier. For thinking that we had all overreacted."

"It's okay."

"No, it's not. You trusted us, Ali and me, by telling us that. And I get the sense that you don't trust easily." My eyes leap unwillingly to his face, which is watchfully, openly earnest. "I didn't mean to throw it back at you."

I look at him and wonder what it would be like to *be* him. To think like him, to believe in Trust and Loyalty and Honor and all sorts of other capitalized Values. "Well," I say, when the pause has gone on an uncomfortably long time. "Thank you. Though I can understand the skepticism." I add, "After all, journalists make careers out of that."

He laughs, as I meant him to, but I'm not describing myself. That's Jonathan, relentlessly holding those in power to account—for him, whoever ends up with the wealth is always at least partly to blame for the world's injustices. For my part, I chase the threads to weave the stories. The stories that demand to be told, that make sense of the people in them.

MY FATHER IS IN MANCHESTER, IN A DRUG REHABILITATION CEN-ter. If you'd told him in his Saint Martin's days that drugs would have been his downfall, he'd have laughed out loud. Back then he had the odd puff of pot, but that was it. And in truth, it wasn't the drugs that were to blame—not at first. It was the horses. And then the dogs, then any form of sport he could put a bet on. He was an addict—he knows that, though he suspects only poor gamblers recognize that: surely the good ones never have any reason to stop? The diamond money bought an awful lot of useless slips of paper; you could have wallpapered a house with them. But then the money was all gone and he had to face what he had done—only he couldn't, and that's when the drugs took hold. If he doesn't kick the habit this time, he likely won't see another Christmas. He knows that. But Christmases don't mean anything without kids, and he gave up the right to his daughter a long time ago.

SIXTEEN

Biscuits. I don't have any biscuits and Callum is coming. It's a potential disaster. Or at least, it is in the mind of a mid-thirties woman with zero childcare experience who has just woken up to the fact that she's offered to look after a seven-year-old. I don't want to dwell on what other disasters might be in store. I jump in the car and nip down to the village shop in short order.

Jean is on the cashier's desk again when I come to pay. "Sweet tooth, hen?" she asks, looking askance at the three different packets of biscuits I've chosen.

"I'm looking after Callum today and I don't know which he prefers."

"That's good of you. He's a fine lad."

"He is."

"Like as not that's down to Glen being there. Stabilizing influence, he must be. A saint, really, given all those kids of his have put him through." It's taking a remarkably long time to ring through three packets of biscuits, a bottle of apple juice, a carton of milk and a news-paper. "Can you imagine being a widower with a small child and then having *another* bairn dumped on your doorstep?" I can see why Carrie took such a strong aversion to her. If I were a better person I wouldn't listen. "There's many who would have demanded a DNA test—and maybe he should have. Jamie looks nothing like Glen." Her lips purse in a way that tells me what she takes from that. "He's a right charmer now, but back then he was an angry wee thing." She nods for effect, the bottle of apple juice in one hand, all pretense of operating the till abandoned. "But that was nothing compared to Fiona as a teenager." She shakes her head. "The drugs, the police, och, the things I could tell you—and it didnae stop after she had Callum. It's a wonder they've allowed her to keep that wee boy at all—"

The bell on the shop door jangles abruptly. "Morning, John," she calls out to the elderly gentleman who has just entered. "I've got your paper here; I'll be right with you." And my purchases are rung through in no time at all.

But now, Callum is here. For a moment after we were left alone in the house, after Ben dropped him off, I felt the onset of panic again: What should I do with him? Won't he be bored? But then he asked very seriously if I wanted to see the Transformers toys he'd brought and the panic cleared before it really had a chance to get started.

Later, when we are on our hands and knees creating an obstacle course out of household items in the living room for the Transformers to navigate, Callum asks, "Do you have a job?"

"Yes, but I'm on a break right now." I can't think when I last watched the news. I've been essentially mainlining it for over a decade, reporting stories, following other stories, never unaware. How is it that I've stepped away so easily?

"A holiday? Here?" He looks around, brow furrowed.

I suppress a smile. "Sort of. Something like that. Where do you go on holidays?"

"We dinnae go away. Mum doesnae like to leave here. She says it makes her worse. With time 'n' all." *With time.* There are so many questions I'd like to ask him on that, but I don't know how to frame any of them for a seven-year-old, so I don't say anything at all. "I'd like to go to Disneyland, though," Callum adds wistfully. "My friend Josh has been and he said it was brilliant." Then he picks up two toys, crashes them together and makes fighting noises before asking, "What were you going to do if I hadnae visited today?"

"Nothing terribly interesting. I was thinking of sorting through some boxes in the attic." *And of getting some security cameras installed.*

"The attic? Cool! Can I see?"

"Sure. Though it's not really an attic. It's just a small storage room on the top floor that I've taken to calling an attic."

But Callum is still intrigued, so we climb the stairs to the attic, and he's endearingly enthusiastic about everything, even the dust. I'm starting to realize that it's an incredibly attractive characteristic, enthusiasm. There has not been enough enthusiasm in my life lately. Maybe not ever.

"There are paintings here!" he says.

"Yes. My mum was a painter. They're just old canvases."

"No, this one is finished," he says. "It's all wrapped up."

I go to see what he's looking at. In among what I had taken to be discarded canvases is a proper packing crate. I've seen enough of them in my mum's studio to recognize them, but this is a smaller size than she usually used. Callum is peering in one end, where it's been levered open. I pull out the crate carefully. It's about three feet by four feet— the piece itself must be much smaller than she usually painted.

"Can I see it?" asks Callum.

"Yes. Let me just . . . Ah, here we go." The crate had been opened and only loosely shoved back together; I'm able to pull it open. "Oh, careful, Callum. Let me be the one to touch it." It's probably worth a fair bit, given most of my mother's paintings are. I pull it out and prop it against the packing crate for us to look at it properly. It's mainly dark, blacks and midnight blues.

"What . . . what is it?" asks Callum.

"I don't know," I say, half laughing. "I think you're supposed to decide for yourself." I take a quick photo of it. Technically it's mine, I suppose. Perhaps I will ask Pete to sell it for me.

He squints at it dubiously. "Well. I suppose it could be a house. Or a storm. Or a sea. At night."

"It could be. Any of those." We are both laughing now.

"Did your mum *sell* her paintings?"

"Yes. Quite a lot of them. For quite a lot of money."

"Really." He reflects. "Maybe she got better at it," he says generously.

I laugh out loud and tousle his hair, and think that I will tell Pete and Carrie about this. It will tickle them both.

Callum moves to a different area of the room to explore. "Who is *M. Cal . . . Cal-der?*" he asks, reading from a label on one of the boxes, and stumbling over the pronunciation.

"*Call-der,*" I correct him. "My father." The box he's reading from is the one that was under the photo envelope. I haven't got to it yet. I pull off the lid, expecting more photos and albums, but instead the box is full of a bulging cardboard folder, ripped at one end.

"Where is he?" asks Callum.

"Who?" I lift the folder out to leaf through the contents.

"Your dad."

"I don't know. He disappeared when I was seven."

"Disappeared." He digests this for a moment. "I dinnae have a dad, neither." I glance up from the folder. "Maybe your dad went into before. Or later."

"I don't . . . What do you mean?"

"Like the bird. Maybe he slipped through."

"Through . . . time?" I venture.

He nods, pleased I've caught on. "Cos it's funny here. I cannae tell anyone at school. They'd think I was mental—the teachers would, anyway. They already think I'm thick because of the reading." I'm so relieved to hear that he's keeping Fiona's nonsense under wraps at school that I'm rather slow in gearing up to reassure him on the reading, but he surprises me by suddenly smiling. "But I'm the best at football, so my friends dinnae care if I cannae read well." He looks across at me. "Anyway, you can see the bird, so you ken it's funny here."

"Well, I can see the bird," I say helplessly. It's all I'm prepared to admit.

"I bet Carrie cannae." He takes my silence as agreement. "She wasnae born here, like us."

"I was born in town at the big hospital, not in the actual Manse."

"But you were here as a bairn."

"Yes."

"I was born actually *here*." He looks around thoughtfully, as if he can see through the walls of the attic. "I dinnae ken which room, though."

I stare at him. "Wait, I thought it was your mum who was born here."

He nods. "And me too."

"What? How did that happen?" Can he be right? Could it really be the case that both Fiona and her son were born in the grounds of the Manse?

His brow furrows. "I dinnae ken, exactly. But Mum says that's how we know about time being funny here. Things slip through."

"Is that . . . is that what you think happened with your dad?"

He shakes his head. "Not to him. But maybe . . ." But he stops, suddenly unsure of himself for the first time.

"What?" I take a step closer to him and put the folder down on top of another box.

"But maybe I did. Maybe that's why I dinnae have a dad. He's before. Or later."

"Callum . . ." I feel helpless as he envelops my middle in the tightest of hugs. It catches me unawares every time, how incredibly free he is with his physical affection. My father was tactile; I remember that. He hugged and he tickled, and he would tuck me into his side to watch television. It wasn't in my mother's nature to hug.

"It's okay," Callum says seriously, lifting his head to look up my torso to my face. "I think we're meant to be here now. I dinnae think we can slip through."

———

After that I bustle us both down from the claustrophobic confines of the attic into the kitchen under the auspices of it being biscuit time, grateful for the cheer of the yellow walls, however artificial. I'm utterly at a loss as to how to address these beliefs of Callum's—and anyway, is it really my place to? Fiona and Callum's theories around the Manse and time seem tantamount to a religion for them, and I wouldn't dare confront someone who, say, believed in creationism rather than evolution. I'm grateful, too, for the single-minded focus of young children when food is mentioned—all difficult topics of conversation have been instantly cast aside in favor of intense deliberating over exactly which biscuits to choose.

Somehow without conscious decision I've brought down the bulging cardboard folder with me. When Callum has wolfed two custard creams, a Jammie Dodger and a glass of apple juice, we leaf through it together. There are several A5 jotters among the loose-leaf papers and maps and photos, and each of them has a familiar phrase written on the front, in blue ink: *Love makes a furnace of the soul.* Carrie's words about the inscription, about my mother, float back to me: *The man she was living with was obsessed by it.* I am holding the evidence of his obsession.

"Look, this is *here*. It's the Manse," says Callum excitedly. I look up from the jotter in my hand to the sepia photograph he's holding out. It's recognizably the front of the Manse, though the oak tree is quite a bit smaller. "Was it taken a very long time ago?"

"I don't know when." I take it from him and turn it over, hoping for a date, or something else in a precise neat handwriting. I can almost see it, a line in faded ink, the way the letters loop and slope, the evenness of the script, but there's nothing there at all. "Perhaps a photography expert could tell."

"Is everything in there to do with the Manse?"

"I think so."

"Do you have any more photos?" asks Callum, clearly much less interested in the jotters. I look around for the aerial shots of the Manse and hand them to him. "Cool!"

I inspect the jotter I'm holding again; one could buy something like it in any newsagent's. It's about two thirds full of decisive handwriting, with a slight flourish to the cross of the *t*'s. *My father wrote this*, I think. *This, and this, and this.* He sat at a table, somewhere in this house, and he set down his thoughts. Not in Biro, in fountain pen, and in the same blue ink. Did he always write in fountain pen? Or was that choice a mark of his investment in the project? "Your grandfather told me that my father was researching the Manse's history. I think we've found his research." I sink into a chair and read a page at random. *Pre-1841, the census report was statistical only. In 1841, the Manse is listed with John Buchanan (41), Mary Buchanan (32) and Christine Anderson (16) in residence.*

I flick through, looking for something relating to an earlier period, to the period of Ali's story. From his notes, it looks like my father had heard that story and was looking for that, too: there's various expressions of frustration in that decisive blue handwriting that he can't find any records naming householders from before the 1800s. The Jacobite rebellion was 1745, and Bonnie Prince Charlie died in 1788. Any pockets of Jacobite rebellion would have died out well before the 1841 census.

"What's this?" Callum asks, pointing near the shore of the loch on one photo.

"Oh, that's a path, surely." The line he's indicating is paler than the green around it.

"But there isn't a path there."

"Well, there might have been one back then. These must have been taken almost thirty years ago." I look at it again. It seems an odd-shaped path, like a tick mark, leading away from the shore at a forty-five-degree angle for a short distance, perhaps only meters, and then turning a right angle to head back toward the shore. But perhaps the shore line has changed over that time too.

"Can I go play?"

"Of course." I follow his dark head out of the room with my eyes, marveling at his comfort here. He seems entirely at ease, more so than I for all this was my own childhood home. And the Manse seems at ease with him.

Picking up the jotter again, I flick through to find a substantial section on window tax, which was apparently introduced in 1748, but my father was disappointed to find that the records contained names only, not addresses. I wonder how he found that out, in the pre-Internet era. Did he have to go to a public records office somewhere? Did he leave Karen and me alone to indulge his passion? I can just imagine my mother's lack of patience with that.

The sound of Callum's footsteps drags me out of the blue-inked jotter. "Hey, you, are you already after another biscuit?" I'm reaching for the cupboard but as he comes farther into the kitchen, I realize he's paper white. "What is it? Callum, what is it?"

"Under . . . under Carrie's bed," he says. There's a catch in his voice. "I was playing a spy game. I was under her bed." Anxiety is creeping in, too. "Was it okay to be there? I wasnae meaning to be naughty, I swear."

He's right beside me now. I kneel down and wrap him in a cuddle. "Of course that's okay. We've told you before that you can go in our rooms so long as you don't touch our things. What's under the bed, Callum?" He's clutching me with a fierceness that worries me more than any words could. "Wait, I can't hear you properly——" I pull back to look at his pinched face.

"There are bones," he says tremulously. "Under her bed."

"Bones?" He nods silently. I open my mouth, but nothing comes out. I close it again. I can't think what on earth he could have mistaken for bones. Or is this the next step in the escalation of the scare-away-Ailsa campaign? How could I have been so stupid to have only moments ago been fantasizing that the Manse is benign with this child in it? But Callum is waiting for me to speak, to tell him it's all going to be all right. "Well, I'm sure this is some kind of confusion, but it sounds like I ought to go take a look, don't you think?" He nods silently, his eyes brimming with words that he can't find a way to utter. "Why don't you stay here—"

"No!" He has grabbed my hand with desperate ferocity. "No! Dinnae leave me! Promise you willnae leave me, promise—" He's almost sobbing. I realize I've never seen Callum cry before. I'm utterly out of my depth.

"Okay, okay, I won't leave you. Callum, honey, I promise I won't leave you." I've gathered him up in my arms again. "It's okay. I'm here. I'm here." I'm stroking his hair, his back, almost crooning to him, for how long I don't know. Minutes, perhaps. Gradually I can feel the tension ease in him and his breathing return to normal.

Finally he lifts his head. I smooth away the tear tracks with my thumbs, feeling close to tears myself. "You have to go see," he says, his face a heartbreaking mixture of dread and determination. "We'll have to go together."

Do we have to? Together? I debate it internally. My first instinct is to keep Callum well away from whatever has scared him. But would that be worse? Would he build up whatever he thinks he has seen in his head until it's the stuff of nightmares, when the truth might be entirely innocuous? But at any rate, it's clear he will not leave my side, and it's equally clear I have to see whatever this is. Reluctantly I nod. "Okay. Together."

So we climb the stairs together, with his little hand enveloped in mine, and I wonder that I ever thought him robust. Right now he feels as fragile as tissue paper. We walk across the landing to the door to the master bedroom—Carrie's bedroom. I find I'm taking a deep breath as we enter.

Carrie's bedroom is as messy as ever. The duvet hangs half off the bed, obscuring the small space beneath the bed on the side we're standing. I take Callum's hand and secure it on the back pocket of my jeans so as to free both of my own hands. "Okay?" I ask him. He nods back silently, his eyes dark pools of barely contained fear. I can feel his hand tightly bunching my jeans pocket material. I pull the duvet up and deposit it all on top of the bed. "Under here?" He nods again. I get down on my knees to look properly. Callum is still gripping my jeans pocket.

The space under the bed is so narrow that only a child of Callum's size or smaller could fit, and the light from the window doesn't penetrate far enough for me to be able to see properly. I sit up for a moment and pull out my mobile phone and switch on the torch function, then put my head back down to peer under the bed again. The pale yellowish light picks up a sock and a red hairbrush and the fact that the carpet under here could really use a pass of the Hoover. And then, at the far end, the pillow end, I can see . . .

Bones. Small bones, yellow-white and clean, looming large against the black shadows thrown behind them by the angled torch. I can't judge their size—the torchlight and the shadows are skewing the perspective—but probably they're no bigger than my hand. A cold thread of dread circles into my belly.

I pull back abruptly and sit up, almost dislodging Callum, who hasn't relaxed his grip on my jeans. "Yes," I say. He nods back at me, once, without displaying any satisfaction in having been proved right, his dark eyes enormous in the pale chalk of his face. "I can see them. I'm going to move the bed." He nods again. Normally he'd be so eager to help that he'd be already moving the bed himself by now, but this time he just shuffles silently along beside me, always maintaining his grasp on my pocket, whilst I yank on the heavy bed myself. When I glance down at him, I see that the thumb of his other hand is in his mouth. After a couple of big heaves, I have moved the bed perhaps a foot and a half away from the wall that it was previously flush against. I have to lean awkwardly over the headboard to see if that's far enough.

It's far enough.

The carpet is heavily indented from where the bed normally sits, and a thick layer of dust covers the inch between the indentations and the skirting board. The bones—five or six of them, all small, not any longer than the main bone in a chicken drumstick—are resting on the hardy woven beige carpet in a loose pile, an inch or so farther from the wall than the indentations from the bed.

Maybe they *are* chicken bones. Though they seem a little thicker. And perhaps longer. I can't for the life of me think how chicken bones—clean ones, with nary a strip of meat on them—would find a resting place on the carpet under a bed. And I can't shake the dread that's settled, coiled snakelike, inside my belly.

"What are you going to do with them?" asks Callum.

I turn back from peering over the headboard to face him. "I suppose I'd better take them to the police, just to be safe. Though I expect they're probably animal bones of some kind," I add quickly.

Callum looks completely unconvinced. "Why would Carrie have animal bones under her bed?"

"Honey, this has nothing to do with Carrie. They've probably been here from before we arrived."

He's frowning stubbornly. "How can you be sure? It could be a black magic thing. I saw it on the telly."

"What?" I stare at him. "What on earth have you been watching?"

"James Bond." He screws up his nose as he thinks. There's a bit more color in his cheeks now, and he has let go of my jeans pocket. "*Die or Go Live*, I think? Or something."

"*Live and Let Die?*" He nods. I have a hazy memory of Jane Seymour and some kind of voodoo in that one. I've never particularly thought about the age certificate for *Live and Let Die*, or for any Bond film for that matter, but I'm sure it must be at least a 12. Which Callum is most definitely not. "Erm, did your mum say you could watch it?"

"Nah, it was Uncle Jamie."

"Right," I say faintly. "Well, I can assure you I've never seen any sign of Carrie being involved in black magic." His jaw remains mutinously set. "Look, Carrie would hardly be fine with you playing in her bedroom if she had black magic paraphernalia to hide, would she?"

"Para . . . ?"

"Paraphernalia. It means stuff, equipment."

He considers this carefully for a moment, then his face clears and he nods. "They could have slipped through," he mutters, half to himself.

I pretend I didn't hear that. "Okay then. I'll just grab these and we can wrap them up and I'll take them to the police station." But then I wonder if I ought to be touching the bones at all—if they are human, would I be tampering with evidence? "Callum, can you grab me some toilet paper from the bathroom there? I'll wrap them in that."

He's off like a shot, then back only seconds later with an entire roll of toilet paper. I shift the bedside table so that I can access the gap more easily. Then I tear off a healthy length of loo roll, fold it and lay it down on the bedside table, waiting to take delivery. I take another length of toilet paper in my right hand, and bend into the gap to pick up the bones.

The paper makes me clumsy; I can only grab a couple of bones at a time. They are simultaneously lighter yet more solid than I had expected. When I'm finished, all six lie among loo paper on the bedside table. It could be a bird's nest, I find myself thinking. A nest of bones. Too small, though, for the raven that lies outside with a yellow Post-it note pinned to its breast. A rising wave of panic is threatening to pick me up. *Dear God, what was I thinking, allowing Callum to come here?* What was Ben thinking, letting him come? How could we expose a seven-year-old boy to this house and the things that go on here? I'm going to be dashed on the rocks of the sheer awful carelessness of it. How could I have? How could Ben? How could Fiona—who seems to know more about the Manse than anyone—have allowed it?

Callum's hand slips into mine again, anchoring me. "Are you okay, Ailsa?" he asks quietly. "I willnae leave you either."

MY FATHER IS WATCHING ME. MY FATHER HAS ALWAYS BEEN watching me. You could say he's a spirit or a ghost, you could say that he slipped into before, or later, but those would just be attempts to put into words what can't be truly expressed or understood. Perhaps years in the future—a century or even two—mankind will possess the language to describe it, but that won't be a language that any layman might comprehend. Mathematicians at the very pinnacle of the field, right at the bright frontier of discovery, will see the elegance of the equations that encircle where my father is, that wrap it and ensnare it in golden threads of Greek letters and symbols. They will be able to spout about quantum entanglement, the reversibility of time and the equivalence of mass and energy, but they still won't actually see my father, because even reversing time in an equation can't create mass from memory.

But nonetheless, wherever it is that he has gone, my father is watching me.

SEVENTEEN

Carrie telephones, as she always does, but I miss the call because I'm outside with Ali's security camera guy. Later I find a text from her, in her telegram style, when I come inside to make a cup of tea for the camera guy.

> Getting lift from station. Will pick up stuff for dinner on
> way x

A lift from Jamie, I suppose. I expect he'll have told her about the bones. The bones that are nothing, of course; almost certainly nothing. I drove to the police station and handed them in once Jamie had collected Callum. The policeman behind the desk listened to my tale of discovery with only the merest hint of a raised eyebrow, looked dubiously at the tissue-wrapped collection then shrugged and found a form for me to fill out. I couldn't have been there for more than fifteen minutes. Surely if he could see the bones were human there would have been a more excited response.

I text back:

Great. Thanks x

I'm at the front door saying good-bye to the camera guy when an ancient Volvo I don't recognize pulls in, with Carrie in the passenger seat. I look across at the driver, but it's not Jamie. It's Fiona.

"Hey. Who was that?" Carrie calls across as she climbs out of the car, then reaches back in for a bag of groceries.

"That's Finley," says Fiona. She has climbed out too, and is eyeing the receding van thoughtfully. She must have come straight from work; she's wearing jodhpurs, a fleece and boots. "He works for Ali." I can only just hear her words. Then she turns back. "Hi, Ailsa."

"Hello." I've lost a sense of perspective on exactly how much warmth I should project. Carrie crunches across the gravel, Fiona in her wake, looking at me rather as if I'm made of glass. Then in a rush, I add, "Is Callum okay?"

Fiona nods. "He's fine. Really he is," she adds, on seeing my dubious expression. "Dinnae worry. To be honest, he's more worried about *you*. He didnae like the idea of you being here alone."

"*Are* you okay?" asks Carrie searchingly.

"Fine," I say brightly. Fiona hovers by the door when I step back to let Carrie in, an indecipherable expression on her face as she glances up at the facade of the Manse.

"Come on in," Carrie says encouragingly, jerking her head, and she does. She's been invited; I can hardly complain about it. And I wouldn't want to either. I'm feeling wretched enough about Callum and the bones that in that moment my uneasiness around her seems exactly what it is: petty and unfounded.

"I can't apologize enough," I say to Fiona when we reach the kitchen.

"Dinnae be daft. You were doing *me* a favor, looking after Callum. You couldnae have known that would happen."

"It's probably nothing anyway," says Carrie. "Most likely chicken bones, right?"

"Right." But even as I'm speaking, I'm looking at Fiona, at her sharp wary eyes and determined chin, waiting for her to agree. She sees me looking, and she doesn't say anything.

It doesn't mean anything that she hasn't said anything. It doesn't.

I offer drinks and start to make tea, because that's what you do when people come to your house, regardless of whether you're comfortable with them being there—which I am, really I am—regardless of whether it's entirely your house. Though I wonder if the Manse has ever truly belonged to anyone. There's an odd expression on Fiona's face as she looks around the kitchen, similar to Callum's: *But . . . but it shouldnae look like this.* I want to ask her about whether Callum was really born here, but Carrie has picked up a block of paint swatches I've left on the table. "Are we redecorating?" she asks, settling into a chair.

"I thought I might repaint the kitchen, at least." I got them from Ali's hardware store, along with Finley and the cameras and a hefty dose of sarcastic repartee.

"Any particular color in mind?"

I lean over her shoulder to pick out a strip and point to one specific shade. It's a strong purple, almost blueberry. "Just for that wall." I point to the wall opposite the window. "The rest in one of the gazillion variations on white."

"Bold choice," says Carrie, sounding impressed. "I like it." She holds it up to show Fiona. For a second Fiona looks startled, but then she smiles and nods in a noncommittal way.

"How was your night in Edinburgh?" I ask. Fiona's eyes shift to me; I can feel their weight, but I'm focused on Carrie. There's the merest flicker on her face, a twitch of her shoulder, and then she replies in an entirely casual manner, "Oh, fine. Nothing spectacular." She's astonishingly good at the lie. I shouldn't be shocked—after all, she's an actress— but nonetheless, I feel the blow land anew, stealing my breath. I had planned to challenge her if she lied to me directly, but I can't do that now, not with Fiona here. I turn away quickly under the pretense of getting milk from the fridge. When I put the milk carton on the table, Fiona is studying me with something approaching unease around her eyes. She doesn't look away when she sees that I'm looking back. *She knows Carrie wasn't in Edinburgh*, I realize. *And she doesn't like the deception.*

"What was the van all about?" says Carrie, when I've joined them at the table. Fiona has shrugged off her fleece to reveal a sleeveless T-shirt. Her arms are an anatomy study, every muscle and sinew perfectly defined.

"Security. He's setting up some cameras for us. He'll be back to-morrow to finish it off."

"Because of the bones?" asks Carrie, looking confused.

"Not really." I really don't want to go into detail on the fox carcass or the raven until I'm alone with Carrie. "Or maybe, sort of. It made me realize how isolated we are out here."

"That's part of the charm, I suppose." She turns to Fiona. "Stay for dinner?"

Fiona looks at me and I quickly add, "You're very welcome. Of course." Carrie glances across at me, warmth in her eyes.

"Okay. Thanks," says Fiona with a nod. "My dad was planning fish and chips with Callum anyway."

"Great," says Carrie brightly. "I'll just nip to the bathroom and then I'll get started."

The kitchen falls quiet without Carrie. Fiona looks at me steadily then reaches out with one hand and rubs the purple paint swatch be-tween her thumb and first finger. I note once again her unusually short nails. I wonder if it's a riding thing. "Are you trying to turn it back to how it was?" she asks, in a musing tone.

"What?"

"You cannae remember?"

"Remember what?" Then I twig that she means what it was like when I was a child. "Wait, do you?"

"Maybe. It's hard for me to tell. I can see it this color, but *when . . .*" She's frowning, like she's trying to catch something in her head. "Ach, I cannae tell."

"Because time is folded here," I say quietly. "Isn't that what you think?"

She cocks her head on one side, her hazel eyes gleaming. "Ben?"
I nod. "And Callum."

"Ah." She absorbs that for a moment. "You want to think it's rubbish, but you live here. What do you *really* think?"

"Carrie lives here too. Have you asked her that?" There's a waspish note to my tone that even I dislike.

Fiona shakes her head. "Carrie wouldnae feel it. Carrie's anchored to *now*. None of it would make sense to her." Except none of it makes sense to *me*. My exasperation threatens to erupt—I fold my lips to stop myself saying anything at all.

She looks at me, and her expression softens, like she's taking pity on me. "Look. It's like this. Imagine you saw a film. And then you saw it again. The second time round, you know how it's going to end, you know who the good guys and the bad guys turned out to be, right? So you feel differently about some of the characters the second time round, aye?" I nod unwillingly. "Sometimes it's like that for me. Not on everything, not even on much, but sometimes. I'm scared of things that havenae happened yet, or I'm not scared when I should be because it's all going to turn out fine. I cannae even get cross with the old biddy who's mean to Callum because I've seen her fall and break her leg, only I dinnae ken if that's happened already or not, and I cannae be polite to the groom at work that's going to run over the dog through sheer stupidity. Or maybe he already did that. I'm not sure. And even when I cannae see anything *later*, *before* is all jumbled up." She looks at me wryly. "You're a journalist. You probably rely on ordered facts."

"If you can't rely on those, what can you rely on?" I try to keep my tone light.

"People. Certain people. For the ones you really trust, it doesnae matter what they do. You're on their side regardless." She smiles. "I can see you think I'm nuts, but you'll come round. You and me are going to be pals."

"You said that before." She's right. I think she's nuts.

"Did I?" It's not really a question; she's not looking for me to tell her when.

"I'm sorry, I just . . . It just doesn't make sense to me. But any friend of Carrie's is"—I stumble over the traditional end to that sentence—"welcome here."

She laughs, short and sincerely, from the belly. "Nicely put."

I aim for a change of topic. "Was Callum really born here?"

She pauses. "Who told you that?"

"He did. Was he?"

"Not according to his birth certificate."

There's a challenge in her words, and her half smile. She wants me to ask the obvious question. "And according to you?"

"Ah, but havenae you been listening? I can never be the gospel. I'm unreliable, I cannae date memories, my recall is questionable." She sees that I don't know what to say, and relents. "I only remember the arrival of one babe, so it would have to have been Callum. And I remember it being here." She shrugs. And then Carrie is back, and in an instant the room is louder and more bustling. She puts the radio on, she co-opts Fiona as a sous-chef and in short order I'm ushered out of the kitchen with orders to *go relax in the bath or something.*

For a moment, I stand outside the kitchen, wineglass in one hand, temporarily at a loss. Then I climb the stairs, but I don't stop on the second floor; I go all the way up to the attic. To the albums, which I flick through quickly, looking for any photos taken in the kitchen. There are plenty in the garden, in the dining room or on various Scottish beaches, but none in the kitchen as far as I can see. If my purple wall idea is less divine inspiration and more the echo of a memory, I can't prove it either way.

For want of anything better to do, I go and run a bath.

———

Dinner is . . . nice. Truly, it is. Carrie's food is delicious, as always, and she has a spring in her step that's infectious. Fiona has a glass of wine in front of her when I come down from my bath, and I try not to think about whether she should do that along with whatever medication she's on. It's brought a flush to her cheeks and softened the sharpness of her eyes. She's talking about Callum when I enter, and that softens her, too.

"The private school, Gordon's—the one at the top of the hill, you ken? It has a great setup for coping with dyslexic kids," she's saying. "But the fees at that place are . . ." She trails off and shakes her head. She lifts the bottle of wine questioningly as I join her at the table, but I shake my head.

"Can your dad help out on that?" Carrie asks from across the kitchen, then adds, "Perfect timing, Ailsa, dinner'll be ready in a couple of minutes."

Fiona is shaking her head. "A police pension doesnae quite run to putting a kid through private school." She pronounced it *po-lis*. I haven't heard that for years. "All he wants to do is work with animals, but without some kind of decent education, he'll end up mucking out horse shite forever." She takes another sip of wine. "Like me."

"You love where you work," protests Carrie.

"Aye. Kind of," sighs Fiona. "But I'd love it more if it, you know, paid me a fuck load of money."

"I hear you." Carrie puts a roast chicken into the middle of the table. It hadn't actually occurred to me to ask what we were having. "Fi, you carve whilst I grab the veggies."

"Was it always going to be acting for you, Carrie?" Fiona asks, as she hacks at the chicken with a total lack of finesse.

"Yeah, though Mum was never keen," Carrie says over her shoulder as she drains something green in the sink.

"Really?" I ask, surprised. "I thought she went to all your plays." *Where did I get that impression from? Was I told it, or did I just assume?*

"She had a ticket to them all. She actually came to very few." Her mouth twists briefly, but then the corners lift. "Dad moved heaven and earth to come, of course. To every one. Though I don't know if he'll make it up to this one; his hip is getting really bad . . ." She trails off, and I see the future that she worries about laid bare on her face. Our mother's death has made her horribly aware that Pete is ten years older than Karen was. "Maybe he shouldn't even try."

"You know we won't be able to stop him." She smiles ruefully at me. We're all seated now, our food in front of us. For a few minutes we busy ourselves with our plates, and the only sounds are the clinking of cutlery and the news bulletin on the radio. I'm trying to remember the last play I saw Carrie in, but I always seemed to be out of the country on assignment. I'd like to think I would have made an effort to get there if I'd known only Pete was supporting her. I'd like to think so, but . . . I was busy, living a different life, a life that was all consuming when I was in it, a life that, now that I am temporarily out of it, seems to have all but consumed *me*. I would make the effort now, though. Now, I definitely would.

And so, dinner is nice. We talk about all sorts of things, and nothing much. Fiona isn't odd or enigmatic—apart from the beeping on her watch every half hour, but even that I'm starting to get used to. She's just a woman having a nice meal and a glass of wine with friends. She's refreshingly blunt and slightly intense when something particularly catches her interest, but there is nothing to suggest she might be fond of the odd cigarette in a stranger's home. I feel myself splinter in two as we eat and talk and start a second bottle of wine. Most of me is sitting at the table, enjoying the evening, one I never expected to happen. But then there's part of me observing, watching, unable to trust what I'm seeing.

"I think I'll head up to bed," I say, when Fiona's beeping watch has alerted me that it's eleven o'clock. They chorus good nights to me. I glance back from the doorway to see their heads together, giggling at the kitchen table. It's so precisely the image I conjured up, mere days ago, that it stops me dead. But Carrie and Fiona are oblivious, in a bubble of wine and shared laughter. I could be invisible. I feel invisible.

My sleep is disturbed by dreams that don't feel like dreams. My father drifts in and out of them—he doesn't look anything like either my memories, insubstantial as they are, or the photos I possess, but some-how I know it's him—whilst I'm looking for something in a house that doesn't look like the Manse either, but I know it *is* the Manse, though the rooms seem to shift and change when I'm not looking at them. I don't know what I'm looking for, and I'm late for work, but I can't stop looking.

I wake suddenly, gasping, dragged abruptly into reality. My bed-room door is open, with the hall light spilling through it, and there's a figure in the doorway.

Fiona.

She's standing there looking at me. I don't know how long she's been there.

"What are you doing? What are you doing here?" I scramble up to a seated position in bed.

She doesn't answer. My eyes are adjusting. Perhaps she never left; perhaps Carrie suggested that she stay over. I grope for my bedside light switch, bumping my BlackBerry in the process so that it lights up. Finally I find the switch. She blinks in the light but doesn't move in the slightest. She's wearing a long white T-shirt—or at least, it's long on her—that I think I recognize as Carrie's, over black jeans. It's her stillness that is the most chilling.

"How long have you been there?" The bark of my words is under-mined by the tremor in them. I glance at the BlackBerry screen. "It's two in the morning."

Finally she speaks, in an oddly thoughtful tone. "Oh. It's not the right time." Then she turns and leaves. Did I see a flash of something silver in her hand as she left? *What was that?* My fevered brain is run-ning through worst-case scenarios. Some kind of blade? *A knife?* Or something more prosaic, like a silver mobile phone? I stare at the empty doorframe for a moment, then scramble out of bed and grab my dressing gown. The hallway is empty and quiet. The Manse is listen-ing, holding its breath.

Carrie. The thought propels me straight through the hallway and through the doorway, the door a few inches ajar, into her bedroom. Instantly I can hear her breathing: *She's safe.* Some of the tension drains out of me. My eyes are adjusting, and I can see her lying peacefully on her back, one arm flung loosely out, her torso only half concealed by the duvet. She's not wearing any nightclothes. I back out of the room quickly, feeling like a voyeur.

Back in the hallway, I try to work out which bedroom Fiona must be in. The remaining one on this floor, surely? It's larger than those upstairs; it's what I would offer to a guest. The door is closed. If there's a light on inside, it's not clear from the crack under it. I stand mere inches from it, then millimeters, straining to hear any noises from within, but I can't hear anything above my own heartbeat in my ears. It would be extraordinarily rude to open the door, but I couldn't care less right now; it was extraordinarily rude of Fiona to open my own bedroom door—rude, and sinister, and so very strange. There's no way I will get to sleep until I've made sure I know exactly where she is, and even then, I'm fairly certain I still won't manage it. Extremely slowly, holding my breath, I carefully depress the handle. It turns, and turns more, and finally—click—it gives. The door opens with the sound of a small moan.

I look at the gap. Three inches perhaps. I can't hear anything from within the room. Reluctantly I push the door open a little more, enough to be able to peer into the bedroom. The bed is opposite the door; I can see the dark gray cuboid of it, a little darker than its surroundings on account of the navy bedspread. My breath is held, but my eyes are beginning to adjust; I can see a pale blob in the bed. There's something odd about it, though. Surely it's not big enough to be a person . . . and I can't hear any breathing. I feel around the doorframe and press the light switch.

And then I start screaming. Because there is a skull in the middle of the bed.

MY FATHER IS IN MANY PIECES. TWO HUNDRED AND SIX, TO BE exact. Six are in a police lab somewhere, undergoing testing. One is laid out on a navy bedspread, as if on a giant presentation cushion, like the crown jewels. It's hard to pin down the other one hundred and ninety-nine. They're in the Manse, certainly, as he was at one time, but they slide in and out of focus and then abruptly, they slip, and they're gone.

EIGHTEEN

We are in the kitchen, Fiona, Carrie and I. The three of us are in the kitchen, while the skull remains on the navy bedspread, propped in the slight gap between the pillows, like a grinning child that has commandeered his parents' double bed. I am not screaming out loud anymore, but inside it hasn't stopped. It may never stop. In my job I have experienced riots, shoot-outs, earthquakes and, once, a volcanic eruption, but I am not prepared for whatever vicious malevolence this is. *The Manse has served this up to me. The Manse has passed judgment and it doesn't want me here . . .* But no, I cannot afford to indulge my fanciful leanings. The skull is solid and tangible and real, and someone very real broke into my house and placed it there. Someone doesn't want me here, but who? There's a list forming in my head of all the people I know round here—Carrie, Fiona, Ben, Ali, Jamie, Piotr, Glen, Callum, Morag, Jean the shopkeeper, the locksmith whose name I can't remember, all the people at Ben's birthday dinner . . . I'm scraping the bottom of the barrel and still the list barely makes double figures.

I distract myself with a quick swallow from my mug. We are British, and this qualifies as a crisis, so obviously we're drinking tea. It's reassuring to have something to do. Perhaps that's the point of it: a way to inject some element of normality in times of extreme stress. *Ben, Piotr, Carrie, Fiona, Callum, Ali, Morag, Jamie, Glen, Jean, the locksmith . . .*

"Are you sure we shouldn't call 999?" asks Carrie again. Her long-fingered hands are wrapped tightly round her own mug, as if she is afraid they might shake otherwise. Her face is sickly white, with bruises under her eyes along with smudged eyeliner.

"We know the house is empty. We've been over every inch." I aim for a reassuring tone, though whether that's for her benefit or to quieten the cacophony inside me, I'm not sure. My first instinct when I stopped screaming was indeed to call the police, but Fiona was more practical. She organized us into checking every room, every cupboard, every crawl space in the house, to ensure whoever put the skull there wasn't still in the house—all three of us together, none of us willing to venture anywhere alone. And once we knew the house was safe, the urgency to call the police had abated. Though since we've retreated to the kitchen, Fiona's control of the situation has evaporated and she's barely said a word. Even now her head is down, her eyes on her mug, as if she can't hear the world around her, as if every ounce of herself is contained and focused within her own skin. "We've been through this—that thing could have been there for days. It's not a room we've been using," I continue. "It doesn't seem like an emergency. I mean, it's not like there's any chance of resuscitation." Carrie grimaces and pulls her dressing gown more tightly closed at her throat. When she burst out of her bedroom, she wasn't wearing anything at all; she had to grab it before we made our rounds. Funny that she woke for my screams and not for the smoke alarm . . . "Did you have your earplugs in last night?"

She shakes her head. "Too much wine. I guess I forgot. I didn't even take my makeup off." Two empty wine bottles are still sitting on the table between us, underlining her point. "Why were you up? And why did you go into that room anyway?" she asks suddenly.

"Fiona woke me up."

Fiona lifts her head at this and looks at me expressionlessly. "What?"

"You came into my room—don't you remember?" She's still look-ing at me. Not a flicker of emotion has crossed her face. "I don't know why. But it woke me up."

Carrie looks at Fiona. "Did you?" she asks hesitantly.

"I dinnae think so," Fiona says thoughtfully. Her head is tipped, and her eyes are looking off to one side, as if she's trying to remember. Or imagine. "But . . ." She shrugs. It's the most expression I've seen from her since she stumbled onto the landing after my screaming. "I cannae think why I would have. Granted I'm never the most reliable on this stuff, but usually I actually *have* the memories, I just cannae tell when they're from. Maybe with the wine, though—"

"You did," I insist. "You were wearing Carrie's T-shirt . . ." I trail off. She *is* wearing Carrie's T-shirt, but this one is maroon, not white, and under it she has her own jodhpurs, not black jeans. If she's playing me, she's a better actress than Carrie, even.

"Maybe you dreamed it," says Carrie gently. She's using the same tone as after the flies incident. My internal screaming grows louder. "You were drinking too. Maybe you—"

"I didn't dream it," I say quietly. Carrie flinches. Fiona looks from her to me and back again. I say it again, louder. "For fuck's sake, I did NOT dream it."

"Ailsa, calm down—"

"Did I dream the skull? You guys saw that, right? You get that somebody crept into this house—*my* house—and put a skull, *a human skull*, in the middle of a bed? You do understand that? So, no, I haven't been fucking dreaming. *She*"—I'm pointing at Fiona now, which is incredibly rude, but under the circumstances, I feel a right to throw away certain social conventions—"*she* came into my room and woke me up, she said it was *the wrong time*, whatever the hell that means, and then she left. It was freaky enough that I got out of bed to check *you* were okay, Carrie, if you must know." I'm so angry I'm almost shaking. Fiona has reached out a hand and placed it on Carrie's forearm. Carrie won't meet my eyes. I look at Fiona. "I knew I wouldn't sleep until I knew where the hell you were, so that's why I checked that room." Neither of them are saying anything. "Why did you take an upstairs room, anyway?" *And why did you change out of the white T-shirt?*

Fiona pauses almost imperceptibly, then shrugs. "No particular reason." Despite my stare, she won't hold my gaze. It's the first thing she's said that doesn't quite ring true.

There's a very long silence. I can't tell what Carrie is thinking. Certainly what I've just said doesn't qualify as *civil*. I drop my head and rest my eye sockets on the heels of my hands, blocking out the light. I wish I could block out more, but I have to lift my head. "It doesn't matter how I found it anyway. The point is that it's there." *Carrie, Fiona, Ben, Ali, Jamie, Piotr, Glen, Callum, Morag, Jean, the locksmith . . .* "Who put it there and when?"

"And who is it?" adds Carrie. "I mean, who was it?"

They both look at me, and I know what they are thinking, because I'm thinking it too, but it's ludicrous. "It could be anyone. There's no point in speculating." My voice sounds brittle. I feel brittle.

"Of course," says Carrie quickly. She's pulled her feet up onto her chair and is hugging her knees. If anything, she's even paler now. Fiona is looking at me with a faint frown, as if she's trying to solve a quadratic equation in her head. In a transparent change of topic, Carrie adds, "You know, I've been trying to remember, and I'm not at all sure that I've been in that room since the first day we got here."

"Me either. Though I suppose Callum might have been in there yesterday." Of course Callum shouldn't be on the list.

"I'll ask him," offers Fiona.

"Let me know. I'll call the police in the morning." There's very little emotion in my words. I may have run out.

"Aye," says Fiona, then stops.

Carrie looks across at her. "What?"

"It's just . . . do you think you could maybe not tell the police I was here?"

"What? Why?"

She has two spots of color in her cheeks and she's looking straight ahead. "I dinnae have the best history with them. I was into some stuff as a teenager—"

"What kind of stuff?" I interrupt.

"Ailsa!" exclaims Carrie, but I won't be deterred.

"What kind of stuff?"

"Drugs," says Fiona succinctly. "I was going through a lot, apparently"—her lips twist ruefully—"and the drugs were . . . escapism. Or so the therapist told me."

"And you had run-ins with the police?"

She nods. "I got arrested a few times. Possession, never dealing. Breach of the peace a couple of times." She looks straight at me now. "The police will have to interview Callum, which means they will have to alert the social services."

"Why will they have to interview Callum?" asks Carrie.

"Because of the bones under your bed," Fiona says, but she's still looking at me.

"But we don't know—"

"Yes," I say quietly. "I rather think we do now." And then I remember Fiona's expression, only last night, when Carrie suggested the bones weren't human. Fiona has always thought they were human.

"Please dinnae tell the police I was here," says Fiona quietly. "Please. It just . . . It doesnae look good. The ex-druggie single mum too bladdered to get herself home . . . They'll tell the social services, and then I'll be on their list, and then . . ."

"But it wasn't like that," protests Carrie. "We'll tell them it wasn't like that."

Fiona shakes her head. "Better to say nothing at all." She shivers uncharacteristically. "I couldnae bear to lose Callum."

Carrie's hand flies to her mouth. "What? You wouldn't . . . Surely they . . ."

Fiona shrugs. "We were on the list before. Callum rolled off a bed as a baby. The system is stacked against you; you wouldnae believe it unless you've experienced it. It took years to get through that." Her fatalistic matter-of-fact delivery is somehow more effective than any emotional outburst might have been.

"Then of course we won't," Carrie says staunchly. "If you don't want us to, of course we won't. Will we, Ailsa?" There's a hard steel underneath her words as she turns to look at me. She repeats herself, softer, but somehow with more emphasis. "Will we, Ailsa?" Her gray eyes are fixed on mine unrelentingly.

"Of course we won't," I agree reluctantly, over the memory of Jean's words: *It's a wonder they've allowed her to keep that wee boy at all.* I glance at Fiona, and for the briefest of moments I could swear I detect a brief flash of triumph. But her expression sags into one of heartfelt relief and the instant is gone.

"Then you should probably go now," Carrie says to her. "So that we can say you weren't here. If you're okay to drive." I look at my watch. How can it only be half past two?

"I should be fine now," says Fiona, and she yawns, then drains her mug. "I'll go grab my bag." She looks across the table at me. "I'm sorry, Ailsa." I lift a hand off the table in faint acknowledgment, though I'm not sure what she's sorry for. Carrie follows her out of the room to help gather her things.

When she's finally gone, Carrie and I sit in silence and drink some more tea and the names run on a loop in my head. Not Carrie, never Carrie. Nor can I fathom a motivation that would fit for Jean, the locksmith, Glen or Piotr, and Morag might hate me, but she can't drive, so she couldn't even get here. It's becoming a very short list: Fiona, Ben, Ali, Jamie. Or some nutcase stranger I haven't even met yet. "I'm sorry I lost my cool, Carrie," I say finally.

She shakes her head. "Don't worry about it. You were pretty freaked out; no wonder you were a bit . . ." Her voice seems to run out of steam.

"I'm still freaked out, if I'm honest. I don't know how we can sleep after that."

"Me neither. Maybe Fiona will have more luck, in a different house."

"Maybe. Though she didn't seem that freaked out." Could it be that she was so calm about the skull because she put it there? The most anxious she had been was when she spotted that I caught a whiff of smoke on the second-floor landing. I expect it will probably irk me enormously later to think she must have been smoking in my house without asking for permission—which I would have refused—but at the present time it hardly seems important.

"Cool head in a crisis," yawns Carrie. "A good quality." She glances across at me. "Are you . . . are you starting to come round on her?"

"Yes," I say. "A bit." And Carrie smiles. I'm not lying, exactly; it's just that I'm still splintered. There's the Ailsa who had a nice dinner with Fiona and Carrie, who appreciates Fiona's forthright company, and then there's the Ailsa who can't do that. The Ailsa with a list of names in her head, the Ailsa who watches.

———————

The police are here.

They've been here all morning; three of them, picking through the Manse, poking into rooms, as if they half expect the rest of the skeleton to leap from a closet and dance a jig, headless and one-handed. The bones from under the bed are human, so very human in fact that it apparently took the forensic department mere seconds to identify them as such. And so, I don't actually have to call the police after all, because they turn up at my door before I even have the chance.

It's a Detective Chief Inspector Something-or-other who's evidently in charge, which he signals by leading the conversation on the doorstep. He's a tired-looking man in an ill-fitting gray suit, perhaps a little shy of six feet. He starts to explain what department he's with or some such detail, but I interrupt. "We found more."

"More?"

"Bones. Well, one more, to be exact. A skull."

He scratches his chin with a thumb. "You found a skull in your house." The weak morning sunlight finds some freckles on his nose.

"Yes. Last night."

"Right," he says faintly. Then, "Where?"

"In one of the spare bedrooms." I step back. "You'd better come in."

"I would think so."

And so I explain, and then I show the detective and his two underlings the bedroom, where we all stand in silence in the doorway for a moment and appreciate the macabre art that is presented by the sharp white of the skull grinning from its pride of place on the navy bedspread.

"Someone put it there, guv," comments one of the underlings. "Like, on purpose."

His boss surveys him with the merest hint of an eyebrow raise. "No kidding," he says shortly.

"This used to be my bedroom." Standing here, surveying the space, I'm suddenly sure of it. My small single bed was against the wall over there. I could see the door without moving my head on the pillow . . . Now that I understand the geometry of it, other pieces of furniture are growing in my mind. There was a chest of drawers, and a toy box, and—

"Miss Calder?" The detective is watching me quizzically.

I shake myself. "Sorry. It is . . . real, isn't it?" I've had all night to think. One of my more hopeful scenarios involved this being some kind of prank, the skull merely a prop. But Carrie, Fiona and I had looked at it carefully after our post-discovery tour of the Manse. It looked very real to us.

The detective turns and looks at me with eyes too washed-out for the color to be distinguishable. "We'll see," he says. "Would you mind perhaps waiting in the kitchen while we go through some standard procedures?"

I leave them to it, suddenly extraordinarily exhausted. My guess was right: neither Carrie nor I could sleep after Fiona had gone. I've already been up for hours and it's not even half past nine. At least I used some of that time to shower and dress, so I was clean to greet the police officers. Sometime later I'm leaning against the countertop in my oh-so-yellow kitchen nursing a lukewarm cup of coffee when the detective comes to find me. "Miss Calder? I wondered if you could perhaps go over again how you came to find the bones?"

"Which ones, Detective . . . ? Ah, I'm sorry, I've forgotten your name."

"Laws," he says. "Do you want to sit?"

"No, I'm fine." I feel simultaneously beyond exhaustion yet awkwardly restless. I don't want to sit.

He stays on his feet, too. "Shall we start with the first find?" I sigh. "I'm sure you've been through this before—"

"Twice actually. Three times if you count when I actually handed them in yesterday." He spreads his fingers, palm upward. I'm not sure what the gesture is meant to convey. "The fourth time is a charm, I suppose?" When he doesn't react, I launch into the same explanation I've given before, and he listens without looking at me or taking notes in the notebook he has at the ready. He's probably only a few years older than myself, but he's a faded man, I find myself thinking, with his pale skin and lean face and the faintest of red hints in his nondescript hair.

"And Callum is Callum McCue?" he asks. There's a hint of a lilt in his voice but he's not Scottish. Welsh, I would bet, if I had to pick.

"Yes." I know it's futile, but I try anyway. "You won't have to speak to him, will you? He's only seven. I bet he's been having nightmares anyway without having to relive it all over again." All I can see is Callum's pinched white face, full of determination and dread.

He looks at me properly for what feels like the first time. "You're fond of him, then."

"I challenge anyone to meet Callum and not end up a fan."

He smiles. There's no wattage in it, but the intent is there. "We will need to speak to him, I'm afraid, but don't worry, we have staff trained for this. They know how to tread gently." I don't say anything, though I rather doubt the staff are trained to deal with the fury of Glen if they upset his beloved grandson. Like a coward, I was enormously relieved when it was Jamie who came to collect Callum after his fateful discovery. Detective Laws considers my expression for a moment, then goes on. "You said it's your sister that's using the master bedroom?"

"Half sister. Yes." There didn't seem any point in her missing her rehearsal; I convinced her to head off to Edinburgh this morning. In truth I'm hoping the work will take her mind off all of this.

"We'll need to speak with her too." He pauses. "Which half?"

I must be tired; it takes me a moment to work out what he means. "Oh. Same mother."

"Karen Innes, the painter." It's not a question.

"Yes."

"I hear she died recently. My condolences." I still haven't worked out the socially acceptable response, so I incline my head and fold my lips in what I hope reads as gracious acknowledgment. Though maybe I ought to double-check that in the mirror sometime. He leaves a respectful pause before continuing. "I suppose that makes your father Martin Calder?"

It can't be merely local knowledge, since he's not from here. He's done his homework. "Yes."

"He's still missing, correct?"

He knows it's correct. I don't bother to confirm it. "Is this relevant?"

"Would you be willing to give a DNA sample for our investigations?"

"I . . . What?" Now I'm staring at him, at his bleached eyes set in skin that seems paper-thin, marked with faint crow's-feet. He's lost weight recently, I note with one part of my brain. Perhaps he's been ill. Perhaps he's still ill. But another part of me is computing his DNA question. "You think the bones . . . You really think it could be my father?" Hearing it out loud doesn't make it any less ludicrous.

He shakes his head. "I don't think anything. But we do have some bones of a person unknown found in the last known address of a missing person. I'd be thought stupid if I didn't at least consider it."

"So, what, you think he's been, I don't know, *under the bed* for twenty-seven years?" I shake my head in disbelief. "With cleaners and rental tenants merrily passing through the building? It's just not feasible."

"Well, no," he concedes, "obviously not under the bed the whole time. Or on top of it . . . But like I said, I don't think anything."

"That's not feasible, either."

My deliberately caustic tone earns a small lift of the corners of his mouth. "It's not helpful if we alight on a theory too early. It leads to a fixed mind-set, and then crucial clues can be overlooked." He raises his shoulders in the smallest of shrugs. "Or so the procedures manual says." It's possible that there's a very dry sense of humor lurking within Detective Laws.

"How long before you know?" I ask abruptly.

He doesn't have to ask what I mean. "It takes five to seven days to get the DNA results back. Depends on how busy the lab is." He pauses, and fixes me with those pale eyes. Pale blue, perhaps. It's hard to tell. "We've been told to expect the finger bones to be those of a male, though. It's not an absolute confirmation, by any means, but men tend to have longer, thicker finger bones."

"Oh," I say faintly. I try to think of something else to say, but my head is filled with my father's skeleton, scattered throughout the rooms of the Manse as if in some kind of macabre Easter egg hunt. I've never imagined a version of my father's life that could have led to that.

Laws eyes me carefully, then goes on diffidently, "There hasn't been time for any analysis on the skull yet, of course. It will take some time to know if it's even from the same person." He looks like he's waiting for me to say something, but nothing springs to mind. He has smile lines, deep enough for the skin to be even paler within them, etched around eyes that don't look like they have smiled for a very long time. After a moment he goes on. "And Carrie was the only one here when you found the skull?"

"Yes."

"What did you do last night?"

I talk him through the evening, or a version of the evening. A version of the evening that has Fiona leaving before any skull can be discovered.

"How much did you have to drink?"

He manages to make it sound like a casual question rather than an accusation, but nonetheless, I have to remind myself that I'm thirty-four years old and entitled to drink as much as I like in my own home. "A couple of glasses of wine with dinner."

"And you say you went to bed at around eleven and it was sometime after three that you found the skull?"

"Yes." Another edited detail necessitated by the elimination of Fiona. We thought it best not to edit the time she left in case anyone saw or heard her car.

He glances at me, and suddenly I have the feeling that his focus has sharpened, though his words are still conversational. "Why were you up? Did something wake you?"

"I . . ." *Yes, something woke me: Fiona, standing at my door.* Except that it was my screaming that brought her to the landing, wearing an entirely different T-shirt of Carrie's. But Detective Laws is waiting for me to speak. "I needed the bathroom."

"And why did you go into that room?"

It's taking more mental agility than I would have imagined to remove Fiona. "I'm not sure, exactly; I was half asleep. The door was ajar, I think . . ."

Laws is squinting, like he's trying to see something. "So you went to the bathroom first—yes? Okay, and then you came out. So you had to turn right to go back to your bedroom"—his hands are gesturing, palms facing each other but twisting from the wrist, as if to show the direction of travel—"which puts you, let's see, opposite the spare bedroom door?"

It would do, if that's what I had done. "Yes."

"And you say you think it was ajar?"

"Yes."

"But you didn't notice it on your way up to bed?"

"Apparently not." I hurry on to cover my flash of impatience. "Or it wasn't open—it's a drafty house. Old windows, you know. Sometimes doors blow open." It's true. The Manse speaks in its own way. Sometimes it shouts.

"Right." He falls silent, though I don't get the sense that he is finished with me yet. I turn and pour my now-cold tea down the sink. "Shame the cameras outside weren't operational."

"You're telling me," I say grimly. "They will be by the end of today."

"Good. My colleague is going to go over security with you. You really ought to get an alarm system. With zones and a night setting."

"Sounds expensive."

"Better safe than sorry." I wonder what *sorry* looks like in his job, and then I wish I hadn't. "We'll need a list of everyone that's been through the house since you got here."

"Of course, no problem."

"First the finger bones and now a skull," he muses. "Have you noticed anything else that's a bit out of the ordinary?"

I almost laugh. There's so much I could say, but how to say it without sounding entirely nuts? "Everything about this house is out of the ordinary, apparently. According to TripAdvisor, at any rate."

"What do you mean?"

"It seems the Manse is haunted. Animals fear to tread the very grounds. Strange bangings in the night, the feeling of being watched. And that's on top of the appalling mobile reception and questionable decor." He looks at me dubiously. "Seriously. Check out TripAdvisor. It's educational."

"Mmm. But have you yourself noticed anything odd?" He flaps a hand to stave off the next flippant remark that he rightly guesses is on the tip of my tongue. "Other than the bones, I mean?" I can't tell him about the flies, or the bin bag, or the dead animals, or the person I did or didn't see in the window, as I have evidence for none of it. And then he will ask Carrie, and Carrie will say I'm overwrought, not sleeping well . . . I shake my head. "Are you sure?" he presses. I can see he's noted my hesitation. "It seems very . . . personal, this. Certainly for the skull. Are you sure there isn't someone who has a grudge against you? Or Carrie?"

"Well, someone threw a stone at me in the garden one night, though it wasn't a big stone and it wasn't thrown very hard, and then there was the newspaper . . ."

One eyebrow rises a millimeter or two. From him, that's an enormous reaction. He actually starts to take notes. I hunt for the newspaper whilst explaining both incidents, but it's not where I left it. Maybe Carrie moved it.

"Is there anyone with some kind of personal vendetta?"

"Believe me, I've been thinking about it. I haven't lived here for twenty-seven years, remember, and Carrie has never lived here before—we barely know anyone round here. If the newspaper is connected, I suppose it could be someone who's targeting me because of my parents . . ." I pull back from mentioning Morag. The poor woman is ill; I can hardly visit the police on her. I splay my hands and exhale heavily in frustration. "But it doesn't make sense to blame me. I was only seven at the time."

"Well," he says, but he's still frowning slightly. I can't tell if he doesn't believe me or if this is what he does whilst he's processing. "Maybe someone sees things differently."

"I don't understand."

"No." He flips over the cover of his notebook, signaling that our interview is over. "I don't either, yet."

A flash of movement from the back garden catches my eye through the window. I turn to look outside, suddenly terrified that the policeman I can now see poking through the garden—literally poking; he has some kind of long white stick—will find the decaying, Post-it note–adorned raven and conclude . . . conclude what? That I am nuts, most probably. At the very least, that I am to be treated as potentially unstable. I suddenly wonder if I have actually committed a crime. Is it against the law to defile the corpse of a bird?

"Miss Calder?" asks the detective. "Are you okay?"

"Yes." I turn round abruptly with a half-hysterical smile, then quickly dim it on seeing his startled expression. "I mean, as can be expected under the circumstances. Of course."

"Mmm." He considers me thoughtfully. His eyes are blue. A pale ice blue.

MY FATHER IS . . . I CAN'T THINK ABOUT MY FATHER. I WON'T, AT least not intentionally. I know I can't dislodge him from the edges of my consciousness, the periphery, where the landscape is amorphous and ill formed. But I won't go there. That way madness lies.

NINETEEN

The skull is male.

Once again, that was immediately obvious to the forensic anthropologist; Laws rang to tell me, in his dry, thoughtful way. I can tell that he's handling me, managing me, trying to gently nudge me into a corner. He drove me to the police station to have DNA taken: swabs from my cheeks—I can still feel the scrape on one side—and fingerprints too, though there is no physical reminder of that. He drove, asking questions, the same questions again but in different ways. Testing me, always testing . . . And new questions, too, about who we've met since we've been here, about my parents and who knew them, about how well Carrie and I get on, how much we see each other. I am discovering that his ability to jump topics with a minimum of fanfare is disconcerting. And exhausting.

Though curiously I'm less exhausted than I have been for a while. Neither Carrie nor I want to spend a night at the Manse without an alarm, cameras or no cameras, and even in a rush job, the alarm company cannot possibly get one installed any quicker than three days hence, so Carrie has arranged to spend a few nights up in Edinburgh with fellow cast members. For my part, I am staying where I might never have imagined I would: I am staying with Fiona. She and Jamie—and Callum—positively insisted, and one of my splintered selves accepted. The long, low three-bedroomed McCue farmhouse is cramped, with nary a clutter-free surface in sight, but it's homely and it's solid and it's the same all the way through. There's no version of it that I'd be afraid to find myself in, and the darkness outside is simply nighttime, not a cloak for an ill-defined threat. Callum is sharing his mum's bed, and I sleep in a narrow single bed with Batman bedsheets and a stormtrooper alarm clock and wake the most refreshed I've felt in days. Weeks even. *It's the Manse,* I think. *The Manse has been leaching my energy, draining my faculties. The Manse has been stealing my very self.*

Everybody is up and moving when I wake, despite it being a Saturday, so I make myself a coffee and then wander outside, cup in hand, to watch Callum playing with Toast in the field closest to the farmhouse. He's trying to train her on a homemade agility course, which currently seems to involve Callum scrambling over the course yelling, "Look, Ailsa, look!" whilst Toast watches him uncertainly, looking rather bemused.

"You're that way," a voice calls. I turn to find Jamie just behind me. "The Manse, I mean," he says. "Just over that ridge there and then down through the woods. If the farmhouse had a couple more stories, you could probably see it from here." I gaze in that direction and wonder if the police are there now. "Sorry," says Jamie, touching my arm gently. When I look at him, his mouth is twisted in remorse. "You probably dinnae want to think about that." Jamie has been incredibly solicitous, though at times I've detected a slight excitement within him. I've seen it before in my job: the self-important glee at being so very close to the action that can't quite be hidden beneath proclamations of shock. But for now he says, "Come on up and let me show you my lair."

Lair. The word jolts me. "Um, sure." Jamie's accommodation is separate to the farmhouse, in a studio-style room above the garage, with its own entrance. I follow him up the concrete steps to his white door, wondering if this is where he took Carrie. It would be child's play to smuggle her in, if they were inclined toward secrecy. Perhaps that thought has my brain expecting some kind of lurid sex cave, or perhaps his use of the word *lair* is to blame, but his room is notable for only two things: clinical tidiness and an enormous flat-screen television on one wall. Other than that, it's exactly as uninspiring as one might expect for a white-walled rectangular space above a garage, even given the large windows at either end. There's a double bed, and a sofa in front of the telly, and a cube blocked off in one corner that presumably houses a bathroom.

"This is nice," I say, out of social convention. Then, looking for something more personal to add, I nod toward the telly. "I bet Callum loves that."

"Oh, he never comes up here," Jamie says easily, from the sofa. "This is my space."

"Oh. Right. Do you work from here?"

"Aye, over there." He points toward the desk, where a sleek black computer sits watchfully, with nothing but a keyboard on the desk. Either he has tidied up relentlessly in advance of showing me his space, or he and Carrie have absolutely no future together—a man this fastidious couldn't ever live in Carrie's chaos. I want to ask him about it—we have a friendship, Jamie and I, that's independent of Carrie or Fiona, but we haven't discussed our love lives. I suspect he's just as private as I am on that score, and why shouldn't he be? What he does with Carrie or anyone else is his business. "I cannae really risk Callum messing around with that, you see. That's why I keep him out of here."

"I see." There's only one picture on the wall, just a small framed photograph. I wander to look at it. "How is it living right by your dad and sister? After all, you could probably day-trade from anywhere." The photograph is in color, of a very thin woman in her thirties with cascading chestnut curls, Farrah Fawcett style, sitting cross-legged in a garden. It's a product of exactly the same early 1980s photography that's in my mum's albums.

"I could; you're right. And it has its moments . . ." He grimaces a touch ruefully. "But I willnae be here forever." I glance at him again, but he's not looking at me; he's looking away, with the same air of suppressed excitement that I picked up earlier. Whatever those plans are, he's not ready to share them.

I wonder if they include Carrie. Or perhaps that was just a onetime thing. Carrie is the one I should have asked about it, regardless of whether Fiona was there or not. I should have cleared the air. I can see it now: Fiona wasn't what stopped me. I was simply too scared to confront her.

"Is this your mum?" I'm suddenly aware there has been a long silence.

"Yes." He leaves the sofa to join me in looking at it. "She was beautiful."

"Yes, very." It's true, the woman is beautiful, though she also looks as if a stiff wind would blow her over. "What happened to her?"

"She committed suicide. About three years after that was taken." He shakes his head on my horrified intake of breath. *How could I not have known this?* "It's okay. I was very young, not even a year old. I couldnae possibly remember her. Though sometimes it feels like I do . . ." He is still looking at the framed photograph, his face oddly still, though I can see all the things he's not saying clamoring in his eyes.

I put a hand on his upper arm. "I'm so sorry."

"I wonder . . . Sometimes I wonder how different things would have been if she lived." It almost sounds like he's talking to himself.

"Same." Jamie is the one looking at me now. "With my dad, I mean. If he had been around . . ." I close my eyes and tip my head back, half laughing at myself. "It feels so . . . *unfair.*"

"Unfair." He repeats my word, as if testing it, to see if it fits. "*Unfair.* Aye, that it is."

———

The farmhouse is welcoming, and its occupants, too, but I'm conscious of not wanting to crowd their space, so mid-morning I head to the hotel leisure club. I didn't think to bring my trainers and sports kit from the Manse, and I'm not sure if the police are finished there yet, so I buy myself a swimsuit and goggles from the shop. There's a revolving rack of Karen Innes artwork reproduction postcards right next to the till. I find myself turning it slowly whilst the woman rings up the purchase, looking at each of the three sides in turn, seeing not the postcards but the actual paintings themselves, the enormous scale of them, the time and the energy they took. I see my mother, her hair scraped back haphazardly, paintbrush in one hand, utterly absorbed in the canvas. She could have been in a different world. I suppose that was the point.

"Are you after one of them postcards, too, hen?" asks the cashier.

"Oh no, they're not really my thing," I say hastily.

"Me neither. All too modern for me. I like a nice landscape. You know where you are with a nice landscape."

I smile and pay and try to imagine my mother painting a nice landscape. It's impossible.

When I get to the pool, it's entirely empty. I sit on the edge with my lower legs in the water, adjusting the new goggles. The water is cool, but not unpleasantly so, though it still makes me gasp when I finally slip in. I used to be on the school team, but it's been a long time since I've swum; it's almost a surprise to me that I remember how. It's more of a surprise how much I enjoy it: the cool caress of the water along my body, the stretch of my muscles as I reach forward to catch the water. It feels clean and fresh and pure, and it makes me feel like I could be that way too. I'm aware of someone else, a man, entering the water, and swimming laps rather quicker than I am, but we keep to ourselves; there's no need to interact. And then we happen to have both stopped for a breather at the same end at the same time, and our polite nods turn to surprise. "Detective!" I say at exactly the same time as he says, "Ailsa!"

"I think under the circumstances you could probably call me Bryn," he says with a mild hint of drollery. He's standing in the waist-deep water, his goggles pushed up on his forehead. I can't avoid noticing his lean muscle, how his collarbones extend like a broad beam placed atop his torso. His pale shoulders are copiously dusted with freckles. I realize he's the same man that I watched swim before, when I was looking for Glen.

"Are you a member here?" I sink myself to my chin in the water, absurdly self-conscious.

He nods. "I swim here two or three times a week. You?"

"I've just joined. First swim."

"Then welcome," he says. There's more of a smile in his eyes than I have ever seen before, as if the water has refreshed him, woken him up.

"Thanks. Actually I'm nearly done."

"I won't be too far behind you." He seems far more at ease than I. "Do you have time for a coffee afterward?"

I pause with my hands on the goggles on my own forehead. "Should I? Is this official?"

He shrugs equivocally. "Look, if it's a bad time—"

"No, it's fine. I'll see you in the café."

"Perfect. Whoever gets there first can order. Mine's a flat white."

"Black Americano."

By the time I've settled my goggles, he's already off, eating up the yards with his long limbs. I swim two hundred meters more, then climb awkwardly from the pool and scuttle for the changing room, feeling as if his eyes are on me, even though I can still hear the steady turnover of his stroke.

I'm conscious of not wanting to tarry in the changing room, but he still beats me to the café; I find him sprawled in an armchair at one of the low coffee tables with the best view over the valley, peering at his phone. He's not dressed in a suit but in dark jeans and a turtleneck sweater. It makes an extraordinary difference. I can't help but view him as I would if I met him in a pub, say, or a coffee shop. I *am* meeting him in a coffee shop. I wish he was in the suit.

He looks up with a ghost of a smile as I approach. "Black Americano," he says, levering himself more upright to push an enormous mug toward me.

"Thanks." I sink into the chair opposite him. It's the kind of low, squashy affair that one can either perch on the edge of or loll back in. I don't feel relaxed enough to loll. "What do I owe you?"

He shakes his head minutely. "I think I can run to one coffee."

"Well. Thanks then." I gesture toward his clothing. "Not in work today?"

"Not today. Not officially." He's looking me over carefully, but it doesn't feel invasive. "You look a bit brighter than when I saw you last."

"You too, if I'm honest." He inclines his head: *Touché.* Suddenly I want to put off the questioning for as long as possible. I force myself to lean back in the chair, cradling my coffee on my lap. "Have you been living here for long?"

"Just over eighteen months. We moved up from Cardiff when Jill—my wife—first got diagnosed. She wanted to be near her family, and I managed to get this job . . ."

There's something about the way he says her name. "Is she—?"

"She died. Brain tumor. It was supposed to be operable, but there were complications . . . She died three months after we moved up." His delivery is matter-of-fact, but there's a bleakness in his eyes that catches at me.

"I'm so sorry." His lips twist in acknowledgment in the smile I've seen on other days, with no warmth in it. It makes a difference that I now understand why, though. I'm coloring him in, in my mind. "Do you think about going back to Cardiff?"

"Yeah, but I'm not sure it would be any better. Maybe I'd just miss her more, in all the places we used to go together . . . This is like starting over, apart from the odd Sunday lunch with the in-laws." He pauses to correct himself. "Ex-in-laws, I suppose."

I raise my eyebrows, grateful for the opportunity to inject some humor. "How is that?"

He spreads a hand in some kind of equivocation. I haven't quite decoded his gestures yet. "Kind of nice, kind of weird."

"I suppose it would be." I look out through the window. There are shadows racing across the steep slopes of the opposite side of the valley, from clouds scudding through the sky above. If I stayed here, I suppose it would be that way for me too: a new start. New friends, a new job, a clean break. Except that the Manse isn't clean. It's rotten and fetid and rank somewhere inside, somewhere I can't see, but I can feel it all the same.

"Are you still at the McCues'?"

"Yes. Which means I get to do bedtime stories with Callum. I may never leave."

He smiles. "He's a sweet kid. Brave soldier too." He pauses. "His mum has an interesting reputation."

He's fishing, though I expect he already knows more than me. "Does she?" He smiles a little at my refusal to take the bait. "Are you done with the Manse?"

"We were done yesterday. Didn't you get the message?"

"No." I automatically look at my phone, and in fact it does have a message, but not from him. It's from Pete: *Call me when you can. It's about the painting x.* "Reception round here can be kind of sketchy." He nods. "So I can go back there?"

"Yes." Then he adds, "Though I wouldn't until you've got a security alarm sorted out."

"That should be in place tomorrow, I think."

He takes a sip of his coffee, and then says, without the merest hint of a change of pace, "Were you going to tell me about the fox and the raven?"

I lean forward to put my coffee down on the table, marveling once again at his ability to jump track with no signal. "Ben, I suppose?"

"Ali, actually. He mentioned in passing that the vet confirmed the fox was poisoned. He assumed I already knew about its existence." He puts a heavy stress on *assumed.*

Ali. To my pals. Of which it seems Detective Bryn Laws might be one. "How do you know Ali?"

"The tri club—triathlon. We cycle together. He was one of the first people I met here." I stare at him for a moment, trying to imagine them both in Lycra. Having seen Laws's lean musculature in the pool, it's easy enough to place him on a bike, but I can't see Ali beside him, no matter how hard I try. He sighs in mock exasperation. "Come on, it's not that ludicrous."

"It is if we're talking about the same Ali."

That brings a twist of amusement to his lips. "Middle-aged men in Lycra. It's a thing these days. Not," he adds hurriedly, "that I'd consider myself middle-aged yet."

"Uh-huh."

"You're buying yourself time," he observes mildly, but there's still a hint of a smile around his ice-blue eyes. "Why didn't you tell me about the fox and the raven?"

"Because there was nothing to tell. The Manse is in the Scottish countryside—take a look." I fling a hand toward the mountains that stand implacably beyond the glass. "Animals die. They have to do it somewhere. What do you want from me?"

"You weren't in the slightest bit spooked?" I look at him warily, sensing a trap. *If he was in a suit,* I think, *if we were in a sterile room in the police station, for example, with thick-painted walls and a crappy coffee machine—if we were there, rather than here as we are with him in jeans, I would have a chance. I might see whatever is coming.* His eyes are holding mine, and there's no longer a smile in their vicinity. "What did the Post-it note say?"

Oh dear God. Now I look like a raving loony. "You tell me. You obviously have it."

"We do. We took another pass at the garden after Ali told us about the animals. It's suffered from water damage, but the lab will figure out what it says in time. Why don't we shortcut that?" He leans forward, his elbows on his knees, exasperation carefully reined in—real exasperation this time—but I can sense it beneath the surface. "Come on, Ailsa, what did it say?"

"I don't remember exactly."

"Roughly will do."

"I thought you would think I'm overreacting. I thought you would think I'm nuts." It sounds like a lament. It *is* a lament.

"Because you received a threat pinned to a bird?"

"What?" Then I twig. "Oh, you thought it was a threat to *me*." It's almost funny.

He cocks his head. "It's not?"

"No. It's a response."

"A response. *From* you?" I nod. His confusion is even funnier. "Saying what?"

"Saying . . . saying . . . yes, okay, I'm going to tell you! It said: fuck off, I'm not scared and I'm not leaving."

I may actually have surprised him. He sits back in his seat, wide-eyed, and takes a sip of his coffee. "And you, erm, stuck it to the dead bird? With a safety pin?"

"Yes. Ask Ben—he watched me do it." Then I add miserably, "Is that . . . It's not against the law, is it?"

He blinks. "No, I don't think so. If you'd pinned it to a dead human, that would be different."

"Good to know," I say faintly.

"Who were you expecting to receive this message?"

"I don't know. Really, I don't." The litany of names cycles through my head: *Fiona, Ben, Ali, Jamie.* And I can't see what any of them would have to gain. The nutcase stranger theory might actually be more realistic. "Believe me, if I knew that, I'd be telling you."

"Really." He's surveying me again, with those ice-blue eyes above a freckled nose. "I know you're lying to me."

"I'm not—"

"You didn't tell me about the animals, yet you were spooked enough to stake a note onto a maggot-ridden carcass. Most peo-

ple I know wouldn't have touched that pile of feathers with a barge
pole."

"I wore Marigolds." He throws up both hands in an unmistakable
gesture. "Okay, yes, I get your point! I was just worried you'd think I
was some kind of neurotic mess." Which I may be. "And anyway, it was
more of an omission, really. I'm not lying now." *Except I am, about
Fiona . . .* I find I'm rubbing my temples with my fingers. "What did
the vet say about the fox?"

"That it must have been transported deliberately to your property.
With that dosage, it couldn't have gone far from wherever it was poisoned."

"Right," I say after a moment when I can't think of anything else
to say.

"Whose idea was it that Carrie come up north with you?"

"Mine. I invited her." But no, that's not quite right. She didn't invite herself, but it was more organic than a simple suggestion from me.
"Why?"

He shrugs. "Families are complicated things."

I laugh out loud. "You've got to be kidding. Carrie has nothing to
do with all of this."

"Maybe not, but you haven't lived with her for years. How well do
you really know her?"

"I know—" I stop. I can see her now, climbing into the jeep, her
coat flaring out around her. "I know her," I repeat stubbornly. She
might be lying to me, but she's not terrorizing me.

She didn't believe me about the flies. Or she pretended not to.

This is ridiculous. Carrie has no grudge against me.

He puts his coffee back down on the table and his elbows on his
knees again, leaning in earnestly. "Ailsa, I don't know what the hell is
going on, but any which way I look at it, you're at the center of it. It
just doesn't make sense that you arrive and suddenly there's dead animals on your doorstep and bones in your house—a house in which you
had all the locks changed, let's not forget. You *have* to be the catalyst—"

"I agree."

"Then why are you keeping things from me? It's written all over your face."

"I'm not, and I can't help it, this is just my face."

He starts to say something but stops himself and takes a deep breath. His next words are down a few notches in pace and volume. "I'm trying to help you. Are you scared?"

I look out at the mountains. It's not a landscape for reassurance. "Yes." I look back at him, but then I have to look away again or the tears that are assaulting my throat might find a pathway out.

"What of?"

Everything. Everything, everything, everything. Never finding out what happened to my father, finding out my father is dead. Throwing away my relationship with Jonathan and never being happy, keeping my relationship with Jonathan and never being happy. Throwing away my career, losing myself in my career, losing the chance to build bridges with Carrie, losing myself, losing my mind . . . and always, always the Manse. I whisper it. "The Manse."

To his credit, he doesn't look skeptical. "Ali says there's some strange tales about it." I nod again. He scratches his chin with a thumb. "I don't blame you for not feeling safe there after all of this."

"I have to go back."

"You really don't."

"I do. I have to. Carrie would think I was running away again." I dash a hand across one treacherous eye.

"Again?" I shake my head minutely and look out at the mountains. He leaves it a moment, his elbows still on his knees, his eyes and his thoughts elsewhere. "I don't have the manpower to put an officer on you for protection."

I nod.

His knee is bouncing as he thinks. "Do me a favor and send me a text when you're moving back into the Manse. I can make sure any cars in the vicinity swing by from time to time. It's not much, but . . ." He grimaces.

"Okay. You haven't had anything back from the lab yet?"

"Not yet. We should have something tomorrow, or the next day. I'll let you know."

"Okay." He's still looking at me, his frustration barely bridled, and I can see that he still thinks I'm being deliberately difficult and obtuse. "Bryn," I say quietly. "It's not that I don't want to help. I just don't know anything that could."

He holds my gaze for a moment, and then says mildly, "If you say so." I wish he was in a suit.

MY FATHER IS DUST AND BONE. THAT'S ALL HE HAS BEEN FOR the last twenty-seven years and that's all he ever can be. He took an earlier flight back from his trip; when he found his car battery was flat, he bused into Edinburgh and then hopped on a train. He was thinking that he would surprise his little girl; he was thinking of the smile that would light up her face (though perhaps not his wife's). But they weren't home, and it was a burglar he surprised instead—a burglar with a crowbar that was used to fatal effect . . .

I won't think about this. I won't.

TWENTY

I call Pete from the car park, sheltering in the warmth of the car to escape the rain that threatens. The clouds have completely overtaken the blue now, and there's a heft to the wind; it means to push and shove rather than play.

It's good to hear Pete's voice, though he sounds older than he did before. Before . . . *what?* I'm not quite sure when the watershed point was. When my mother died, or some point before? I've missed out on more than just Carrie by chasing every news story around the globe. But Carrie has clearly brought him up to speed—I spend at least the first ten minutes of the call dissuading him from getting on a plane, trying to reassure him that he needn't worry, that I'm fine, that Carrie's fine, that we are keeping ourselves safe.

Stay safe, Jonathan would say. But Jonathan hasn't got on a plane. He hasn't even offered. We spoke last night, a snatched conversation given it was still his working day in DC. He's horrified, of course. I thought he might at least *offer* to come, even if that offer was based on a calculation that I would tell him to stay put. But no. There were things I wanted to say but he had to get off the phone, and I looked at my silent Blackberry for several heartbeats after he hung up, thinking that every thought unuttered, every sentence unsaid, moves us further apart. Our DNA cannot handle the strain. Already I see it like a fraying rope, the liberated ends of the broken fibers swaying gently in any breath of breeze.

"When will you hear?" Pete asks. I know he means about the identity of the bones. It has become like a Schrödinger's cat experiment in my head. Right now the bones are both my father's, and not my father's; both possibilities exist simultaneously. Even though whichever outcome does in fact come to pass is already determined, has possibly been determined for twenty-seven years, it will somehow only come into effect at the point that Detective Laws—Bryn—calls me. Until then my father is both alive and dead.

"A day or two more. It depends on how busy the labs are. A current murder would take precedence over this." New bones, with flesh and dried blood on them. As these must have been once upon a time, regardless of who they once belonged to.

"I suppose that's fair." I can picture him tugging on one of his long-lobed ears. "I expect you can think of little else."

"Something like that." The Schrödinger's cat experiment extends to my feelings about the potential outcomes, too, and my feelings about those feelings . . . I simultaneously want the bones to be my father's, because then he never voluntarily left me, and I hate myself for feeling that; and I don't want them to be my father's, because then he could still be alive and I hate myself for not knowing better than to cling on to such pitiful hope. "Though it does help actually being out of the Manse." I can at least breathe again. I can sleep again.

"Your mother hated that house, you know."

"I have some sympathy with that," I say wryly, and I hear a breath of a grim chuckle from him. Though in truth, I couldn't say that I hate it myself, not all of it. There are versions of it I could perhaps grow to love, if they could find a way to stay fixed. I hesitate to ask my next question. "She wasn't . . . scared in it, was she?"

"I don't think so. She just said that she could never sleep properly. Why, were you scared there when you were little?"

"I don't think so." I've tried to give it proper consideration. "I don't have a lot of memories, but in the ones I have, I think I was . . . at home." At home in the Manse. I'm surprised by a wave of longing. "But it's certainly an odd place. Mercurial, I suppose."

"Mercurial." He sounds amused. "That's a strange description for a house."

"It's a strange house. You should come and see it sometime." It's easy to imagine Pete in the Manse. I fancy there would be a sort of mutual respect between them. "Was it . . . was it just the house she hated, or was it everything here?"

He blows down the phone, thinking. "I don't know, pet. She wasn't much for talking about it. The past is another country and all that . . . But I don't think she was very happy then. If your dad hadn't disappeared, I doubt they would have lasted much longer." He gives me space to say something, but he doesn't press. I appreciate that about him. He's always been happy to let me come to things at my own pace. When I don't speak, he moves on. "So, no safe place."

"What?"

"That's the name of the painting you sent me a snap of. *No Safe Place*. Never my favorite piece."

I tell him about Callum's reaction to the painting, and he laughs uproariously, like I knew he would. My cheeks are aching with smiles at hearing him, but my eyes are curiously blurry. *I miss him.* I will miss him enormously if anything should happen to him. These little hooks, they catch and hold me; I feel them bite. I'm no different to Carrie after all: my mother's passing has made me all too aware of Pete's advancing years. "Anyway, it's the oddest thing," he continues.

"What is?"

"Well, I checked the books, and it's supposed to be in Denmark. She sold it in the mid-eighties. For a pittance, if I'm honest; it was one of the first. She got barely enough for a decent supermarket shop out of it."

"Then how come it's in the Manse?"

"I haven't the faintest. I've put a call in to the chap who bought it. Perhaps he'd swapped it for another, and we didn't record it, or we were supposed to be selling it for him and somehow it fell through the cracks. Though I'd be surprised." I would too. Between them, Karen and Pete were very on top of all the business aspects. Pete still runs an extremely reputable gallery and art dealing has been his life's work. Both of them knew that you could never afford to neglect a customer.

"Wait, Carrie said a guy from Denmark came to the funeral—is it the same person?"

"That's right. I'll let you know if I hear anything. Speaking of Carrie, um, are you two getting along all right?"

I blink. "Fine." He doesn't say anything. "Were you expecting that we might not?" I add a half laugh to make the question sound like I'm teasing him.

He laughs a little awkwardly in return. "Well, it's been a long time since you spent any time together. You're both grown-ups now; you're different people from when you last lived together. And you can both be . . ."

"Delightful. Charming. Stormingly good company."

"That's exactly what I was trying to say." His chuckle is genuine this time. "You know she only took the Edinburgh part because of you. She could have been doing a Tom Stoppard thing instead."

"Really? I didn't—I didn't know about that."

"Well. Anyway. *No Safe Place*: mind you keep it stored properly in case we've got to ship it back. No direct sunlight—"

"I know, I know, I've not forgotten." I change the subject quickly before I get a long lecture on the proper care, storage and transportation of oil paintings. "Anyway, tell me what you've been up to." And he does. He tells me lots of things, and I read in each of them the message he's trying to give me: he's keeping busy and there's nothing to worry about. But I will, and so will he.

It was easier, when I was away. No hooks to catch me, no bonds to tie me. Stories to tell, but none of them of people I love, none of them mine. Easier, certainly.

———————

I'm back at the farmhouse, in the yard, having popped out to rather inelegantly retrieve my phone charger from under the driver's seat of my car—head down, bottom in the air—when I hear something from the direction of Jamie's flat. Raised voices, perhaps? Though more likely he has that enormous television on particularly loudly. But when I emerge triumphant with charger in hand, I spot a familiar figure descending the stairs down from Jamie's rooms.

"Ben," I call.

He looked like he was about to head off across the fields, but he turns. "Oh, uh, hi. I . . . uh, I didn't quite expect to see you here." He visibly regroups, and strives for his trademark affable charm, but it's a far cry from his usual effort. "Which is silly of me since Fiona said you were staying."

"Yes, she and Glen have been very kind." I look at him more closely. "Are you okay?"

He raises his eyebrows. "Shouldn't I be the one asking you that?"

I find a smile. "I'm okay. Have you been out for a constitutional?"

"What?" I gesture at his muddy shoes. "Oh, yeah. Right. Getting some fresh air. Then I thought I'd come and see if Fiona is around."

"She's in the house, but she's about to take Callum to his football match, I think." Why was he looking for her in Jamie's digs? I wonder.

We turn for the farmhouse together, then he puts a hand on my arm to draw me to a halt. "You know, I wanted to ask you: did you tell the police about the animals?"

"No, I couldn't think of a way to do it without sounding nuts. But Ali told them anyway."

"That's good, right? It's part of the overall picture, surely? That someone is targeting you?"

"That seems to be the conclusion."

He falls quiet and we move toward the farmhouse again. "If it *is* your father . . . I'm so sorry, this would be no way to find that out. Though I suppose it might offer some kind of closure . . ."

"To be honest, I think it would offer more questions." We're just outside the farmhouse door now.

"Yeah," he says. Then, more quietly, "Yeah, I suppose that's right."

I touch his arm. "Are you sure you're okay?"

"Of course. All good." He smiles and opens the door without knocking in a way that speaks of years of familiarity. "Hello, hello—ah, Glen! How are you?" The kitchen seems smaller with Ben in it, shaking hands vigorously with Fiona's father, and tousling Callum's hair whilst Fiona attempts to pull a tracksuit top over Callum's head. It's already apparent to me that Callum is the beating heart of this house. Fiona and Glen revolve around his timetable.

"Is it Doune we're playing?" Callum asks, when his head emerges.

"Aye," says Fiona, her head bent as she ties Callum's lace. He's only wearing one football boot.

"Oh no!" he groans. "Then Stuart Davidson will be there. He's a wee gobshite."

"Callum!" exclaims Fiona.

"Well, he is," he says stubbornly.

"Go and find your other boot. And some better language," she says sternly.

"Who's Stuart Davidson?" I ask as Callum disappears through the door.

"A wee gobshite," says Fiona, to a bark of laughter from Ben that sounds overly loud. "And he's going to be on particularly special form today when Doune wins."

"What?" Callum is already back in the doorway, a boot in his hand. "Mum! We're not going to lose *again*, are we?"

I glance at Fiona, expecting to hear *I meant if*, or one of the many encouraging things that any parent might say, but all she manages is, "Just play your best, wee man. Do that and you'll have a great game."

"Hey, Callum, shall I come and watch?" Ben says, in a transparent distraction attempt, but it works. Callum erupts in an enthusiastic cheer. "I'll drive you, shall I?" Ben says to Fiona. "We can catch up."

"Uh, sure. Thanks," she says casually, but her gaze stays on him until Callum asks her for a water bottle. Then there's a crescendo of noise and bustle as Callum, Fiona and Ben clear out of the kitchen, leaving Glen and me alone in the loudly silent farmhouse with Glen's black Lab, Sheba, and a sleeping Toast. Glen smiles at me awkwardly. Since I arrived, he's been gruffly welcoming and quietly, genuinely horrified by the circumstances. I can see that he can't quite believe the bones can be those of his old friend, and yet he's thinking what we are all thinking: who else could they belong to? All except Fiona, that is. I know she has always believed they are his.

"I've been meaning to show you something. I'll be back in a second." I nip off to my bedroom—Callum's bedroom—and return with the box of my father's research.

"Goodness," Glen says, as he leafs through the contents. There's a reverence in the way he holds the book that touches me. "I knew he was taking it seriously, but this is . . ."

Obsessive. "Yes. I know."

"Well, he did seem fair passionate about it." He reads on. "Window tax records! Smart man, your father."

"All done pre-Internet. I suppose he must have actually gone to public record offices or something." All that effort. A labor of love, surely. Or a way to avoid the breakdown of love.

"Aye, he did that. Wee research trips." He reads out loud from the front of the jotter. *"Love makes a furnace of the soul.* I remember that. He wanted to find out who wrote it." Me too. And why. And what they meant. "And the kirk, he wanted to find the kirk. It's not short of secrets, that house. Though it doesnae seem about to give them up."

I fish out the aerial photos. "Here, take a look at these. I think they came just after he disappeared." He puts the jotter down carefully to take them. "Callum says the path on this one—see here?—isn't there anymore."

"He would know; he loves to take Toast round there. I dinnae let him go alone, though, not by the water." He flips through the photos again, then pauses on the last two, that don't contain the Manse. "Now that's interesting."

"What?

"This is the falls—see here? You cannae get up there now, with the landslips. But these must have been taken before. Martin thought there was a memorial up there."

I grab for one of the jotters. "Yes! I read that somewhere. He found notes on a Sunday collection for an unspecified memorial. He thought it might prove the church fire story, right? Yes, look, here—he thought it might have been in memory of all those that died. But . . ." I read the date in his notes. "1802. That's far too late. That would have been years after the actual fire."

Glen takes the jotter off me. "Aye, but that doesnae surprise me. The English would never have allowed a memorial at the time. It would have been a lovely spot for it too. I remember it from before the landslips. Fair overgrown, though. There could easily have been something up there somewhere." He turns a page, then frowns. "Now that's interesting."

"The list of names? Yes, I saw that. Turn the page—" He gives a short, surprised bark as he reads the entry I'm pointing to, written clearly in my father's decisive script. *Callum McCue, babe in arms.* "I don't think my dad knew if they were donors for the memorial or names to go on it. The church records weren't clear."

"I didnae think there were any McCues round here until the nineteen hundreds. We were mostly in Ireland and then Lanarkshire before then. What a coincidence!" He frowns slightly. "Seems odd to list a babe as a donor, though."

"Maybe those are the names on the memorial then." We fall silent together. I'm thinking of the raging inferno inside the church. My mind skitters away from imagining the final moments of those trapped inside; it's simply too horrific. *Babe in arms.* Whose arms, though? I take the jotter from him and read the list of names again. There isn't another McCue.

Glen shakes himself, then peers at the photos of the falls again, then hands them to me. "I cannae see anything on these, though." I don't know what I should be looking for, but whatever it is fails to jump out at me.

Glen glances at Sheba. "She could use a walk. Shall we go and take a look for the path by the loch?"

His immediacy takes me aback, but I don't want to seem rude, which is how I come to be walking through the wood with Glen, his black Labrador running ahead of us. There are clusters of bluebells at the base of some of the trees, and in one area, a full carpet of them in a sun-dappled grove. "It's beautiful here. I always think I should get a dog when I'm walking through here."

He snorts. "Not if you're living at the Manse." I glance sideways at him. "You willnae get a dog in there."

"You've tried?" When would he have tried? Has the whole bloody McCue family been wandering through the property? A comic book–style image jumps into my head of Glen trying to shove poor Sheba through an open window.

"Sometimes Callum and I walk the dogs that way."

"Ah." That's more feasible. "Fiona's lucky to have you around to help."

"Aye, well." He doesn't take a compliment easily. "It was a bit of a shock when she turned up with him, but it's easier being a grandpa, I can tell you."

"Were Fiona and Jamie that bad?" I ask lightly.

"Well. I wasnae the perfect dad, either. It took a long time to get Fiona diagnosed. And Jamie . . . well, he was Jamie." He grimaces. "If

I'd known that Fi . . . I like to think I would have handled things different. Been gentler, maybe. Fewer thrashings and more talking. Like all these modern dads I keep hearing about."

"It was a different time, I suppose."

"Aye, it was. And I was a different man, in many ways. I hadnae learned to cope with missing my wife." I look over again, surprised at his honesty. He's very determinedly not looking at me at all. This walk was never about finding the path. "I'm partly to blame. Just like the way you are, the way your life has turned out, is partly because we never found your dad. That was my job and . . . I didnae do it. And I'm sorry for that."

"Well." I'm caught off-balance. Once again, I've failed to appreciate that my parents' story touched more lives than mine. "Well, I . . . I believe you did everything you could."

"I did."

"And my life isn't *that* bad," I say drolly. "When I'm not being terrorized out of my own home, that is."

He expels air sharply in what might be a laugh. We've reached the loch already, and we search the edge for a few minutes, looking for any sign of a path that might match the photo. But there's nothing to be seen there now.

Later, back at the farmhouse, Callum comes home red cheeked and muddy. I ask him what the score was, and he tells me they lost 5–3, but he was the one who scored all three. And Stuart Davidson was an absolute gobshite to him afterward.

MY FATHER IS . . . I DON'T KNOW, I CAN'T THINK, I WON'T THINK about it. He's dead, or alive; he's a thief, or a victim; he's . . . I won't think about it, I won't think about any of it, because whatever else he might be, my father is not here.

TWENTY-ONE

It's done.

The DNA of Jonathan and me, those intertwining strands and bonds that made we two into an *us*, has been torn asunder. Actually, not torn, exactly, since I more or less took a knife to the sections which were still holding together. A clean break, a neat slice, if there ever could be such a thing in matters of the heart.

I miss you, he said.

You could always get on a plane.

Carrie calls me just as I'm waving off the man who has fitted the Manse with an alarm. I texted her that Jonathan and I had a fight, though *fight* is not the right word—it suggests fire and fury, whereas this was a study in measured statements, at least until the last few exchanges. I'm not sure whether I texted her because I wanted her to call me or because she would have wanted me to reach out, but it amounts to the same in the end. "Are you okay? What happened?"

You know I can't do that, he said.

I know you won't do that.

"We spoke this morning. It went badly." A wry laugh escapes me. I think it's a laugh. "I made sure it went badly." I'm wandering through the ground floor of the Manse as we talk. When I got here, the alarm guy was already waiting for me, and this is the first time I've been alone in the house since I found the skull.

The skull.

"Are you sure it's over?" Carrie asks hesitantly.

"Yes. It's been coming a long time. We worked because I would make the effort, I'd bend my life to match his." The rooms are very quiet, but the Manse is listening to me. "I'm tired of doing that."

I don't want to fight, he said.

Sure.

Oh, come on, Ailsa, what do you actually want from me?

Maybe I do want you to fight. Maybe I want you to fight for me.

Jesus, Ailsa, what does that even mean?

"You shouldn't have to bend," she says. "It should be more . . . organic than that. Honey, I'm really sorry." I hear her blow out a breath down the phone. "I'll get back as quick as I can tonight. Just . . . be kind to yourself today, okay?"

Be kind to myself. I don't know what that equates to in her mind. Chocolates, a trashy magazine? A hot bath with scented candles?

I climb the stairs to the second floor and stand in the landing. If this was a television series, there would be some kind of police tape hanging limply from the doorframe of the spare bedroom, but there's nothing to show that someone once carefully placed a human skull in there. I head into my own bedroom instead.

Detective Laws still hasn't called. The bones are still in both states: they are my father's and they aren't. And I am, too, though I think I have splintered into more than two states. There's the Ailsa that believes there's nothing to fear, that every oddity can be explained away, and there's the Ailsa that sees the layers beneath the Manse. There's the Ailsa that's suspicious of each and every person here: Ali, Jamie, Fiona, Ben—Jesus, even Carrie (*How well do you really know her?*). That's the Ailsa that scares me most. She might be the one I can never shake.

I sit on my bed and look around the room. Even with the alarm, I don't know how I'm going to be able to sleep here tonight. A sudden shiver runs through me, and it occurs to me that the house is cold. Perhaps the flame on the boiler has snuffed out again. I really ought to get it serviced.

A door thuds.

I know it will be the bathroom door. I know that even if I go and close it, even if I test that it's so tightly shut that I can't force it open, only minutes later it will be thudding again. I sit and listen to it. *Thud. Thud. Thud-thud.* If Carrie was here, the Manse wouldn't be clamoring for my attention in this way.

It's a day for bold decisions. When Carrie comes back, I will tell her we should leave.

The phone in my hand suddenly rings again.

"Ailsa, I need to talk to you."

"Ben?" I know it's Ben—it says so on the screen—but it's not the usual Ben. He sounds ragged and flustered, a far cry from his usual laid-back demeanor. "Are you okay?"

"Yes, but I need to talk to you."

"Fire away." *Thud.*

"No, I mean in person. I can't do it now," Ben says. "Fiona too. Will you be home tonight?"

"Uh, sure." I pause. *Thud.* "Are you sure everything is okay?"

"Fine, of course, nothing to worry about. I just need to chat something through with you. I'll come round later."

Nothing to worry about? Really? "Wait—can we meet at the pub? It would be good to get out of the house." The house I just got back into. The house I've just discovered I can't stay in alone. I thought I could, but I was wrong.

"The Quaich? Yes, okay, fine. Six o'clock?"

"See you then."

Six o'clock. I just have to survive the Manse until six o'clock.

_____

The Quaich.

I dither over whether I should walk there or take the car—it's not at all far, but the car would restrict me to one drink, and in my current far-from-balanced state, perhaps even one drink is too many. But in the end I leave early and decide to walk without analyzing the reason for that decision, admiring the play of the light on the heather, searching out the winking river at the bottom of the glen and feeling the chill breeze gradually win out over the diminishing strength of the evening sunlight. *If I go back to London*, I think, *I should make sure I don't work with Jonathan.* And then I think, what is there for me in London now that I've cleaved myself from Jonathan? What is there for me here once Carrie's play is over? What is there to tie me to any place at all?

Despite the fact that I'm a good fifteen minutes early, Ben is already seated at a table when I get there, nursing a pint with half an eye on the door whilst he chats to the waitress. A different waitress tonight, but one no less smitten with him. "Ailsa," he calls, climbing out of his chair, and I lift a hand and head over. He must have showered after work: his hair is damp and there's a strong smell of his aftershave when he kisses me on the cheek. He's exactly the relaxed, at-ease character I first met, except he's not, quite. Something is off. I try to figure out what as he asks me what I want to drink. There's a tightness around his eyes, perhaps, and I find an answering tightness developing in my chest. *Nothing to worry about.* I knew that was rubbish.

"So what is it you wanted to talk about?" I ask as lightly as I can when I have a glass of wine in front of me.

"Best wait for Fiona and Jamie," he says easily. "Save me having to say things twice." So, Jamie too. Earlier it was only Fiona. "Oh, here they are."

I glance up to find them both crossing toward us. They pause to give a drinks order to the waitress and then I'm enveloped in the ensuing hellos. Jamie kisses me on the cheek and, after a slight hesitation,

Fiona does the same; I have to bend my head to facilitate it. Ben gets a hug, though. I sense that's more natural for her. She's dressed in jeans and a light fleece, a thoroughly no-effort attire, but she has mascara on. I'm not sure I've ever seen her wearing makeup before. It suits her.

"Callum's missing you already," she says with a smile. "He doesnae think you should be on your own."

I don't think I should be alone, either. Not in the Manse, which is why I won't be staying there. But if I say that, there will be twenty minutes of discussion before Ben tells me why I'm here. "Bless, I miss him too."

"Is the alarm set up now?" Jamie asks. "Ah, thank you," he says to the waitress who has just delivered the drinks. "Does it go straight to the police?"

I nod. "Yep. I'm terrified I'm going to set it off by accident and look like a moron." A thought strikes me. "God, I'd better text Carrie the code, otherwise she might set it off." I grab my phone.

"Aye, you'd definitely look like a moron if it goes off the very first day," says Fiona.

It's small talk, this. They are filling the gap, waiting for Ben to start. A small silence falls, and we all look at Ben, who looks round the table at each of us then clears his throat. "Okay. So." He turns to me. "Ailsa. There's something we need to tell you." His gaze drops to the table. "It's . . . it's not an easy thing. Just please try to hear us out."

I look around the table at the three of them. Jamie tries for a reassuring smile. Fiona looks like she's simply watching. "I . . . Okay."

"When Jamie and Fiona were little, sometimes they'd play up the river. You know, where the waterfalls are?"

"I haven't been there. Didn't you tell me the river path is unsafe at the moment?"

Ben nods. "It is. In summer you can usually get up to the waterfalls quite easily, though. You used to be able to get a lot farther, but there were landslides after a storm one year, and the path has been officially closed, right from the bottom, ever since. Any of us would have got our arses tanned for playing there, which I guess was part of the appeal. Fi and Jamie went there a lot. They would even climb the rocks and head up way past the falls." Why is Ben relating this story when it's about Jamie and Fiona?

As if Jamie can hear my thoughts, he takes up the tale. "We found something. It didnae mean anything to us; we were too wee, I suppose. It became part of our game." He stops.

"What?" I prompt. "What did you find?"

"We found a skeleton," Jamie says.

I stare round the table wordlessly. Jamie and Ben are leaning in, shiningly earnest. Fiona is sitting back, her mascara-rimmed eyes still watching. "A skeleton," I say quietly. A skeleton. My father, and not my father. Schrödinger's cat, again.

Jamie nods. "There had been a storm when we found it. I dinnae ken if some of the earth covering it had been washed away. Anyway, it must have been there for years; it was just bones."

A skeleton. By the falls. Where my father thought there might have been a memorial. I can imagine him now, perhaps home early from his trip, taking advantage of some free time to do a little research on foot. There's a heft to the image that scares me. It won't budge easily. Somehow, my journalistic training kicks in. "Were there clothes? Shoes? Anything?"

Jamie shakes his head.

"You didn't tell anyone?"

Jamie shakes his head. "We would have had to admit we were up there. We were only kids. We couldnae grasp that it was more important than a skelping."

"How old were you?"

"Seven, maybe?" He looks at Fiona, but she shrugs. "Around that. We hid them in a sort of mini cave; it was part of our game."

"Jesus, what kind of game do you play with a skeleton?"

"We were pirates. Or sometimes Jacobites," Jamie says. Fiona is frowning slightly, but he carries on. "Ben followed us up there one time. That's how he found out, but we swore him to secrecy."

"I wanted to tell," Ben explains. "I thought we ought to tell the police, but Fiona convinced me not to. She made me promise." He glances at Fiona with a slight smile. "I swear to God, I was scared of your father for years. You went mental when I wanted to tell. You had me thinking you'd be skinned alive."

Jamie's mouth twists. "Aye, well, he's far more mellow with Callum than he ever was with us."

"So you think . . ." I find I'm rubbing the bridge of my nose. "What, you think this was my father?"

"We didn't. Not at first. Everybody thought your dad ran off with the diamonds." Ben shrugs. "And we had no idea how old the bones were. They actually *could* have been from the Jacobite era for all we knew; no clothes remaining suggests *really* old. When we got older, we did start to wonder . . . I thought about going to the police, but I'd promised these two I wouldn't, and they didn't want to, and anyway the longer we left it, the harder it seemed . . . I don't know, it all seemed very *abstract*. And then you arrived and it wasn't so abstract anymore." He looks at the table. "Ever since you got here, I've been wondering. It's all I've been able to think about." The misery in his face is entirely genuine. Ben has failed himself. He's fallen short of his capitalized Ideals.

"I don't . . ." I shake my head.

"The point is this," Ben says. "After the bones started turning up in your house, I went to the cave." He grimaces. "Bloody lethal getting there; they're right to have closed the path. I was only there that one time, but the cave was just as I remembered it—a bit harder to climb up to now I've got a lot more bulk to haul, but otherwise the same. Only it was empty. The bones were gone. And then I went to see Jamie, to find out when he last saw them; no point in asking Fi." He directs a small smile at her to show no offense intended. "And he said . . ." He stops and looks at Jamie, who obligingly fills the gap.

"I was up there three weeks ago—nearly killed myself getting there, mind. But the bones were still there."

All three of them wait for me to speak, though that's not exactly a change of pace for Fiona. I can't think what to say.

Ben fills the silence. "I don't know whether they're your father's bones, but I think—we think that someone has taken them and is using them to terrorize you. We're going to go to the police tomorrow and explain. But we wanted to tell you first." He looks like a man who has finally got something off his chest. "I'm so sorry that we didn't do it before."

I take a sip of my wine. I still don't know what to say. Suddenly Fiona speaks, as if she's finally woken up. "It's your father," she says quietly. "It's always been your father."

"What?" Ben is staring at her, grabbing her shoulder. "Are you sure?" he asks shakily. "You've never said so before."

"I'm saying it now," she says to him, with an odd dignity. "It's her father. She ought to know."

"How do you know?" The words are mine, but I don't recognize the voice.

Fiona turns to me. "You know how I know."

"Fiona," says Jamie warningly.

"She's going to find out sooner or later. Sooner, I think. Maybe tomorrow." She turns her hazel eyes on me, bluntly sympathetic. "He died, Ailsa, all those years ago. I'm so sorry."

I leave.

———

Ben catches me when I'm maybe a third of the way home, stomping along the roadside. He slows his BMW to a walking pace with the window wound down. "Ailsa," he calls. "Please, get in. I'll give you a lift home."

"I'm happy walking." *Happy.* That's a joke, the universe's bad joke, and I'm the butt of it.

"We don't have to talk if you don't want to."

"Believe me, I *really* don't want to."

"It's raining."

"I daresay I'll survive." I walk on, pulling my coat tightly closed around my neck. What was originally a few meager drops of rain is rapidly becoming a very heavy shower. It's still light—it's not even seven o'clock—but the rain clouds are making it feel like dusk. Ben's headlights are on, painting the raindrops they can reach with a silver light.

"Come on, Ailsa, jump in. You're getting soaked."

He brings the car to a stop the moment I turn to face him. "Do you have any idea how completely fucked-up the lot of you are? Who on earth plays with a *skeleton?* At seven years old?" I have a vision of the three of them as children—Ben, Fiona and Jamie—sitting cross-legged in a circle around a toy tea set in a cave, with a grinning skeleton sitting upright as the fourth member of the gang.

"Believe me, I get it," he says earnestly. "I only saw it the once, and that was enough." Then he adds, wretchedly, "But I *promised.*"

"Jesus Christ," I mutter. It's not even him I'm upset at. Or maybe I am. Maybe I'm upset at absolutely everyone right now. I open the car door and get in. I'm probably soaking his luxury seats, but I really couldn't care less. To be fair to him, he doesn't seem to care either.

He drives in silence for a moment, sneaking nervous glances at me. It's too murky to see clearly across to the other side of the valley. The mountains that I know are there are an ominous dark shadow, crouching like a giant beast ready to pounce. "You know what Fi said . . ." he starts hesitantly. "About it being . . ."

"Yes. What kind of person would *say* something like that? Without a shred of evidence?" Except I know why she would say it—and I know she believes it. I hate that one of my splintered selves believes it too.

"The thing is . . . The thing is, she's always right."

"Is this another piece of crap like time folding at the Manse?" My delivery is brutal. My filter has gone; it's been blown sky-high by the roiling fury within me. I can't even begin to describe how completely I want to wash my hands of Ben, Fiona, Jamie, the Manse, everything, everything, everything. I wish for the rain to wash me clean and clear and pure again, but it doesn't seem to be that type of rain.

"Look," he says patiently, but stubbornly. "The Manse is . . . whatever. The Manse is the Manse. But I can tell you, you're just shooting the messenger. Fi is right. She's always right. You can believe it or not, as you like. But if you choose not to, then you're just ignoring the evidence. You've seen it yourself. We all have. Everyone round here knows it, whether they acknowledge it or not. She might not have a bloody clue what time it is or when things happened, but if she tells you something, she's right." He glances at me. I'm thinking of a drunken Fiona outside the Quaich: *A Fi fact. Incontrovertible.* I'm thinking of Piotr and the accident in front of him; I'm thinking of Callum's football score. *Callum. I will miss him,* I think, and something twists in my chest, *but we have to leave.* I'll tell Carrie; I'll convince her to leave too. I should have left weeks ago. I should never have come back here in the first place.

Ben goes on after a moment. "So I wanted to say . . . I'm sorry. I should have gone to the police all those years ago. I know I should have. It would have made a difference in your life for you to know."

That's too big a topic to try to pick at right now. "You said you promised." We're already turning into the drive of the Manse. He parks in front, only meters from where he found the fox, with the engine still running, then looks at me, waiting for my question. "Why? Why didn't they want to go to the police?"

"They were scared of getting into trouble with Glen. I mean, *really* scared. He was pretty tough on them." He shrugs. "Parenting was different then: nobody was afraid to spank their kids; the school still used the belt—do you remember?" I do remember. I remember our collective fear of it as pupils. I don't know if I ever actually saw it, but in my head it was a broad thick strip of brown leather. I remember the horror that the thought of it elicited in me—and the burning outrage. "Jamie was a wee shite. He hadn't learned to play the system like he does, so he was on the receiving end of some harsh discipline. And Fi had her own problems, but none of them had been diagnosed then, so sometimes she just seemed willfully difficult." He looks forward through the windscreen with a shrug of his shoulders. The wipers are working in a steady continuous sweep, but they can't quite keep up with the deluge. The raindrops that I can see falling through the silver light of the headlamps are fleetingly sharp then they blur and bleed. "Cause and effect was especially confusing for her back then, before she figured out coping mechanisms. Can you imagine having your arse tanned but not being able to work out why? It must have been terrifying." He shakes himself and turns back to me. "Anyway. On top of that, I just don't think they were as scared of the damn thing as I was. Both of their mothers had died; maybe they thought about death differently to most kids. They still do—certainly Fi does."

There's nothing I can think of to say to that.

"Anyway," he says again. "Thanks for at least hearing me out. And I really am sorry." The hand farthest from me is on the steering wheel, in the twelve o'clock position. "I wouldn't blame you if you wanted nothing to do with the lot of us ever again."

"It's not . . . That's not . . . I was never planning to stay anyway. And I'm not going to stay here tonight. When Carrie gets back we'll be leaving."

"Does Carrie know that yet?" he asks neutrally.

Instantly I realize he knows about Carrie and Jamie. Has everybody known? Has everybody been talking about it? I ignore his question. "We can stay in the Quaich or a Travelodge or something tonight. Then she can get organized to stay in Edinburgh for the rest of her play."

"If you say so." His tone is still neutral, pacifying. He glances at the Manse, a touch uneasily. I didn't leave a light on, and in the gloom, it's an indistinct dark mass, an enormous crouching shadow. "I'm glad you're not going to be sleeping in it again, though."

"Have I lost my buyer?" My anger has entirely dissipated, I realize, at least where he's concerned. We're talking like we ordinarily do.

He shakes his head. "I still love it. It's Marmite, this house: you either love it or hate it, I think. I meant that I'm glad *you* won't be sleeping in it. All of this weird stuff revolves around you."

"That's encouraging, seeing as I'll be taking my own self with me."

He does at least crack a smile. "You and the Manse then."

"Yes." Me and the Manse. The Manse and me. Ben is hesitating. I sigh. "Come on, spit it out."

"Fi is worried." I bristle slightly, and he sees it but carries on regardless. "When I ask her, she says that it's going to be okay in the end, but . . . she's worried, I can tell. So—I don't know. Be careful, I suppose."

I climb out of the car, wondering exactly what *okay in the end* means for Fiona. It's alarmingly nonspecific. Okay for whom, and when is the end?

MY FATHER IS TAKING TEA. HE'S SPRUCED UP IN A DARK BLUE suit, complete with pocket handkerchief and matching tie, that perfectly sets off the white of his bones, so white that his fingers are virtually indistinct from the fine bone china of the cup in his hand. The cave he's in is dark and musty; it surely won't be doing his suit any good. He's grinning, but I can't tell if he's happy. Skeletons always grin.

TWENTY-TWO

I'm packing when I hear Carrie at the front door, but I immediately stop and head down the stairs to greet her. She shakes off her raincoat and pulls me wordlessly into a hug. My face fits into her neck.

"Are you okay?" she asks into my hair.

"It's been a pretty strange day." Pulling back, I press the heels of my hands to my temples. "Carrie—I don't think we should stay here."

"What? I thought you said the alarm was sorted."

"But I still don't think it's safe. We should get a room in the Quaich for the night or something. You should stay in Edinburgh for the rest of your play."

She looks me over searchingly. "You're scared."

"Yes. I thought . . . I thought it would be okay, I wanted it to be okay here, but it's not. It's not safe."

"You really think we could be in danger?"

I nod silently.

"Okay." She's thinking, but whatever she's considering doesn't show on her face. "Okay. I'm sure we can stay with Fi. I'm seeing her tonight anyway—"

"Not Fiona. Anywhere but there." Why do Carrie's thoughts always jump to Fiona?

She looks at me, her exasperation more than clear. "What is your problem? You've just been staying there."

"Well, that was before all the things I heard tonight."

"What are you talking about? I'm sure you've got the wrong end of the stick. Why are you always so down on her?"

"What?" I'm missing something. I know I'm missing something. "Why are you always defending her?"

"I'm not—"

"Yes, you are. You haven't even heard what she said yet, and you're already defending her. It's like she can do no wrong in your eyes."

"And it's like she can do no right in yours," she shoots back. But she won't meet my eye. "You're wrong about her. I *know* that you're wrong about her."

Perhaps it's the way she says *know*. Perhaps it's a million little things connecting that I hadn't connected before. Whatever the reason, I suddenly understand what's been going on. "Oh my God." It's out before I can stop myself. "Are you in love with Fiona?"

"What?" she blusters. But the flush across her cheeks and the way in which her eyes leap to me, as if caught with her hand in the cookie jar, tell me I'm right.

"Jesus. You and *Fiona*?"

"Who the hell are you to tell me who I can be with?" There's no volume in her words, but somehow they crack like a whip.

"Why aren't you answering the question?"

"Yes!" she explodes. "I am with Fiona! And it's absolutely none of your business."

"Indeed." I'm still shocked to hear it confirmed. Carrie and *Fiona*? "You made that abundantly clear when you lied to me." Fiona was driving Jamie's jeep. I assumed the wrong McCue.

"I didn't—"

"I saw you. At the village shop, when you were supposed to be in Edinburgh. When you *told me* you were in Edinburgh." She drops her eyes, her righteousness slightly dented, red spots of embarrassment in her cheeks. Ben knew, I realize. Did everyone know except me? "So yes, you lied to me."

"You're right: I lied," she rallies. "Of course I lied. I didn't know how you'd react. Turns out I was right to lie to you. I thought it might take you time to adjust to the idea, but I never thought you'd have this level of homophobia."

"Homo—" It never occurred to me that she would think my aversion was because of homophobia. "You've got to be kidding. I couldn't give a monkey's if you sleep with men, women or sheep; you can fuck the entire animal kingdom in alphabetical order if you want. I just don't want you anywhere near Fiona."

"What—"

"That woman just finished telling me she knows my father is dead, despite having no evidence, which is twisted and fucked-up beyond belief, on top of being just plain nasty, and her favorite game growing up was playing dolls with an actual skeleton. *An actual skeleton!* Which, incidentally, may or may not have been my father, and which she utterly failed to tell the police about. And that's not even mentioning her obsession with this place." I fling an arm out as if to sweep the Manse into the ring. "Did you know she even thinks my father was her father?" There are hot tears spilling down my cheeks. Carrie is frozen, staring at me with wide eyes. "So excuse me if I feel slightly ill at the idea of her in bed with my sister. But hey, you don't even think enough of me to tell me the truth, so I guess it's not my place to care." A sudden thought occurs to me. "Wait, was she sleeping in your room that night? When I found the skull?" I can see from Carrie's flush that I'm right. I looked in, I saw Carrie; how come I only saw Carrie? But I already know the answer: because Carrie was naked and that made me feel like I was invading her privacy, and I had no reason to look past her. Fiona could easily have been beyond her in the dark.

Unless she was elsewhere in the house. Placing a skull on a bed, perhaps.

Carrie's phone has started to ring, faceup on the table in front of us. Both of us look at it involuntarily as the caller ID lights up the screen. *Fi M.* Of course it would be fucking Fiona. Carrie looks at me, then at the phone again, then back at me. It's still ringing. "Take it." The words are crimson and savage; they seek to rip and tear. "Ask her about it. Ask her about it all."

"Ailsa—"

"Take it."

And she does, like I knew she would, like I told her to, but it still feels like she's made her choice as she reaches out for the phone. I leave the room.

———

Sometime later I hear the door slam. The instant she's gone, the Manse abandons all pretense of silence. The wind has picked up outside, and I can hear it throwing rain at the windows, rattling the glass in its lead casing and whistling through the eaves. Closed doors strain at their frames. The bathroom door bangs.

As I pack, with very little method and all amounts of haste, tears run down my face unheeded to drop from my chin. I don't understand where the urgency has come from, but it's rising inside me, an inexplicable drumbeat that's picking up in pace, exhorting me to leave, leave now, leave while I still can. At least Carrie has gone; she is safe—but it doesn't seem like she will be someone I will have to worry about again. Perhaps it was a fool's errand all along, to think we might salvage a relationship after all these years. Other people might have managed it, but not me. I haven't had the training. I was stupid to even try.

The bathroom door bangs. Again and again it bangs. I have to go,

I have to go. The Manse is telling me to go. I don't know where the threat is coming from—*Jamie, Ben, Ali, Fiona . . .* or someone or something else entirely—but the Manse is telling me as plainly as it can. I have to go.

I won't return to London, to my job—that life is over for me. Perhaps it was over for some time; perhaps it took my mother's death for me to recognize it. For a little while, I thought that meant I could have a different life, but now I see that I've completely unhooked myself. I could slip my skin and disappear, like my father did before me, except in my case, nobody would care.

I have to go. I must go. I must go, I must go, I must go.

Toiletries—I need to clear out my stuff from the bathroom. It's colder in there, but it often is. Possibly the pilot flame on the boiler has gone out again. I don't bother checking; there's no point when the house will be empty. I stand at the bathroom door and run my eye over it for a last check. I can't see that I've missed anything. Though the bathroom window is open and there's a pool of rainwater collecting on the sill. I don't remember opening it, but it doesn't matter now. I turn to the landing.

Jamie is standing in the middle of it.

I manage to cut off my half scream. "Jesus, Jamie, what are you doing here?"

"Sorry, sorry," he's saying. He's holding his palms out placatingly. "I wanted to—"

"How did you get in?"

"The usual way," he says impatiently. "But look, I wanted—"

"Jamie, it's not a good time. You can't just come into people's houses uninvited—"

"Have you been crying?" He drops the tote bag that was over his shoulder and takes a step toward me, pushing back the hood of his dark raincoat. The shoulders are soaked through.

"I'm fine, it's just . . . it's not a good time." I push past him and head down the stairs. How *did* he come in? Most of the houses round here don't even have automatic deadlocks on their front doors, but the locksmith installed that when he came.

Jamie hitches his bag onto his shoulder and follows me down the stairs. "I just wanted to apologize," he says behind me. "For what Fiona said." I stop in the hallway of the ground floor. "It was horribly insensitive of her. I just . . ." He descends the last step and stands in front of me, then puffs out a breath. "Sorry."

"Well. Yes. But thank you." Even apart from the fact that I want him gone, so I can be gone myself, there's an awkwardness now between us. I can still see a younger him in the cave tea party, though Ben is no longer in the circle. Just Fiona, Jamie and a grinning skeleton that's now wearing a smart blue suit and has a toy tea cup in one hand with its pinkie crooked sardonically. I feel sick.

Present-day Jamie smiles a little ruefully, then gestures at the alarm panel in the hallway. "All going okay? I spotted the nice security tech outside."

"I haven't quite got it linked up yet. The Internet keeps dropping out." I move toward the front door, not so subtly trying to herd him out. Ordinarily he's very good at picking up nuances. Not so much today.

"Well. Keep trying. You cannae put a price on safety." We're by the front door now. "Listen," he says, with his hand on the deadlock. "I know you've probably had enough of, well, everything today, but there's something I wanted to tell you. Two things, actually."

"Jamie, please, it's really not a—"

"It'll just take a minute," he wheedles. "And I think you'll really want to hear it. Please?"

"Now?" I have a headache, I'm exhausted, I'm starting to feel sick and I really, really have to leave this house.

"Better now than when you've packed up and left Scotland for good. That's what you're doing, aye?"

He holds my gaze, and I can't dissemble. I cave. "Come through to the kitchen."

Once in the kitchen, my gaze falls on the paint swatches on the table. *That's one job I don't have to think about anymore.* Jamie pulls out a chair, and I'm reminded of the first time I ever met him, here in this kitchen, what feels like ages ago but could only have been six weeks or so. Only this time he's sitting where I was and I'm the one boxed in.

How did he get in? "Did Carrie leave the front door open?"

"Aye, she must have. She ought to be more careful."

"So what did you want to tell me?" I'm desperately eager to get him out of here. I haven't even offered him a drink. There's an air about him that's extraordinarily discordant with how I'm currently feeling. Like a low thrum of electricity is running through him.

"I know who's been terrorizing you."

"You do?" He certainly has my undivided attention now. "How? Who?"

He pauses for a beat, enjoying the buildup of suspense. "Morag."

"What? But . . . why?" *Morag.* Now I know, surely, it can be over. Can it really be over?

"I dinnae ken, exactly." He shrugs. "I think maybe she's nuts."

"I thought she couldn't drive." I'm trying it take it in. Is it over? It doesn't feel over.

He snorts. "She cannae. Still does, though—she's a bloody liability. She was doing near seventy the other day on the back road." *The Land Rover.* "Anyroad, you can stay now," he says earnestly. "And that's important for the second thing—"

But I'm still trying to make sense of this. "How do you know it was Morag?"

"I saw her leave the fox."

What? "That was days ago. Why didn't you say anything?"

He shifts in his seat. "Well, I wanted to speak to Ali first. It is his mother, after all." He sees my expression and moves on hurriedly. "But you're missing the point. You can stay now, and I wanted to show you—"

"How did she get in?" How did she get access to move the bin bags, to place the skull? How did *he* get in for that matter?

"Never mind that. Something—"

"Seriously, Jamie, how did she get in?"

"Who cares?" he explodes. My mouth is agape in shock. He makes a show of exhaling slowly, like an adult deliberately moving past frustration with a toddler. "I told you I wanted to show you something," he says in a more reasonable tone, reaching inside the pocket of his rain-sodden jacket. Designer, obviously. Like all of Jamie's clothes. "Dinnae worry, it's a good thing." He draws out a folded sheet of paper. The hood of the raincoat is stiff; it sits half upright, flared out behind his head. Something about it is nagging at me. "Ailsa? Ailsa, are you listening?"

"Ah . . . yes." I don't know what's going on here. None of this is making sense.

"Aye. Well. As I was saying, the full report is, like, fifty pages or something. But the gist of it is here." He passes the paper across to me. It's a letter, on headed notepaper: *Genetica Biolabs*. A sudden noise from upstairs whips my head away. "Ailsa, *look*." His frustration is boiling up again. I've never seen Jamie like this.

"Sorry, I . . . I thought I heard something." The Manse breathes in its own way. And if anything, the wind and the rain outside are increasing in intensity. I turn back to the letter. Underneath the logo, in smaller font, is written:

MEDICAL DNA TESTING AND LEGAL BIOMEDICAL TESTING

"What is this?" Once again I have the feeling that I'm missing something, something I should have seen.

"Read it." I'm trying to scan it, but I'm only getting snatched phrases. *Close relationship DNA testing. Combined Relationship Index.* "It says what I always thought. Read it," he says, grinning, but he doesn't give me any time to do that; he can't help himself. "It says we're siblings."

"*What?*" He's grinning and nodding. I look back at the letter.

*Tested relationship: half sibling. Conclusion: The DNA
from the samples labeled as James Calder and Ailsa Calder
support the biological relationship. This means that the
individuals from whom the samples were obtained are
highly likely to have the relationship which was tested.*

"How did you get my DNA?" I ask him shakily. *James Calder and
Ailsa Calder.* Since when was Jamie a Calder?

"Hair." He's still grinning. "From your hairbrush."

"You took my . . ." He took my DNA without my permission.
Expressly against my wishes, in fact. "But Jamie . . ." When he asked,
he said he was asking for Fiona. But now I think he was twisting the
truth, asking for himself. What else was he twisting? "But . . . but this
can't be right." My voice is not my own. It can't find a definite pitch.
"How could this be right?" *What has he done? Who is he?*

"I always felt it," he says, an odd mixture of earnestness and something approaching intoxicated elation. "Surely you felt it too, when you
met me? The connection between us? I always kent I couldnae be
anything to do with Glen or that nutjob everybody thinks is my half
sister." He looks across at me, his eyes gleaming. He's almost bouncing
with the frenzy of it all. "Our father would be so happy, aye? You and
me, together in the Manse? I used to think that it was so *unfair*, that
this place would be yours. But I was missing the point. It can be *ours*.
You and me together here. Can you just imagine it?"

"Jamie . . . I . . ." I look at his eyes, and everything I thought I
knew, every iota of trust that I thought we had between us drops away,
and I am suddenly, paralyzingly, scared. He's not the biggest of men,
but he's a lot bigger than me. I start to reach for my phone, which is
on the table, but he reaches out and grabs it first.

"I get it—it's a lot to take in. But let's not be jumping the gun."

He drops my phone casually into the inside pocket of his jacket. His jacket . . . I can see it now. The way the hood sits up, flared, I can just imagine the silhouette it would make in dim light. It wasn't Fiona at all in the box room. It was Jamie. The bathroom door starts to thud like the Manse has something to say. "You should meet your father before you go spreading the good news."

"What are you talking about?" I whisper, but I know. The skeleton. Jamie has it. Not the skull, surely, but the crossbones, and all the rest of it bar a few fingers. *We were pirates.*

"It wasn't Morag," I say shakily.

"Oh, it was. Mostly." He sounds unconcerned. "She did the newspaper, and the fox and that manky bird." *He's been watching*, I realize. *He's been watching all along.* He shudders. "You couldnae pay me to touch that thing. Come on upstairs, to your bedroom. Come on. Up you come," he says, as if encouraging a small child. "Ailsa," he barks sharply when I don't move. "I ken you're my older sister, but you are going upstairs if I have to drag you by the hair to get you there. And believe me, I will." He comes round the table as if to pull me up himself, and that's enough to spring me into action. I can't bear the thought of his hands touching me. There's a rottenness within him that I can see, now; it's his rottenness that I sensed in the Manse. I don't know how I never saw it before. I don't know what he means to do with me, but I can't imagine that anything is out-of-bounds in his head.

Through the kitchen we walk, with me two steps ahead of him. I begin calculating whether I could make it to the front door before he brought me down—but he's bigger than me and faster, too. When we pass by the alarm pad, with its panic button, he calls out sharply, "Dinnae," and I know that for all I might now pretend to be delighted with him as a brother (*Can it really be true?*), however much I might play for time, he won't be fooled. He's too smart for that. I climb the stairs slowly, and for once they don't creak. Perhaps this is exactly what the Manse has been waiting for.

At the top of the stairs I turn for my room, but he calls out sharply.

"Uh-uh, Ailsa. Your room, I said." I stand blinking for a minute, and then it dawns on me that he assumes I've been sleeping in the master bedroom. It would be a natural assumption. *He didn't see that in all his watching,* I think, and it feels like a small victory. He hasn't quite been the omniscient observer he thinks he is. I turn for Carrie's room, and he says encouragingly, "In you go." The tote bag over his shoulder isn't quite empty, but it doesn't seem to have much in it. The bones must already be in place.

How did he get in? Not that it matters now.

It's already dark outside, and Carrie's curtains aren't drawn, but for once I fear what's in the Manse far more than the blackness beating at the windows. I take a small step forward, then Jamie pushes me and I stumble forward two more. I don't think I have the courage to look around the room, yet I know I have to. Jamie has switched on the small lamp on Carrie's bedside table. "You're a clarty besom, you ken," he's saying disapprovingly, but I have eyes only for the heap on the bed. My brain is slow to resolve the lights and shades into recognizable shapes, even though I know what I'm about to see. "I had to make the bed. You'll have to be much tidier when we're living together; I cannae abide a mess. Anyroad." He flings out a theatrical hand. "Say hello to Daddy."

It's a skeleton, just as I knew it would be—or at least it's most of one. The major bones have been laid out in a decent approximation. They're very clean, but an off-white color. I wonder if there's a color in the swatch downstairs that would match, and press a hand to my mouth to dam a hysterical sob. I've been avoiding looking toward the head of the bed, but as my eyes travel up past the pelvis, past the collarbones, I see that there's a skull after all, turned sideways on the bed as if waiting for whoever might enter the room. "The skull . . ." I whisper. Now I can't take my eyes off it. The weak lamplight is throwing cavernous shadows into the eye sockets and the disturbing nasal gash. There are some slightly crooked teeth still attached in the mouth.

"Oh, this is the real one. I got the other one on eBay. I bet you hadnae a clue you can buy human remains right off the Internet. Some people are fair sick in the head." He shakes his own head. "The finger bones Callum found were his, though. I cannae think how I missed them." He frowns, evidently annoyed at that slip. "This is his favorite place to be, you ken. I like to bring him here as much as I can."

"How do you know . . . that it's him?" My mouth is too dry; it's difficult to speak. The teeth, a whiter shade of ivory than the bone in which they're set, humanize the skull in a way that makes it even more disturbing.

He laughs. "I always kent it. I found him first, you see. I ran away, and that's when I found him. It was fate. Glen was furious at me for running away; he fair lost it when I came back. More than tanned my arse, Fi will tell you that. Child abuse, it was." His jaw is tight. "No wonder I ran away. But the point is, I found him first, as I was meant to, and I found his wallet. Credit cards dinnae biodegrade." He smiles a slow, secretive smile with the half of his mouth that's nearest the lamp; the rest of his face is in shadow. "D'you ken what else I found?"

I do. I'm already ahead of him. "The diamonds." I doubt he's ever traded a day in his life. I should have made the connection already; he had none of the paraphernalia—extra screens, Bloomberg keyboards and the like—that I saw at the desks of the financial geeks in the newsroom.

"Top of the class!" he crows. "You're a smart one, Ailsa. Runs in the family, I guess. I didnae ken what they were or what they were worth until I got older. And it took a fair while after that to figure out where to go to trade them. If I'm honest, I spent too much at the beginning. And the way house prices have been rocketing . . . But I've kept enough to buy this place if it doesnae get bid up. And let's face it, who else would want it with all the stuff that goes on here?" He suddenly grins again. "I should really thank Morag; she gave me the idea."

"What idea?"

"To scare you so you'd sell at any price. But now I dinnae need to buy it after all. You and I will share it."

I should tell him he can have it, he can have the whole thing—except that he can't. The thought runs up against an unexpected wall inside me. *He cannot have the Manse.* This house is not for him. I look at the door again, assessing my chances, but he's moved a step or two to block my exit. "Pull the curtains," he orders sharply, and I do, wondering if I can leave some kind of sign at the window, except there's no point. Nobody travels along this road. We are a mile from our nearest neighbors, one of whom happens to be the person terrorizing me, and he has my phone. Even if I could get it from him somehow, the reception is abysmal in every room but this one. I need to find a way to take the upper hand from him. It's not going to be through strength. What if I stand up to him? What if I refuse to play his games?

The bathroom door is thudding. Actually, it's not the only one thudding now. The wind must have shaken another loose in its frame.

"I have a suit for him. A blue one, pin-striped, very smart. I didnae have the time to put him in it tonight . . . But aye, I always knew it was him," he says, as if answering a question I haven't asked. "Fi didnae know who he was; I threw his clothes and shoes in the river. But Glen wouldnae let me go anywhere alone for a wee while after that, so I had to pretend to find him again with her. I had to make it our secret." He smiles, and says conspiratorially, "You could convince Fi of anything back then since she couldnae tell what was real and what was made up. I told her I took the blame for something she did when he tanned me. I told her it would be even worse for me next time, and it was all her fault, that she owed me." Oh God. Poor Fiona. She's been living with a psychopath all these years, and yet she's the least well equipped person to figure that out. I feel a wave of shame about every piece of blame I have laid at her door, but now is not the time to dwell on that. I need to figure out how to get away.

Jamie frowns with half a forehead. "You should lie down."

"Wh-what?"

"You need to lie down. Is this any way to greet your old man? Lie down."

"No." It's not convincing enough. I try again, and the word comes out with a strength I don't feel. "No."

He sighs. "You dinnae want to make me cross with you, Ailsa."

"Or what?" I demand. I glance at the en suite bathroom, calculating my odds of getting in there and locking the door—if it has a lock?—and he smiles at me.

"Ailsa," he says, shaking his head. The golden lamplight moves across his face and back as he does so. "You're smarter than that." He frowns a little. "I expected to have to gie you some time to adjust, but even so, you're disappointing me. I didnae want to do this." He reaches into the empty tote bag—the almost empty tote bag—all the while keeping his eyes on me, and pulls out something long and dark and metallic.

Dear God, he has a shotgun.

Adrenaline races across my skin in an electric wave. "Jamie, you don't—"

"Dinnae presume to ken what I want to do. Shut it and get on that bed."

I sit down on the bed, hard, then awkwardly lower myself onto my back, trying not to disturb the bones in the center, but my weight spills them toward me. I want to close my eyes, but I daren't look away from Jamie. "That's right," he says encouragingly, the shotgun held casually in one hand. He seems very relaxed with it; I can't imagine he wouldn't know how to use it. I know absolutely nothing about guns. I can't tell if it would shower me with pellets or blow me in half. Is it even cocked? How would I know? He leans over me and adjusts the skeleton; I can feel him placing some of the bones into a macabre embrace of my torso. A wave of extreme revulsion hits me, like the feeling I had with the fly carcasses, only one thousand times magnified. "Now, aye, that's it . . . Now, turn your head." I start to tremble uncontrollably, straining my face away from the bones. "The other way."

I turn my head back to find that the skull is mere millimeters from my face. My own nose is almost in the gaping nasal cavity. There's a roaring in my ears. My head is blocking most of the lamplight, but for a moment I think I see something moving within the eye socket, something glistening and white, wriggling and writhing like the larvae from the broken branch, and then I can't help it: the roaring increases and the panic breaks through and I can hear myself start to keen in terror. And Jamie starts to laugh.

MY FATHER IS WAITING FOR ME. I THOUGHT IT WAS THE OTHER way round.

TWENTY-THREE

Breathe. And again. And again. Slowly the roaring recedes.

Oddly, it's Jamie's laughter that brings me back to myself. The skeleton is not the horror here. That skeleton is my father; he would not and could not hurt me. The horror is Jamie. There is nothing writhing in the skull. These bones can't hurt me. They are just bones.

I hear Jamie behind me, still laughing. "You shoulda seen yer face. But now, that's better, aye? We could be happy here." He sounds wistful. I wonder if he has ever been happy. But in an instant, his mood flips. "You're not being very grateful. You should be thanking me: I've kept our dad for us for all these years, so we can be together." I wonder when he removed the bones from the cave. Not three weeks ago, that's for sure; Jamie probably hasn't been to that cave in over a decade. I would think he has been taking very special care of this skeleton for a good long time. "You, me and our dad—it's how it's meant to be. We can be happy here in the Manse."

"Jamie—"

"Say it."

"Say what?"

"Say it!" He's yelling, and it's terrifying. He's armed and unhinged and unpredictable, and it's utterly terrifying.

"It's how it's meant to be, we can be happy here, it's how it's meant to be, it's how it's meant to be . . ." The words are tumbling out of me on repeat, so fast they barely make sense.

A sound comes from outside, a purr of an engine. "Shut it!" snarls Jamie, and then seconds later, I hear the unmistakable crunching of gravel. I turn my head from my father's, and Jamie snaps off the lamp and crosses to the window, flicking the curtain aside. I start to get up.

"Not so fast," he barks, and the faint gleam along the shotgun's barrel pivots in my direction, freezing me in the darkness, half sitting, half on one elbow. Some of my father's bones have slipped against me. One knobbly bone end has slipped under me, pressing into my hip.

My father's bones. A Schrödinger's cat experiment no longer. *He is dead, he has long been dead, he can only ever be dead . . .*

Now is not the time for that.

"It's Fi. Took ma fucking jeep again. Bint." His accent is getting stronger, and he looks flustered. He hadn't counted on an intrusion. It would be the perfect distraction to use to somehow get the upper hand, except that if Fiona is here, Carrie will surely be with her . . . "And Carrie, looks like."

"She has a key," I find myself muttering, horrified dread pooling in my stomach. Should I shout, scream? What can I do to safely turn them away? The jeep's engine has already cut off. Now there's the sound of a car door slamming, once, twice, and footsteps crunching on the gravel.

Jamie visibly makes a decision. "C'mon, we'll have to go down. Put that lamp on again. Hurry up!"

I make a show of fumbling for the lamp switch, trying to buy time to think. *How will he hide the shotgun? Will he even bother to hide it?* The bright light of the hallway after the dim lamplight makes me blink. As I start down the stairs, Carrie and Fiona have already entered the front door and are on their way to the kitchen. "Ailsa? Ailsa?" Carrie is calling. "Have you seen Callum?" She turns when she hears me on the lower stairs and comes back along the hallway, Fiona at her shoulder. They're right by the alarm panel, with the utterly useless panic button. "There you are. Oh, Jamie, too, hi. It's Callum—he's disappeared. Is he here?"

"No, I haven't seen him." What is the right amount of concern to portray? I glance back at Jamie. I think he has the shotgun hidden against his side, inside his jacket.

"Let's go into the kitchen and attack this logically," Jamie suggests. Carrie and Fiona turn for the kitchen, and as I follow them, passing the alarm panel, Jamie breathes into my ear from behind me, *Dinnae you be doing anything stupid.*

"How long has he been missing?" I ask when we get in the kitchen. Nobody sits down.

"Not long, I think," says Fiona. She can barely stand still; she's almost pacing on the spot. Carrie puts a gentle hand on her upper arm. "Dad said an hour max. I was so sure he'd be here. He was really worried about you being here on your own . . . Maybe he's somewhere between here and home; it's wild out tonight." Her eyes won't stay still, as if they need to keep roving, searching. She runs a frantic hand through her thick hair and breathes out unsteadily. The two doors upstairs thud, and her eyes flick upward, startled.

"We'll find him," Carrie tells her earnestly. "We will."

"He's a smart cookie. He's not going to have done anything stupid." I don't know if Fiona even hears me. She's suddenly much more still. Only her head moves, looking round, as if trying to make sense of something. "We should go out and look for him. With torches. We should go now. Split up and cover more ground." *If only I can get us all outside. Outside, surely Carrie will be safe.* "Carrie . . ." I'm willing her to look at me, as if I could somehow telegraph the danger we're in through my eyes, but she refuses to turn away from Fiona. "We have to go."

"Safer in pairs, actually," Jamie counters. He's leaning against the kitchen doorway. The gun must be propped just out of sight, perhaps resting against the doorframe on the hallway side. "Ailsa and me, and the pair of you. With mobiles—for all the bloody use they are round here."

"Shouldn't we leave someone here?" Carrie asks.

"No, we should all go," I say quickly. There's not a chance Jamie will leave me here, and I can't see Carrie separating from Fiona, the state she's in. "If we leave the front door open, he can come straight in if he comes here. We can even leave a note to explain."

"Well, dinnae write anything complicated," Jamie says, and I hear the meanness in his voice that's been hiding all along. Carrie looks at him in slight shock, then her eyes pass briefly over me, but she won't allow them to stop. The fight still hangs in the air for her, but I am far, far past that. Centuries past that. In contrast, Fiona's eyes are entirely fixed on me.

"Let's go," I insist.

But Carrie catches sight of the genetics report that Jamie left on the table. "What's—?" she starts, but Fiona breaks in.

"Oh my God," Fiona says quietly. She's still staring at me, the blood draining out of her face. Even before she says anything, I can see that she *knows* what's going on. I don't know how, but she *knows*. "It's that time."

I whirl round to Jamie, hoping I can shove him, knock him off-balance, anything to get him away from the gun, but it's too late. In one fluid movement he's reaching behind him and slightly to one side, grabbing the smooth barrel, hitching it up into firing position in the same hand, then reaching for me, an easy grab because I'm moving toward him anyway. Which is how I find myself with my upper arm in his grasp and a shotgun butting at my stomach. I close my eyes briefly then look across the kitchen at Carrie's shocked face, her hand at her mouth, half cutting off a shriek.

"I'm sorry," I say helplessly. Her eyes have finally met mine. She shakes her head mutely, one hand still at her mouth. In my peripheral vision, Fiona is reaching out an arm to her, murmuring something, but my eyes can't leave Carrie. For a moment, the Manse is entirely still, shocked, but then the creaks and bangs and loud rasping breaths return, more frenetic than ever before. The Manse is furious.

Carrie removes her hand from her mouth, and her shoulder moves in that strange wriggle it does whenever she slips into another skin, and for a moment I think I might break in two, because I *know* her now. I know who she is and what her movements mean, I know the trail she leaves through the house, I know how she sleeps, I know all of these things, and yet I have a shotgun trained at my stomach. "What is going on, please?" she asks, very politely but very calmly. It's the persona she has chosen to assume. I suppose it's as good as any other.

"Yes, what's the plan, Jamie?" I say, taking Carrie's cue. Find a person to be, someone capable. Someone tough. Surely one of my splintered selves is up to the task. "Or should I say, little brother?"

"I'm not sure I understand," says Carrie, again in her absurdly polite tone.

"Jamie has been getting a little genetic testing done. Apparently we're siblings. Half siblings, anyway."

"I don't . . ." Carrie starts, but she trails off. She does understand. She's worked it out.

"Surely you can see that this is over? You're not really going to shoot all three of us, are you?" I ask him, aiming for a conversational tone. I don't pull it off. There are cracks in my delivery.

"He isnae going to shoot you," says Fiona. The certainty of her words is echoed in her pale, fiercely determined face. She wears the same expression as Callum when we climbed the stairs together to find the bones under Carrie's bed. There's a part of me that believes in her, that believes that she *knows*. I wish all of me could. "That isnae how this ends."

Jamie laughs contemptuously. "Like you'd have a fucking clue. If you know so much about what's coming, how have I been playing you for years? You cannae even tell what day it is tomorrow." He nudges me with the gun, and my stomach feels extraordinarily, unforgivably vulnerable. Surely evolution should have put an armor plate there. How can there only be skin and muscle to protect my insides from a shotgun blast? "We're in the back of beyond. I could shoot all three of you and hide your bodies and nobody would be any the wiser. There's thousands of acres right outside; I could dump you just about anywhere. They didnae find our dad, did they, Ailsa?"

"We'd be missed," Carrie says. She looks very young. Under her smudged eyeliner, she could be fifteen. "People would look for us."

Missed. Carrie and Fiona would be missed, by the future they should have had, by each other most of all. I am not certain I would be missed.

"Or I could set it up like Fiona went nuts and killed the pair of you, then turned the gun on herself." I look at him, trying to gauge how serious he is. Very, I think. He likes this plan. It tickles him. "Aye, that story everybody would buy. Maybe that's the way to do it."

The light in the center of the ceiling flickers. Fiona glances up at it thoughtfully. "You want to be careful, Jamie. I dinnae think it likes what you're doing." She looks at me with meaning. I don't know what she's trying to tell me.

"What?" he says irritably.

"The Manse," she says. "You cannae feel it? It's furious with you."

"For Christ's sake." His face twists in disgust. "It's a fucking house! It cannae feel! It cannae speak!"

"Oh, but it can," I say, suddenly catching on to Fiona's plan. She gives a small nod. "It's been speaking, but I haven't been listening carefully enough. It's been trying to tell me that you've been coming in through the bathroom window. It's been trying to tell me that you stole the picture of your mum from the album in the attic." The light flickers again as thuds come from upstairs. There must be three or four doors slamming now. The shotgun is still trained at my stomach. His hand is still clamped round my upper arm, so tightly that I will have bruise marks. If I'm alive to have them.

"The bathroom window?" asks Carrie faintly.

"There must be a ladder hidden somewhere. He's hardly Spider-Man. I'm guessing he used to have a key, from when he worked at the estate agent's, but then I rather unhelpfully got the locks changed. He's been coming in with my father's bones. He likes to lay them out and have a cigarette. Sometimes he's not so careful about collecting up all the little bits."

Jamie's jaw clenches at the revulsion that crosses Carrie's face. "*Our* father's bones, mind." A gust of wind strong enough to rattle the kitchen windowpanes blows for a few seconds, accompanied by flickers of the light overhead and a string of thuds and bangs.

"How would our father feel about you pointing a shotgun at me?" It's a misstep. For the briefest of moments, I see how much he wants me to believe in a fantasy future of the three of us living here, Norman Bates style. But I'm not the actress Carrie is. And he's not stupid. "Stop trying to play me, you cunt," he says brutally. "Dinnae think I willnae end you just cos you're my sister. I will. I'm gonna."

Carrie's gray eyes leap to mine. I can see her horror and there is nothing I can do. I'm all too aware of the metallic barrel at my stomach. I'm helpless. *I'm sorry*, I say soundlessly. The kitchen door starts to swing farther ajar with a loud creak behind Jamie. He glances round quickly, then lifts his foot and boots it firmly closed behind him, like a horse kicking out.

"Sister," says Fiona suddenly. "Based on what?"

"I told you," says Jamie impatiently. "DNA testing."

"You gave him a sample?" Fiona asks me, frowning.

I shake my head, but very carefully, given the proximity of the shotgun. "He took one anyway."

"Hairbrush," Jamie says, almost gloating. *Too easy*, I can see him thinking. "From your bathroom," he says to me.

"What color?" Fiona asks. There's something about her manner, a sudden excitement. It catches Carrie's attention too.

"What the fuck does that have to do with the price of fish?" Jamie asks irritably.

"A blue one, right? A blue one? From the master en suite?"

"Aye." Inexplicably Fiona starts to laugh. "What?" he says. Then louder. "What?"

"Ailsa isnae sleeping in the master bedroom. Carrie is."

"But . . ." He looks at me, bewildered. "But Carrie and me cannae be related."

"Carrie couldnae find her hairbrush the other day. I lent her mine. It was blue." Fiona is laughing again, doubled over with it, crowing. "You took *my* hairbrush; my DNA. You've just proved *we're* the half siblings: you and me. You've just proved yourself *wrong*."

"No. I dinnae believe you." The words scrape his throat on the way out. He's almost white with fury and disbelief. Outside the wind is rising to another crescendo.

"Everything you thought is wrong. You're not Martin Calder's child. You're not Ailsa's brother. You're the product of a suicidal mother and the man who found himself in her bed when he was grieving for his wife." She's not laughing anymore. "And you thought you were so smart." She stands up squarely and faces him, and I finally see the full extent of her disgust laid bare on her face. "Fucking eejit. The Manse won't stand for it." And she hawks up a globule of saliva and spits at him.

It's too much for Jamie—he swings the shotgun toward her, and in the same instant the lights flicker and die and a wind begins to blow, so fiercely that I can hear it screaming through the eaves, only it sounds like it's coming from inside the Manse rather than outside. I'm conscious of moving toward the barrel that is now mercifully not pointing at my stomach, but I want to knock it away from Carrie— and Fiona, too. There's a pressure in my ears as I'm moving, as if they need to pop, and then they *do* pop, as the kitchen door blasts open with astonishing force, whacking Jamie on the side of the head as I ram him from the other side. The shotgun discharges with an enormous bang as he goes down, and my full weight follows through the space he was in only milliseconds before, so that I crash shoulder first into the wall, then tumble on top of Jamie. *Carrie*, I think desperately. There is shouting. I'm not sure if some of it is coming from me. My elbow connects with a thump against some part of Jamie's head, but he doesn't make a sound.

There's no light whatsoever in the kitchen. The wind has dropped; the Manse is silent and dark.

"Carrie, are you okay?" I call.

"Ailsa?" asks Carrie. She sounds like half of herself. Not even half, not nearly as substantial as that. "I'm okay, I'm okay—are you okay? Fi? Fi?"

"Here," comes Fiona's voice, reassuringly steady.

My eyes are adjusting to the dark now. Fiona is standing beside me, but she has three legs—and then I realize one of them is the barrel of the shotgun, and it's in contact with Jamie's head as he lies crumpled, half on his side. I look at Fiona. I can't see much except her glittering eyes, staring unflinchingly down at Jamie. "Um. Fiona . . ." I struggle to get upright, but one shoulder isn't working at all. There was a *crack* and a wave of heat around my collarbone when I connected with the wall. I can't imagine that was a good sign.

"We don't shoot him. That's not how this ends," she mutters. Then more loudly, "Carrie, can you find something to tie him up with?"

Carrie has activated the torch function on her phone and is playing the light over us all. "Is he . . . is he unconscious?" she asks. She's found a little more of herself.

"Aye. The Manse gave him a fair old smack."

"The . . . the Manse?" says Carrie hesitantly, but neither Fiona nor I answer her. Part of me believes it. A much bigger part than before. I've shuffled myself into a position where I'm seated on the floor, my back against one of the kitchen units, my bad arm cradled awkwardly in front of me. It aches enormously in an oddly muffled way, as if my body knows the damage is too severe for me to cope with. Carrie's torchlight slides over my face. "You're hurt!" she exclaims.

"Collarbone," I say briefly. I must have hit my head, too; I feel as if my brain is still ricocheting inside. The wind is still howling without, but we seem cocooned inside now. There's no banging. The Manse has said its piece. "I'll live. Find something to tie him up." Her light slides off me as she turns for the drawers.

"Nothing here—oh, but I've found some candles!" Carrie says. "I wonder if the power is out everywhere. Matches, matches, where are matches?"

"Fiona, don't you have a lighter?" I ask.

"Nope. Dinnae smoke," she replies. "Not for years."

"But I saw you . . ." It's an effort to speak. "With a cigarette. Outside the Quaich."

I sense rather than see her shrug. "I must have been holding it for someone else. I dinnae smoke. Not even when drunk."

"She doesn't," says Carrie, still rummaging through drawers, and I start to laugh, though it hurts so much I could cry at the same time. Jamie. She must have been holding it for Jamie. I can see him now, leaning on the bonnet of his jeep, the glow of a cigarette in his cupped hand. Then he went to help Carrie get her jacket—he must have passed it to Fiona. Fiona doesn't smoke.

"I bet you're not on any medication, either."

"I take an antihistamine for hay fever, if that counts."

I find I'm laughing again. Carrie sweeps her phone light over me anxiously. "Are you sure you're okay?"

"Yes." *No.* Trust the people, Fiona said, not the story. She was right; I've been building a false narrative. I've probably been doing it all my life. "Light the candles off the hob."

In a minute or two she has three lit candles held more or less upright in a pint glass, like some kind of abstract art version of a vase of flowers. The yellow light forms a glowing sphere by the table but deepens the shadows elsewhere. On the floor, mere feet away from me, Jamie groans. Carrie's hands cease moving as she looks across at him anxiously, then at Fiona, then she resumes the search more frenetically.

"Try the boot room," I suggest. My voice sounds as if it comes from a place very far from me.

"Yes. Right. Good thinking."

Carrie steps into the boot room, and I turn my head very slowly toward Fiona, maintaining contact between the back of my skull and the cabinet unit. She's chewing her lip, the gun still trained on her brother. "How does this end?" I ask her quietly.

"We dinnae shoot him," she says, just as quietly. "But—"

"Got it!" Carrie returns, holding aloft a roll of garden twine, which she puts on the table. She's very pale, but it's obviously helping her to focus on tasks. "I'll call the police now. And an ambulance." She frowns at her phone. "Oh, for fuck's sake—no reception. I'll have to go upstairs."

"Call my dad first, will you?" asks Fiona. "See if he's found Callum. But dinnae tell him about . . . all this. I need him focused on Callum."

"Yes. Okay. Yes." She eyes Jamie dubiously, then mutters, "Right, here goes," and picks her way gingerly past his supine figure on her way out of the kitchen.

I start getting to my feet, which is more of a struggle than anticipated with one working arm. I have to grab at a drawer handle to get enough purchase to lever myself up. Jamie groans. Fiona glances wordlessly at me.

"I'm on it," I say, reaching for a knife from the wooden knife block. It has a black handle and long blade. Something about it catches at my brain, but I don't have time to follow the thought. I cut some lengths of the twine, expecting it to be an awkward exercise with my arm, but the wickedly sharp blade slices through the twine as if it offers no resistance. What *is* awkward is trying to tie his hands. I don't even want to touch him, but I force myself to reach out, to lift each hand in turn to loop the twine around it. *I'm scared of him, even though we have the gun and he's only half conscious.* I hate that I'm scared. It belittles me in my own eyes.

"Should we swap? Can you hold the gun?" asks Fiona.

I shake my head. "It's my right arm." And I have no idea how to fire a gun. But it's taking me too long; he's starting to stir, faint movements at first. I just manage to tie a secure knot as he jerks against the bonds. I glance at his face, lit in macabre fashion from the pint glass of candles. I see the situation dawning on him, as Fiona places the barrel of the gun very deliberately at his throat. Slowly he breaks out in a grin that's chillingly manic. His teeth are smeared with black. It takes me a second to realize that it's actually deep scarlet blood suspended in his own saliva—at some point he has cut his mouth, presumably in the fall. Perhaps my elbow was to blame.

"You willnae shoot me," says Jamie to Fiona. I wonder how he can be so sure of his words. Ignoring the barrel at his throat, he turns his head and spits out a spray of scarlet. I see a tooth in it and I think of the teeth in my father's skull upstairs. "If you shoot me, you'll go to jail," he says.

"I willnae," she says steadily, but there's a flicker in her face.

"You will. Disproportionate response. It's murder." An icy leaden mass starts to form in my belly. This is what I was afraid of. How can it be that we have the weapon but he's in charge? "The police will be all too ready to believe it with your record."

"So what do you think is going to happen, wee brother?" she asks. The stress on *wee brother* makes him grin once again.

"You'll let me go."

"You've got to be kidding. Why on earth would I do that?" says Fiona, at the same time as I say, "The police are already on their way." I really hope I'm telling the truth.

"Because you've got no choice. Kill me, and you go to jail, and leave that lad of yours without a mammy. You cannae even have me arrested because I'll tell them about Callum."

I look at Fiona. Her face is utterly still. "Tell them what?" I ask. "Fiona, what will he tell them?"

Jamie starts to laugh, his teeth scarlet where the candlelight touches and black otherwise. "I'll tell them Callum isnae yours."

"Don't be . . ." I start, but I trail off as I catch sight of Fiona's face. He isn't being ridiculous, I realize. He's not being ridiculous at all. I can't even begin to process that right now. "We can't let him free," I say urgently to Fiona. "He's just trying to play you."

"Of course he is," she says, her eyes still on Jamie. Her jaw is set. "He's always played me. I'm never able to defend myself—how can you defend yourself when you cannae sequence events? Who would believe me in a trial? He's always played me. I'm done with it."

Jamie's smile fades. He spits again, another scarlet-streaked stream of saliva. "So. You're willing to lose Callum."

"Ailsa, go check if Carrie has any news on Callum." I look uncertainly from one to the other. Their eyes are locked. She glances at me when I don't move. "Please?"

"Okay." I turn for the door, but something isn't right; I can *feel* something isn't right, as if I've been here before and I know that something's coming, something bad . . . I get through the hallway and put one hand on the staircase banister, and then I hear a faint shout and a hard thwack, and I have to turn back. I walk as soundlessly as I can. Through the half-open door I can see Fiona crouched over the prone figure, doing something to his hand. I reach the doorway in time to see her move toward his head, a flash of silver in her own hand, and then . . .

"Fiona!" I gasp, but it's too late. She has stabbed into his neck. A pool of blood flows out unevenly as I watch.

She looks up at me. Her hand is black with blood from the knife. "He got free and knocked the gun away from me," she says. "He was going ballistic." I'm leaning against the doorframe, too stunned to move. "He had a knife," she adds, gesturing at his hand. A silver steak knife is in it. The twine I tied is still looped round his wrist, but it's been cut through. "Look. There."

There's so much wrong with what she has said that I don't know where to start. Jamie's throat is spurting, but his eyes are closed. She must have knocked him out with the butt of the gun first. Fiona is getting to her feet, the black-handled knife in her hand, the blade extending down her side, glinting silver against her black jeans. I've seen this before. "The knife . . ."

"He must have brought it from home. I recognize it," she says, but I meant the other knife that she's holding, the one I used to cut the twine. I've seen her before, holding it. When she came to the door of my bedroom. Her face is calm; her voice is quiet. "He was going to hurt me. He was going ballistic."

"No." My words are quiet. "No, he wasn't."

She considers that. "But he was going to hurt me."

"I . . ." It's true. Any way this played out, Jamie was going to hurt her. "Yes." I should be trying to stop the blood. I move quickly to grab a couple of tea towels. "Is this how it ends?"

"Now you believe me?" The irony in her question doesn't escape me.

"Maybe." I'm on my knees, awkwardly pressing the tea towel to the gash in Jamie's throat.

"There's no point."

"I know." I'm already too late to save him. It was always too late to save him; Fiona did a remarkably effective job. But it has to look like we tried.

"What will you tell the police? And Carrie?" she asks, kneeling to help me press the tea towels. She's blocking the candlelight and Jamie is in darkness now. Not that he's Jamie anymore. Maybe he was never the Jamie I thought he was.

"Don't you know?"

She shakes her head. "I saw this. I dinnae ken what happens next. Carrie . . ." she falters, and closes her eyes briefly. "I dinnae want her to have to lie."

A dozen different sentences start in my head, but I can't complete any of them. I don't want Carrie to have to lie either. And she would. I know she would do that for Fiona.

Carrie appears in the doorway. "Callum is safe—Glen has him. The police are . . . Oh my God." Both hands are at her mouth. Clean hands, not a spot of blood on them. I look at mine. They're clean too, actually—it's the tea towels that are sodden—but they don't feel it. "What happened? Is he . . . ?"

"I think so," I say. I can hardly believe this is happening.

"He got free. He had a knife," Fiona explains. "He was going—"

"Are you okay? Are you hurt? Oh my God, you're bleeding." Carrie rushes to her side, standing over her. One of her clean hands is on Fiona's shoulder. Her enormous eyes are fixed on Fiona's face.

"It's okay. It's not my blood." Fiona has turned toward Carrie, but her eyes keep flicking across to me. "I was checking the ties; I didnae think they were tight enough, and then somehow he was free. He had a knife."

"Maybe I didn't tie him properly, with my shoulder and everything." I look up at Carrie. "It was self-defense."

I don't think I'm lying.

MY FATHER IS DEAD.

TWENTY-FOUR

We huddle on the floor in a corner of the kitchen, as far away from the body as possible, but somehow unable to leave the room. Carrie sits in the middle. I drop my head onto her shoulder.

"I'm sorry. I was wrong about Fiona—sorry, Fiona," I add. "Jamie said things . . ."

"Aye, he was good at that," says Fiona quietly, from the other side of Carrie.

"But I shouldn't have presumed," I continue. "I'm sorry."

"Thanks," she says.

"It's okay," says Carrie. She bends the arm that belongs to the shoulder I'm leaning on to stroke my hair gently with one finger. "I know you were only thinking of me."

"Under the circumstances, Ailsa," says Fiona thoughtfully, "I think you could maybe see your way to calling me Fi."

I start to giggle, but it hurts too much, in my head and in my collarbone.

"Listen," says Carrie suddenly. She left the front door ajar. The sound of a car on the gravel reaches us.

"Ailsa? Fi?" calls a familiar voice. It's Ben. I can hear him clomping down the hallway. He must have a large torch. Or two: there are two circles of stark white light, much stronger than our three puny candles, dancing over the kitchen units before training on Jamie's body. "What the—?"

"Fuck!" comes Ali's voice. That makes more sense. Ali is here, and has a torch too. The sense of relief that someone has arrived to help is overwhelming. Almost immediately after it floods through me, I realize I don't feel well.

"We're here," calls Fiona. "We're okay. Sort of."

"He's not," I hear Ali mutter. I can see the dark shadow of him bent over by the body. Taking a pulse, presumably, though there's none to take. How many times a minute does Jamie's pulse not beat? Ben's light explores the rest of the kitchen and finds the three of us. "Jesus Christ," he says. I can't see his face behind the circle of light, but he sounds like someone just punched him. "Are you hurt?"

"We think Ailsa's broken her collarbone," Fiona says. "But it's not our blood."

"What happened?"

"It's . . . it's a long story. The police are on their way. How come you're here?"

"We were just doing the rounds, checking on folks given the power's down everywhere. Your dad and Callum are okay, Fi; they've got the generator going. He said you might be here." He plays the torch-light over to Ali, who raises a hand to shield his eyes.

"He's dead," Ali says shortly, shaking his head. The light pauses, then swings away.

"Where was Callum?" I ask into the silence.

Ben clears his throat. "The barn. The cat had kittens. He was fascinated and lost track of time."

Fiona—Fi—gives a short rueful laugh. "I'm not really in a position to get mad at him for losing track of time. How many kittens?"

"Never mind the fucking kittens. Why is Jamie dead?" Ali's voice is rising, both in pitch and volume.

"There's a skeleton upstairs too," Carrie pipes up. "It's Ailsa's dad."

"Jesus, fuck." The shock in Ali's voice is unmistakable now. "Cannae one of you give a straight answer to a question? What happened? This is like the fucking three witches."

"*Macbeth*." This is Carrie.

"And look how that turned out," I murmur. I don't feel well. I don't feel well at all.

Carrie turns to me. "Are you okay—"

"I might throw up," I blurt. And then I do.

It's three days before I'm discharged from hospital, not on account of my collarbone, which is indeed broken, but because it's discovered by my very thorough doctor that I have carbon monoxide poisoning and therefore need to be oxygenated for at least forty-eight hours. Apparently the boiler in the bathroom has been silently pumping out invisible lethal fumes right next to my bedroom for who knows how long. Yet another thing the Manse was trying to tell me, with the smoke alarm incident—if you believe in that sort of thing. More of me does than before. The doctor lists the symptoms and I nod to almost every one: headache, fatigue, nausea, depression, confusion, feeling better whenever out of the house. Ever since I got to the Manse, I've been slowly undergoing poisoning. Carrie has only the mildest of symptoms, because her room is farther away and she sleeps with her window open, but she still has to spend twelve hours on oxygen to be safe. We both endure several lectures on the importance of testing smoke alarms and how stupid I was not to have replaced the batteries after the fly incident, about which Carrie and I feel equally guilty but for different reasons—her for not believing me, and me for putting her at risk by not immediately buying new batteries.

Bryn and other officers come to the hospital to speak with me, but it's fairly clear they have no intention of pressing charges on Fiona, or anybody else for that matter. Jamie threatened us with a gun and then fired in a confined space; his guilt is not in doubt. And neither, apparently, is his mental state—we have Jamie's computer to thank for that. It holds some fairly odd stuff that Bryn doesn't want to detail for me. And despite sophisticated efforts at hiding his tracks, the police easily prove that he bought the skull—which dates to the sixteenth century, and probably originated in Asia—from the Internet, which is not illegal (*How can that not be illegal!* I exclaim to Bryn), though the breaking and entering to lay it on a bedspread certainly is. With all that evidence corroborating our story, nobody is interested in a different narrative, procedures manual be damned. I get the impression that Fiona's story and mine don't quite tally exactly, but I have carbon monoxide poisoning, and she has always had her own issues; slight inconsistencies are apparently forgiven. Instead, Bryn lectures me about the smoke alarm. He seems oddly stricken at what has happened, as if he should have been able to stop it.

Callum comes to the hospital, too, immediately scrambling onto the bed to snuggle into me despite his mother's protestations from the doorway. He has the sense to at least climb on the side without the sling. "Hey you." I smile at the little face tucked against me. "How are you?"

"Good," he says, then stops as if unsure he's allowed to say that. "Uncle Jamie died."

"I know. I'm sorry." *I'm sorry.* The words sting as I say them. *He didn't need to die,* I think, or one version of me thinks. I try to quash that version. No matter how many times I tell myself it wasn't my fault, I still feel like I let it happen. When I stepped away from the kitchen, I *knew* something was wrong; I knew *something* was going to happen.

Clearly nobody has yet told Callum what Jamie did, because he says, "Grandad says he's gone to a better place, but it cannae be that good." He's frowning. "Otherwise everyone would kill themselves right now and go there."

I glance at Fiona, who is trying not to laugh. "I think life here is pretty good. Probably worth living that first."

"Aye. Oh!" He brightens. "The cat had kittens! Four of them!"

"I heard."

"You can have one now. You can have the cutest. It's fine, Toast says it's okay to go in the Manse now."

I raise my eyebrows. "Toast can speak now?"

He giggles. "Dinnae be daft. She's still a dog."

Fiona speaks from her position in the doorway. "Remember, Carrie is buying sweeties in the shop, Callum—if you want to help her choose, you'd best go now."

He scrambles off in a shot, then pauses by the door. "I'll be back," he promises me. His mum tousles his hair and he races off.

"Do you think it was the carbon monoxide?" I ask Fiona. She shrugs but doesn't move from the doorway. She's wearing mascara again, and rather a nice V-neck jumper over her jeans. I think it's for Carrie. "You can come in, you know," I say.

"How's the collarbone?" she asks, pulling a chair across to sit near me.

I grimace. "Remarkably sore."

"Aye. I've broken mine a couple of times, falling off horses. I cannae recommend it."

"My head is so much clearer, though. I can't quite believe I didn't even realize something was wrong."

"Carrie feels awful that she didnae pick up on it." She's looking at the bed, not at me. I don't know what it is that she's reluctant to say. There are too many possibilities.

"Can animals detect carbon monoxide?" I press again. "Is that why they wouldn't come inside before?"

"I dinnae ken. I suppose it's one theory."

"What's yours?"

She meets my eyes calmly. "That the Manse was trying to tell us something." I wait for more. "We used to be able to walk the dogs through the Manse grounds, when I was much younger. I wonder if that stopped when Jamie started taking your dad's bones there." She smiles wryly at something in my face. "But you'll come to your own conclusions in your own time." She could tell me more, I think. She's waiting for the right time. It must be even harder for her to gauge that than for everyone else.

I check that the doorway is clear of listeners. "Are you going to tell Carrie what happened?"

"She knows what happened." I raise my eyebrows with my best skeptical look. She relents. "All right, she mostly knows. I will tell her one day, I promise. It's just . . . it would be too much, now. Too much to put on her and the relationship."

I nod. "She'll hate that you lied, whatever the reason."

"She'll get over it." Her words are blunt.

"Is that a Fi fact?" I ask lightly, and she shakes her head, smiling, her triangular fan of hair bouncing around her.

"Nope. Just blind faith."

I hope for both of our sakes that she's right. "Why did you do it?" I ask hesitantly.

"I didnae have a choice."

"You did."

She shakes her head again, her mouth a thin line. "Not once he threatened Callum."

"Was he . . . right?" I've been turning it over in my mind. If he's not hers, whose is he?

She takes a long time to answer, but I don't press her. I can see that she's considering it—her eyes track around, thinking, remembering, perhaps seeing the things that only she sees. She's the oddest package, Fiona. Blunt practicality and capability mixed with extreme vulnerability, and all set slightly off-kilter, like she's out of phase with the world and trying to figure out how to catch up. "I dinnae ken," she says at last. "I dinnae remember having sex—with any men, I mean—but with the drugs . . . well, who knows? Sometimes . . . sometimes I wonder if he slipped through to me. Or maybe I slipped back to him for a spell and brought him with me." *Callum McCue, babe in arms.* I find I'm holding my breath. But I'm being ridiculous; Callum is a common Scottish name . . . Fiona cocks her head and says fiercely, "He's all mine now, though."

I nod and wait until a little of the tension has left her. "You know that sounds completely nuts, right?" I'm not sure if I'm trying to reinforce it to myself or her, but I add a smile to stop my words biting.

"Aye. Well. No more nuts than the Manse kicking Jamie in the head, and we both saw that happen," she replies pointedly, though with a touch of humor, and I incline my head to her—*Touché.* I can't help wondering how Fiona remembers that, and for a second I'm back there, in the kitchen of the Manse, as the lights go out and the Manse roars its fury at Jamie. But in my hospital room, Fiona's face sobers. "I couldnae take the chance. And"—she shrugs—"I kent he died. I've always kent that. No matter what he did to me, no matter how he manipulated me or everyone else, I kent he'd be found out in the end. Not the details, mind, but the gist of it."

"Why didn't you *say* anything?"

"Like you'd have believed me." *True.* "And anyway, I knew it was going to turn out all right in the end." I look pointedly at my arm in the sling and raise my eyebrows. "You'll live," she says dryly. "I kent we'd be fine. And I kent he would be gone."

Jesus. It occurs to me that it became a self-fulfilling prophecy for her. Killing Jamie to protect Callum, I can understand. Waiting silently for years for your manipulative half brother to get his just deserts is somewhat more chilling. "Please tell me you don't see Carrie or me dying in strange circumstances." I'm not entirely joking. Though of course it's more likely that Fi has no more foreknowledge than an astrology chart, and is simply trying to make sense of the memories in her tangled brain as best she can . . . But at least one of my selves doesn't believe that, can never believe that. Because I was there when the Manse expelled its fury on Jamie.

Fiona smiles. "I already told you. You and me are going to be great pals."

"And Carrie?"

She looks down as if she's fighting something, but when she looks up at me again, I see what's inside her—the hope, the excitement, the fear. "I cannae see it. I dinnae think I'm meant to. You have to leap blindly into love."

"*Love makes a furnace of the soul,*" I mutter. I'm thinking of Carrie, of Pete. Of Callum. The people I would jump into a fire for. The people I want to play a part in any life I fashion for myself now. Perhaps Fi will be one of those too, one day, though I'm still a little splintered where she's concerned. Maybe I always will be.

"Aye, well. A wee bit melodramatic, but I cannae argue with it." She pauses. "Ali wanted to come see you but he wasnae sure if he'd be welcome."

"What? Why? Because of his mum?" She nods. "But that's not his fault."

"He feels guilty; he thinks he should have twigged. Especially with the fox."

"Does he know why she—"

But Fiona is already shaking her head. "He thinks she was blaming your folks for the business going under, but she willnae talk about it." She grimaces. "She's going downhill pretty fast now."

"Does Ali know I'm not pressing charges?" She nods again. "Tell him to come. Tell him . . . tell him we're not our parents." That's not quite right; that's not quite what I want to say. "Tell him I'd like him to come."

The next day, Carrie arrives to drive me home from the hospital. *Home.* I don't yet know if the Manse could ever feel like home after what happened there.

"It's your sister," says a cheery nurse, popping her head round the doorway of my room. I'm all packed up and sitting in a chair. The nurse surveys us both, in turn. "You two are nothing alike," she marvels.

"We're half sisters," I say, and her face clears in understanding.

"Will you shut up about the half sister thing?" says Carrie irritably. The nurse looks at her face, then mumbles something like, *I'll leave you to it, then*, and makes a hasty exit. "It's such a stupid phrase. It's not as if anybody has the other half of me."

"It's not like that." I'm genuinely surprised. "I didn't . . . I've never wanted to presume."

"Oh." She absorbs that for a moment and smiles, the wondrous smile that so rarely comes. "I choose whole sisters, then."

"Whole sisters it is."

We talk on the way home without covering anything meaningful, but I know she'll get to the things that matter in her own time. It's a bright day, with patches of sunlight painting the slopes of the glen, but it doesn't feel fixed; the weather might change at any moment. After a while Carrie tells me that Pete has been going spare, and he's flying up at the weekend. "Oh, I forgot to say, he gave me a message for you. In connection with the painting—what was it? *No Safe Place*? Morbid title."

There's something in her voice. "Yes. From the Danish guy?"

She shakes her head. "Not Danish, Scottish. I never said he was Danish; he just lives in Denmark. Hang on." She changes gears for a roundabout with a series of alarming lurches. "I bloody hate driving a manual," she mutters.

"I'm not so keen on you driving one either." She sticks her tongue out at me. "But go on," I press her, when the road looks thankfully clear of any obstacles. "The Scottish guy living in Denmark?"

"You'll never believe his name." She pauses for dramatic effect. "Gordon Jamieson."

"Wait . . ." She is nodding beside me as the penny drops inside my head. "No! Ali's dad, I'm guessing?"

"The very same." She glances across at me, which worries me slightly, as she needs to make a turn up ahead. "Does that make any sense to you?"

"I'm not sure yet." But I'm beginning to have an inkling.

"Well, he's coming to the funeral, apparently, whenever it happens." The police haven't released my father's bones yet. "You can speak to him then." She glances across again. "Does it feel different? Knowing after all this time your father is dead? That he didn't . . ."

"Abandon me?"

"Yes."

"I guess it does." I feel lighter, somehow, though that could be due to no longer being slowly poisoned. "Though it also makes me feel bad for ever having doubted him."

"Don't be silly. Anyone would have, under the circumstances."

"Maybe." Logically she's right, of course she's right. But it may take some time to reconcile that within myself.

We're turning into the driveway now, with its familiar crunching gravel. Carrie doesn't so much park as stall the car, but I'm too busy looking at the Manse to comment. "Are you sure about coming back here? We could still go to the McCues' place instead."

"I'm sure." The words sound clear, definitive. Believable, even. "Wait—are *you* okay being here?"

"I'm fine," she says unequivocally. "I wasn't the one forced to lie in bed with my father's remains."

"I bet Jean is having a field day with that bit of gossip." But I'm talking to delay the inevitable. I climb out of the car carefully, my eyes fixed on the building. It knows I am here. I can sense the thrum that goes through it, just beyond the range of hearing.

Carrie grabs my bag for me and heads for the front door. "The boiler was replaced yesterday," she says. "Bryn lit a rocket under the company."

"Bryn? First-name terms?"

She shrugs. "He's been really great. Fi thinks so too, which is saying something, given her past experiences with the police. Though we're all starting to wonder how much of that was Jamie's doing. It's all coming out now; he was quite the master of spin. It was so easy for him to blame Fi, given she couldn't defend herself."

I don't allow myself to hesitate at the front door. I step straight in, though I feel like I'm waiting for something, but what, I don't know. There's an odd smell in the corridor leading to the kitchen. *Toast says it's okay*, I remind myself. Then I consider the lunacy of relying on a small boy who believes he understands what his dog is thinking.

"Ta-da!" says Carrie. The kitchen is not the kitchen, or not the kitchen I expect. The walls have been painted white, except for one, which is the purple of the swatch I selected. The linoleum on the floor has been completely replaced with some kind of faux tiling—not quite what I would have chosen but perfectly inoffensive, and absolutely preferable to what must have been left there after they moved Jamie's body. I look at the spot where he lay, and there's nothing there. I reach out a hand to one of the walls. "I wouldn't touch," warns Carrie hastily. "I'm not sure it's dry yet. Ben and Ali worked all night after the forensics unit finished up. They couldn't start the painting until the plaster was dry where the shotgun had blasted the ceiling . . ." She trails off, as if remembering, then turns to me. "Is it . . . is it okay? Do you like it?"

"I love it." It's hard to speak.

"It made them feel better. Neither of them can believe they hadn't realized what Jamie was really like. And what with Ali's mum, too— you know," she says thoughtfully, "if you are planning to stay for good, I think you could do pretty well out of this if you really milk it." I laugh, as she means me to, and it warms her gray eyes, which warms me too. "Tea?" she asks.

I leave her making the tea, ostensibly to go to the bathroom, but really to walk through the Manse. It feels different, but Carrie is here.

I can't tell how I feel about it with her pottering in the kitchen. Belatedly it occurs to me that I missed her real question: *If you are planning to stay . . .* I know what I want to do, but I don't know for sure if the Manse wants me. In the dining room, I cautiously touch my fingertips to the golden lettering, ready to snatch them away at the slightest hint of a buzzing in my ears, but the inscription remains inert. *A furnace*: I wonder again what kind of love my parents had. Enough to marry, enough to have me, but beyond that, neither of them can ever tell me. Though perhaps I should see that as a gift: I have a clean slate, with no pattern to fall into. Any mistakes I make will be my own.

In the middle of the night, I wake with the pain from my collarbone gnawing at my consciousness, and lie still for a while, listening for sounds. There's the low hum of a car engine that must be coming from the main road a couple of miles away. It dies away into silence, and somehow I can feel that silence; I can feel the space that extends beyond me in my bed, the way the landscape within which the Manse sits spreads out and soars. The Manse itself doesn't feel silent, even though I can't hear anything. It feels like it's breathing steadily—not at any pitch my ears can detect, but I hear it nonetheless. It's reassuring, like the feeling of a cat purring on your lap.

Eventually I realize I won't go back to sleep without a painkiller, or ten, and reluctantly leave my bed. Now that summer is just around the corner, the wood of the stairs holds no chill for my bare feet. The faint green light of the alarm panel glows reassuringly at me when I pass it. I lay a hand tentatively on the doorframe of the kitchen. The Manse doesn't stir.

In the kitchen I smile inadvertently at my purple wall, then fill a glass at the tap, looking out over the back lawn. A flash of red catches my eye: a fox. He trots insouciantly across the back lawn, pausing halfway to turn his head toward the house. But whatever has caught his attention is too inconsequential to delay him and he resumes his journey, leaping lightly onto the wall to exit the garden. I breathe out slowly when he's gone, only now aware I've been holding my breath. Then I take two painkillers and go straight to bed.

In the morning, I tell Carrie that I'm staying, that I'll get some kind of producing job in Glasgow, that I won't be selling the Manse. And that she's welcome to call it home for as long as she likes.

MY FATHER IS DEAD. THERE IS NO LONGER A MYRIAD OF POSSI- bilities for my father's life: all that could have been, might have been, has collapsed to nothingness, because my father is dead, because he has always been dead. There's a clear-eyed solidity to that knowledge that might, in time, give me more peace than all the lives I could invent, but not just yet. I've lived with those lives for a long time; I've scoured each of them for what they might tell me about myself. I am grieving for them, too.

TWENTY-FIVE

There's an inquest for Jamie, which records a verdict of lawful killing. That seems remarkably apt. But the inquest can't answer the questions that really matter. Like when did he lose his grip on reality, or did he never really have one? Were there signs, and if so, how were they missed? Glen is the most troubled by it; Fi says he picks over it constantly. He blames himself for being too hard on him, or for not being hard enough when Jamie twisted facts against his sister—half sister. I don't think she has told him that she saw it coming. I'm not sure he would forgive her for keeping that to herself. For that matter, I'm not sure all of me forgives her either. My splintered selves have mostly amalgamated, but the one that always watches Fiona can't seem to fully merge. It sits like a shadow behind my shoulder even as Fiona spends more and more time at the house, something I don't begrudge in the slightest, because she and Carrie are so lit up by each other that it warms those around them. And both Carrie and I can see that the Manse itself is a tonic to Fiona. She can almost keep time when she's there.

There's an inquest for my father, too, which concludes "death by misadventure," though nobody can say for sure what his misadventure might have been. Perhaps when he discovered the flat battery he left the airport by taxi, or perhaps by bus or train. Perhaps he wanted to put off another fight with his wife and went for a walk up by the falls, or perhaps he was researching the memorial. Did he slip and hit his head, or suffer a heart attack? His bones weren't inclined to say.

The funeral of Martin Calder takes place two weeks later. Pete flies up for it; there are no malevolent volcanos thwarting plane travel. Carrie helps me buy a black dress and heels, then lends me some "statement" jewelry that somehow makes the dress a thousand times more stylish. Glen gives a eulogy, and this time I give credit to what he says about his old friend. Carrie holds my hand, and I wish beyond reason that I had been at my mother's funeral to hold hers, but I don't cry until Callum leaves his mum to sneak his little hand into my free one. And then it's hard to stop.

We invite everyone back to the Manse for the wake. If I was being uncharitable, I might say that half the villagers have come purely to get a peek inside the Manse, and the other half out of guilt at thinking my father was a thief, but I don't feel uncharitable. I'm too overwhelmed by the enormous number of people who have made an effort to honor his memory. At one point I squeeze through the crush to find Ali and Ben in dark suits by the kitchen table, laying waste to the salmon sandwiches. "You two scrub up well." My smile may be tenuous, but it's genuine.

"I could say the same about you." Ben gives me a one-armed hug on account of the other hand being occupied by food.

"It's the sling that really makes the outfit," says Ali, through a mouthful. He's not a hugger; I've learned that now. Occasionally he manages a squeeze of the arm. Occasionally. He nods at my shoulder. "How's it doing?"

"It's just annoying more than anything else. I hate that I can't drive."

"She has to rely on help from other people," says Carrie, coming up from behind me to slip an arm round my waist. "She can't be totally independent. It's a learning experience for her; she has to *trust*." I wrinkle my nose at her and she laughs.

"My dad's been looking to speak to you," Ali says, in a quiet aside, as Ben asks Carrie something about her play. "But maybe now is not the time."

"Do you know what it's about?" My words are equally quiet. I noticed a big man in his sixties next to Ali in the service; I've been expecting this. We've both been expecting this. Ali's jerky gaze flickers around my face.

"Aye. He spoke to me."

"Is it what we thought? Was he . . . Were they . . ." I make some kind of gesture, but he breaks in abruptly.

"He should tell you."

"I'd rather you did, actually."

"Oh." He thinks about it for a second. "Then . . . aye."

"Aye, you'll tell me, or aye—"

"Aye, they were having a torrid extramarital affair."

"Oh." Even though I've been expecting it, even though it was the only thing that could make sense of Morag's hatred of my mother and the return of a potentially valuable painting, I have to let that soak in for a minute. My mother and his father. My mother sleeping with her husband's boss; his father sleeping with his employee's wife. Unwise, in the extreme. Neither of them could have been happy with who they were to choose to do that.

"Are you okay?" Ali asks. "He doesnae know anything about what happened to your dad, if you're wondering."

"God, I never thought that." It occurs to me for the first time that for all those years that my father has been missing, I've never once thought that my mother was directly responsible. It would have been logical perhaps to wonder if she'd killed him—it would be logical to wonder it now—but I never have. I feel a little lighter, realizing that. "Are *you* okay?" The flippant words—*torrid extramarital affair*—lead me to suspect he isn't quite at peace with it yet.

He shrugs. "Like I told you, I always knew there must have been someone." But his face is bleak, and his heavy eyebrows almost obscure his eyes.

"Do you think he'll want the painting back now? It must be worth a bit." Even if he still can't bear to look at it, he could always sell it.

"Ask him." Over Ali's shoulder I see Glen. There's nothing I can put my finger on, but somehow his years are sitting heavier on his frame, though at least he looks less hollow cheeked than at Jamie's funeral. Ali follows my eyes. "He's in a bad way, right enough."

"I know." A thought occurs to me. "Ali, would you do something for me?"

"It's your father's funeral. I cannae exactly say no."

"That's the spirit. Come with me." I drag him through the crowd to Glen, who can barely meet my eye. "Glen, have you got a minute?"

I lead them both into the dining room, where my father's research box lies on a sideboard. "Glen's seen this, but Ali, I thought you might be interested."

"What is it?" He picks up the jotter I hand him and starts to leaf through, then looks up with dawning realization. "Who did this?" I knew he'd be intrigued.

"Martin," says Glen.

"This is detailed stuff." He turns a couple of pages. "This must have taken him ages."

"There's photocopies of papers, and all sorts of related articles—oh, and there's these, too." I hold out the aerial photos. Glen explains about Martin's theories on the memorial, and about us looking in vain for the path.

"But it's not a path," Ali says immediately, squinting at the photo. "It's a negative crop-mark. You can only see this sort of thing from the air. You get positive crop-marks over old ditches and trenches, where the soil is deeper so the plants get better irrigation and nutrients, and the opposite over walls and foundations. The negative crop-marks are harder to spot; you're lucky this photo was taken in the summer."

"How d'you ken all that?" Glen asks him, visibly impressed.

Ali shrugs. "I watch a lot of documentaries. Mum likes them." He glances at me quickly, as if checking my reaction to the mention of Morag, and then looks again at the photo, this time with rising excitement. "Ailsa, this might be where the kirk was. You should dig. This could really be something."

"You two should dig. And if anything comes out of it, my dad's name goes on it too."

Glen and Ali look at each other. "Aye," Glen says gruffly. "I'm game if you are, Ali."

"Of course I'm game." He turns to Glen. "It might be nothing, but if it is the kirk, I wonder how the loch came to be there? Was a river maybe diverted? And if so, when?"

I'm about to leave them to it, but I find myself turning back. "You should try and get up by the falls, too. In case he was right about the memorial." I showed Fi the entry in my father's notes only a few days ago. *Callum McCue; what a funny coincidence*, I said casually. I don't know what reaction I was expecting, but she simply nodded.

"Aye, lass, if it's safe," says Glen agreeably, his eyes still on the photos.

I bite my lip to keep from insisting, but Ali has caught a glimpse of my face. "We will, Ailsa," he says quietly. "I'll find a way."

I leave them to it.

Later, Bryn finds me outside, leaning against the Manse, purportedly watching Callum and Toast playing in the front garden. I haven't seen Bryn since he visited me in the hospital, though we've spoken on the phone a few times. He's in a suit, of course—not black; dark gray instead—but this one seems to fit. Perhaps he bought it very recently. "How are you doing?" he asks, squinting a little against the bright light. His face seems healthily lean now, rather than gaunt, and he has more freckles and more color than I remember. His hair could be any part of the brown spectrum—auburn, sandy, chestnut, plain old brown—depending on the light, but his eyes are a definitive pale blue.

"Everyone is asking me that. Right after they tell me what a lovely service it was."

He tips his head, the smallest of movements. "Well, it was. And they all care. Which is surely preferable to the alternative . . ."

He's teasing me. Very gently, but he's teasing me. I stick my tongue out at him.

"How about I ask you something different then? It's probably not the right time, but life is short." He grimaces. "As days like this prove."

I'm intrigued. "Go on, then."

"Are you still with Jonathan Powell?"

"Oh." My head swings round to him. Bryn doesn't falter under the weight of my full attention. I'm starting to think I know where this is heading. "Um. Actually, no."

"Would you like to get a drink sometime?" His eyes are smiling in the way that I can only detect now that I know him better. It's exactly the kind of invitation that I think it is.

"I'd quite like to get a drink now."

His mouth curls up at the corners. I like that I made it do that. "I'm not sure absconding on all these guests is really the best idea." He pauses. "But I can hang around until they've gone if you want me to."

"I'd like that." We watch the small boy and his dog playing together for a minute. Callum is throwing a Frisbee, and Toast is leaping for it, twisting with incredible agility in the air to snap at it, yet somehow the Frisbee remains in pristine condition. I close my eyes and tip my head back against the stone of the house. The sun has a warmth to it that cuts through the breeze, a promise of summer to come. I may have more freckles of my own after today. "My father died," I say quietly to Bryn, opening my eyes. It occurs to me that I may be standing exactly where my father was in the photo I have of him.

Bryn nods. "I know."

"And my mother."

"Yes. I'm sorry."

There are tears slipping soundlessly down my cheeks again. I didn't think I had any left in me. "Me too."

———————

We scatter my father's ashes in the wood a few weeks later. The remaining McCues come along, with Sheba and Toast in tow. The wind is flighty that day; it's prone to sudden changes of heart and direction, which is how a most indignant Callum and the two dogs come to find themselves showered in some of the said ashes. It's frankly hysterical, if not exactly respectful.

It's late when we all head back to the Manse, and the light is fading. Callum and I are a little ahead of the others. As we approach the garden wall, I can barely see Toast. "Look," he says suddenly.

"What?"

"The cat."

"I see her." The gray cat is prowling on the wall as before. As we get closer, she turns her head to us, her tail swaying menacingly as she stalks. "Can you see what she's stalking?"

"The bird, of course."

"Wha—" But we're close enough for me to see through the bars of the iron gate to the injured bird. As we watch, the cat leaps lightly down from the wall into the garden and starts to stalk the bird from within the walls. I've been assuming it was the carbon monoxide poisoning that led me to see the bird. I don't know what to think now.

Callum takes hold of my hand. "Dinnae worry," he says, anxious to reassure me, though he misconstrues the source of my consternation. "I dinnae think the cat will get it. It will slip away in time."

"Time folds here," I murmur. I don't believe it, and yet there's a splinter of myself that can't entirely reject the notion. Just like with my feelings on Fiona, there's a part of me that can't quite subsume into the whole.

"Aye."

"I wonder what could make it do that."

Callum looks surprised. "It's the Manse," he says, as if speaking a self-evident truth. Which he may be. *Callum McCue, babe in arms.* I think of Fiona, weeks ago in the Quaich: *He put them out of reach.* "But it's okay now. Look, the animals go into the grounds now." He gestures at Sheba and Toast, waiting impatiently for us at the gate.

I open the iron gate, the dogs slip through and we follow, and the Manse watches us all. I suppose I'm glad of it now. The Manse will always be watching us.

ACKNOWLEDGMENTS

Writing a second book is not like writing the first. I don't mean that every book is different, though of course there's an element of that. The crucial difference is that when you write your first book, you don't have a publisher, which means you don't have a deadline. Deadlines—well. Deadlines put a whole new spin on this writing lark.

Consequently I must offer my heartfelt gratitude and thankfulness to my family, who all bore the brunt of a hollow-eyed, half-crazed wife/mother/sister/sister-in-law/daughter/daughter-in-law with remarkable equanimity and understanding. Without their help and support in keeping the home fires burning, *The Missing Years* would not have come into being—or at least, not for another twelve/fifteen/eighteen months or so . . . I still find it remarkable that the dreaded deadline was in fact met, and that is entirely due to these lovely people I am so fortunate to have in my life. Thank you all, you have my heart.

To my extraordinary agent, Marcy Posner—who coped with more than my usual levels of insecurity and neurosis on this project—I am, as ever, hugely indebted and enormously grateful. On the countless times when I felt unworthy to type even a single word, Marcy was able to offer advice and encouragement and keep me writing. Marcy: a million thank yous, I couldn't have done it without you. And to Abbie and Rachel, also from FolioLit, thanks so much for your helpful comments and insights.

ACKNOWLEDGMENTS

To Kerry Donovan and the wonderful team at Berkley and Penguin Random House: you are so much more than a deadline! My sincere thanks go to all of you for your encouragement, dedication and unstinting enthusiasm. I am so grateful, in what often seems like a world of instant gratification, to be working with a team of such talented professionals who are committed to nurturing long-term careers for their writers. Thank you for your commitment to *The Missing Years*; I am more than a little humbled by it.

Thank you to my lovely friend Faye Raincock, for a fabulous lunch laying out for me all the goings-on in newsrooms. The book took a turn away from that, but I think there's something in there, and I think you, Faye, might be just the person to write it. And to all my friends, thank you for the unending supply of empathy, support, help with the kids (special mention to the wonderful Laura Dent, who took the boys to the school bus every day when I broke my leg), catch-up coffees, lunches and raucous dinners (another Not-New-Year, anyone?!). And thank you all for getting behind *The French Girl*. I've been so touched by how involved you've all been in generally getting the message out, and in buying the book for multiple family members. Same again for *The Missing Years* please, if you'd be so kind!

And lastly, thank you to all my readers. In an era when time is a precious commodity, it's an enormous privilege that you've afforded some of yours to reading my novels. I've had the opportunity to interact with some of you via e-mail or social media, and I think I can safely say that my particular readers are the nicest, kindest and most thoughtful people on the planet. It's been a pleasure to make your acquaintance.

Clinical Judgement & Decision Making in Nursing

4th Edition

Clinical
Judgement &
Decision Making
in Nursing

Mooi Standing

Learning Matters
A SAGE Publishing Company

Learning Matters
A SAGE Publishing Company
1 Oliver's Yard
55 City Road
London EC1Y 1SP

SAGE Publications Inc.
2455 Teller Road
Thousand Oaks, California 91320

A SAGE Publishing Company
B 1/I 1 Mohan Cooperative Industrial Area
Mathura Road
New Delhi 110 044

SAGE Publications Asia-Pacific Pte Ltd
3 Church Street
#10-04 Samsung Hub
Singapore 049483

Editor: Laura Walmsley
Development editor: Richenda Milton-Daws
Senior project editor: Chris Marke
Project management: Swales and Willis Ltd,
Exeter, Devon
Marketing manager: George Kimble
Cover design: Wendy Scott
Typeset by: C&M Digitals (P) Ltd, Chennai, India
Printed in the UK

Library of Congress Control Number: 2020930950

British Library Cataloguing in Publication data

A catalogue record for this book is available from the
British Library

ISBN 978-1-5264-7833-7
ISBN 978-1-5264-7834-4 (pbk)

At SAGE we take sustainability seriously. Most of our products are printed in the UK using responsibly sourced
papers and boards. When we print overseas we ensure sustainable papers are used as measured by the
PREPS grading system. We undertake an annual audit to monitor our sustainability.